The Invisible City
The Stolen Future Trilogy
(Book 1)
Brian K. Lowe

DIGITAL FICTION
PUBLISHING CORP

To Marlene. I would wait a million years for you.

Chapter 1
I Depart

Notwithstanding all of the fantastic things that have befallen me since the last day I spent on this Earth in the service of a king and country not my own, none has had the same nerve-destroying effect as the shelling.

When I came to war in the spring of 1915, with tales of German atrocities ringing in my ears, hell-bent to defend the land where I had spent a magical year researching the legends of Robin Hood, I still saw war as the romantic adventure of centuries gone, hardly changed from the days of stout yeomen and knights in brightly-beribboned plate armed not only with steel but with the religious certainty that God fought by my side. In that I resembled no one as much as our own generals, who still believed that messengers from both sides should ride forth the night before the battle and arrange for a mutually agreeable starting time the next day. I had not anticipated (nor had they) the changes wrought when the battle ceased to be one wherein you saw with your own eyes the men you killed. They had still to come to grips with the shells and the gas.

In that we differed, for I had first-hand knowledge of what they refused to see.

That morning, the shelling had stopped after three straight days and nights. It was March, and our company was pinned down in a long straight trench dug just east of the town of Pont à Mousson. If you had asked me who first excavated that trench, I couldn't tell you, because we had been trading the Germans the same strip of land for four months. We'd dug in right before what would have been Thanksgiving, in the States, and huddled in frozen hell through the winter. The German lines had been barely forty yards away when we started. When it wasn't snowing, one side or the other might try to gain ground: those who weren't cut down in the open were met with hand-to-hand combat.

On occasion, we would push the Germans out, usually when they were too tired or cold or sick to fight us effectively. The next day, fresher troops would arrive, and we would become the defenders. If we won out, we stayed; if not, we fled for our own original position while bullets whined around us, or stopped with a flat smacking sound that meant another empty spot on the line. Sometimes we simply abandoned our prize and crawled back through the snow under cover of darkness.

By now I didn't know if we occupied their position, or our own.

"Corporal Givens reporting, sir."

I wearily returned the sloppy salute of the courier I had sent down earlier. If he hadn't spoken, I wouldn't have recognized him, covered with the swampy mud that coated the sides and floor of the trench. The company commander was situated less than half a mile away; it had taken two hours to get there and back.

"What orders, corporal?" I asked in a voice a good deal steadier than I felt.

"Captain MacLean instructs you to choose a small detachment of men to cross no-man's-land and survey the enemy's position. He says Headquarters thinks the shelling may have been a cover for a withdrawal."

I bit back my first comment. "Right," I said. "Pick two privates who aren't too ill and report back here."

The corporal didn't move. "Beggin' your pardon, sir, but the captain gave me strict orders that you wasn't to lead the patrol. 'Lieutenant Clee is not to undertake this mission under any circumstances,' he says. Sir."

This time I didn't muzzle myself. Captain MacLean knew that I would want to take the scout party out myself; we both knew what it meant to venture into no-man's-land if the Germans *hadn't* retreated. But commissioned officers were in short supply on the line, and he couldn't risk losing me, particularly on a mindless mission that was probably the result of a bet between two half-drunk colonels in a Paris brothel.

Angry as I was, I couldn't say that to the corporal. Normally I would be his sergeant's problem, but that poor devil lay thirty yards into no-man's-land, taking his orders now from God. The simple solution to my dilemma came to mind quickly enough.

"Good job, Givens. Give the captain my compliments."

He frowned. "And…?"

"That's all, Givens. Just give the captain my compliments."

"Ah…yes, sir." With a heavy sigh he adjusted his gear and turned to go. Then he stopped, turned again to look at me queerly, and said: "Good luck, sir."

I cobbled together a patrol out of three random soldiers whose names I have since forgotten. One was a Canadian boy, but more than that I cannot recall.

I ordered them to spread out, and climb over the edge only after I had cleared it. Captain MacLean to the contrary, I was not about to order one of my men into a situation I would hesitate to go into myself. First, though, I raised my helmet above the lip of the trench, balanced on a borrowed rifle. An old trick, and one the Germans had caught onto, so I was not surprised when it was not blown back by a burst of machine gun fire. I lifted it again with my head still well below the line of fire, and when it drew no attention a second time I decided the coast was as clear as it might be.

The third time my helmet showed itself to the sight of God and everyone, my head was inside of it. Ten seconds later, finding myself still alive, I clambered out into no-man's-land.

Perhaps "clambered" does not properly describe the mechanics involved. The rain had eroded the lip of the trench to the point where no man could climb out unaided, and even with a ladder the footing was treacherous. While I scrambled for purchase on level ground, my Canadian pushed from below in a fashion that would have earned him a court-martial in different circumstances. I tried to keep my muddy boots out of his face, but I am not sure I succeeded.

Before I had covered a score of feet I found myself nose-to-nose with one of the men who had failed to survive the last retreat. I held my breath and moved past. If Headquarters was right and the Germans had withdrawn, he would be buried today. If not, I would soon look just like him.

The shooting still had not begun, so I looked back for my men and cautiously waved them forward. What remained of my uniform was unspeakably fouled with mud, and in a moment of inspiration I smeared it on my face and helmet as well. As my patrol drew abreast of me, I pantomimed for them to follow my lead, and I was pleased to see that it did seem to help them blend with the ground. I confess I was most pleased because it meant that I blended in, too.

Thus disguised, we wormed forward. Every few feet we would stop, our eight eyes anxiously roaming the near horizon for any bit of movement, any hint that we were lambs being lured to slaughter. None came.

All at once we were peering down into a German trench—and no one was staring back.

The trench was not set out in a true line; we could see only a few yards in either direction. Fearful of any sound lest it alert a thousand Huns huddled around the next bend, I tapped the

Canadian on the shoulder and motioned him to follow me. Signaling the remaining pair to remain, I slid into the trench. Like our own, there was no way out unaided. If it was a trap, I was committed.

With my guard at my back, I crept forward, straining for every sound. The pernicious rain, eager to heap upon me the greatest amount of suffering, began again to drop its offerings into the ankle-deep puddles, fogging both sight and hearing. The wet squishing of our boots made a mockery of our stealth.

After a short time the trench straightened, and as far as I could see the Huns' retreat was confirmed. We retraced our steps, passing our original ingress, which spot we anticipated by softly calling to our companions lest they take us for the enemy. I reported our findings and moved on, but we returned even more quickly than before: The Germans were nowhere to be seen. This line, at least, had been abandoned.

I sent the two men up top back to Captain MacLean with my report and kept up my search. Truth to tell, now that I had apparently survived my fool errand I was none too eager to face him and admit my flouting of his orders. It surprised me to realize that I had not planned my life that far ahead—that I had in fact expected to die in no-man's-land. A wave of relief swept over me that almost made me forget the mud—a feeling quickly stilled by an unmistakable wisp of movement up ahead.

The Canadian boy gave a start beside me, so I knew that he had seen it too. Again I took the lead, hugging the side of the trench, unpleasant as that was. Cold mud sucked at my back as well as my feet. I had not seen much, only that it was too large for an animal, and my mind retained an after-image of grey. Without that I would never have noticed it at all, but it stood out even in the rain against the universal muddy brown of the surrounding earth. Only the sky was grey, leaden where it was not black.

Where the path straightened again, we saw him, a lone German soldier striding strongly but unconcernedly away from us—*his grey uniform unspotted by mud and his black boots gleaming where they showed above the water line.* I stopped suddenly and pulled the boy up against the wall with me, fearful that the Hun would turn and see us.

"They must have a secret tunnel somewhere up ahead," I hissed in his ear. He nodded dumbly. "We'll follow him."

By some miracle we kept out of sight, although at no time did the German stop to look behind him. More astonishing, however, was that his uniform seemed impervious to mud or weather, as did he himself. He seemed no more concerned about nature than he did about anyone following him. Overall his appearance began to take on a supernatural air, and I am not sure how much longer I could have taken the strain when he turned a bend and vanished.

Throwing caution to the winds I scrambled forward to keep him in sight. As I drew abreast of the curve I saw that this disappearance, at least, lacked anything magical: The trench had been built to take advantage of a small natural cave at the base of a hillside. Beyond the cave mouth it stretched on ahead, but the perfection of placement made the underground grotto the best candidate for a secret German redoubt. I congratulated myself on my perception—and very nearly into an early grave.

Thinking to listen at the cave mouth for guards, I crept forward and bent down toward the entrance—and the first shot spat up mud on the wall behind me. The enemy wasn't in the cave—he was fifty feet further down the trench!

The mud stole my footing from me and I went down, saving me from the next volley. Wallowing like a crippled turtle, I shouted at the boy to get back.

"I'll hold them here! There was a ladder back there—get back to our lines and tell them it's a trap!"

To be sure, I was no more certain that I could hold back the Huns than I was that he could cross no-man's-land alive, but neither of us had any choice. I brought my revolver around and fired blindly; the Germans were so thickly clustered that I couldn't miss. Perhaps they'd thought they had hit me, because the shot panicked them and they fell about themselves as helpless as I.

Helpless or not, they outnumbered me one hundred to one and I was in the open. Blind luck had run out and left me only one option. I gathered my feet and dived into the cave inches ahead of the next hail of gunfire.

I landed on blessedly hard ground. It sloped up from the entrance, keeping the water out past the first few yards. I rolled to my feet and stumbled away from the entrance, hoping there were no Germans inside because I knew there were far too many outside. I didn't have time to adjust my eyes to the dimness before I trained my pistol on the light from the opening.

It took several moments before the first of them blocked it, and I rewarded his efforts with a single shot. Before they had dragged his body back I was shifting my position. Still no one came at me from behind—could I have been wrong about the soldier I was following? But then where had he come from?

A rifle muzzle showed itself at the opening, firing randomly, but it couldn't reach me any more than I could reach the man holding it. For the moment we were at a stalemate: they couldn't get to me, or past me, and I couldn't get out. It was critical that I hold this spot if my men were to have any chance of returning to our lines alive, but sooner or later my time would run out. And if the Huns had another way to reach no-man's-land, my sacrifice wouldn't even make a difference.

If sacrifice I was to be...

Another rifle showed its muzzle at the entrance, and I fired at it just to keep the Germans honest. As it drew back, I did the same, retreating further into the cave, dividing my attention between the outside and my new home.

The ceiling rose as the cave deepened, and I grew more sure that I had found something. No one would have allowed this natural shelter to lie unused... I learned later that they had never known it was there. It had been hidden from mortal eyes by a device undreamt of in our time, and the only reason I ever saw it was a simple malfunction brought on by relentless rain and cloying mud.

At the time, however, I was convinced I had stumbled onto some secret Hun headquarters, and felt my way every step while I kept a wary eye on the outside. For this reason alone did I find the passage to the deeper cavern.

Keeping an eye out for the enemy, I reached behind me for the wall and felt nothing. I turned that way just as the cave entrance exploded with gunfire. The Germans had decided on a full frontal assault—a decision fueled no doubt by their surprise at finding this cave in the middle of their own lines. At that moment I stepped backward and I, too, disappeared from sight.

I found myself in a passage screened from the front chamber by a curtain of rock, a camouflage only penetrated by my forced feeling of my way. A man with a lantern would not have spotted it, I am sure. But the twisting path I took explained to me a more important mystery: why no one had been drawn by the sounds of war. The stone acted as a baffle for sound as well as sight. I lost track of my pursuers the moment I entered the stony corridor— and the sight I beheld at its end drove all thought of them from my mind.

The man I had been following sat at a desk near the back of this chamber, which was roughly the same size as its predecessor. He was facing away from me, and toward a doorway in the wall of the cave. I call it a doorway because that was how it seemed to me, even at first glance, but a doorway such as I had never seen before.

It shimmered, like mercury pinned in a vertical suspension. It stood higher than a man, and wider, but there was no evident frame, nor could I see any handle or knob. Yet it struck me undeniably as a doorway, a portal to something deeper inside the rock. Whatever it was, it was beyond my understanding of any German or Allied science, and it frightened me.

Tearing my eyes from it, I fell to examining the desk where the man was seated, oblivious to my intrusion. From all that I could see, he sat before a plain wooden table, head bent over several objects that I could not discern. While he was so engrossed, I was hesitant to move, believing myself safe for the moment, but I roused myself with an almost physical shake: If this was an enemy base, then the men behind me knew its secrets and my safety was but a sham. My only hope was to keep moving, my first task to subdue the man at the desk.

My wet clothes and soggy boots betrayed me only a few scant feet from my goal. He heard me approach and spun about, rising from his chair with a look of utter shock. Clawing at his side, his hand came up with a small box he pointed at me even as I lunged for him, but my muddy feet slipped on the stone floor and I fell. What the box would have done to me—for I had to believe it to be a weapon—I did not see nor did I wait to give him a chance to show me. I scrabbled forward and knocked him off his feet.

We did not struggle long. Rough hands pulled us apart. The Germans, knowing I had not left the cave as I had entered, had found for themselves the passage to the inner chamber. I was stunned to see there were only four or five where I had expected hordes. Two held my arms. I could see my sidearm on the floor nearby, but it might as well have been on the Moon.

The rest ganged up on the other man, whose garments now resembled less a German uniform than they did the strange door itself, seeming to slide and gleam like liquid metal. To their dismay the Huns found that this appearance was not deceiving, for the man slipped from their grasp and unleashed his box-weapon once more.

This time I saw the beam that struck down two of the Germans, and so did the men holding me. At once they both released me to use their guns; I saw the stranger stagger as the first shot rang out, then I slugged one of the Germans and broke free, and seized my revolver.

I had but two choices. Outside the cave was the enemy army; through the silver door might lie anything.

I made the wrong choice.
I chose the door.

Chapter 2
I Arrive

If any time passed while I journeyed through that portal, I was not aware of it, and if there were any sensations, I did not feel them. It was no different than the door into my parents' parlor, but one moment I was in rainy, war-torn France, and the next I was standing in the hot sun of a quiet countryside.

Had I known then the true extent of my travel, I might have given leave of my sanity right on the spot.

Fortunately I did not know, for what I could see was already taxing my reason—and my faith in my own eyes—to the limit. My surroundings were serene, warm, and had I but the wit to notice, beautiful. The air smelled clean and slightly sweet, with none of the bitter scents of blood or gunpowder, or the heart-rending cries of dying men. I stood in a small depression among several low hillocks; in fact I stood at the base of one such hill, into whose side the door must have inserted itself, in parallel fashion to the doorway through which I had run. Suddenly I recollected my flight, and spun about to see if anyone pursued me—only to stagger back in shock at finding the hill behind me blank but for tall green grass spotted with small, unfamiliar red flowers.

Slowly, over the course of several minutes, I slowed my heart and breathing. I am a rational product of the twentieth century, I told myself, and can find a rational explanation for my situation. Presently I did so: I had fallen afoul of a German experiment in gas warfare, such as was always rumored on the front. I was victim of some fantastic hallucination, my mind being forced to twist familiar objects into disorienting fantasies. The more I thought along these lines, the more convinced I was that it was true—surely I was wandering the corridors of a secret mountain laboratory, and not the soft green hills of a summer forest.

But the effect on a man—! All around me arose the vision of a peaceful glade, while further back in the rolling landscape massive trees rose to a cloudless blue sky. Like sentries, the trees and hills surrounded and protected my little meadow, except to my left, where a mound of rocks rose like a giant's throne twice the height of a man. How could any soldier think of war in a place such as this?

The imagery was so overwhelming that I fancied I could feel the hot sun already beginning to dry my clothes and the mud starting to itch against my skin. I reasoned that while I remained under the effect of the narcotic, I could hardly navigate properly, and so, hoping that what my eyes perceived corresponded in some fashion to reality, I resolved to treat my wonderland as though it were real until I could recover and make my escape. This might allow me to alleviate my growing discomfort, and if I strode blindly into the enemy's hands—well, it was no worse than if I stood still and the enemy came to me.

As they formed the highest nearby point, I climbed the rocks to gain a vantage upon my personal world. The mud caking my uniform made climbing difficult, and once my wet boots nearly slipped; I had to grab suddenly for a handhold. The rock was rough and skinned my palm painfully. It was astounding how the human mind could be compelled to construct such detail!

My efforts proved their worth, however, when I gained the top of the rocky promontory and gazed down the other side. There, not ten strides from the bottom of the hill, ran a shrub-lined stream as wide and deep as a hotel bathtub. Without another thought I began to step and slide my way toward it. I no longer cared about fantasy or reality I hadn't had a bath in weeks.

My haste to be clean very likely saved my life.

Peeling off my filthy, sodden clothes, my sidearm, and my heavy helmet as quickly as I could manage, I plunged into the stream to wash. The icy water was nothing after the rainy hell I had lived through these past months, and it stood as no barrier to my zest to be clean. After a few moments I simply submerged my entire body while I rubbed vigorously all over.

When I burst again into the open air I felt a new man. I picked up my shirt from the bank and soaked it until the water downstream turned brown, then wrung it out and turned to lay it out to dry on a bush. Then, shirt in hand, I stopped. On the crest of the hill above me stood a man dressed in the same silver garments as the man in the cave in France.

I was at first unsure whether to hail him or hide from him. My mind was still of two opinions as to the reality of this land in which I seemed to have been dumped—was this a savior to return me to my own world, or a Hun soldier determined to dispatch me to the next?

His own actions dictated my course. In each hand he held what appeared to be a small device about the size of a cigarette package. The device in his left hand looked to me, at that distance, disquietingly like the weapon that had subdued the Germans in the inner cave. With his right hand he cast about in the air before him as though trying to catch a scent. I was certain of one thing: If he was looking for something, it could only be me.

Very quietly I knelt down and picked up a small stone from the water's edge, and when his attention seemed elsewhere, I tossed it downstream, where it landed in the water with a plop.

Immediately he whirled, his left hand extended. A beam of light, pale against the sky, shot out and incinerated a bush near where the rock had struck.

I no longer had any doubt as to his intentions.

He did not move from his spot on the ridgeline as his right hand swept the air in the direction of the smoking shrubbery; if he was a German, he was extraordinarily careless. I quietly retrieved my Webley, sighted carefully on his breastbone, and shot him. Without a cry he fell back behind the hilltop.

I was on the bank in an instant, forgetting in the urgency of the moment both my nakedness and my concomitant lack of shoes. Numbed by the cold water, my feet hardly noted the rocks, and it was only later I saw the bloody trail I was leaving. I reached the crest of the hill knowing he must be dead, but the instinct born of months of trench warfare bade me pop my head into view only just long enough to see the field below without exposing myself to enemy fire.

His ray-weapon charred the ground black not six inches from my nose.

He was standing near the center of the natural amphitheater whence I had come, watching the top of the hill where he anticipated I must appear. He had not sought cover; either he was confident that he could shoot me before I could react, or (as I realized belatedly) his silver tunic had the characteristics of a suit of armor, and my bullets would not penetrate it.

This cat-and-mouse worked vastly more in his favor than mine, as it began to dawn on me that far from wearing a suit of armor, I was wearing nothing at all. The numbness in my feet had worn off with the return of heat and circulation, replaced by the pain of cut and bruised soles and toes. A soft wind ran shiveringly across my back and legs, a product of the waning afternoon and prelude to the coming of night. And most urgently of all, I was pinned down with no way of knowing when my enemy might burst over the hill and sear the flesh from my bones.

Gritting my teeth against the pain, I retraced my steps to the stream. With only a moment's delay to rinse them, I stuck my bare and bleeding feet into my boots, broke a branch from the bush, grabbed my helmet, and made my way once more up the hill, dreading every moment being caught in my extremely exposed position.

Deep in my mind the idea had already taken hold that this was no ordinary soldier I was fighting; had the Huns developed such weapons and armor they would have overrun Europe long ago. I still could not come to conscious grips with the consequences of such logic, but my hindbrain had grasped onto the practical reality that it presented. Gingerly placing myself flat against the hillside again, I poked the branch up under my helmet, pushed it into view of the man below—

—and pulled back half a stick. There was no sound, no smoke—and no helmet.

I waited.

True to my assessment of him, the silver-garbed stranger walked straight up the hill without hesitation, pausing at the top to survey what he expected to be my headless corpse. This time I shot him above the line of his suit. I don't think he had time to realize his mistake.

I was upon him in a moment, steadfastly ignoring the horrible mess my bullet had made of his skull while I examined his body for any clue as to his identity or origin. The silver material felt thin and smooth, like tinsel, but unlike tinsel it would not crease, instead flowing along the lines of the body. Suddenly it began to glow softly. I pulled away my hands with a grunt of surprise, and thankfully so, because the body vanished with a soft *pop* as air rushed in to fill the empty space. I cast about for his possessions, but they were likewise gone.

Slowly and inexorably the truth forced itself onto my unwilling mind: I had fallen into something even beyond the imaginations of Mr. Verne or Mr. Wells. I was a very long way from home.

Over the next two days I was to learn several invaluable lessons about this new world. In the morning, having found a small cave in which to pass the night, I sought after food. Months in the trenches had bred out of me any particularity for the shape of my nourishment, but I was an active man and as such I craved meat. Craving, however, is not the same as having.

Game was not especially difficult to find. The stream drew animals from all around, as I had surmised it would from my limited skills in forest craft, but these were not the beasts I had expected to see. My first shock was how similar they were to the hares and foxes and badgers to be found in the woodlands of my own country; my second shock was how different they were.

The first who chanced by was, I believe, a rabbit—but a rabbit such as no hunter of my acquaintance had ever bagged. The size of a small dog, its ears towered above it like wireless antennae, and with much the same effect, for it clearly spied my presence from two score yards away, though I made no sound louder than an indrawn breath. Its feet were of such length that it bounded six feet at a leap. When it stopped and fixed its gaze on my position, there was an intelligence in those eyes that clearly indicated to me that it knew I was there, waiting. But unlike the skittish animal I was used to, this rabbit calmly continued down to the bank of the stream and drank its fill, ears gently waving in the breeze. I was so bewildered at its appearance that, ignoring my growling insides, I let it be and simply watched.

The growling only increased as the morning wore on and the parade passed by. A fox trotted by not long after the rabbit had left, intent on its trail, but a fox such as I would have hesitated to confront, even with my pistol in hand. Other creatures followed. In every instance, recognizable species had undergone incredible changes, all obviously designed to fend off predators or to enhance predatory ability, and all of which worked wonders on me. Although some of the beasts passed quite near my ambush, and knew of me, none paid unwonted attention, as though Man was but another animal, and lacking any evident hostile intent, was ignored. I could have killed any one of them, but I was loathe to waste limited ammunition on dinner.

At last caution overtook me, along with the belated realization that I had no way of cleaning that which I would kill, and I fetched myself berries that I had seen others eat. They were surprisingly sweet, and fortunately quite edible. The only distress they caused was due to my own overindulgence. I spent the rest of that day exploring my new demesne, but no sign of civilization could I find.

On the second day I drank as did the animals, ate their berries, and forgot about them. The herbivores ignored me, and the carnivores had apparently decided that I was too large to challenge. I had ranged north the day before, so now I set off to the south. Beyond the first small hill I stumbled onto a vague path. Whether it had been trodden by animals or men I did not know, but the very idea that it might lead somewhere brightened my spirits immeasurably, and I set off upon it.

In common with the nature trails in the Santa Monica Mountains of my boyhood, this one dipped and weaved like a prizefighter. Thorny plants overhung at almost every step, and I, reminded of the poison ivy of my earlier hikes, avoided them with care—such care that when half the trail fell away under my feet in a miniature crevasse, I nearly fell in and broke an ankle.

I had hardly avoided this fatal mishap when I saw the men in silver.

There were three of them this time, standing in single file in the middle of the path. Their heads seemed to be bowed over some apparatus, likely similar to that used by the man I had killed the day before. For this reason they had not seen me, and I quickly stepped into the underbrush.

Thus concealed, I watched them walk past me, muttering unintelligibly in their own tongue. I had of necessity learned a smattering of both French and German, but this was nothing like any language I had heard. In thin, webbed belts they carried the small weapon that had been directed at me twice before, but in addition two of them carried longer tubes that reminded me of nothing so much as rifles. I did not doubt that I was correct, any more than I doubted their intentions toward me. I resumed my journey some minutes after they had disappeared, staying off the path and moving as quietly as haste would allow.

It was due entirely to these precautions that when I reached civilization I did not fall immediately into the hands of the Nuum.

Chapter 3
I Become a Monster

They say that first impressions are the most lasting; they could not have been speaking more truly than of my first sight of a member of the race known and reviled across this world, the Nuum. Although I did not know, of course, what I was seeing at that time, there was something about them from the very start that set them apart from other men—but only made them seem different to me, not greater. Perhaps this first impression had as much to do with the path my life was to take as any other factor since my passage through the silver door.

Passing through a cleft between two ridges, I looked over an entire vast valley overlaid with a great haze, grey in color, and from where I stood, curiously flattened on top. But beneath the haze was an object of far more interest: a city. Long and narrow like the valley itself, it stretched for miles to a line of barren, half-seen mountains forming the horizon.

The streets were straight and geometrically aligned as though the entirety had been laid out beforehand by a mathematician. I saw massive structures rising in isolated groupings, which I took to be commercial centers, surrounded by vast tracts of variegated buildings of all sizes—all in all not unlike the cities I was used to, save on a grander scale. Although I could not, at that distance, make out vehicles on the roads—or any living souls at all—I rejoiced that I had at last found civilization, where the answers to my questions could be found.

The slopes leading down the city were steep, but not unmanageable, and covered with sufficient shrubbery and plant life that a handhold was never far, thorny though it might be. An occasional nearby rustling as I scrambled down told me that these hills were not untenanted by other creatures, but evidently my hasty passage frightened them and none showed itself.

My path had ended abruptly in a garden. So familiar was the pattern of neat rows with small green sprouts rising from the soil, that it gave me a momentary thrill of homecoming. There was no one tending the garden at present. I stepped carefully across its short width and up to the small building to which it belonged.

The structure was a single dun-colored story, with a peaked roof only slightly less dreary. The masonry was smooth, so even that it almost felt wet to the touch, and I had to admit for all its ugliness it appeared as though it would hold out against the harshest weather conditions.

In my own world, the wall of this home (as I assumed it to be) would have been comprised largely of glass, the better to gaze out onto the garden and the wilderness beyond. This house, however, boasted only the most miserly and cloudy windows. I quickly discovered one that was open, allowing me to witness one of the most astonishing conversations of my life.

There were four people inside the room. The room itself was unremarkable, furnished with several chairs and a long sofa that looked more like a bench with a very low back. There were pictures on the wall, but the light was so dim compared to outside that I could not pick out the subjects.

The people themselves were likewise not so unusual as to stand out in a crowd, save that both of the women and one of the men seemed extremely thin. Their features were regular and not unpleasant. The women sported short coiffures that curled in well above the collars of their single-piece coveralls, but the man's head was almost shaven.

They were apparently in argument with the fourth person, a man whose stature and build seemed much like my own, so that while he was not imposing to me, he overwhelmed the others. He had a full head of red hair and a red beard. He might have been called handsome, in a slick, snooty fashion that I did not take to, his nose being too pointed for my taste. His coverall was shiny dark green, with red stripes down the pants; had the situation not been so odd, I might have laughed to call him a walking Christmas tree.

To describe what they were having as a "conversation" would strain what I know of the term, and in this lay the astonishment to which I have alluded: While they waved their hands in the air like Italians, they spoke only three or four syllables in an entire minute! By their expressions and movements, I know that they were engaging in protracted discourse, but hardly any spoken words could be heard. Those sounds I did hear, I could of course not understand, but all through the time I watched, I could almost sense a buzzing, tingling sensation in my brain, as though some meaning went whizzing by at speeds too fast for me to comprehend, tickling my mind in passing.

Later I was to learn that this was very close to the truth, but for now I only watched. Wherever I was, it was like no place else in my experience, but plainly I would have to learn to communicate with the natives sometime—unless I wanted to spend the rest of my life living in a cave.

The argument stopped without warning and the red-bearded fellow took his leave. Those he left behind fell to muttering (I supposed) amongst themselves, and I noticed that the verbal proportion of their speech seemed to increase, but for what reason I could not guess. In all the time I remained, they never once looked out the window and saw me. I was to learn that these people placed far more reliance upon their intellect than their senses.

Finally the three departed the room, and I backed carefully away from the window. There was no telling but that one of them might come out into the garden, so I slipped into the brush, and thence back to my cave in the hills. On my way I saw none of the men in silver. I was glad of that, for the strange buzzing sensation persisted even after I left the city behind, growing into a headache that persisted until I fell late into a fitful sleep.

I had never thought of myself before as a monster.

Like most young boys, I had read *Frankenstein*, but I had always sided with the creator, and not the creation. Now I found myself crouched each evening outside the home with the garden trying to decipher the inhabitants' speech, even as the monster had done in the novel as he tried to learn how to be human.

In the past week I had gone on various scouting trips—from the hills above the city I could see a great deal of the coming and going of its inhabitants—but I had been careful to avoid meeting anyone. This was especially true after I saw a Silver Man again, on a hill some distance away, waving his small box about and wandering apparently at random. I hid until he had gone, and I did not see his fellows. Still, they seemed much less concerned with stealth than I and were easy to elude. In time they were simply one more danger to beware, like the gigantic foxes and the occasional bear. Nor did any hazard keep me from my nightly appointment.

Each night, the headaches and the buzzing were less and less onerous. The buzzing changed character, too, becoming softer and after a while changing pitch on occasion. It wasn't long before I began to be able to understand the gist of conversation, and within a few days I could discern individual words.

The chamber I had first spied upon appeared to be some sort of dining room or parlor. The family gathered there most evenings, and as the weather remained mild, usually the window was open. Now that I had an idea of upon whom I was eavesdropping, I spent my time sitting with my back against the wall and listening, instead of watching. Their words came just as clearly, and I did not fear discovery. I was fortunate that they never thought to bring their palaver into the garden.

The family was composed of three: Bantos Han, the man of the house; Hori Han, his wife; and Hana Wen, Hori's sister. I have to admit that at times I had difficulty separating Hori and Hana in my mind, for to me all the women of this land appeared largely similar, particularly in the matter of hair, which was worn uniformly shorter than I was used to. But Hana's hair was of a reddish tinge, where her sister was blond, and her voice had a younger, softer tone. It wasn't long before hers was the voice I most longed to hear.

When I arrived, on the seventh night of my new life, in the garden, I could hear an argument in progress.

"—no right!" That was Hori.

"He carries all the rights he needs with his name," Bantos Han replied bitterly. "Farren is a Nuum; he doesn't need any more right than that."

"Tell that to Hana! My sister is in her room right now crying her eyes out because she doesn't want to go with that—that alien! What's happened to the law? How can he make her marry him?"

"Marriage," her husband answered dryly, "is not what Farren has in mind."

His words chilled me to the bone. Who Farren was, I could only guess, but Hana plainly wanted nothing to do with him. Farren, on the other hand, just as plainly would not take "no" for an answer. I was at a loss what to do, or even if I should do anything at all. It wasn't my house; I didn't even know these people.

At times my hands and feet will carry me into action before my brain has had a chance to vote. Before I quite knew it, I was sneaking around the house looking for the window into Hana's room.

Her sister was correct. Although the window was shut tight, I could see Hana was, or had been, crying on her bed. This was the first time I had spied on another room—let alone a bedroom—but my eyes were not so glued to the girl that I could not take in her surroundings.

Her bedroom was suffused in a soft light, too even for gas or electric lamps, of which I could see none in any event. The bed and dressing table were familiar in a way dictated by their function, but the walls were covered by the most esoteric artworks I had ever seen. What appeared at first to be merely swaths of color actually seemed to move on lengthier examination, so that a painting was more like a kaleidoscope in its effect. The whole effect was at once attracting and repelling; I wasn't at all sure I liked it.

I turned my attention back to Hana. Unlike the painting, she had not moved. Behind the glass, she was like the tragic heroine of a motion picture, silent but communicating all by the language of her pose. To me she fairly cried out in despair. Again my limbs moved in direct opposition to all reason—I tapped on the window.

She jumped up, her tear-streaked face drawn with anxiety. "Who's there?"

Now it was my turn to jump, for she had been facing me when she spoke, projecting her words directly past the window glass like it wasn't there—and her lips hadn't moved. So startled I was that I stood paralyzed while she approached the window and finally her lips moved—she screamed like an Irish banshee.

By the time Bantos Han had rushed out of his door into the garden and around the house, I was already hidden in the bushes. But I fled no further. As chance would have it, this was the first opportunity I had had to observe people up close, outside. From a distance, the town crowds had always seemed to me the slightest bit odd, as though they moved too slowly. I wanted to see if that held true up close, for I had realized over the last few days that wherever this strange world was, it was not the one on which I had been born. What Jules Verne or H.G. Wells would have made of it, I do not know. I only knew that if I wanted to survive, I had to know who might be hunting me.

My earlier surmises had been correct. As I watched Bantos Han poke through the brush several yards to my left, I could see how thin were his limbs; in fact, in the America I had left behind, he would have been considered sickly. But there was no tremor in his movements, no uncertainty, and he seemed perfectly in tenor with his wife and sister-in-law. If I was right, then I had nothing to fear from these people physically.

Not from these people, no, I corrected myself quickly, but there were the Nuum, and the men in the silver suits. In my experience, neither shared the physical shortcomings of the Hans and their neighbors—and in fact, were the only persons from whom I had seen any hostility, whether directed at me or another. If I had anything to fear, it was from them. Time was to prove me right...

But if I counted the Nuum among my enemies, did these then become my friends? I couldn't live the rest of my life in the hills. Bantos Han was slowly making his way toward me. I would never have a better chance to speak to him without fear of interference. I readied myself and stepped out of the bushes.

He was startled, but he didn't run. He stopped short, staring at me curiously—but no more curiously, I suppose, than I had been staring at him for the past several days. He said something short and unintelligible, and at the same time the buzzing increased in my head to an almost intolerable degree. For a moment I was helpless, bent over and blinded by something that was less than pain, but just as debilitating. Had he wanted to, Bantos Han could have ended my life there and then without difficulty.

When the discomfort had passed once more into the background, I slowly straightened to find him still in front of me, his curiosity mixed with concern. He searched my face minutely, reached out to touch me gently on the temple, and gasped at what he felt there. Then he took my arm and lead me into his house.

I followed docilely to find the women awaiting us. I expected the same sort of reaction Bantos Han had shown, if not worse, but they seemed to know I was coming. Moreover, they didn't try to speak to me; Hori motioned me to a stool. When I sat down, so did they.

Their glances were silent, but the buzzing rose and fell in my head in no apparent pattern, something it had never done before. At length Hana slipped off of her stool and stood beside me, her liquid blue eyes staring steadily at me with most unladylike directness. Under normal circumstances I would have found it uncomfortable, but I had been through so much that I actually began to relax under her gaze. Before I realized it, I was slipping off my perch, and would have fallen if Hana hadn't steadied me. At the same time, the buzzing in my head vanished as though it had never been.

"Who are you?" Hana asked. "Why were you at my window?"

Her English was flawless.

Chapter 4
I Am an Alien

The sound of someone speaking my mother tongue was so wonderful to me that at first I was not as surprised as I should have been, but was momentarily overcome by the idea that perhaps I was not be so far from home as I had thought.

"My name is Charles Clee," I said excitedly. "I'm a lieutenant in—" Suddenly my brain kicked into gear and put a brake on my mouth. Unconsciously I stiffened. "I am Lieutenant Charles C. Clee of the Allied Forces." My rank I had already blurted out, and the fact that she spoke English meant she knew my allegiance, but further information could wait until I knew more. Insane as it might sound, this *could* still be an elaborate German trap.

She frowned, her eyes darting back and forth across my face.

"I understand what you're saying, but the words don't make any sense. Is all that just your name?"

It was my turn to frown, as an intuitive sense of dismay began to form deep in my mind. Her manner was unreal, almost bizarre. It looked more and more a trick of the enemy—but I felt almost as if I could read her mind and literally see the sincerity behind her words. I made up my mind to trust her; whatever I was experiencing, it was not a German trap. A small part of me wished it could be.

"My name is Charles Carol Clee," I said slowly, then waited.

"Charles?" she repeated. "That is an unusual name."

I blinked. "Not where I come from."

"Carol is much nicer," she said, as if we were simply meeting for the first time at a concert in the park. With her flattened accent it sounded like "Keryl."

The incongruity of the conversation left me no option but to follow her lead.

"My mother called me Carol—because I was born on Christmas Day."

She stared at me, and shook her head. She said she had no idea what Christmas was, and I believed her.

I knew then I was very far from home, indeed.

After introducing me to her sister and brother-in-law, Hana lead us into another room, where we sat and tried to make sense of my intrusion into their lives. As best I could, I described how I had come to be there. None of my experiences, nor my description of the silver door, rang any bells for them. When I told of my fight with the man on the hill, however, Bantos Han leaned forward anxiously, interrupting me for the first time.

"Are you sure of what you saw? He had machines?"

"I was entirely too close for my own comfort. If he had done to me what he did to that bush, I'd not be sitting here right now."

Bantos Han slumped back on the couch, shaking his head. "This is bad. Only the Nuum are allowed to have machines that you can carry with you."

His wife grasped his arm. "Bantos, Lord Farren could come here at any time. If he sees Keryl…"

"No," Bantos Han said firmly. "If Keryl had killed a Nuum, they would be out hunting him by now—and we would have heard about it. No, whoever he fought with, it wasn't one of the Nuum." He glanced at me. "But we will have to hide him when Lord Farren comes. He doesn't look like he belongs here."

"Is Lord Farren the gentleman I saw here the other night, in—?" I stopped, but the damage was done. I had caught their full attention.

"So you've been spying on us for a while, then?" Bantos Han asked.

I nodded, the heat was full in my face—and then I saw an matching blush on Hana and I realized the full horror of what she was thinking, of what they were all thinking.

"Oh no! Please!" I blurted. "I wasn't spying on Hana—I mean, just that once—I mean..." I fought down my shame and I struggled to rise. "Excuse me."

Hori reached out and touched my arm. "Don't go. Please. There's a great deal going on here that we don't understand."

I smiled in rueful agreement. "The first thing I don't understand is how I can hear you speaking when your mouths aren't even moving."

"The same as we can understand you," Bantos Han explained. "Through your mind. Long ago, people spoke verbally, just like you do, but now it's mostly through thoughts. We can broadcast and receive for short distances, but someone like you, whose mind is untrained, can broadcast emotions much further—and more wildly."

"Through my mind?" It was unreal, and yet totally consistent with what I had seen. "But how? Where I come from, no one can do it."

"Hana taught you. When you first came in, she helped you relax so that she could reach into your mind and teach you."

"I didn't really do anything," Hana said. "The pieces were there; you just didn't know how to put them together."

"You can read my mind?"

Bantos Han hesitated, then frowned, turning to his wife. "Is it just me, or—?"

"No," she said. "I can't hear him now either. I didn't have any trouble when he was speaking, but now—nothing. Not even a mental shield."

All three of them looked at me as though I could explain it. To the contrary, I was at a loss to explain what they already knew.

I took a deep breath to calm myself. "Can I talk to anyone this way?"

Hori smiled. "I wouldn't try it yet. As far as we're concerned, you're shouting."

"Can they hear me outside?" I asked, glancing at the walls.

"No," she said. "The walls are insulated. But once you've had a chance to practice, you'll be fine." Suddenly she leaned forward. "Are you all right?"

I was not, and I hadn't even known it. My eyes began to blur and I was rocking slowly back and forth in my chair. I felt so tired I didn't think I could stand up, and I said so.

"He's been through too much," Hori snapped. "You've exhausted him. Bantos, let him have the couch. Hana, get some blankets." I'm sure all of her instructions were carried out, but by that time I was out on my feet.

When I opened my eyes, Hana was sitting by me, reading. Hori and Bantos Han were there almost as I awoke, though I didn't hear her calling them. When they had told me that I had a lot to learn, they were not joking, for it was like learning to talk all over, although much faster.

They all continued to call me "Keryl." Telepathy is largely based upon one's own language: everyday concepts can be expressed easily, but proper nouns and more technical terms are incommunicable unless both parties have a common understanding—and in fact are more likely to be expressed verbally.

Within a few days they had taught me how to "whisper" my thoughts so that not just anyone could hear and how not to "shout" (which was something else entirely). Shielding myself from unwanted eavesdropping, a necessity in a telepathic society, proved exceedingly simple—as far as they were concerned, when not speaking, my mind was virtually invisible! Evidently my more primitive brain structure rendered it as transparent to them as the mind of an animal. (A humbling simile, but it would prove a useful trait.)

When I say "they," I mean mostly Hana, for both Hori and Bantos Han had jobs outside the home. I asked what they did, and they politely described it to me—with the end result that I had absolutely no idea what they were talking about. Bantos Han seemed to be a cross between an insurance salesman and a haberdasher, and Hori worked, as near as I could tell, in a library. What she did there, I couldn't understand.

They were delighted with my progress. After a few days Bantos Han confided to me that he had initially feared I was no more than a blond-haired Nuum, because the Nuum were known to be less telepathically agile than his own people, and he was glad to find that this was not the case.

I took the opportunity to ask him about the Nuum. To me they seemed almost identical (if better-fed) to the Han family and their neighbors.

Bantos Han lead me into the sitting room and made sure the window was shut. When he spoke, he used his voice more than was usual, as though he didn't trust his own walls not to reveal his thoughts to the world.

"Thousands of years ago, we had a highly-evolved scientific civilization, and we established colonies among the stars. The forefathers of the Nuum were colonists. Ten generations ago, they returned.

"We had found other life out there. Some we traded with, some came to live here, and once in a while there were wars, but mostly it was peaceful. Over time, our colonies became self-sufficient, and sent out their own colonies, and so it went. We became more and more backwater. When none of the original colonists who had been born here were left, we ceased to hold any special meaning. To their children, we were just one more planet."

Thanks to the wondrous clarity that I had gained through my telepathic powers, I could feel, even in his spoken words, the utter truth of Bantos Han's story, and although I had thought I had truly accepted before this the fact that I had stepped through that silver door into another world, listening to his matter-of-fact recitation of things that should have been beyond my imagination still had the power to chill me and touch off a chord of despair deep in my soul. Whether because I had learned to hide it, or because he was too much a gentleman to notice, Bantos Han kept right on speaking.

"For centuries we lived quiet lives, trading with those who came to trade, but seldom venturing away ourselves. We thought of ourselves as the parents—or perhaps the grandparents—of the children of the stars…and like any grandparents we occupied our time with our own pursuits.

"After hundreds of years of not bothering anyone, and no one bothering us, we began to turn our weapons to other uses. By the time the Nuum came, we had nothing left to defend ourselves."

"What did they want?" I asked.

He snorted softly. "It didn't matter. I don't even know if they intended to conquer us all along, or if it was just so easy, they went ahead and did it. In either event, they took everything. And they've owned us for three hundred years.

"Every generation they become more and more ingrown, less and less interested in what we're doing—and more and more like us, at the same time. This town, for example, they call it Vardan, after somebody's grandfather. But the grandchildren aren't taking very good care of it. Vardan is falling apart."

I shrugged. "I'll admit I haven't seen very much, but it doesn't look run down to me. Your house is very nice."

"Thanks, but you probably can't see it—" He broke off, chuckling suddenly at some private joke. It was odd to hear him laugh, because the sound came entirely from his mouth. It gave my heart a lift to know that something as simple as a man's laugh was still the same wherever I went. "Of course you can't see it," he went on more reasonably. He gave a jerk with his head in the direction of town. "It's over there. Where all the big towers are."

I had to stand up to look, since the bushes were in the way, but even then I couldn't see where he was indicating. Frowning, I looked to him for confirmation. He was trying with little success to keep from laughing again.

"You can't see it," he advised me when he had himself under control once more. "You can't see the city because part of it's invisible."

"*Invisible?*"

"Well, not really invisible, more like transparent. But from this distance it's the same thing. Once you get into town you can see a little better. And if you did, you'd see what I was talking about.

"It's ironic," he went on. "We could help them a lot. But it's a capital offense to have access to any machines we can carry. They're afraid we'd make weapons."

"Would you?"

Bantos Han's narrowed eyes were his only reply.

I reached slowly down to my holster and drew forth my Webley. Heavy as it was, I still wore it at all times in case Farren dropped by to see Hana, which he seemed to do every chance he got.

"What would the Nuum do if they saw me with this?"

Without touching it, he looked the revolver over carefully.

"It's a machine; that's enough for them. They'd confiscate it and execute you. Is it a weapon?"

I nodded and described to him how it worked, and what it could do...what it had already done once, in fact, since I'd been here. He said nothing in reply, and we sat, staring in the thing in my hand as though it were an odd creature we had found in the garden. After a while, I put it away.

Chapter 5
I See Wonders

Within a few days, I had progressed sufficiently in my studies that my teachers thought it was safe for me to go outside and see some of the city.

"Won't I stand out? I'm too tall to be one of you."

Bantos Han frowned. "Don't they have tall people where you come from? Just because we're all shorter than you are, doesn't mean everybody is."

"You'll be fine," Hana Wen assured me. "Just slouch a bit. Don't walk like a soldier. Relax."

That, of course, was the hardest advice to take, but I pretended I was back in the trenches where no man stood tall unless he wanted a German sharpshooter to make him permanently a head shorter. The role was easier to assume than I thought.

Since personal transportation was, naturally, forbidden, the four of us walked to the corner to await a trolley. I was pleasantly surprised to note that some things had improved over time—the open-air trolley arrived almost as we did. We boarded and sat down; if there was any mechanism for collecting fares, I could not see it.

The ride was smooth and utterly soundless, and since my hosts had decided that conversation in the close quarters of public transportation was best avoided, lest any "accent" on my part be detected, I was free to watch the passing scenery. Amazingly, I quickly grew bored: The more things change, the more they stay the same.

Human beings required the same food, clothing, and shelter as in my day, and the shape of their shelter, the only aspect of this equation I could observe from the trolley, had not changed dramatically over the years. Perhaps also it was due to centuries of oppression that made each dwelling seem so like its neighbors, drably earth-toned single-story houses with rounded corners and windows. Most boasted only the most minimal of yards, with almost no plant life, let alone gardens. Bantos Han's house was plainly an exception in a land where exceptionality bred danger. Most humans seemed content to kneel before their conquerors and hope for the storm to blow over.

As we approached the city proper, however, the view changed for the better. Soap bubbles in the shapes of buildings seemed to grow out of thin air, more solid the closer we came, but never more than ethereal, glinting like muted diamonds in the sun. The closer to the center of the city, the taller the buildings, so that the entire scene resembled a fairy giant's ice sculpture. I had never seen anything so beautiful.

But as we passed inside the city limits, my gaze was wrenched from the skies and fixed upon the *people*—if people you could call them. A woman paraded down the street in broad daylight wearing nothing but flowers in her hair—I was so shocked that I could not tear my eyes from her swaying body, until I realized that she was not wearing flowers *in* her hair, they *were* her hair!

Only a profound revelation could have drawn my eyes away, and one was not long in coming. A bull moose was parading down the avenue—on his hind legs.

He was dressed in a dark brown suit, not too unlike what I might have worn in his position—except that I was a human being.

Head and shoulders above the crowd, he held a small device up to his ear…and then he spoke into it! He must have felt my eyes upon him, for he stared at me most queerly as he passed.

I stared in turn at his retreating head and antlers, remembering Bantos Han's story about visitors from other worlds. I had assumed at the time they would all look like men, as did the Nuum. Suddenly my sense of my own naiveté washed over me like a cold bath. It was followed by a colder drenching of pure dread. What else was walking these streets?

My companions seeming perfectly at ease with our surroundings, I forced myself to relax. If I lost my new-found mental control and broadcast my fear of these everyday sights, I would like find myself in a latter-day Bedlam before lunchtime.

The sudden thought of food cheered me, reminding me as it did of our destination. After much discussion, my adopted family had decided that a communal meal would allow me ample opportunity to observe the manners and customs of my new world, while at the same time giving me the camouflage of hiding in plain sight. We were to eat breakfast at a small but well-known restaurant, in the city where I might see a variety of sights, but away from the best sections, where the Nuum tended to congregate. There was nothing to be gained by courting trouble.

The Hans' wisdom proved true. Nothing is more universal than the human (or alien!) need to eat, and in every society, it seemed, the communal meal was a cultural staple. The restaurant sat on a corner, above a market whose windows advertised foodstuffs of a dozen planets. I stared at them, overcome by the sheer number of colors—never before had I been so acutely aware that earthly food comes mostly in shades of green and red—until Hori Han took my arm.

"Don't worry, you'll find plenty of food you recognize upstairs."

She lead up a short flight of stairs to a dining room that could have easily come from London or New York. As I have noted, the necessities do not change: tables, chairs, silverware all looked familiar. The walls were not hung with curtains; the walls themselves, being transparent, had somehow been tinted so that the sun was tempered and gave enough light to see while causing no discomfort to the diners. The diners themselves, I was happy to see, were nearly all earthmen. There was not a moose nor a walking hedgehog to be seen. The room was quiet, though nearly full, with most conversation being carried out on a telepathic level. The only sounds were those rare words that must be said to be understood.

The only exception, I was charmed to see, was an infant whose burblings and occasional cries appeared to be accepted in good grace by all. Apparently I was not the only one for whom telepathy was a learned activity. I smiled; it gave new meaning to the term "born yesterday."

As we reached our table, I automatically stood behind Hori Han's chair, holding it for her, expecting Bantos Han to do the same for his wife. Instead, the other three seated themselves, turning as one to stare at me, standing up alone like a lighthouse in the middle of the desert. Quickly I sat down before anyone could take curious notice.

"It's a custom where I come from to hold a chair for a lady," I whispered in response to their furrowed brows and puzzled looks. They exchanged glances, shrugged, and turned to their menus. Again I nearly betrayed myself; I couldn't find the menu, but Hana, alert for just such an eventuality, put her hand on mine, in the process subtly activating a button I had taken to be a table decoration, but which actually caused the menu to appear in the air before me. Rather than commit any further errors, I graciously allowed her to choose my breakfast for me.

Despite her earlier assurances, I didn't see a single dish I recognized, although the fruit juice was similar to an orange-pineapple mix, and the meat dishes were more than palatable.

I have said I was struck by the quiet, mostly telepathic conversation; at our table we were even more so, to give me the chance to watch the people, but all at once even that low hum of sound faded almost completely away. Hori Han looked up at something over my left shoulder, and her face froze. I risked a look myself.

Sitting down, three tables away, was a Nuum.

He was a study in indifference. When everyone at each of the adjacent tables decided, almost simultaneously, to leave his breakfast unfinished, pay his bill, and leave, the Nuum paid no attention. When every waiter in the restaurant bringing in food changed course and carefully lined up, out of his sight, awaiting his order, he did not notice. And despite my open staring for several moments, he was oblivious to my presence.

No sooner had he made a choice than one of the waiters swooped in to serve him another diner's meal. He accepted this as his due, albeit with some small look of annoyance—whether because the food was late, or too prompt to allow for complaint I could not say.

The remainder of the waiters swiftly and quietly rerouted their dishes to their original destinations. My companions' were among them; mine was not. I had the distinction, it seemed, of having given up my meal to my superior. I hid my anger with difficulty.

My breakfast arrived late and without apology. Gradually the conversation increased, but never to its previous level. My frequent glances showed the Nuum eating steadily and mechanically, as if my breakfast were only the most palatable of an array of distasteful choices. My anger began to be overtaken by my offense at his rejection of my taste.

We both looked up when the baby began to cry. Its mother picked it up immediately, her eyes darting to the outworlder, but the baby was not satisfied. If anything, its cries grew more insistent. The mother fumbled at her blouse, and I realized with some consternation that she planned to try to nurse right there in the restaurant in front of a room full of strangers. Fortunately for my outraged morality, she was too nervous to work the fastenings.

Fortunate for me, but not for her or the baby.

The Nuum lifted a single finger, and a waiter appeared at once. He nodded at the mother and child, muttering something unintelligible, and the waiter blanched. He walked unsteadily toward the mother, but she had already seen the by-play. She bolted out of her seat, baby clutched desperately to her bosom, and ran from the room, leaving her companions and belongings behind.

The Nuum resumed his meal. All around me others did the same. I pushed my plate away. My appetite was gone.

I went to bed that night worried that I would not sleep, electrified as I was with anticipation and trepidation. I had been a soldier, and a good one, but now I was operating as a spy, and like a spy I could expect no mercy if I were unmasked. But it was not my well-founded fears that interrupted my slumbers.

It had been a long while since I had spent time with a woman— before I left for France, in fact. Not that the French girls were uninterested; by the standards with which I had grown up they were downright forward. Most of the men in my company had taken advantage of French hospitality while waiting their orders to the front, and I might have as well, given the possibility that I would not return, but a veteran sergeant had made me a gift of a few well-chosen words about the hazards of "dippin' in the same well" as so many others, and I had abstained.

But my abstinence had been born out of common sense, not principled morality. That night my chamber door slid quietly open and a figure slipped inside. I was already familiar enough with her thoughts to recognize Hana. She stood at the foot of my bed, her breath audible to my straining ears. Her robe slid to the floor; there was nothing underneath.

Withal the details are private, I said words that night which I had never spoken before; nor had she, I believe, ever heard them.

I was doubly reluctant to leave my bed the next morning; not only was I was loathe to leave Hana's side, but to add insult to injury, I needed to be out of Bantos Han's house before dawn.

So with some red hair dye Hori had obtained, and a pair of red coveralls whose origin I did not question, I magically transformed from slave to master. An early morning departure had seemed wisest; although none of the neighbors would dare remark openly upon the sight of a Nuum departing the Hans' residence at any hour, still the rumors would fly and I was loathe to harm their reputations.

I regarded myself in the mirror, clad in unconventional scarlet from my head (literally) to my toes.

"I'm ready," I said to my reflection.

I was never more wrong in my life.

Chapter 6
The New World

My adventure began, however, innocuously enough. Following explicit instructions, I took automated transportation into the city center. Its visibility, or lack thereof, did not present a problem because the sun had not come up; the city was lit up just as one would expect any large urban center would be.

I found myself in the local "business park" where Bantos Han had his office. Once there I was able to loiter with impunity, since no one would dare to question one of the Masters as to his doings. Only about the Nuum themselves did I need to worry, and Bantos Han had assured me that they paid as little attention to each other as any passing pedestrians on the streets of Los Angeles or London.

"They've been here for three hundred years, and they're spread all over the world," he had said. "You can't expect them all to know each other."

As I had expected, the pre-dawn streets were quite deserted, populated only by those whose toil required them to be up and about. I mused about the universal nature of their jobs, for though I could not very well ask them what they were doing, the work of the trash collector, the street sweeper, and even the delivery man is the same no matter where he may be found. If they noticed me, I failed to concern them.

I used the time to myself to conduct some investigations. The architecture and construction of the buildings, for example, were completely foreign to me. Since no one was about to remark upon it, I was able to pay the kind of close attention that would have attracted stares in broad daylight. These office complexes (as I correctly assumed them to be) were tall, perhaps ten stories on the average, but quite narrow to my eye. Their surfaces were slick and cool to the touch. Every building boasted windows by the hundreds; some seemed to be made of nothing else. At first I wondered how glass could hold their weight, but when I touched a ground-floor window I found it was not glass, but rather the same material of the walls, rendered transparent. This discovery awed me considerably, and I am sure had the streets not been deserted my stupefaction would have made me a magnet of unwanted curiosity.

Just then, the sun, which had been betraying its coming by the graying of the eastern sky, hove into view at the end of the street. For a few moments the entire city was transformed into a fairyland of sparkling diamonds, the sunlight catching glassy corners and cornices that dazzled and delighted.

My breath caught at the sight of ten thousand points of sunlight catching and refracting off the walls and windows, a galaxy of stars that by some modern magic did not blind, but only enchanted.

Then, as if by more magic, the street sweepers and the drivers—and the buildings!—faded away to be replaced almost in the same instant by throngs of office workers. Suddenly I was in the middle of a vast open space among crowds of people—and others!

Although I had realized that there were to be many astonishing, mind-wrenching sights to behold, I was nonetheless unprepared for them. This part of town seemed to court the alien trade more aggressively than that where the Hans had lead me before, and glad I was that I was backed up against a solid wall, else I might have run.

Another moose—or the same—in a brown suit of overlapping leathery plates; a black woman who might have caused no tremor walking down Broadway, save that she was over seven feet tall, with ten-inch fingers, and gaunt almost to the point of transparency; a three-foot high cross between an iguana and a parakeet...

It was all at once too much. I wrenched myself away from the sight, colliding with oncoming pedestrians. For a moment I was carried along with them on the sidewalk. Suddenly the shoving stopped and an island of calm surrounded me. All the people were edging away from me, trying to escape without attracting my notice, making small motions and noises of excuse. Waves of embarrassment, fear, and longing, the latter tinged with envy, wafted toward me as they moved out of my way, out of the way of their master.

Their emotions made me sick. I spun again and found myself up against a door. I pushed it open and went inside.

The lobby I found myself in was high and cool. Lights filled out every shadow, but where they were coming from I couldn't see. The crowd outside had already moved on, and those coming behind didn't even know I was here. I took a deep breath, feeling more relaxed in my oasis, even though I knew it was only temporary: I had to go back outside to meet Bantos Han so that he could give me a tour of the city. Moreover, whoever worked in this building would arrive soon, and I would have to leave before I attracted more attention.

Still, it was another opportunity to learn. Directly ahead of me was a tall interior shaft, constructed of the same shiny material as the walls—although I noticed now that under the indoor light, they did not shine but gleamed quietly, like soft wood.

To my right as I entered was a tall lighted screen. I couldn't read the script, but from the order of the lines I guessed it must be a building directory. Each line had a circle next to it, where a summoning bell might go, but when I felt the screen it was flat, without a button or bell of any kind that I could see. Curiously, I touched one of the circles. Immediately a door silently opened in the shaft ahead of me, revealing a small room. I almost laughed—an elevator! It chimed to me softly, but before I could decide to take it up on its invitation I was startled to hear a small noise on the other side of the screen.

I froze. The noise did not recur, nor did anyone peek around the screen to see who was there. It could be a watchman, stationed in the lobby during the night—but then why didn't he present himself, asking my business?

When I was very small, I picked up a sharp stick in a field and used it to poke inside a tree trunk, just because I wanted to know what was inside. I found out very quickly—a beehive—and if not for a handy pond nearby I would have paid dearly for my intrusion. As it was I had to bury myself in the muddy water for a long time before they went away, and when my parents, frantic with worry, found me at last, wet and filthy, my father gave me a treatment that even the bees would have been proud of.

That incident taught me about bees, but it did nothing to cure my damnable streak of curiosity. Before my rational mind could overrule the little boy inside, I peeked around the screen.

There was a desk back there, with a man hunched over it. The elevator was invisible from where he sat, and he must have thought I had boarded it and gone, because he was speaking softly at the desk, as I had seen Bantos Han and his family do at home. Bantos Han had tried to explain a "computer" to me, but I had no idea what he was talking about. It was one of those things that we had decided was best left for later.

What this man was doing on a computer in a deserted building at sunrise was a mystery to me, but then again it was none of my business, either. I should have left him alone and slipped away, but

I couldn't stop staring. I stared for so long it was inevitable he would notice me, and at last he jerked his head about and looked straight into my face.

He was one of the Silver Men.

Thinking me a Nuum who had caught him at his mischief, naturally his first thought was to murder me.

Chapter 7
I Give Chase

The pale red beam flicked out at my head. Having learned from my previous experience with the Silver Men, my head wasn't there when it arrived. The ray only bored a smoking hole in the wall behind me.

Instantly, a siren began to wail, activated by the smoke or perhaps the firing of the weapon itself. I crouched alongside the desk waiting for the Silver Man to poke his gun around the corner, but he never did. I stuck my head up in time to see the elevator door close behind him.

Over the door an indicator read off the floors as the car whizzed by. He stopped at the top floor. I ran into the next car in line. There was no operator and no lever. Jumping up and down in my impatience as the door slid closed I was nearly frightened out of my skin when the elevator said:

"Please do not rock the car. What floor, please?"

I said, "Top," and when the doors opened I found myself in a small penthouse hallway, framed in the elevator like a man in a shooting gallery.

The corridor was short, with only a door at the other end and one door halfway down its length. There was no knob in evidence on the nearer door, and a small light off to the side only blinked at me when I passed my hand over it. As near as I could tell, it was locked. Unless my quarry had a key, he was somewhere on the other side of the other door, which probably lead out to the roof.

The siren was still shrieking, quieter on this floor but still much in evidence. I had no time to wonder what it meant, but I was sure it had something to do with me—and that someone was coming to answer it.

I passed my hand over the light next to the second door, and it obediently slipped aside. The early morning sun struck me full in the face and saved my life—as I involuntarily stepped back a murderous beam missed me by inches.

The corridor behind me was a trap, with no cover. I ducked and ran forward even as my eyes were watering from the sun and I couldn't see my attacker. More by instinct than design I found a sheltering vent and huddled behind it, blinking my eyes to clear them.

Even after I could see again, I stayed motionless and listened. The vent I crouched behind was about five feet tall, with an inclined top that angled downward away from me, and the same smooth finish as the rest of the building. Under my feet, the roof was flat, and years of dust, rain, and birds had worn the surface of even this fantastic material. I had felt the fine grit under my shoes as I ran, and I knew that no one could walk up here without making a noise.

My nerves tightened until I could hear the wind scraping my clothing against my skin. The unending siren seemed miles away. The breeze played with my hair, waving it before my eyes, and rasped across my ears. I turned my head into the wind and twisted at a sudden noise behind me—but it was only a large black bird, watching me with an unnaturally intelligent stare, as though he wanted a ringside seat to the drama that had unfolded beneath his wings.

I'll bet you *know where he is*, I thought bitterly, but the bird only cawed at me and took wing—eliciting a startled grunt from the other side of the vent.

He had to know where I was; what he didn't know was whether or not I was armed. I was the only one who knew the answer to that, but I knew it was the wrong answer. I couldn't attack him without a weapon; he couldn't attack me without me hearing him. Sooner or later, though, he would have to risk it, and I was stuck here, unless...

I scraped up a handful of tiny pebbles from the area around my feet, slipped them into my pocket, and stood up slowly. Peeking over the top of the vent, I saw what I had hoped to see: The angle of the top of the vent had kept it relatively clear of debris. Carefully I lifted myself to the top of the vent. I had to bend my knees to keep my shoes from scraping, and all my weight was supported by my arms for what seemed like several minutes. I breathed only through my nose lest I make a noise.

Finally I gained the top and gathered my feet underneath me, crouching on the vent. I couldn't see him; fortunately, the morning sun was still in front of me, or my shadow would have stood out across the roof and I would have been cut down in an instant. I reached into my pocket and flung the pebbles across the roof. I heard the scraping of feet below me, and I jumped.

I landed behind him, wrapping an arm around his throat before he could react. He grabbed my arm and twisted from the waist, but instead of throwing me off he only slammed me into the side of the vent. With my free hand I clutched for his arm. He was wearing a long, flapping coat which kept getting in the way, but it hindered him as much as me.

He tangled his leg with mine and I went down hard, but I wouldn't let go and he fell on top of me. He tried to twist away and I turned his trick on him, tangling his own leg between mine. Growing up, I had often been forced to defend myself from my three older brothers, and those lessons were coming back now.

I tried to turn us over, but it was no use; he was twisting like a snake and writhing like a maddened tiger, and it was all I could do to hold on. I was bigger and heavier, but we were trapped, neither able to gain the upper hand. Were we both unarmed, I might have overwhelmed him, but the minute I let him go he was going to shoot me. Then he got a hand free and grabbed my ear.

What he did I don't know, but I screamed and jerked away. This time he let me go, scrambling to his feet. He raised his weapon and fired—directly over my head. For a moment I thought he was stunned, but then he ducked behind the vent housing which suddenly burst into flame!

Not knowing what was behind me I rolled away from the flames as fast as I could. When I dared I rolled to my feet and looked up. The siren had been answered. The sky was full of men.

There were at least a dozen round platforms floating in the air above the street before me. Each one held a Nuum. They buzzed about like bees attacking a bear, gouts of orange light spouting from their cumbersome rifles to split into flame against the roof and walls of the building.

Though I couldn't see him, I knew how my foe was responding from the way they would suddenly dart and weave, avoiding a death that I could not distinguish against the pale morning sky. Suddenly a flier failed to move fast enough, and platform and rider plunged earthward in one sodden mass.

It came to me in a flash that none of the combatants had any time to worry about me. I could gain the elevator in seconds and be on the ground before they knew I was gone. Yet I stood planted in my place. This could be my only chance to talk to one of the Silver Men. Left to his own devices he would be dead within a few minutes, and my opportunity to find out what had happened to me might be gone. On the other hand, if I interfered, I could be dead in a few minutes, and it wouldn't matter a damn.

But for now it did. It mattered a whole lot.

I ran for my former shelter, still bubbling and smoking from that first hit. But now it was out of the line of fire, and unless the

Nuum were terrible marksmen, it was as safe as anywhere else. I stood poised for a few seconds, catching my breath, wracking my brain for a way to get the Nuum to stop firing long enough to keep from shooting me while I subdued the Silver Man. Again, Fate took my choice away.

The Silver Man whipped around the corner, running straight for the penthouse. Without a thought, I shot out of concealment after him, doubtless the stupidest stunt of my short and reckless life. But somehow the Nuum held their fire, and with my outstretched hand I clutched at the other's flapping coat. He pulled up short. I fell into him and he pushed me away. I could hear the low humming of the platforms as they dropped toward us. The Silver Man spun, sprinted for the edge of the building, and leaped into space.

Surpassing the briefly-held "stupidest stunt" record, I jumped after him.

Chapter 8
The People Rise

The God who protects fools surely protected me. I slammed immediately into the man's body and held on for dear life as we both plummeted to the ground. How I knew that we were not about to die is a mystery to me to this day.

He battered me about the head and shoulders while the wind snatched at his frantic shouts and swept them away.

"Let go, you idiot!" I wouldn't; why would I? "You'll get us both killed! You're fouling the outlet jets!"

I could feel something encircling his body where I clutched it close to me. I took a chance, releasing my grip ever so slightly so that I was holding his coat. He had only to shuck out of it to be rid of me forever, but now that I had freed him, he was too busy to worry about me.

He fumbled with something around his waist—I couldn't see because my eyes were tightly shut, but I could feel his movements.

"We're going to hit!" he shouted, but I could feel our descent slowing. I opened my eyes in time to look down and unlock my knees. We hit the ground and rolled: battered but alive. In the impact I tore the Silver Man's coat clean off his shoulders.

We both lay there panting as a stunned crowd gathered. I tried to catalog the pains in my legs, shoulders, and back. Far above me I could see the Nuum, descending far more slowly than we had. Suddenly the Silver Man scrambled to his feet and shoved through the crowd.

I was a second behind him, throwing aside creatures that until now I had never imagined existed, and would never have touched in a dream. But each of them reacted as any human being would, scattering before us with a rising cry of bewilderment and fear.

I ran full bore down the avenue, still holding the man's coat in one clenched hand, aches and pains and coat forgotten in my desperation. I had risked death by fire and by falling to catch this man, and I wasn't going to lose him now. Up ahead I spotted him bouncing off startled pedestrians. For me, they parted like the Red Sea. They thought I was a Nuum, and at that moment, I was perversely glad. The feeling did not last.

A shadow passed me by, skimming the crowd until it overtook my quarry. The Nuum hovered overhead and in front of him, cutting off his escape. The Silver Man raised his weapon, but the Nuum fired first, aiming hastily from his unstable floating platform. The shot went wide into the crowded sidewalk—striking a pedestrian who flew backward through the air, dead before he hit the ground.

A woman grazed by the same shot screamed and kept on screaming—but her hoarse shouts met with a vacuum. The entire street was frozen in horror. Even the fugitive and I had stopped dead in our tracks. Suddenly the tableau was broken by the swooping arrival of the other Nuum. Guns drawn, engines roaring, they landed their craft on the sidewalk and the street heedless of the people underfoot. They had almost reached the Silver Man when the first rock flew.

The whole block went up like wildfire. Office workers and passersby and people of all walks of life suddenly became a hysterical mob armed with fists, lunch boxes, and carryalls. They descended on the Nuum like a wave, and the few shots that the conquerors got off only incited them further. Three hundred years of untold degradation and mistreatment erupted on a quiet city street all about me—until a frothing young woman clubbed me with her briefcase and I remembered too late that to these people, I was also a Nuum…

I hardly remember how I survived that day. The mob surrounded me like an ocean wave; it beat mainly upon the Nuum, but I was battered and kicked and slapped. I have vague recollections of being knocked to the ground and realizing that I still held the coat, I threw it over my head and red coverall as best I could, concealing the color that to the mob was as a red flag to a bull.

I was stepped on and kicked still, but it was the mindless movement of the crowd, and not any deliberate abuse. I curled into a defensive ball and prayed my bones would hold. In a few minutes, the noise died away and I risked raising the coat far enough to see.

It was no-man's-land all over again. I saw the civilian dead first, most lay on their stomachs, facing the Nuum's last position, those who had died storming against the foe. But others lay facing opposite, black scorch marks on their backs, arms, necks and heads. The air was obscenely perfumed with stench of burnt flesh. In their panic, the Nuum had fired on everyone and everything. It had done them no good.

At first I could pick the soldiers out solely by the dead that surrounded them. It was difficult to make out the bits of red cloth, among all the blood. Of the bodies, little remained; even the flying platforms had been torn to bits, or perhaps set upon with the Nuum's own weapons. There was evidence that the mob had torn them from the soldiers' hands and turned them on their owners. Even now, as I listened in the eerie silence, I could hear the sounds of superheated air sizzling not far away.

I was the sole man standing in that graveyard avenue, the sole survivor of the slaughter I had helped to cause.

Suddenly my eye was attracted by a silvery glint on the ground. Stepping forward, I gingerly moved a dead man out of the way—and found my quarry unconscious, but still breathing. My boot slipped in fresh blood as I freed him. His face was bleeding, but his metallic suit must have saved him from more serious injury. Now I had him; what was I to do with him?

All at once I found myself in shadow. I looked up to see two large floaters above me, their decks crowded with men and guns. Many of the latter were pointed in my direction.

"Ay, there!" a man called from above. "Stand slowly."

I obeyed, and realizing that I was still partially covered by the now-ruined coat, I let it slide away from me. Immediately the man's face changed and the guns were moved away.

"Hold on," the man called again. "We'll pick you up."

"I have a wounded man here."

"Leave him."

"I can't," I answered, shaking my head. "He's a prisoner. We were chasing him when the riot started."

By this time the floater had descended to only a few inches above the ground. Its commander grimaced, plainly nervous to be here. With my officer's eye, I could see his men's eyes were rolling, their attention diverted and their concentration weak. This was not what they had been trained for.

"Bring him, then, but hurry up," the commander said, but when he did not offer any assistance, I was obliged to pick the Silver Man up myself and haul him aboard.

There was a small cabin in the center of the flying disc, and by the time I had dumped my unconscious burden there with whatever gentleness I could muster, we were again airborne, heading by my guess toward the ongoing fighting. I had never flown before, and I admit that the experience would have been unnerving even without the grisly events of the past hour.

As it was, the buildings betwixt which we flew caused updrafts and cross-winds that kept the little craft bobbing like a sailboat on a rough sea, and when, on approaching the disturbance, a random flash of weapons-fire prompted the commander to order immediate evasive maneuvers, I was thrown from side to side of the cabin and hard-pressed not to spread my breakfast all over its floor. At that I was lucky; had I been standing on deck, unprepared, I would surely have been thrown overboard to my death.

The upper half of each wall was clear, so that I had an unobstructed view when I was not being tossed to and fro. I saw the crowds below, milling, not marching, point upward as we appeared. Whence the earlier gunfire had come I could not see, and none greeted us now. I breathed a sigh of relief that these were only onlookers, either drawn here by the noise, or else driven here from elsewhere by the riot, but in either case not part of it. I looked down at my prisoner to see how he was faring and thus missed the command to fire.

The sizzling shrieks of weaponry and the screams of the trapped people below hit my ears at the same time. I leaped for the window to see every man on deck, weapon to shoulder, knuckles white from effort, firing randomly and at will at the crowd.

I tried to get outside, hoping somehow to ameliorate the slaughter even if it meant my own life. I was partly responsible for this. It was my pursuit of the Silver Man that had attracted the Nuum's attention. But the pilot threw the ship into another dive, swooping over another part of the crowd to afford easier shooting, and I was slammed against the opposite wall, where I slumped, senseless.

When I woke a Nuum helped me swallow something for the pain, and bade me lie down. But I couldn't. The noises of the crowds, the high far-off cries that had echoed in my mind at the height of the madness, had stopped. I staggered to my feet; I needed to see again the devastation, the dead, innocents and rioters alike strewn about like just another kind of garbage to be swept up by faceless men in the pre-dawn darkness. The dead, who would be walking still had I not brought down on them the wrath of their conquerors.

That was what I feared to see; the truth was much worse.

The Nuum had brought in even greater weapons. They left no bodies, nothing but dust; the silent streets were seas of black ash, stirred occasionally by the breeze, piled against an overturned vehicle or the cracked walls of high semi-transparent buildings now stained by the shadow-bodies of atomized souls. Nothing else moved. The weapons of the people into whose hands I had stumbled left little trace of those who fell before them.

The central and highest tower of the entire city lay directly before us, its sparkling spire silhouetted against the low clouds that I had never seen so clearly—or so near. Away from disturbances, the sensation of flight that had unnerved me earlier now seemed so smooth I felt no fear. Perhaps my emotions had simply been drained out of me. They might have thrown me from the top of the tower and I wouldn't have felt a thing.

They flew directly into the building. Inside it was completely normal and visible. The hangar must have occupied an entire level, and was several floors high, with flying craft of all sizes and descriptions squatting on platforms on varying heights. Many of the one-man flyers were in use as elevators. The room buzzed with so much activity I wondered how they could dart about without mishap, but gradually the design of the place became clear and I could see that horizontal flight was allowed only at certain levels, and through defined corridors. It was as if bees had been gifted with human intelligence without sacrificing their organization. It was a Jules Verne novel come to life.

My return to reality was quick and sudden. Someone clapped me lightly on the arm.

"Let's get this prisoner of yours put away." The Nuum commander shifted his weight slightly from side to side, as if eager to get away. The adrenaline of the hunt wearing off, he was reluctant to look me in the eye. "Then I'll see you down to the doctor."

The Silver Man lay where he had slid up against a wall during our aerial maneuvers, to all appearances still unconscious from his injuries. For all we knew, he could be dead, but the commander seemed oblivious to his plight. Between us, the commander and I hoisted the prisoner so that we could drag him along to the elevator.

Please make your floor selection. The words sounded mechanical, even in my mind. *This elevator is in service.*

"Detention," said my companion to the air. The doors obediently slid closed and there was a faintest sense of downward movement. We stood without speaking, the Silver Man hanging limply between us. I found the silence most anxious, but at the same time I was praying for it to continue. If the Nuum exhibited the slightest curiosity—about me, or about the prisoner, what would I say? I had an assumed name, but no serial number, no unit, no idea how to answer any one of a thousand innocent questions he might pose.

For all I knew, if he asked, and I could not answer, the elevator itself might reach out and render me as helpless as the man we carried.

Sub-level four, the disembodied voice announced. *Detention.*

"Let's get him settled so you can see the doctor."

"No, thanks," I grunted as I rearranged our burden. "I'll be all right. I can get there by myself." Five minutes' examination by a doctor and I'd never leave this building.

He sighed heavily, giving me a grieving look.

"No, look, really," I said. I lowered my voice. "What are they going to think if you have to help me? What kind of duty do you think they're going to give me? It's just some scrapes. I don't want to be stuck in bed for a week."

He stood there for a minute. We were two trench veterans with the same disdain for the rear echelons. Wherever you go, men fight. And wherever men fight, some things don't change.

"All right," he said at last. "But I'll take him the rest of the way. You get back upstairs and get some sleep. That's an order."

I walked away and let myself breathe. It was a short reprieve. Within sixty seconds I had gotten into trouble again.

I wasn't lost...exactly. I knew where I was; I simply didn't know where I wanted to be. This is a fine distinction that can only truly be appreciated by those who have experienced it.

I had put aside for the moment any thought of the massacre I had lived through. It wasn't the first; it might not be the last. But those who dwell on such things do not survive long.

Thinking there might be some way to track my movements, I had returned to the hangar, whereupon I had strolled straight into a corridor which lead directly to another elevator. For those few seconds while I waited for a car, I struggled to stand nonchalantly while the spot between my shoulder blades itched intolerably in anticipation of a sizzling red beam that could turn me into dust before I could blink.

When the doors opened and I was still alive, I stepped into the car and said: "Lobby."

Obediently, the car took my weight away as it dropped through the shaft hundreds of feet toward the ground. This made me much more nervous than flying, and I tried not to think about how fast I was going. Not as fast as the last fall I'd had, certainly! And with less worry about stopping, to boot.

Then some hideous demon inside me changed my life forever and I could only watch in horror as I heard my own lips form the word:

"Stop."

I have mentioned how in moments of extreme duress my mind unhinges itself from conscious control of my body and allows itself to be taken for a ride. This was one of those moments. My brain had formed one rebellious thought, fed it into my nervous system, and stepped back to watch the fun...

I might never be in this position again. The Nuum were the overlords and guardians of all technology and science on this world. If there were answers, they would be found here, in their headquarters. If I had left then, I might have returned to the home of Bantos Han, washed the dye out of my hair, and sought work with the garbage collectors. How my life would have been different!

Would I have made same choice, had I known that the fate of two worlds rested upon it? There are very few truly courageous men. Most of us simply rise to an occasion when we have no other choice, and if we live through it, we are hailed as heroes. But how many of us ever do something like that again?

Had there been another option, I feel sure I would have taken it. Unfortunately there was not: Necessity is a poor substitute for courage, but a compelling one nonetheless.

Please make a selection. This elevator is in service.

The mechanical voice shocked me out of my introspection. It was time to make a decision.

"Sub-level four."

Had I been so naive to think that the events of the past few days—or even the past few hours!—had been sufficiently astounding as to subdue my capacity for surprise, the detention section would have steered me straight from the moment I walked through its unlocked doors.

Yes, I said "unlocked." That was only the first surprise to greet me, but in a way it was very nearly the last of my life. Before I was to learn that valuable and dangerous lesson, however, I was to see and hear things that would age me a great many years and threaten to obliterate my very sanity.

I quickly forgot about the curiously inviting door when I stepped through and found myself in a medieval dungeon. Having imagined this scene a great many times in the course of my history researches, I think I might be excused for saying that this discovery stopped me dead in my tracks.

The change was immediate and total. Far from the gently gleaming white walls of the administration building with their indirect lighting and pristine floors, this corridor reflected the most primitive imaginable surroundings. Narrow and low-ceilinged, the corridor didn't so much "stretch" before me as yawn like the decaying maw of a beached leviathan. The walls were narrow, dank with groundwater and slimy moss. Wet straw coated the slick floor, doing nothing to soak up the muck but contributing a great deal to the smell.

Light was provided by widely-spaced ill-smelling torches whose flickering created more shadows than it dispelled. The Nuum had gone to great lengths to create as disagreeable an atmosphere as possible, a trait I was to learn was popular among them. As my eyes became more accustomed, I was able to pick out darker packets of shadow at regular intervals, midway between each pair of torches. The distances had been cunningly calculated so that the light never reached the doors themselves, never presenting even a symbolic ray of hope to the wretches entombed behind.

But the prisoners themselves were silent. As the muffled booming of the door behind preceded me down the haunted hallway, I heard nothing else but my own breath. I had lived this tableau in fiction and study so many times that I expected them to start wailing whenever someone came near. But where I would have anticipated the pleas of the wrongfully taken and the moaning of failing sanity, there was nothing but dying echoes and the belated fear that I might have trapped myself alone in hell.

Chapter 9
The Dungeon

The itch between my shoulder blades was beginning to seem like an old friend. At that moment it was telling me that if the door should open and someone should find me standing here, I would have a very hard time explaining myself. That thought communicated itself to my reluctant feet, and I stepped into the dungeon.

As I advanced the floor dropped in a gentle incline that ended just short of the first cell, where the floor leveled once more. At the same time, the temperature rose uncomfortably. The moss on the walls grew more lushly here, droplets of moisture gleaming even in that uncertain light, and the straw underfoot was little better than mud. The architect of this dungeon had gone his forebears one better: He had designed the entire floor to flood at regular intervals, transforming a hot, dismal cell into a steaming jungle with a locked door.

Inside the first cell I heard something move.

True to form, the doors appeared to be fashioned from thick beams with only a head-sized barred opening. As I stuck my torch near the opening I could smell the rotting wood adding its own aroma to the miasma of muddy straw and perpetual dankness.

"Hello? Who's in there?"

"It's still me," grunted a surprisingly strong voice. "I haven't escaped since you put me in here."

I could have danced. It was he! I'd found the Silver Man! Only now, in the excitement of my discovery, did I realize that I had no idea how I planned to convince him to tell me what I needed to know. If he was trapped inside, I was no less trapped outside. And he could at least explain to the Nuum why he was here...

I only had one card, so I played it.

"I've come to get you out of here," I hissed.

That provoked a reaction. I heard the sound of a body moving across fabric, as though he'd been lying on a bunk, then his footsteps, and then his face appeared in the opening.

"Quick," he whispered. "Open the door. There are no keys; it's only locked on my side." When I didn't reply, he got excited. "Hurry up! They might come back."

"First we have to talk." I fetched a torch and placed it so that he could see my face. His voice flattened.

"What do you want?"

"I want some answers. You want to get out of here. Can we make a deal?"

He backed away, but not before I saw all the hope drain from his face.

"Wait!" I brought the torch back to where I could see into the cell, but it didn't help much. "Do you want to spend your life in there?"

"No, but I don't think you're going to do anything about it." I could almost hear his shrug. "'Course, if you want to stay, I could use the company."

I nearly cursed his obstinacy until I realized its inspiration. He thought I was a Nuum. No wonder he wouldn't talk to me.

"Listen! I'm not who you think I am."

"Oh? Who are you?"

"I'm the man you've been chasing."

After a moment he returned to the door. I held the torch so that he could see my face again. He stared at me hard.

"Okay," he said uncertainly. "What's the deal?"

"I told you. I need some answers. If you give them to me, I'll get you out of here."

"Then talk fast. I want to be out of here before they come back."

"All right. First: where am I? Is this Earth? Am I on some other planet?"

He stared at me a moment and sighed deeply. "You do get right to it, don't you? No, you're not on another planet. Do you know what time travel is?"

I think that in some deep portion of my soul I was actually relieved. At least I was still on Earth! To answer his question, I nodded.

"I've heard of it."

"Well, you're a time traveler. And I think you set a record. I don't know what you did to the displacement grid, but I don't think anybody's ever gone this far before."

I am proud that I kept the trembling from my voice. "How far?"

He sighed again. "Near as I can tell, about 900,000 years."

It was too big a number; I couldn't focus on it. It was more than astonishing that I could believe in time travel! I passed on to the more important question.

"How do I get back?"

"Sorry. You don't."

"What do you mean? Aren't you going back?"

"Well, yeah, course we are," he replied, scratching his head. "But not until you're dead."

For some reason this seemed far less an impediment to my would-be assassin than it did to me.

"Tell you what," he said in a tone as normal as if he had not just pronounced my death warrant. "You let me out of here, and then we'll talk."

I believe I was excused to stare. "Are you mad? Why should I let you out at all?"

He actually laughed. "God, you're paranoid. Listen, I'll answer all your questions as soon as we're both outside this cell. But I just showed you my good faith by telling you why I was here, so now it's your turn to show me some. How do I know you won't just leave me here?"

Someday, when the final horn sounds and the multitudes of Mankind gather around the Lord's throne for judgment, He will rise up to His full magnificent height, and He will point His majestic finger, and He will say:

"Behold the irony of Man, that I should grant him reason, and he should squander it."

And He will be pointing at me.

The cell door, I was told, would resist a lifetime of effort from inside the cell, but like the door at the dungeon entrance, could be opened at a touch from the outside. I tried it, and it was true. The door swung open, the prisoner offered a friendly handshake, and I instinctively returned it.

That's when he hit me.

Chapter 10
The Library

As glib as he was, I didn't trust the Silver Man any more than I did the Hun. So when he hit me, I was waiting for it. I grabbed his arm as I fell into the cell and in the struggle one of us kicked the door closed.

Now we were both trapped.

I came up fast, mindful of his intent to kill me, but he was standing at the door again, looking through the bars. After a moment he spoke.

"You would have let me go, wouldn't you?"

I backed up until I felt a wall behind me. "Yes, of course. I said I would."

"Damn!" He hit the door with his fist. I winced. "Well," he said, "we might as well get comfortable."

I watched him as he sat down on what I presumed was his bunk, though I couldn't see it in the dimness. For several minutes we sat silently. He seemed to have nothing else to say and I doubted that he was going to answer any of my questions now.

"What do you want to know?" he asked abruptly.

I swallowed my surprise and tried to order my thoughts. He had already disclosed my location, but it was so fantastic that I don't think my mind had yet embraced it. I tried to force myself to concentrate on practical considerations.

"How did I get here?"

His face barely glowed white in the shadows; his words appeared almost as if from a medium's spirit. It seemed altogether too apt for this setting.

"From what I know, you accidentally screwed up a historical survey mission. You weren't supposed to see anything, but the rain in your location was heavier than anybody thought it'd be, and it must have shorted something. Nobody knows why you went through the co-continuum."

"What's a co-continuum?"

He snorted. "I knew you were gonna ask that. I haven't the slightest idea. It's the interface between time periods. The door you went through is technically called a displacement grid. It lets you go from one time period to another. That's what the survey team was doing in the middle of your war."

"The survey team? Those were the men in the silver suits."

I could barely make out his face nodding up and down. "Yeah."

"I was afraid they were the Germans—the enemy. Especially when one of them shot at me."

There was a short bark of laughter. "You don't have to tell me. Once the Time Board found out about that, there was hell to pay. Those guys'll be lucky if anybody from that university ever tee-tees again."

"I beg your pardon?"

"Tee-tee. Time-travel."

"Ah. Uh, what's the Time Board?"

He shifted on the bunk and I tensed, but he did not get up.

"Why don't you ask me your real questions, mister? You don't give a damn who the Time Board is. You want to know why they sent us here to kill you."

I let my silence be his response. He sighed.

"It's my job. The damned Time Board is so paranoid about anybody messing with the time stream that their number one rule is nobody prior to the 24th century travels through time. That's when the whole thing was invented. Anybody goes through the co-continuum before that, they have to be executed."

"You don't sound too happy about it," I hazarded.

"Like I said, it's a job. But every time these damned professors bring back an aborigine or something—" he jumped to his feet—"you'd think they'd know better!"

"How about me? How could I have known any better?"

"You couldn't," he admitted. "But at least now you understand. And besides, you're not exactly a helpless Cro-Magnon. You're already one up on us."

"He shot at me first."

"'Course he did. He figured, walk through, find you, do you, and walk back. He'd done it a dozen times. Like I said, those history geeks think they can smuggle people in and out without anybody noticing. And don't even get me started on the religion researchers—!" By now he was pacing. I forced myself to relax. Killing me wasn't going to get him out of this cell. "Not often one of you guys gets the better of us. That's why they sent me. I'm the best."

"What about your two friends?"

"Oh. You saw them?"

Again I let him supply his own answer. This was supposed to be my interrogation; unfortunately, I was running out of questions.

"Your friend couldn't seem to find me. I wonder why?"

"He was probably tracking you by your residual particle radiation. Were you still wearing the same clothes when you saw him?"

"I had taken them off so I could take a bath. They were muddy."

"That's it then. I knew they must've worn off by now because we couldn't track you either. When you saw me I was trying to interface a datalink for information."

I had no idea what he was talking about, but there were more important questions rising in my mind.

"What do you know about this world? Do you know anything about the Nuum?"

"Not a blessed thing—about either one. Nobody's ever gone near this far ahead before. Whatever jammed up the camouflage field also messed with the displacement grid. This is way out of my league."

I doubt that we sat there, neither one willing to start a friendly conversation, for more than an hour before someone came to see my cellmate. In the dark, it was simplicity itself to reenact the trick that had ended with me trapped inside, only this time I stood at the back of the cell while the hapless guard opened the door, completely oblivious to my presence. In seconds we were in the hall, robbing the unconscious Nuum of his keys and weapon.

"A sword?" I hefted it for balance. It seemed too light to be real.

My former cellmate eyed me cautiously. "Looks like. It's made out of plastic or something. You know how to use that thing?"

I waved it around, more for effect than anything else. "I've used one before." No sense in telling him how long ago…

"Don't think I like the idea of you having a weapon."

Without taking my eyes off of my companion, I relieved the Nuum of his belt and girdled it on. Then I sheathed the sword and faced him empty-handed.

"Would you like to try to take it away from me?"

From my brief clutch of his arm, I could tell that the men of the 24th century must be less physical than those of the 20th. He couldn't fight me and we both knew it.

"Let's just get out of here," he said at last. "None of this'll mean a damn if we can't out of this building."

I told him I agreed and we set to work figuring the lock-and-key mechanism on the outer door. When we had it undone, I held out my hand.

"Thank you."

"For what?"

"For letting me know where I was. For letting me know there's a way back."

Although he looked unhappy, he took my hand. "My name's Buchwalter."

"Charles Clee."

"Good luck," he said, and I believe he meant it. Then he turned, and my best chance of ever getting home walked out of my sight forever.

"Directory."

Directory. Please make your selection.

"Does Hori Han work in this building?"

Hori Han works in the library, level seven.

"Please take me to level seven."

The lobby on level seven was equipped with its own directory, naturally, and just as naturally I couldn't read a word of it. But by this time I was beginning to get an idea of how to find my way around. I asked for directions; it gave them promptly, and I set off down the hall feeling very pleased with myself.

Hori Han worked alone in a small room, sitting at a flat table with various lighted buttons and some kind of moving picture screen set into its surface. Behind her several doors lead to other rooms, each one marked by a single character. Hori Han looked up as I entered.

"Yes, can I help—?" Her automatic greeting faded away as she realized who I was. In an instant she was around the table and flinging her arms about my neck.

"We thought you'd been killed!"

I disentangled her gently and shook my head. "No. I was

caught by a mob, but I was rescued." I indicated our surroundings. "They thought I was one of them, so they brought me here."

Hori leaned forward to get a better look at my face and shock gave way to horror. I hadn't had a chance to look in a mirror since I was beaten and it only now occurred to me that I must look frightening. If a Nuum saw me like this, it would be hard to argue my way out of a visit to the doctor a second time. Thank heaven I hadn't tried to walk through the lobby to leave the building.

"You've got to see a doctor about those bruises."

"I can't. The minute he performs an examination, he'll know I'm not who I say I am—which raises a good question, now that I think of it. If they ask me, what name should I give?"

"You can use your own. It's unusual, but it won't arouse any suspicion." She glanced at my left temple, not for the first time, and I wondered just how big a bruise I was sporting there. Whatever the Nuum had given me for the pain on the flight was still working, so I had no idea how badly I was hurt.

"You'll have to stay here tonight," Hori decided. "You'd attract too much attention looking like that. You can use room number two; I can fix the records. Just stay inside until I come get you."

"But what if someone comes in?" Her face froze with an expression as if I'd suggested using a Chaucer manuscript to line a birdcage. It took a visible effort for her to speak.

"No one will bother you." She shuddered. "The very idea is disgusting."

"My God," I gasped. "What's in there?"

"It's a library." She lead me to one of the rear doors and hustled me through. There was no light inside.

"A library? But I can't read!"

"The librarian will take care of you."

"The librarian? But I thought *you*—" The door slammed and I was alone in the dark…

"Hello. I am the Librarian."

…wasn't I?

One moment all was dark, the next there was light. But not all of a sudden; it rose softly, more gradual than dawn itself, springing from the very air and gently impinging on my eyes, the darkness now merely a mist, now dispelled altogether. And when the last had lifted, I could not but survey my surroundings and gasp with pleasure.

Stretching further than I could have imagined, the room was lined floor to ceiling with books, broken only by faded medieval tapestries and a fireplace fit for roasting—well, me, had I been so inclined. Each shelf was dark with a shine mahogany can only achieve when rubbed by generations of scholarly hands. A second gallery wound about above my head, similarly lined with thousands of volumes.

On a tabouret alongside the leather chair near the fireplace a brandy snifter stood ready to welcome the contents of its companion Waterford decanter. I lifted the latter, inhaled the deep aroma of its amber treasure, and swayed on my feet.

It wasn't until I put the decanter down again that I noticed the fire, reflected in its facets. But I wasn't just unobservant; it hadn't been there before.

Then I remembered the voice, and the warmth of the room abandoned me.

"Hello?" I ventured.

"Good morning," said a friendly voice behind me.

I forced myself not to spin around. I hadn't been shot; this had to be a good sign. Instead I turned as though I had every right in the world to be exactly where I was.

"Good morning," I responded. "You're the librarian?"

He nodded, once. The Librarian was the oldest man I had seen since my advent through the co-continuum. With his watery blue eyes, furrowed, kindly face, and white hair, he reminded me much more of an Oxford don than a Nuum. Even his robe complemented the comparison. Only later was I to learn how accurate my initial impression was.

"Have you helped yourself to a brandy, sir?"

My gaze darted guiltily back toward the decanter behind me.

"I'm sorry. Was that yours?"

"Not at all, sir." Stepping past me, he decanted a glass of brandy and handed it to me. "I put it there for you."

The warmth of the liqueur seeped into my hand through the glass while the fumes drifted into my nostrils. It was as heavenly as before. When I finally succumbed to the temptation of tasting it, I could only close my eyes and let my palate savor the moment. All outside sensations slipped away, until only the grandfatherly voice of the librarian remained.

"I am glad to see you enjoying it, sir. It has been many years since I have been asked to entertain anyone but a Nuum."

Chapter 11
I Receive My Education

The glass didn't break when I dropped it. It simply hit the floor and vanished. I stared stupidly at the spot until the librarian spoke again.

"I apologize if I startled you, sir. My appearance was designed to make you as comfortable as possible, but your brain structure is so unfamiliar that I may not have gotten everything quite correct."

I looked up. "My brain structure?" I repeated. "You can read my mind?"

He smiled disarmingly. "Of course not, sir. Not in the sense that you mean. But I am able to interpret the emanations of your mind and take certain impressions. I then use those impressions to sculpt the library environment to the most useful setting. I must say, however," he added, scanning the room, "that I have never used anything like this before." I watched in complete bewilderment as he walked to the nearest wall and plucked a volume from a shelf. "What are these things?"

"They're books."

"What are they for?" he asked, turning it over in his hands.

"You read them. There's writing inside... What kind of a librarian are you?"

Opening the book, he ignored me. "Fascinating. I've never heard of such a thing."

"How can you call yourself a librarian if you've never seen a book before?"

He seemed to recall me with a start and put the book away.

"I'm sorry, sir. How can I help you?"

"You can start by answering my question!"

"I call myself a Librarian because that is what I am. Since until I met you I had never heard of a book, I don't know how else to answer you."

I had to sit down. The chair made a comfortable place to ponder, but the librarian's hovering made it difficult. He put another brandy on the tabouret. He pulled more books from the shelves and made a point of pretending to examine them while he examined me. Eventually he went away, but I couldn't shake the feeling he was always right over my shoulder.

Sure enough, when I stood up, there he was.

"Where am I?"

"You are in Library Two, Nuum Administrative Tower, Vardan, Thora."

"Vardan? Thora?" I repeated, pronouncing the latter in the German style. "What are those?" Of course, I was already familiar with the terms, having heard them from Bantos Han, but the librarian might provide more information.

The librarian seemed not at all nonplused by my questions. "Vardan is the name of this city. Thora is the name of this planet."

"I thought this was Earth."

This did seem to give him pause. He stood perfectly still for at least two seconds, not long in most situations but quite noticeable in a conversation.

"This planet has not been called Earth for approximately 800,000 years. Yours is the first contemporary reference to that name of which I am aware since I was initialized."

As with so many facts I had recently become to know, I believe that I had already decided that the librarian was not a man, but the confirmation did not fill me with any sense of satisfaction. Rather it filled me with apprehension. I knew now how Alice felt when she fell down the rabbit hole.

"Where I come from," I said in what I believed to be a remarkably normal voice, "it is called Earth. I am a time traveler from the 20th century."

"Really," he replied distantly. "Time travel is number thirteen on the list of those subjects whose research I am instructed to report to the Nuum."

"However," he continued, "my human programmers have blocked that instruction."

I breathed a sigh of relief, even though I wasn't completely sure why. "Initialized?" "Programmers?" There were gaps in my education that needed to be remedied immediately. Belatedly I realized that Hori Han must have had exactly that thought in mind when she left me here.

"Librarian, where can I find books that will help me to live in this century?"

"That is a wide field." He placed one hand on his chin, supporting his elbow with the opposite hand exactly as one of the dons in my college had done. Now that I looked, I could see that don's features on the librarian, mixed in with those of other men I had known. The effect was pleasant, if unsettling when you dwelled upon it. At least, for all that he was a machine, he sounded far more human than the elevator. "I can give you a general education, but much of it will depend on concepts with which you are unfamiliar: hierarchical mathematics, biosoftware conceptualization, psycholinguistics, genetic engineering, dataspherics, atypical physics, prescient causality…and of course, more history than your brain might absorb."

I stared at him. "I can't learn all that—I'm only going to be here one night!"

True to his form, he *tsked*, then gently lead me back to the chair. He took a book off a shelf.

"Since you are familiar with these books, I can use them as your interface. Just open it as you would normally."

"But I can't read it. I don't understand this alphabet."

"Then that will be the first thing we teach you. I will transfer the information directly into your unconscious mind while you sleep. Some things you will retain better than others, because you have already studied them. Those neural pathways are established and can be expanded upon. And muscle memory, for example, can only be learned over time."

I opened the book...

There was no sensation of awakening other than the knowledge that I had been asleep. The librarian stood over me in the same position he had been in before. He was smiling again.

"Don't try to get up just yet. Your neural networks are not as developed as were those for whom this program was written. It might give you a headache."

He was right about that. My first winter in England had greeted me with snow and a terrible head cold, and that was how I felt now. My skull was throbbing all over. The librarian handed me a pill and a glass of water, both of which I took with thanks. Immediately my discomfort began to fade into the background, but I was content to let him speak on.

"I gave you as much basic general knowledge as I thought safe. Your brain is more disposed toward artistic than logical endeavors, so your grounding in mathematics is quite limited. This was particularly necessary since your own education was very primitive in those areas." He bent down to peer into my eyes before continuing. "On the other hand, given your dilemma, I thought it superfluous to feed you a deep understanding of contemporary art and literature."

"My dilemma?" Any attention I was paying to my headache

was now diverted. "What dilemma?"

"My original programming goes beyond simple data input and output. I was designed to assist patrons in sifting through research and synthesizing outlines. Moreover, I have been operational for over 600,000 years. In that time I have continued to develop through self-programming. It is my analysis that once your presence here is known, you will immediately become the most valuable man on Thora."

I felt a warning chill. Even though I knew the answer, I had to ask, "Why?"

"Time travel is a highly-prized commodity, sir," the Librarian informed me. "Both the Nuum and the Thoran resisters would pay dearly to possess it. Once they learn of your origin, they will want to take you into their custody."

"But I don't *know* anything... What about the men who followed me here?"

"If the presence of additional time travelers were known, they would rank equal to you as a goal."

I paused to consider my options. "Then if anyone finds out about them, I'll lose my chance to get home."

For the second time, the librarian did not answer me immediately, but this time instead of freezing, he paced slowly before the fireplace. It made him more human, more familiar; had he done more while I was asleep than simply give me information? Had he taken information from me as well?

"That is not necessarily true. I am only a branch librarian, but the main library in Hebrone might have more information on time travel. It is even possible that a time machine still exists."

"Are you sure? Where?"

"I don't know. The only information on time travel in my database is very old: The last known incidence of a time traveler arriving from the past occurred approximately 100,000 years ago. And I cannot access Hebrone mainframe on a classified subject through the datasphere. It could be picked up by the Nuum, and traced to you."

The datasphere was a worldwide information network telepathically accessible only by the Nuum—and by the Library. That information came automatically; I had not known it before, but I did now. Its existence contributed to the fact that the Library was empty, since most of the data useful on a day-to-day basis was directly available to any individual authorized to have such information. Thorans, naturally, did not, which explained why it had never come up in my conversations with Bantos Han and his family.

"What if I went to Hebrone? Could I download the information from the library there?" I didn't even notice when I started using new words; they were simply there for me.

"Yes, but Hebrone is a very long way from here." He handed me a book, whose title I could now read: World Geography. I opened it at random and saw a map of the Northern Hemisphere with my location and that of Hebrone clearly marked. I noted in passing that time had changed the face of the earth, but I saw much more clearly than that how far I had to go. If I were still in what was once France, Hebrone was what in my time had been called California. "I must also warn you that, if the Nuum were to conduct an audit of the library records, they would discover your search."

That slowed me. "And that could lead them to me."

"Researchers' identities are private," he assured me. "But the results of your research are not."

I considered this for a moment. Even were I to find a way back, it might take time to use it. I might even have to build a machine from scratch—assuming I found the plans for one. And I would be leaving behind a roadmap for an alien race to conquer not only this planet, but all of Time, as well…

He who hesitates is lost.

"Can you give me a copy of this map?"

"I can do better than that," he replied. He held in his hand a metal sphere about the size of a large marble. "This is a mini-branch library. It contains information that your brain couldn't hold. I have programmed it with geographic, political, and other data that will aid you on your journey. You can access it by voice command."

"Thank you."

"Don't thank me yet," he warned, shaking his head. "This machine is forbidden by the Nuum. If they catch you with it, it is a capital crime."

I thought of my pistol, hidden in Bantos Han's house. That, too, was a capital offense. Suddenly I thought of Hori Han, and I asked the librarian how long I had been there. It was far less than it seemed, but there was still much to learn, so little time! The irony had never been more poignant. Just a few hours ago I had witnessed the aftermath of an incredible bestial atrocity, and now I as I looked around I saw myself surrounded by the summit of knowledge of almost a million years of mankind.

Surely in this library were the answers to more than my simple problems.

"Librarian, given your grasp of history, can you estimate the how long it will be before the Nuum empire falls?"

"Given the current trends and allowing for no significant outside forces, the Nuum will be absorbed into the Thoran population in approximately 253 years."

I squinted at him suspiciously. "That didn't take you long."

"You were not the first person to ask that question."

I attempted to learn the identity of the other researcher, as much to test his resolve as to discover an answer, but try as I might, he refused to divulge the name, and I eventually gave up. Time was fleeting and there was much else to learn.

Following the Librarian's advice, I finally satisfied myself with picking random volumes and skimming them for what I could understand: Tantalizing glimpses of scientific discoveries, bizarre cultures, pioneering space colonies, unimaginable human atrocities. I learned in one night about the rise and fall of human civilizations in eerily consistent cycles of one hundred thousand years; of the constancy of man's devotion to love and hate; of the similarities of alien races spawned on opposite sides of the galaxy. When Hori Han opened the door in the morning, I walked out of the library with my head in the clouds.

When we arrived back at their home, Bantos Han and Hana were awaiting us. When they had heard how I had survived the rioting and how Hori had found me in the Nuum's own headquarters, they had both notified their employers that they would not be in that day. Following the disturbances, many businesses had closed, so there was no problem with their decision to stay home. Hori had gone in as usual, solely to retrieve me, then made her excuses and left early.

They greeted me with hugs such as I would have expected from my own family upon my return from France. Hana threw her arms around my neck in a fashion I found especially enjoyable. When she pulled back to look at my face, tears streaming down her cheeks, she kissed me right there before her siblings, God, and everyone.

"You've found something! I can tell," she said breathlessly.

"Perhaps," I replied. "Perhaps not. Let's go into the living room so I can tell you about it."

As we sat down, I used the time to consider my words. The Hans, especially my Hana, had earned the right to the truth, but now that so much more than my own life hung in the balance, in, could I trust that this mind-reading, tyrannical society would allow them to keep it to themselves?

As usual, my hosts were far ahead of me.

"If you did find something, maybe you should keep the details to yourself," Bantos Han suggested. His caution surprised me, until I recalled our conversation in the garden, his hatred of the Nuum and his covetous looks at my Webley. Perhaps Bantos Han had secrets of his own that the Nuum would pay to discover…

In general terms, then, I outlined my visit to the Library, my assumption of so much useful contemporary knowledge. I told them that a way to return to my own time might exist, although uncovering it would engender its own dangers. The existence of my branch library remained a secret. I also described for them the advent of the riots, but for Hana and Hori's sake I stuck to an outline of that subject as well. I could give the details to Bantos Han later; from his look I believed that, given a chance, he would soon press me for that information regardless.

"So what will you do?" asked Hori. "If you find your information, it could place a terrible technology in reach of the Nuum, and if you don't, you're stuck here forever."

"Unless the Silver Men find me and kill me," I said. "Or the Nuum find out who I am and kill me. If it exists at all, the time travel technology has been locked away for ages. No one has stumbled across it until now, and there's no reason to suppose anyone will find it because of me, if I don't attract any attention to myself. Maybe I can even destroy it before I go." And if not, I reminded myself, the Nuum will be gone soon. That knowledge had been lost for 100,000 years. It would stay hidden another two hundred. "All I have to do is keep a low profile."

We were interrupted by the buzzing of the door. As I was the nearest, I passed my hand over the light which activated the visitor screen. When I spoke of what I saw, it was as though my voice were coming from far away.

"It's the Nuum," I said. "They've found me."

Chapter 12
Kidnapped

Farren strolled into the house as though he owned it—which in a sense he did. During the period in I had been learning how to carry myself as though I belonged in this place and time, Farren had been a frequent, if unwelcome, visitor. His attentions upon Hana had never varied: insistent, boorish, and in vain.

Had I not witnessed his visit that first night, I might have taken Hana's present reaction to him as reassurance that her heart leaned toward me, but having seen them together before I made my appearance, I knew beyond a shadow of a doubt that in this, at least, my presence was immaterial. She despised him, man or Nuum, and he just wouldn't take the hint.

It seemed that now, however, he had comprehended his problem and was prepared to use the force typical of his race to remedy his other shortcomings.

On his prior visits, moreover, he had aroused in me only the relatively impersonal outrage that came from seeing a woman subjected to unwanted attentions, the kind of seething anger any gentleman would experience when he was helpless to step in and halt the injustice. Now, however, my rage was infinitely more personal—this time he was threatening the person I held most dear in this utterly alien world. If he were to lay a hand on Hana in my presence now, one of us would soon lie dead on the floor.

Yet this visit was different in another sense. Always before, Farren had arrived alone to pursue his vain ambition; this time he brought another. The second Nuum stood back from the proceedings at all times, his eyes flickering ceaselessly between the family members, and me. Me most often of all. Speculation as to why Farren suddenly foresaw the need for a bodyguard gnawed anxiously.

Now he strode brusquely straight to Hana as though the rest of us did not exist. She grasped her sister's arm as he spoke.

"Hana Wen, gather your things. You are coming with me."

For a moment, the world stood still, then Bantos Han stepped forward—to protest, to strike, I did not know, but Farren's bodyguard did not wait to learn. He flashed before his employer and struck at my friend's head with a short club he had carried at his waist. It was a wicked, swift blow designed to incapacitate or worse, and likely would have split Bantos Han's skull.

I got there first.

Farren gaped and the bodyguard frowned when I grabbed the club in mid-swing, holding it fast. The effort nearly broke my hand, but I kept the pain of my face by concentrating on my overwhelming anger. I easily twisted the club out of the other man's hand and flung it aside.

"What is the meaning of this?" I demanded before Farren could open his mouth to do the same.

It doesn't matter whether you are right or wrong as long as you take the initiative. His self-control faltered in the slightest degree. He had not expected to find another lion guarding the sheep-pen, nor did he find looking up at me a pleasant experience. Men like Farren are used to looking down their noses at others, regardless of height. I refused to let him.

"I am Farren ten Paset," he announced, not without a heavy touch. "Ten" indicated a Nuum of high noble state. If he expected me to retire from the field at the sound of his name, however, he must have been quite surprised when I did not move or speak. "I'm here to speak to Hana Wen. Alone."

I laughed softly, glancing from his retainer back to him. My continued silence goaded him into impatience.

"Whatever your business here, it is done. Move aside. Better yet, go. The woman is mine, now."

Oh, that was his game! He thought I was another of Hana Wen's suitors, a powerful man in the eyes of the rabble, but sure to step aside when a true lord of lords such as he entered the picture. It did seem a convenient way of explaining my presence.

"I believe my claim takes precedence over yours, my lord. The lady prefers me."

Anger, defiance, and disbelief battled across his weak features.

"The lady—?" he sputtered. "This is no lady, this is a common Thoran! Who are you to speak that way?" Then he actually turned to his bodyguard, and asked, "Who is this man?"

The bodyguard closed his eyes for a half-second. Bantos Han grabbed my arm, but I didn't need him to tell me what must be happening. The Nuum was accessing the datasphere, apparently because Farren could not be bothered with such a menial task himself. But the Hans and I knew what he would find...

His eyes opened and focused on me and he leaped forward, all in an instant.

The impact of his face into my clenched fist made a satisfying sound, but it nearly broke my hand. I had the advantage of knowing what he was going to do before he did it, by virtue of knowing what he would find when he researched me in the datasphere, which was to say, nothing—but it must have looked to Farren as though I had the reflexes of a cobra, so quickly did I counter his bodyguard's attack.

I hid my pain as I turned on Farren, reaching with my left hand to grasp for his throat. But I had underestimated him; he blocked me, and my hand went numb. I jumped back in surprise, and he opened his hand to reveal a small black tube that seemed to crackle with unseen energies. Behind me, Bantos Han hissed in horror. Now it was I who acted as though he had seen a poisonous snake, and Farren smiled cruelly as he advanced, confident in his superiority once more.

"My lord," gasped out the bodyguard, his voice rough from his smashed nose. "My lord, be careful! He's a *ghost*!"

Farren flinched and hesitated, and I seized the moment, charging him with my aching right hand, the left still useless. I knocked the tube out of his grip—he was nowhere near as strong as I—and moved in. I had no idea what I planned to do to him, but that it would be violent he could read in my eyes and he retreated until he backed into the door, his face white with fear.

"Keryl—look out!" There was a scuffle behind me, but as I turned all I could see was the bodyguard, blood streaming from his nose, cuff Bantos Han aside and sweep the black tube from the floor. He pointed it toward me, my limbs went numb, and I knew nothing more.

I awoke slowly and painfully, to find Hori Han crouched over her husband. She moved to see to me when she heard me, but I could see that her concern, rightfully, was with him and I waved her away.

Bantos Han recovered soon after I did, to my relief as well as Hori's. For a moment, we all sat there, sprawled on their floor, none wishing to be the first to admit what had happened. Although Bantos Han and I had been unconscious when he left, we knew Lord Farren was gone, and that Hana Wen had gone with him.

"Where will he take her?" I asked gently. A plan was already forming in my mind, vague as yet, but focused in its purpose.

"We knew this was coming; it was only a matter of time," Hana assured me hurriedly, as though explanation could wipe away the feeling of loss.

"*Where will he take her?*"

"To his palace," Bantos Han replied with resignation. "The same as the others."

"Once he gets tired of her, he'll send her back." We both looked at Hori with surprise. "She and I talked about this, Bantos. I told her not to resist, but not to cooperate, either. She knows what to do. He'll soon tire of her."

Try as she might, she could not hide the desperate note in her voice that told me she was trying to keep her husband or me from doing something that she feared would only make matters worse. She had lost her sister, her protestations to the contrary, and she wanted badly to hang onto what was left her. I felt more than a touch of gratitude that I was included in that category.

But gratitude faded to insignificance in light of the more volatile emotions that played within my heart.

I heaved myself to my feet, noting with satisfaction that my dizziness passed quickly. Bantos Han stood as well, though he required his wife's aid. I saw now that she had applied a compress of some type to the side of his head.

"Where is my weapon?" I asked him. He indicated where he had hurriedly hidden it at Farren's arrival, and I retrieved it, checking the action.

Hori started to protest anew, but Bantos Han stopped her with a gentle but firm gaze.

"You're right, dear, she's gone. But she doesn't have to spend her life as Farren's play-doll. If anyone can get her out of there, it's Keryl."

"What about the server scans?"

"What are server scans?" I asked. The words were familiar, but their meaning eluded me. Bantos Han hastened to explain. His words were rushed, and I wondered why.

"The palace is protected by mental scanners. But I don't think they can detect you. None of us can hear you unless you're speaking to us."

I nodded. "It's a chance I'll have to take."

But Hana Han was not finished. "And where will they go?" she demanded. "They can't come back here."

I had to admit that my plan had not progressed so far.

"You couldn't stay here, regardless," Bantos Han explained. "Farren has seen you; he thinks you're a ghost. A 'ghost' is someone who doesn't appear in the planetary datasphere; he has no official existence, because there are no records of him. Keryl, ghosts are almost always assassins. Farren thinks you're here to kill him. The only reason he didn't kill you is because he fears retaliation."

I tucked my revolver into my tunic. "Farren didn't kill me because he's a coward. And as much as I would like to validate his theory, I won't unless I have to."

"It would be best if you didn't; the city is going to be in a panic as it is. Lord Farren probably has men on their way here now, but we can tell them you threatened us and used Hana for bait. I just don't know how you're going to get in touch with us later. You don't know your way around, and Hana has never been out of the city."

Now I understood why he had hurried his explanations: time was short. "Don't worry about that." I thought of the branch library safely and secretly tucked into one of my pockets. The less Bantos and Hori Han knew, the safer we all were. "Just tell me how to get to Farren's palace."

"You can summon a vehicle from here," Hori told me, her surrender evident. "You can charge it to our account. It's what the Nuum do."

"That's right," Bantos said. "And remember, you're one of them now, not one of us. Act like you own everything. And one more thing, don't let anyone see your pistol. Remember, we're not allowed to carry mechanical devices of any kind."

"Don't worry about that, either. I'm not one of you."

The cab Bantos Han had summoned arrived quickly, and on

impulse I instructed its driver to take me away from the center of town. He obeyed without comment, nor did he so much as express curiosity in the small crowd of vehicles that swept to a halt outside of the Hans' residence just as we were turning a corner two blocks away, other than a flicker of his eyes in the mirror that I all but missed. We took a leisurely drive through the outlying homes of the district, I actually enjoying the comfortable view of the hills that had briefly been my home. I wondered if the men in silver hunted for me there still, and the notion made me sit back in my seat to escape any chance notice. I soon directed the driver to return to the city and take me to the palace.

He left me within sight of the main gate and drove off without requesting payment. The palace itself was tall, open, and translucent at this distance, though even from the ground I could see that many of its walls and windows were hazy, due to some process that left the material simultaneously opaque and transparent and allowed for the occupants' privacy. I shrugged off this latest wonder and walked to the gate as though I were Lord Farren himself. The Thoran guards nodded politely as I went by, but made no move to intercept or question me.

I passed through a long, wide hallway, with a cold marble floor, and abstract paintings adorning the walls on either side. I mixed with Nuum and Thorans on their own errands. The former ignored me, the latter acknowledged me only insofar as they must to avoid impeding my progress, or even crossing my path to the extent they could. As my boots softly slapped the smooth floor, an inadvertent thought came to mind: This was the hall of the servers, the mental sentries whose constant scanning was the greatest, and technically, the only defense against violence the Nuum possessed in these walls.

As I walked, my new learning, absorbed in my sleep, arose to my conscious mind, and what I suddenly realized almost made me stop in my tracks.

The servers were alive.

Almost as though I were reading from a text, the concept materialized before my mind's eye. The servers were Thorans, generally taken from the ranks of the terminally ill, who had volunteered to have their brains separated from their bodies and immersed in nutrient tanks, placed behind these very walls. Unfettered by the old demands of a body, they could create (with the use of Nuum technology) whatever world they desired in which to live, and yet enough of their mental potential remained to be harnessed by the Nuum for their own purposes, including security for this and other important buildings.

Each person passing through this gauntlet was scanned by these disembodied minds, searching for any indication of hostile intent. Finding such, the perpetrator would be immediately paralyzed by a telepathic jolt whose nature was only vaguely described. Moreover, any weapon he might carry was rendered useless, although by what means was not detailed. Had they recently been warned to watch for a ghost?

With an effort of my own will, I kept walking as though nothing were troubling me, but the thought that just behind those artistically-decorated walls lay tank after tank of naked human brains, hurried my feet despite my best efforts at nonchalance. After a long few minutes, I reached the end of the hall, and the palace proper.

Not being a commercial building or a tourist destination, there were no directories; every person there seemed to know exactly where he was going. I hesitated to ask directions, but then it came to me: Everyone had to come here for the first time; no one was born knowing the architecture. I marched straight up to the next guard I saw.

"Where are the elevators to Lord Farren's quarters?" Being a Thoran, he should neither require nor expect an explanation, but what if Farren's trust in his disembodied watchdogs was less than absolute? If he had warned his staff against intruders, I was likely to lose this battle before it was fairly joined.

But my fears were unfounded. "That way, sir," the guard responded immediately, pointing out the direction. "Around the corner to the right." Having said his piece, he snapped back to attention. I bit back my thanks and proceeded, as instructed, "as though I owned the place," although I itched intolerably between my shoulder blades all the same.

For the first time in my life, I took an elevator to the top floor of a building and emerged outside.

Roof gardens were hardly new to me; they extended back to Babylonian times. Still, I had asked the elevator to take me to Lord Farren's quarters, not his gardens. Yet before me stretched a spacious plaza of softly winding paths wending between profusions of lush foliage that tended largely to leafy palms, creepers, and mosses, copiously splashed with red, blue, purple, and orange flowers. I could not see clearly more than a few yards in any direction. Somewhere invisible birds sang softly; a breeze sprang up to cool my face as if on command.

On impulse, I turned to examine the elevator door that had silently closed behind me, and I was less than surprised to find that I had, to all appearances, stepped out of a thick stand of green bamboo. Nor was it merely a drawing or set piece; as closely as I looked, I could see nothing but thick green shoots of vegetation. The technology used by the Nuum made anything available to their Thoran serfs seem as primitive as...well, as I seemed to the Thorans.

An attitude which could serve me ill, should I be found gawking like a doughboy on his first leave in Paris. Just because I saw no one did not mean that no one saw me. I stepped forward along the first path I saw, apprehensive suddenly that I had not seen anyone here. I realized it had been naïve of me to expect that Farren would be in his own rooms when I came calling; Bantos Han's personal opinion of him aside, it was natural to assume that he must have some business that took him away during the day.

Still, I would have thought to see servants—unless everything was done mechanically?

No. I shook my head. Farren was the kind of man who would want others fawning over him and catering to his whims; witness his kidnapping of Hana Wen for his harem. Yet here were no maids—or gardeners. And yet the elevators had delivered me directly to Farren's private quarters when I could state no legitimate business—not that anyone had asked. I had been left alone to wander at will. I saw no movement of any kind except myself, heard no sounds, not even the phantom birds—save for a sinister scurrying through the leaves of the overarching trees...

The hairs on the back of my neck told me nothing that was not already obvious. The trap was sprung, and I was caught.

Chapter 13
The Garden of Death

"It's called a tiger spider," advised a voice from nowhere and yet everywhere at once. "It comes from the southern jungles. Its bite is invariably fatal, and there is no antidote."

Finding the location of the voice was of much less concern to me right now than locating the creature of which it had just warned me. While some rational part of my brain was trying to maintain composure by reassuring me that anything I heard could be broadcast in the same way as the strange voice, and anything I saw could be as false as the bamboo elevator, it was fighting a losing battle with my Neanderthal hindbrain. Caught between the urge to run and the need to hide, my feet were glued to the floor. By an effort of will, I removed my Webley from my tunic.

Out of the corner of my eye, I saw a spindly stick-like object emerge from cover—then another, and another. My lips were dry. The thing sidled into view not two feet from me and the urge to run became almost overwhelming. I have never been fond of spiders, and this must have reigned as their king.

I would estimate its legs spread twelve full inches across, yet it balanced its yellow and black striped body on a single leaf as though it weighed nothing at all. Its segmented eyes watched me intently, as though measuring the size web it would require, and despite every sermon I had ever heard pronouncing that Man was the only living creature with a soul, I would defy any priest to deny that this foul arachnid held evil in its gaze.

A single drop of sweat rolled down my throat.

Then it leaped.

I jumped backward in sheer instinctive fright, but it was not leaping at me. It stood on its eight legs blocking the path forward, tensed every so slightly forward, like a mastiff guarding its master's house from a burglar.

"It's not real, of course," said the same voice, only now it belonged to a man, a man who stepped out of hiding and stood behind his hideous bodyguard: Farren. He sneered at my obvious fear. "It's only a robot. I couldn't possibly have the real thing; it would kill everyone, even if I could find a way to capture one and bring it here. You don't want to know what it cost me to have this one made. It's an exact duplicate." He smiled like a chess master who has just determined the move that will give him the match. "Well, almost. It's also completely ray-shielded and telepathically activated." He indicated the Webley. "I assume that's some sort of weapon. If you try to shoot me, it will leap to my defense. And then it will kill you."

I could see now. Every living thing moves, however slightly, at every moment. This spider did not have that quality. Yet I would not doubt its lethality.

"How did you get in here, by the way?" Farren's question sounded genuine, and that was no surprise; he had a great deal invested in my answer.

I, on the other hand, had no intention of satisfying his curiosity.

"Where is Hana Wen?"

Farren blinked. "What do you care?"

I lifted the revolver and pointed it straight at the bridge of his nose. "I'll not ask again."

"I've already told you: If you activate that weapon, you'll die." His words were cold and precise, but he couldn't keep the smirk off of his face. "The same trigger that fires it will set the spider on you—and it's impervious to hand weapons."

I hadn't had an opportunity before to study the man, to see who he was. Now I stood curiously detached, a soldier facing an enemy whose humanity I had discounted, reduced to an abstract to facilitate the act of killing him.

His age I estimated at thirty, but it was impossible to be sure. I had noticed since my arrival in this time that no one seemed old, gray or decrepit. Perhaps Farren was my age, perhaps he was old enough to be my father. Once he had been an athlete, but now his love for easy living was betraying him through the softness of his jaw and the bags under his eyes.

Those eyes were staring into mine now, blue where the spider's were black, but otherwise the same. They both held contempt, utter disdain for anyone who could neither help nor harm them. But in Farren's face I saw too the smirk of a man who was used to his own way, all the time, no matter the cost to young women or their families—or the planet. It was the cocksure ghost of a smile of a conqueror who had never felt a hand in anger.

I lowered the barrel, taking careful aim on the robot. His twisted pride and joy, he had taken pains to show it off and tell me how much it had cost him, despite believing that I was a specialized assassin sent specifically to kill him—or perhaps because he believed it. The epitome of millennia of destructive engineering, the spider was telepathically triggered and impervious to modern weapons. I carefully squeezed the trigger of my million-year-old revolver and blew Farren's deadly toy into a hundred pieces. The noise staggered him, hands over his ears. I raised the gun to his face again. I had warned him I wouldn't ask about Hana Wen a second time, and I kept my promise.

He was trembling now, his eyes darting between my eyes and my Webley. A man of the kind I knew would have begun to sweat, his forehead would be moist and glistening, but Farren's was neither. Perhaps Nuum did not sweat. I had no doubt, however, that they would bleed. Still not speaking, my aim shifted to his left knee.

"All right! All right!" He fairly screamed, like a woman. "I—"

And in that moment, when I had unconsciously relaxed my guard, thinking the battle won, he jumped wildly to the side and disappeared into the foliage. Cursing, I fired wildly, but the bullet itself disappeared and I do not know what I hit. I plunged after him, entering the plants at the same spot, hardly surprised by now to find that there were no plants at all, but merely an illusion hiding another twisting path. Farren was nowhere to be seen, but I did not need to guess where he had gone. In seconds, this entire floor would be flooded with armed guards.

A hand abruptly appeared out of nowhere at my side, seizing my arm and pulling at me. When I resisted, a voice hissed:

"Come with me if you want to live!"

What choice did I have? I found myself in a small area half-filled with gardening implements—items I recognized because their basic utility had never changed. Evidently some of the plants in Farren's garden were real, and here was where his gardeners kept their tools. And where, it appeared, his gardeners spied on him.

My rescuer put a finger to his lips, another sign that had not changed at all.

"If you don't know where the door is," he whispered, "it is almost impossible to find."

The area outside exploded with noise, men—many men—bursting into the apartment, spreading out in a search pattern, looking for me. I heard them shouting instructions, suggestions, and finally questions as I was not run to ground. Farren's voice I did not hear.

While we stood unmoving and silent, I had a chance to appraise the Thoran who had saved me. Typical of his race, he stood only to my shoulder, dark-haired, elfin of features. His smock was irregularly smudged with dirt, a rarity in this world where dirt seemed as conquered as air travel or telepathy.

He was the first Thoran whom I had had an extended opportunity to study, other than Bantos Han and his family. Heretofore I had assumed that the similarities between them were simply familial, and where observed elsewhere, I did not ascribe a great deal of importance to them because I was trying not to stare, but without such a prolonged study, deductions become difficult.

Here, however, was a completely different person from my friends, different of background and breeding, perhaps different of racial origin, and yet he appeared in most respects quite similar to them; his skin, for example, was the same dark milky color, as though all of the races of Man had long ago coalesced into one. I confess that even I, who had grown up in America and felt no greater racial antipathy toward others than did my neighbor, found the idea of such melding a trifle unsettling. Lost I might be in a far-advanced era, but I was still a man trapped in my own time. I was glad that my unique brain physiology allowed me to keep such thoughts entirely to myself.

At length, the sounds of the search died away, but even then neither my rescuer nor I moved to leave our hiding place. By this I appreciated that he was no fool, and I fancy that he understood the same of me. In such a necessarily brief and uncommunicative friendship as our was to be, this kind of unspoken bond is the most to which one can aspire.

"I think they're gone," he whispered at last. "Let me go first."

"If they see you, they will know that you were here all along," I objected. "I won't stay hidden if they arrest you."

"If anyone sees me, I will stall as long as I can. You can either come to my rescue or try to escape, whichever seems best. But you can't be caught."

He turned to leave but I took his arm. Gentle as my grasp was, I doubted he could easily break it.

"What do you mean? Who are you? How did you know I was

here?"

He shook his head. "Names are dangerous—but Bantos Han sent word you would be here. You're a ghost; you're more valuable to Thora than I am—than any of us."

"What are you talking about? I came here to find Hana Wen, that's all. No matter what Farren thinks, I'm not an assassin."

He looked me straight in the eye. "You're a soldier, I know that much. You could help. You can go places where we can't, carry machines that we aren't allowed to own. You can help us take back Thora."

I thought back on Bantos Han now with greater clarity, and respect. What a weapon he must have thought he had found in me—and yet he was willing to give it all up to allow my quixotic adventure, rather than deny me my freedom. Or was it the life of his sister-in-law he held above all else? I doubted I would ever know, since I was unlikely to see him again. But my own path, dictated by my heart and my own sense of duty, was unchanged.

"I'm sorry, I can't. I came here to find Hana Wen, and I'm going to." His disappointment was evident on his face and in his thoughts. "Look," I continued on impulse, pulling out the Webley. "I can't carry this around anymore; they'll be looking for it. But if you can smuggle it out of here…"

His despair evaporated in an instant. He had witnessed, in some sense, the entire exchange between Farren and me; he knew what my Webley could do, and how it could operate where more sophisticated machinery was useless. I quickly showed him how to use it, paying special attention to the importance of never pointing even an "unloaded" gun at anyone you did not plan to shoot. He accepted the gift with alacrity.

"This is wonderful," he said as he hid it among his tools. "Now we can both be shot on sight." I must not have appreciated his wry humor, because when he spoke again it was with utter earnestness. "Look, Farren's probably gone back to Dure. That's where his family is. It's thousands of miles away. We can use you here. You don't even have any way of getting there."

"Leave that to me." *Assuming I can get out of here, of course…*

Chapter 14
I See War

There was no sound in the cabin, no rush of air or roaring engines, nothing but the steady soft rasp of my own breath. Common soldiers didn't merit outside berths with breathtaking views of the tops of the clouds, and as my bunkmate Harros had joked right before he went off to mess, if you climbed to the observation deck at this speed the wind would sweep you straight off the ship.

I had begged off from breakfast, citing my injuries, although they were just memories now, and even the scars were fading fast. But Harros hadn't argued; I think he was put off by my manner. I am normally much more gregarious with my fellows-in-arms, but under the present circumstances I thought battlefield friendships both unnecessary and ill-advised.

Especially since I was not at all sure which side I wanted to fight for.

How had I come to be here? To put it succinctly, I had been shanghaied. This worked in my favor; I was able to put on a show of total ignorance of where I was going, and why, without rousing any suspicion. Even the fact that no one knew me had so far not posed a problem.

Escaping Farren's palace had proven far easier than I could have hoped; his security, to give it perhaps a better name than it deserved, was unused to actually needing to do more than stand and look mildly menacing. As with so much of their culture, the Nuum had placed too much confidence in their machines to have any experience in the real-life tracking of men.

How ironic, then, that such was my own goal, to track Farren down wherever he might run and wrest from him that which I desired with my heart, and which he desired with only the basest animal emotions: Hana Wen. Whence he would fly, I knew not, but the answer would likely be found in the midst of his fellows.

With that end in mind, I marched boldly into the aliens' headquarters, planning to elicit advice from the Library. Hardly had I stopped before the elevator than two Nuum pulled up even with me, seized me by the arms, and whisked me away.

At first I thought I had been arrested, but in the space of the few words they vouchsafed me, they made it clear that they thought I was merely one of their own, whose blind obedience and cooperation were expected. I immediately discarded any impulse to break free, although I am certain I could have done so with ease. Although their bulk was nearly the equal of my own, their muscles seemed less developed, as if generations of allowing mechanicals to do their heavy work had softened them.

They ushered me back to the hangar whence I had first entered the building days before, loosening their grip when it became obvious I was not going to resist. Docked there was what I could only presume was a large airship. It was a silvery white oval, not unlike a large zeppelin, but without any gondola that I could see. I was marched up a gangplank to an officer holding an electronic clipboard who presided at a hatchway at the top. After a few words with my escort the officer waved me inside.

"Hey, wait a minute!"

I stopped and turned slowly, still in the hatchway. "Yes, sir?"

He spent a very long moment staring me up and down.

"What's your name?"

As much as I had been expecting this, it was still hard to form the words.

"Uh, Keryl Clee, sir."

Again he studied me closely, his eyes narrowing.

"Good to have you aboard. We're going to need men like you." He made an entry on his clipboard, and waved me inside, where more officers stood to direct me to my bunk assignment.

I tried not to stare, but the few open doors I passed were full of banks of machinery whose blinking lights and buttons that were very nearly frightening to a boy barely out of the dusty Southwest. Electricity was still very new where I grew up, and Bantos Han's house had featured few machines of any kind, or at least any that I could recognize as such. Knowing that this was a war vessel and that some of those lights and panels probably represented weapons beyond my comprehension did nothing to soothe my nerves.

One—and not the least—of the evils of trench warfare had been the hours of waiting until your orders came up from the rear echelons, knowing that when the waiting ended the dying and the killing began. As I sat on my bunk in the belly of a war machine the likes of which I could not have imagined a few weeks ago, I felt that same anxiety—except that this time I didn't have any chums to help pass the time away in song, or family reminiscences, or just plain companionable silence. I was alone, and only one person could make that any better.

Finally overcoming my own self-pity, I got off my meager bunk and wandered off to find food. The mess room hit me like a sharp, cold wave at the beach. All of my previous experience with the Nuum had shown me an efficient, aloof people in a cold, streamlined environment. I had dismissed Harros' attempts at camaraderie as an aberration, only what was expected of civilized men trying to make the most of uncivilized conditions. One minute in the mess hall plainly revealed that this time the uncivilized lout had been me.

Only three-quarters full, the room could not have held more noise. Arching over all was the music—at least I think it was music. To me it was loud, chaotic, and discordant, but from the number of tables rocking back and forth under the timely pounding of Nuum fists, to them it was prime entertainment. I resisted the urge to put my hands over my ears with some effort and found an empty seat as far from the others as I could. I was still being unsociable, but at least I was being unsociable in a crowd. And I was still an alien among aliens—I wasn't even sure I knew how to order a meal.

Suddenly I realized that I was famished. When had I last eaten? I couldn't remember for the life of me—unless it was in the Library, and I didn't know just how far the food provided by the Librarian might satisfy me. Without a thought I swept my hand over the table, and a menu glowed to life beneath the surface. The Librarian had plainly taken wide latitude with the knowledge he had implanted: The operation of the food service machines seemed to flow straight from my fingers with no direction from my brain. My facility was that of any Nuum born and bred, nor did my familiarity stop there. I had never seen a single one of the menu items before, yet I made my selections with alacrity and confidence. While I waited, I took in the room again.

No eyes at all were directed toward me; no one had heard me walk in over the noise. The music stopped abruptly—I breathed a sigh of relief—only to crash back as twice as loudly and incomprehensibly as before. This time I couldn't help putting my hands over my ears.

"Loud enough for you?"

I jerked my head up. I had heard the question as clearly as if the music hadn't been driving straight through me. For an instant, despite abundant evidence to the contrary, I thought it must have stopped—then I remembered the magic of telepathy and its independence of my ears.

Harros stood across from me, a tray of food in his hand and an inquiring look on his face. I nodded and he sat down.

"Sorry if I startled you," he said in my mind. It was an odd feeling, this communication through telepathy alone, but it seemed to block out normal hearing, and soothed the headache I was getting from the music. "I didn't realize you had come in here because it would help you concentrate."

He had a smile on his face, and he conveyed it with his thoughts, so I grinned back. With the music softened, it seemed easier to smile. Harros' timeless offer of friendship had helped me delude myself into believing for the moment that we were merely two more soldiers fighting a war we pretended to understand.

"It's all right," I said. "I really came in here for the company. I just wasn't prepared for the music."

"First time, eh?"

"Hm?"

"First time on a fighting ship?"

"Yes." At least on a flying one. "How did you know?"

"Easy. You hate the music." He grinned. "This is all they play. After a while you get used to it. What did you do before?"

I hazarded a guess. "I was in the library section."

"You?" His eyebrows shot up. "You sure don't look like a librarian. How'd you land a job like that?"

"Just lucky, I guess."

He leaned back in his chair and laughed, the sound lost in the music. It didn't come through his thoughts at all. I just kept grinning like an idiot. I had no idea why he thought it was so funny.

And then the music halted again, abruptly as before, but this time it didn't start back up. Harros' laugh came out full force, odd like a sound that is cut off in reverse. He brought himself under control with an effort and swiveled in his chair.

I expected an officer to address us, but in the air over our heads in the center of the room an image began to take form. It was a map of a hilly plot of land that I didn't recognize. The accompanying voice emanated from no particular direction.

"You are viewing a map of the black sector. The Thorans have taken advantage of the local topography to mount an unusually strong terrorist offensive." In the next sentence I thought the voice deviated noticeably from its even pedantic tone. "The blacks have been unable to contain the problem."

The image glided to a ground-level view of a rolling jungle crisscrossed with what had looked from the air like roads.

"The local eco-system is highly fragile and highly valuable, which prevents our using our heaviest firepower, a fact that the rebels have used to their own advantage. Witness."

The next scene was reminiscent of a motion picture battle scene, save that the pictures were in color, and far more vivid than anything I had ever seen in the cinema back home. Our point of view started at ground level, then rose straight up like a man coming to his feet. It was only when our vantage point moved forward that I realized it was a man, evidently carrying a camera—although where he held it I could not fathom, since at intervals either of his hands might be seen.

Something bothered me about his hands, and distracted me from the action. I tried to concentrate, but at the moment the camera was simply moving through tall grasses toward a line of overwhelming trees. We could see helmeted men to either side carrying what appeared be staffs of some sort, and hear the swishing of many legs cutting through the rushes, but no one spoke, and there was little to keep my attention. What was it…?

Of course! The voice had spoken of "the blacks" being unable to handle their own problems with the rebels. I had assumed that the Nuum to whose aid we were speeding were dark-skinned…but the hands in the picture were white. I breathed a sigh of inward relief that I could dispose of my irrelevant concerns—obviously the man carrying the camera must be an officer, a white man commanding a Negro company. It was comforting in a way to see that some of Nature's orders remained the same no matter how else Man might change.

Like so many other cherished illusions of my existence, this would soon be shattered by a truth far more astonishing than any I could imagine.

I jerked my head back to the screen as a flash of light scored across it. The camera began to zig-zag back and forth. Occasionally a small explosion would burst off to the side or in front of us, return fire as I supposed, but there were few of those, and as we approached the trees the firing from our side halted altogether.

But it was not until at last the camera burst through the grasses onto a seared strip of land, and a line of men rose up to meet us in hand-to-hand combat as if Jason himself had sown them from dragon's teeth, that I realized how cruelly correct my observations of humanity had been. Those were not roads I had seen earlier. And this was not war with buttons and levers and death rays from the sky.

This was trench warfare. And I was headed straight for it.

Chapter 15
I See Battle

The mess room briefing was only a short overview of the problem; after a few minutes of watching the kind of warfare any intelligent species would have banned millennia past, we were ordered back to our bunks for what turned out to be some kind of sleep learning, similar in process to what the Librarian had done for me.

Harros seemed more disposed to conversation on the way back to our room; apparently he had forgiven me my earlier rudeness.

"That looked like fun, didn't it?" He winked as though he didn't believe I would understand his stab at humor.

"At least it wasn't raining," I answered, which earned me an odd look.

"Are you sure you haven't done this before? I thought you were in the Library section."

I couldn't help it; he seemed so gullible.

"Do I look like someone who's spent his entire life in the library?" Actually, up until a year ago, I had.

"You mean you have been in combat?"

"Years ago." Inwardly I cringed at my own understatement. "But it was all on the ground," I added, sensing his confusion. "No flying."

He seemed satisfied to take me at my word. "Then you know what this kind of stuff is like—all this running back and forth and jumping into holes in the ground."

I nodded unhappily. "Like I said, it's worse when it rains."

"I heard somebody say it rains down there every day. I guess it would, from all those trees we saw." He stopped as we came abreast of our compartment. "We must be pretty far south, then."

Pretty far, I agreed to myself. An unexpected stroke of Providence, that. But was it far enough?

I was awakened by the cessation of a motion I hadn't been aware of before it stopped. I awoke clear-headed, a notable phenomenon for me under any circumstances, with the feeling I had just emerged from a dream—and the entire tactical situation of South Equator in my head. Across from me, Harros was rousing himself with somewhat less celerity than I; I used the few moments this gave me to myself to acquaint my conscious mind with what my sleeping brain already understood.

South Equator was what the Nuum, in the exercise of their limitless imagination, had christened the southern equatorial continent. I suppose that it most closely resembled northern Africa of my day, but only in geographic placement. The flora and fauna were more akin to that I had read of in certain explorers' accounts of Central America in my own time. When I read them, I had frankly dismissed many of their tales outright; I found their tales of jungle fever and delirium more than an adequate explanation for imagined man-eating mosquitoes, plants, and just about anything else that crawled, slithered, or oozed.

After dreaming of South Equator, I viewed jungle fevers as almost friendly.

The political situation was clear enough: Less of a rebellion than a strike, the Thorans had abandoned their plantation duties for the trenches. Apparently believing soldiers were merely pawns to go and to fight where and when ordered without access to the higher reasons behind the fighting itself (another practice I was sad to see had survived the centuries), the Nuum had not bothered to describe why the workers had revolted. They told us that the harvest of a number of plant species was being interrupted, plants that served important purposes we were either assumed to know or weren't entitled to be told.

Still, the pictures they did show us were instructive.

Along with many other animals I had seen in the hills during my first few days here, the beasts of the jungle had climbed up the evolutionary ladder in almost one million years. Most obviously fearsome were the lions. In addition to increasing in size fifty percent, their forelimbs had developed longer and more useful claws until now they were almost arms, and the King of Beasts walked nearly upright, like an ape. In my day they had climbed trees like ladders—now they climbed walls.

Our lessons touched upon my friendly fevers, but only to the extent that we would be vaccinated against them before we were allowed out. More ominous were the myriad bites and stings that awaited us, "all of which can be made harmless with immediate treatment." I thought about the immediacy of medical aid in the trenches and resolved not to be stung or bitten.

Amazing, in hindsight, that anyone besides me ever stepped off the airship. That I did so could be traced to but one fact: On the other side of South Equator and perhaps a thousand miles further south from this spot stood the city of Dure.

But step off every man did, and purposefully, for we had a job to do. The local "blacks" had failed to keep order, and now it was our job. I still had not seen one of the "blacks." We stood at parade rest outside the ship, in the sun, while our officers stood about deep in conference about matters far beyond the ken of their troops. As an officer myself once upon a time, I had participated in those conferences, and I knew they first and foremost consisted of tossing about ideas as to how to get ourselves out of the hot sun.

As far as I was concerned, the officers could twiddle their thumbs all afternoon. I hadn't asked to be part of this army, I didn't believe in this army, and as soon as humanly possible I intended to separate myself from this army. And although I hardly needed my sleep-briefing to tell me that nighttime was a bad time in the bush, it beat being shot in the back trying to escape during the daylight. So I suffered in the heat. The longer we stood here the less likely it was that I would ever find myself in hand-to-hand combat with my own kind.

Nor was I planning any pitched battles with the men around me. True, they had enslaved my planet, but I was here only by accident, and I had my own fight. As soon as I could, I would strike out by myself across country and find my way to Dure and Hana. That was my well-laid plan…

…which I had plenty of time to reflect upon while I crouched in a trench awaiting the order to charge. Our officers hadn't wasted away the afternoon in idle chatter; they had formed us into smaller units and marched us straight onto the field of battle. We were armed with staffs, just as I had seen in the moving pictures. I examined mine as carefully as I could without arousing suspicion, but as far as I could tell it was no more or less than what it appeared to be: a long, heavy stick. I looked about; only the officers carried sidearms.

I shook my head in disbelief. The Nuum were so afraid of damaging the local jungle plants that they sent their own men into combat with…sticks. I knew what crossing no man's land was like. If the Thorans had gotten their hands on a single sidearm, they would wipe us out.

The order came to advance.

And it started to rain.

In my months in France, I had learned of the concept of *déjà vu*, or living through the same event twice. It had come over me again and again in those ancient trenches, and it hit me now. The rain, the men, the uncertainty of enemy fire were all the same elements I had faced the day I left France for this place. Only now I wasn't in charge.

We clambered over the slippery lip of the trench and began walking. Other than my mood, which was blacker than the Kaiser's mustache, it wasn't all that bad. The rain was warm, and the ground seemed to absorb as much as it could drink, so that the mud was only mud and not soul-sucking pools of sludge into which a man might disappear without so much as a cry. It made sticking sounds when I lifted my boots but at least I could lift them.

To the left and right of me men walked with a certain caution, sniffing the wind like a dog that knows the bear is in these woods but can't pick him up yet. But they stood straight up like reeds before a storm, or the armies of the Continent before they met the hideous reality of the German machine gun. Only I approached the enemy bent like an old man, ready to dive to one side or another at the first sign of the withering fire that would turn the other men into stalking-horses.

Some of my comrades looked at me oddly, but they had their own business to mind. The officers were different. One whose name I had never known and would never find out walked straight over to me with a parade ground strut and planted himself in my path. He opened his mouth to speak and took the blast that had been meant for me.

I was rolling madly away from that spot before his ashes settled. I began to shout at the men to get down, to take whatever cover the grass offered, but because they were still in shock or because I wasn't an officer, they ignored me. The Thorans had found more weapons somewhere, and all around me Nuum died.

The grass all around me cut off my vision. Mud was caked all over my uniform and my face; I had to clear my ears to hear what

I couldn't see. A sudden shout went up and the ground vibrated under me. I knew what had happened: the Thorans had used their ray-weapons in a surprise attack, panicking the Nuum, and now they were following up their advantage. If I stood, I would be shot; if I didn't, the enemy would stumble over me in seconds.

I have said that my body has always possessed the ability to act independently of rational thought, and that on odd occasions I find myself acting in ways that on later reflection even I find completely lunatic. I have also said that such lunacy has saved my life, and it did so now.

I leaped straight to my feet and charged the entire Thoran army single-handed.

Screaming at the top of my lungs and waving my staff about my head, I plunged right through their line and kept on going. Somewhere deep in my unconscious a small voice had reasoned that no one would shoot me if their own men were in the way, and that same voice had convinced me, for the most fleeting of instants, that these rebels were likely a small "army;" there would only be enough of them for a thin battle line, not a massed attack. That little voice was right. When I burst past the startled Thoran troops, there was no one between me and the jungle. I wasted no time in putting the jungle between me and the Thorans.

As soon as I felt I could, I slowed to a stop. There was no pursuit, of course. Who would be so insane? I congratulated myself for escaping my merely human enemies and placing myself in the hands of animals less known for their merciful qualities than for their large appetites and poisonous fangs, the antidotes for which I had just neatly rendered unavailable to me.

My breathing once more under control, I undertook to examine myself. In the heat of battle and flight, I could have suffered wounds all unknowing, but serious nonetheless. Happily, I had escaped, the most annoying injury being a persistent throbbing on my right thigh. It felt as though I had rolled over a rock—in fact it felt as if the rock were still there. I felt a cold thrill of fear. There was something in my pocket.

The jungle fauna briefing had not been encyclopedic in its scope, but it hadn't mentioned any small round animals with hard shells. Did that mean none existed? Slowly, carefully, I forced the unseen object from my pocket from the outside, protecting my bare hands.

The miniature library fell out of my pocket and plopped to the ground.

It greeted me in a voice I recognized. "I will be of about as much use to you down here as I was in your pocket, young man."

"I had forgotten you were there," I breathed, picking it up.

"I will accept that as an apology, under the circumstances." It was still the old librarian's voice, but the tone was different, less deferential. There was also an undertone of humor. I liked it better.

A distant roar followed immediately by an agonized, short scream recalled me to my situation.

"What do you know about my current circumstances?"

"Not a great deal," the small metal sphere admitted. I marveled at the clarity of its voice. "However, I can extrapolate from the ambient temperature and humidity, and what sounds like a lion's roar, that you are either in a zoological habitat dome, or you have traveled *very* far off the course I prescribed for you back in the Library."

"I'm afraid it is the latter. Can you help me find a way out of here without getting any closer to that roaring?" I was trying to watch every direction at once, and the effort was making me dizzy.

"Not likely. My video capabilities are limited by my size. I can't see much better than you can—although at night I'll still be able to see even when you can't."

"That doesn't leave me with a whole lot of choice, then." My rampage through the trees had left some signs; not much, but enough given the virgin nature of the territory. Gripping my staff with one hand, and apologizing to the library unit as I slipped it back into my pocket, I set off the way I had come. By picking my path carefully, I might be able to reach the battlefield again. Then, if I could just avoid both sides, something might present itself.

And something did. I simply wasn't prepared for it.

I had gone far enough to be completely lost when I froze at a noise from ahead of me. It did not recur, and I took a step, only to freeze again at a noise *above* me. I looked up as a dark blur plunged toward me from a tree branch. I jumped back but the blur leaped out of the brambles and seized me. I had no time to level my staff before I was helpless.

I stared directly into the eyes of a full-grown bull gorilla whose hand encircled my throat. There wasn't even room to swallow one last time. With its free hand it ripped open my pocket and removed the library.

"That's a very nice toy you have there," said the ape. "I think I'd like to own one."

Chapter 16
Tiger Spiders

My grandmother used to say, "Sometimes you want to kick God in the ankle, just so he'll know you're there." And that's what I did.

The gorilla's grip on me had loosened as he examined the library. He hadn't let go, and he still could have killed me in an instant, but at least I could breathe. As soon as blood began to flow back into my brain, I knew I had had enough. From the moment I had stepped through the silver door, I had been chased, shot at, kidnapped, and used—and now to be robbed of my one useful possession by a talking gorilla? I had had *enough!*

I reversed the staff and jammed it as hard as I could into his foot. He might not have been God, but he sure knew I was there.

Roaring with pain, he tossed me through the air. If I had hit a tree in my flight, all my worries would have ended right then. They almost did anyway.

I hit the ground and skidded to a stop in the damp loam, shook my vision clear and saw the gorilla bearing down on me, eyes red and hands clenching with rage. I scrambled to my feet, leveled the staff, and stood my ground. He might have been mad, but he had nothing on me.

The ape stopped short. We stared at each other. The moment stretched on without end.

"I think you broke my damned foot."

I cleared my throat painfully. "You should complain." I nodded at the library. "I'd like that back."

The baring of his fangs may have been meant as a smile, but it was ferocious in any event. I stayed my ground by sheer will.

"You willing to take it from me?"

"If I have to." *Lord*, I prayed, *don't make me have to.*

He laughed. I had never heard a gorilla laugh before, had never even considered such a thing, but if I had I wouldn't have expected this. Out of that gargantuan chest, from which growled the lowest voice I had ever heard, leaked a feminine squeaking, a pin-pricked balloon of a laugh, that abruptly exploded and sprayed me with gorilla spit. He laughed until he could not stand up, and had to support himself on his knuckles like his ancestors. As soon as he realized what he was doing, he straightened up in a hurry, but he couldn't keep the giggles from escaping.

"You are the *biggest* damned fool I have ever met!" he boomed, and tossed me the sphere. Like an idiot, I caught it, leaving myself off-guard and completely defenseless. If he hadn't been so busy snorting between mumbled editorials about my sense—or lack thereof—he might have crushed me.

I placed the library in another pocket and waited with what remained of my muddy dignity for him to stop. The formality of my upbringing rescued me.

"Keryl Clee," I offered, extending one hand. He stared at me for a moment, then held out his own. That's when I took hold of my staff and swung straight at his head. "Duck!"

He ducked as I screamed and my stick caromed off the tree trunk, almost vibrating out of my numbed hands. I managed to stagger partway around the tree and away from his inevitable counter-attack, barely in time. I heard him rush me and cleared my throat frantically.

"Look at the tree!" I croaked. He frowned, backing away, quickly glanced at the wood where my blow had landed, and saw a large yellow-and-black smear, pulpy with red, where none had been before.

"Tiger spider!" he gasped.

It was a tribute to the dead creature that he had recognized it even in its altered form. Tiger spiders frightened even the lions— or, as in this case, the great apes. Here in the wild, they were primarily tree-dwellers, and they didn't spin webs like the garden varieties I had known in my own time, they *hunted*. Tiger spiders routinely attacked creatures several times their own size, including human beings. The power of their venom was unquantifiable because no researcher could capture a specimen; few even wanted to try. But the most horrifying thing about them was that *they traveled in packs*.

The gorilla jumped back away from the shelter of his tree, shivering as he realized that the thing must have been in the branches below him while he was watching me. If he hadn't fallen on me from that height, he probably would have stepped on it.

Our minds were traversing the same path now; he looked at me with a new expression in his eyes.

"You aimed high on purpose. You saw that thing ready to bite me."

"I would've warned you, but there wasn't time," I replied tersely. "We'd better move. If it was ready to attack something your size…"

"It wasn't alone. I know. Follow me."

He took off through the underbrush, whether because he knew a path away from the tiger spiders or simply because it was more dangerous to stay put, I don't know. I didn't stop to ask.

Needless to say, I had never observed a gorilla in the wild, nor had I had much chance to visit them in zoos, but from what I had heard, this one moved more nimbly on the ground than his ancestors. There was none of the knuckle-walking I had been lectured about, although his gait was less limber than mine, and there was no question I could outrun him in a sprint. We never got that far; even our fair trot was only attainable due to his familiarity with the terrain and the faint paths that I was only beginning to discern. Trying to keep up this pace on my own in the jungle would have had me down with a turned ankle inside of a mile.

We couldn't make it that far; within two hundred yards he was slowing, his breath coming in heaving gasps from his bellows-like chest.

"When you're my size," he wheezed, "you don't have to run very often."

I looked back the way we had come, nervous at even this short rest. With their black and yellow banding, tiger spiders blended well with the sun-dappled branches, and the few, short studies ever done on them had carelessly failed to measure either their speed or their tracking ability. They could be preparing to drop down on us as we spoke.

"Just another moment," my companion begged when I said as much to him. "I'm really not used to this kind of exercise."

"Well, perhaps they are." I was literally hopping from one foot to the other in my anxiety. I imagined a horde of huge spiders dropping from the trees onto our heads, covering us with webbing like living mummies—never mind that these spiders didn't spin webs. As though reading my thoughts, the great ape straightened with a groan and we were off again, if less agilely than before.

"Is there a clearing anywhere nearby?" The pace we were making now hardly impeded my ability to talk, however taxing it might be to my guide. He raised one arm in what I hoped was a sign and trotted on.

Then the birds stopped singing.

Through redoubled efforts we reached the clearing ahead of the spiders. It was smaller than I had hoped, too small to dissuade the tree-dwellers from pursuing us through the tall yellow grass, which I realized belatedly would only allow them to blend in better. On the far side of the clearing one liana-strung tree stood alone, and it was toward that I pushed my comrade-in-peril.

We stood on its exposed roots, the grass on all sides of us unable to grow within a few feet of the tree itself. Even now the impatient spiders were dropping out of the shade we had just quitted—in their eagerness they could not be bothered to climb down their trees. Their bloated bodies made a soft thud as they hit the ground. The grass began to weave evilly.

Glancing upward, a slim hope was born. "Up the tree!" I didn't wait to see if my friend complied; there was no time for noble sentiment and he climbed faster than I anyway. Startled questions died on his lips and he took the only course open to him. Not until we were quite a ways up (and not without his help), did he address them with me.

"What are we supposed to do now? Those things *live* in the trees!"

"So did you, once—or at least your ancestors," I replied, casting about for what I needed. Had I the time, I would have laughed out loud at the irony of my idea, an irony, had he but known it, more suitable to my companion. If we lived, someday I would have to explain it.

"What are you talking about?"

I thrust aside the consideration of how long it must have been since the apes had come down from the trees that they would not even remember their own heritage. I had less doubt that he could accomplish what I intended than that I could; my only consolation was that if I failed, the tiger spiders would cease to be a worry.

"Take a vine," I instructed hastily. "One that's secured to a branch. We're going to swing on them into those trees over there."

"We're—" words failed him. "If—" he sputtered again. "Are you *insane?*"

All the time I was arguing I was trying on vines for a secure hold and length. This was not as easy as I had read. I resolved to have a talk with the author when I got back to my own time.

"I've read about this. You can swing on the vines into those trees. The spiders will have to climb back down and run after us, but we should be able to get away."

"Are you crazy? You'll break your neck! I'd rather stay here with the spiders!"

"Then have it your own way!" I pointed behind us. The first of the monsters had reached our branch, and I didn't have to look down to know that the trunk beneath us must be swarming with venomous eight-legged demons. The gorilla screamed and tried to bounce up and down on the branch to dislodge the spider. I myself nearly fell to a merciful death, but it only stood and watched with unconcerned evil certainty. Suddenly my companion whipped about, seized the first vine to come to hand, and launched himself into space. If tiger spiders have breath, I swear that I felt this one's frustrated exhalation as I recklessly followed suit.

We both survived our amateur jungle lord experience, and not surprisingly (to me, at least) I was less eager to try it again than my new anthropoid friend. In the face of its unarguable advantage in speed over walking, I did consent to two more airborne voyages, though they were successful more by chance than design. At last determining that our luck was merely finite, we once more descended to *terra firma*.

My friend was a new man...er, gorilla.

"That was incredible!" he repeated over and over again with frequent longing looks skyward. "What was it you said about my ancestors?"

"It's a long story," I said cautiously, "but from what I have read, once long ago, gorillas and apes were tree-dwellers, or at least some of them were." To be honest, I was about at the end of my zoölogical rope. And despite what we had been through together, almost everyone I had met in this world had treated me as an enemy or a prize. I did not want to show off knowledge that might brand me as an outsider.

"No kidding," he breathed, never taking his eyes off the high branches. "That must have been something."

Somehow, I had held onto my staff throughout our ordeal. I shouldered it and nudged my new friend. Reluctantly he left off his daydreams and struck a path.

"The name's Timash," he said as we fell into our pace. "Alin Timash."

"Keryl Clee," I said again. The last time I had offered my hand I had followed it with a swing at his head. As the gesture seemed unfamiliar to him anyway, I restrained myself this time.

He acknowledged my introduction with a distracted grunt, not seeming inclined to take the conversation any further. The silence stretched on painfully; unlike the companionable quiet of a long hike, there felt here as if there were an obstacle between us, something unsaid but floating in the air. It was the silence of tension. Something was wrong.

"Thanks," I said.

It took him a moment to answer. "For what?"

"For not leaving me behind. You were better at swinging through the trees than I was; you could have left me behind and gone on your way."

That stopped him, and he turned to me. He had been walking slightly ahead, but now he waited until I had come abreast. He stood, hands on hips, and leaned into me.

"Are you *ever* going to make sense?"

I opened my mouth but he cut me off.

"Every time you want to talk about something, you just jump right into the middle of it. Now that's fine when we've got tiger spiders on our butts, but now we've got nothing to do but walk and you don't have time to start a conversation at the beginning. What's your hurry, anyway?"

If you have never been berated by a gorilla with a chip on his shoulder, take it from me, you are blessed.

"Are you listening to me? Hello? Is anyone home?" He shook his head. "You are the strangest Nuum I have ever met."

"I'm not a Nuum," I said automatically. It took only a second for my brain to reach down and strangle my tongue, but the words were out.

Timash (as I learned to call him) stepped back and looked me over carefully. Then he inched forward again, squinting at my eyebrows.

"Damn," he whispered presently. "You're a yellow, aren't you?"

In for a penny, in for a pound. "What's a yellow?"

"That's a damned good question," he acknowledged, "because I've never heard of one. Which means maybe you're telling the truth. So what's a Thoran doing running around disguised as a Nuum?"

I sighed. "It's a long story. Let's just say it's not something I want spread around—especially to the Nuum." *Or the Silver Men*, I added silently, but that would take a *very* long time to explain.

Timash nodded thoughtfully. "All right. You saved my life, I owe you something. But when we get back home they're going to want some answers."

"Home. And where's that?"

He pointed off to our left. "About three hundred yards that way. We've been circling it until I figured out what to do with you."

I opened my mouth to protest but didn't get the chance. There was a terrible pain in my head and I never heard the shot that brought me down.

Chapter 17
In the City of the Apes

I dreamed that I was lying on a table, naked. A crowd of people had gathered near my head, digging in my skull, removing little bits of my brain with very tiny spoons. Not surprisingly, it being a dream, no one found my nudity the least bit odd—except me. I felt a vague sense of vulnerability from my nakedness, all the more odd as I felt none at all from the removal of my brain.

At last one of the faces glanced down at me and frowned. It said something I couldn't make out and the dream faded away. I slept on for another century.

When I woke up, I was naked under a blanket, on a table, with the unsettling sensation that someone had taken out my brain and stuffed my head with cotton balls. I started to worry immediately. Strangely, the fact that the gorilla looming over me was not Timash was not uppermost in my concerns.

"Good morning," it said prosaically enough. It wore what I was learn passed on an ape for a smile. Whatever evolution had brought them to the point of Man's speech had not elevated their ability to assume facial expression to the same level. Smaller than Timash, its fur was tinged on the ends with silvery grey.

I smiled back, very weakly. I had to swallow a couple of times before I could get words through my throat.

"Good morning."

"Are you in any pain?" I shook my head, rather surprising myself to learn that I was telling the truth. By its voice, I guessed this to be a she-ape, although it was not a distinction at which I was practiced. "I shouldn't think so," she said, "but your brain is a little different from anything I've encountered before. I wanted to make sure the blocks were working properly. Here, let me help you up."

As she did so, the sheet fell and pooled around my waist. I grabbed automatically to keep it in place, the sudden movement making me dizzy for a moment. The room was comfortably warm on my bare skin, but my head seemed a bit off-center, as if it weren't quite situated correctly on my neck. I shook it to clear my senses, but the fuzzy feeling remained. When I reached up to touch my scalp, I couldn't feel my hand.

"I'm Dr. Chala," my helper informed me, gently moving my head from side to side. I couldn't feel her hands, either. "You've been ill, in a coma, for about two days." She stopped, holding my face directly before hers. "You've contracted a telepathic virus."

She might have been explaining the interior structure of the sun for all I understood her. I reached out for the only anchor I had.

"Where's Timash?"

With a toss of her head toward a door behind her, she said: "He's been waiting. You must have made quite an impression on him. Timash isn't known for hanging around any one place for very long."

"Could I see him?"

She shrugged. "There's nothing else I can do for you. I'll let you get your things. But we'll need to talk before you leave." She left and I looked about for my clothes.

Someone had cleaned and repaired my Nuum uniform while I was unconscious. Even so, as I put it on I resolved to get some new clothing as soon as possible—and to wash the red out of my hair. I was starting to feel like a leper—or a target.

Timash was obviously glad to see me, but he approached me as though I were made of glass. He stood back, afraid to touch me, almost afraid to breathe on me.

"Thanks for bringing me here. I guess we're even now."

Hesitantly, still without speaking, he placed the library on the cot beside me. I realized guiltily I hadn't even noticed it was missing. I picked it up and glanced at its irregular surface, covered with crooked lines and tiny indentations whose function I could not begin to guess.

Timash watched me silently, not moving away, but carefully avoiding me nonetheless. I gave him the distance he seemed to crave and spoke directly to the library.

"Tell me about telepathic viruses."

"I am scanning medical equipment nearby," the library responded obliquely. "If you place my sphere into the indentation on that imaging diagnostician in the corner, I can more easily manifest my visual persona."

I did as instructed, or at least as well as I could make out. The library fit into a cuplike depression in a small, squat machine in the corner. Although there were no obvious catches on either component, an experimental tug proved that it was there to stay. A moment later, the familiar figure of the Librarian materialized before us. Timash jumped a foot in the air.

"Good morning, sir, Mr. Timash," he said with a small bow to each of us. He assumed a pedantic pose. "Telepathic viruses. A self-explanatory term. Although viruses were unknown in your time, you will be familiar with the concept now, after your general course in modern topics." I spared a glance for the gorilla. If he understood the implications of what the Librarian was saying, he wasn't giving it away. Well, the cat was out of the bag now. The Librarian continued: "Telepathic viruses are so small they can be passed literally by thinking about them.

"Telepathic viruses were invented in the Fifth Age, when

telepathy was finally grasped as a learned behavior. Before that, it was the province of mutations and the occasional religious mystic, but when it began to be available to the normal human population…well, someone always finds a way to make a weapon out of any example of progress. And so it was here.

"Fortunately, it was never used in actual warfare; as soon as its existence became known, it was outlawed. There was no cure for it, and no escaping it without giving up this new ability that Man had sought for so many generations and now had within his grasp. Not that the development of telepathy itself was so smooth or easy—not at all. For a generation the asylums were filled to capacity with the untrained and the poorly-trained, not to mention the victims of early forms of telepathic dueling. Often as not both duelists ended their days drooling in their porridge behind padded walls on a robot-tended asteroid. No one could—" He trailed off at the look on my face. "Oh, sorry. I am a librarian, you know. Once I get onto a subject, I can simply beat it to death."

"You were telling us about viruses," I prompted.

"Although they were outlawed, some specimens were saved for research, naturally. A laboratory was established on the dark side of the Moon. There were many who lobbied for the virus' total destruction—they protested that something so small could never be completely contained, and unfortunately, they were right. A mutated form of the virus infected one of the researchers, driving him mad before it killed him. But by the time the symptoms manifested themselves, he had journeyed back to Earth. He lived on a small Pacific island. They say it was beautiful.

"At first they thought they were simply seeing a return to the early madness, but soon the virus had mutated again—it can mutate simply by its host's thinking about it—and entire households began to die on a daily basis. Ironically, it was the originally-infected scientist, the Patient Zero of this particular plague, who realized the danger. Before he died, he called for an air strike that destroyed the entire island and everyone on it."

"Easy enough for him to decide, since he was dying anyway," Timash commented.

"The island's entire population was descended from a single couple," the Librarian replied quietly. "He signed the death warrant for his entire family."

Timash retreated, abashed, but I put aside the millennia-old tragedy to focus on my own.

"How did the virus survive?"

"The virus apparently had spread so quickly only because of the genetic similarities between the people infected; they thought they had engineered out all of their recessive weaknesses, but Nature proved herself more ingenious. By the end, however, the virus had mutated in such a narrow fashion that it was far less contagious than anyone would have believed, and since the island was declared off-limits and remained radioactive for centuries, it could only lie dormant until eventually it found a new host.

"That took many years, and by then humanity had developed its telepathic abilities to an extent that the normal, routine barriers that everyone erected to preserve the privacy of thoughts were sufficient to ward off infection by the virus. In fact, for many years scientists thought the virus had died on the island. Nowadays, attacks are very rare, usually occurring only in the very young, the extremely old, or victims of certain types of brain injuries." Suddenly he stopped, smiling, awaiting my next question.

I wanted to hit him, but it wouldn't have helped. "And —?" I challenged.

"And that's all. I would judge, based on what I know of your own history, that you compare with the very young in terms of telepathic ability. You must have been infected before you learned to raise the proper barriers."

I fought down the cold lump in my stomach. I knew that if I allowed this latest horror to fight its way up my throat to manifest it in a single sign of fear it would overwhelm me, but of all the terrors of this horrific tomorrow, this was the most personal. I was a victim of my own mind.

"Is there a cure?"

"I don't know. My databases are strong on geography, language, anthropology, and zoology—subjects that the main library foresaw as necessary to you on your journey. My medical database is not equipped for complicated diagnoses and treatment."

The horror lurked at the base of my throat. My breathing came harder and faster and I fought it down. *Think*, I told myself, *think!* There had to be a way out, a cure… I swung to face Timash.

"Where is the doctor?"

He fetched her without a word. She stopped short at seeing the Librarian, and he bowed as he launched into a new introduction, but I cut him short.

"Doctor, how long do I have?"

She looked from the Librarian to me, and back to him, plainly flustered. I had already gathered from Timash's earlier machinations that strangers were neither usual nor welcome in the apes' city, and this one had appeared without notice. Eventually she would grasp the hologram's true nature, but for now I did not care. As it had with the Librarian, my urgency brooked no delay from her.

"How long?" I snapped.

Her professional instincts came to the fore in time to save me from giving her what would have been an ill-advised shaking.

"That depends on you. We have installed nerve blocks throughout almost your entire brain. You may have noticed that you are not telepathically active even now." Truth to tell, I hadn't. I wondered if that was why Timash had been so quiet. Although I was to learn that apes used words more than humans, he still wasn't used to talking completely verbally. "Fortunately, the virus attacks brain functions that you don't use in everyday situations. But your telepathic abilities are completely blocked out, and some of your higher brain functions with them. That can't be helped. Still, you can go about your normal tasks as long as you don't try anything too technical or straining.

"Your virus was triggered by exposure to an extremely strong telepathic source. We know it wasn't Timash, and he swears there was no one else around you when you collapsed. But someone nearby awoke the virus, and that someone is an extremely dangerous telepath." She paused, as if weighing how much to reveal. "We have had search parties out for almost two days with no luck. Do you have any idea who that person could be? Have you been in contact with any powerful telepaths?"

I returned her anxious stare with my own blank look. "How would I know? By now Timash must have told you everything he knows about me, and you've been inside my brain enough to know even more than that. You tell me!"

"Is this a symptom of the disease?" the Librarian asked with clinical interest.

"Yes, he's becoming over-stressed. This is exactly what I told him he needed to avoid."

"Maybe if you stopped talking about him like he wasn't here...!" Timash interrupted, earning my gratitude.

Dr. Chala flashed him a look of irritation, but then she turned her attention back to me.

"I'm sorry, but your case is extremely unusual, Clee." She lowered her voice. "And I was surprised to find --" she jerked a thumb at the Librarian --"him here. Who *is* he, anyway?"

"He's a librarian." At her puzzled expression I tried to elaborate. The words didn't come easy. "He's a—holographic projection. I picked him up from the Nuum."

I knew when I said it that I shouldn't have mentioned the Nuum, but it was only a vague feeling and I couldn't work up the energy to formulate a reason for it. Dr. Chala's eyes narrowed, but she examined my skull again as though nothing had changed. I was happy to let her examine me; she smelled warm and sweet. I suddenly realized I was very tired.

I said as much, and Dr. Chala helped me to lie down again. I asked Timash not to go away, and vaguely heard him promise he would not. The room began to spin but by then my eyes were already closed.

When I woke up again, my head cleared more quickly than before, and I barely felt the fuzziness that was confined now solely to my forehead and temples. I swung into a sitting position and stepped onto the floor for the first time. It was warm and yielding under my feet, a far cry from the cold that I had expected. I found my boots in the closet and felt ready to leave. Straightening up, I took a deep breath, and with a guilty sigh turned to where I had left the Library.

It was gone. I checked the cabinets and even the floor, although I knew it could not have fallen from its perch; it had been fastened too tightly to be removed any way other than deliberately. On a sudden inspiration, I tried to open the door.

It was locked. I was a prisoner.

Chapter 18
I Am Given a Vision

The opening mechanism was a simple knob, just like those I had been used to back home. I thought that perhaps if I broke it off, I might find a way to manipulate the latch. Where I would have gone if I had succeeded, being to my knowledge the only human being in the entire city, I do not know, but as events transpired it never fell to me to decide.

In casting about for a way to break the knob, my eye fell on the diagnostic machine; it was on wheels and appeared quite heavy. I crossed the room, laid my hands upon it—and stopped dead in my tracks, struck dumb at the simple and obvious ramifications that had escaped my clouded brain until now.

It was a diagnostic *machine*. The apes had *machines*.

I returned to the cot, sat down, and waited like a good lad until they should come for me.

By the time the door finally opened, I had poked through every cabinet twice and examined each and every object inside until I almost understood their purpose. The only thing I found was that, for something that I had barely become used to, I missed my telepathic abilities. Time and time again I wished I had them to probe beyond the locked door and solid walls of my medical prison.

There was a knock at the door, and Dr. Chala came in. Timash was at her heels. He handed over the Library.

"Your friend told us everything about you," the doctor said, gesturing to the Library. "Once he had finished speaking to the authorities, they agreed that you should be allowed to stay here. I'm sorry we had to lock you in, but we had no way of knowing who or what you were." She extended a hand. "Welcome to Tahana City."

I took her hand with automatic politeness; it was soft and supple, like a favorite leather glove.

Timash was fairly bouncing on the balls of his feet in the background, as does a child who has news that he will be allowed to tell, but only when his mother allows. It was distracting, and I was already distracted from the whirling thoughts and ideas that were bubbling near the surface of my disease-hobbled mind. Quite frankly, I was having trouble keeping them there. I shook my head to clear it.

"Timash, would you please stop doing that? It's making me dizzy."

He settled to a stable position, but not before Dr. Chala had turned to bestow upon him what could only have been a forceful look.

"I just want to talk to him," Timash muttered.

The doctor turned back to me. "You'll have to excuse him. You're the most unusual thing that's happened around here since the Nuum came."

The fog was starting to descend again, but I fought it back.

"So you know—I'm not one of them…" I said. She nodded. "I suppose if I had been, you wouldn't be so friendly to me. Those machines…"

She glanced at the console where I had attached the Library. "Yes, exactly. If the Nuum were to find us, it would be very bad."

I tried to speak, to carry on with my questions, but the effort was overwhelming me. The edges of my vision were darkening and I couldn't keep my eyes focused. Dr. Chala motioned to Timash.

"Son, help me with him. He needs rest, and this is not the best place for him to get it."

The gorillas each put a hand under my arms and lifted me off the table, hefting me like a child. When we were out of the room, Dr. Chala left me with Timash while she fetched a wheelchair. Whatever she had told him, he took it to heart, propping me up without any repeat of the excitement he had exhibited earlier. With my carriage secured we set out of the hospital.

I had no preconceived notion of how the apes lived, having seen nothing of their city outside of my examining room, and having had no time to formulate opinions from the meager clues provided by Dr. Chala. Despite this lack, and despite my enervated condition, when the full uniqueness of Tahana City presented itself to my eyes, I forgot my fatigue and surrendered wholly to my supposedly jaded sense of wonder.

Tahana City was contained entirely inside of a mountain.

To call it a "city" was perhaps an exaggeration. It was more of a small town, encompassing at most ten thousand souls. But although I lacked any pretension to engineering, I could see at a glance that the construction of this hamlet had required more skill and more technical knowledge than the greatest metropolis of my Earth. I stared skyward, or where I had assumed the sky to be, and the only word that finally came to convey the majesty of this achievement was "cathedral."

The builders of Tahana had not sought to make the inside of their mountain resemble the outside world; that would have been too obvious, and too cruel. Their genius had suggested a far more elegant solution, one that incorporated, rather than denied, the uniqueness of their setting. Through some exotic process, they had altered the very composition of the mountain itself so that parts of it, in a dazzling pattern that drew the eye ever onward until it curved in on itself, actually admitted the light of day.

Dr. Chala explained to me that the mountain itself was solid rock, and that the process of admitting light, called "photonic integration," was a gift from the original architects, gone to dust a thousand years ago, their knowledge lost with them. From outside the mountain appeared to be, and was, entirely normal. But inside the golden light shone as through clear glass, diffusing until the city suffered not at all from its subterranean milieu.

All this I absorbed in the first breathless moments that I stared, transfixed, as I exited the hospital. Later I asked the Librarian what he knew of photonic integration, but it was outside of his programming. I was disappointed, having hoped to repay the apes in some way for their assistance. But that disappointment soon melted in the warmth of their genuine friendship.

Dr. Chala took me to her home, which was, I was surprised to learn, Timash's as well. They were mother and son. No sooner did we arrive than she informed him that I would be using his room and he would be banished to guest quarters. Like any son, he averted his eyes, muttered under his breath, and obeyed.

Timash's bed seemed large enough for my entire family, built as it was to support his greater bulk. When I crawled out into the middle of it and spread-eagled, I could not touch any of the edges. The first night I took advantage of this fact to wrap the huge but thin blankets tightly around me, but I soon learned that Tahana City's stable temperature rendered most night coverings unnecessary and I slept quite comfortably indeed.

I soon had reason to be glad of my comforts, for Dr. Chala's residence suddenly became a social watering hole, as civic leaders, scientists, friends, relatives, and curiosity seekers began beating a path to her door. She had been granted a leave of absence from the hospital, with the understanding that she would use her home office to keep up with some of her patients, but the endless parade of visitors quickly made that impractical. In self-defense, she began to encourage Timash to take me on tours of the city.

Following the contours of the mountain itself, Tahana's buildings became taller the closer one came to its center. It made for a pleasing symmetry, even if the tallest of them rose only four stories. The pattern of light from above, diffused by distance, created a warm glow about the city that complemented the quiet way the apes went about their lives. Quiet, indeed—with the mountain all around them loud noises would forever be echoed back upon them. Londoners and New Yorkers could never have survived!

The city streets were narrow, but the apes had no vehicles to speak of, and in a deliberate contrast to the rocky precipices that formed their horizon, they had lined their avenues with trees and their buildings with color. Along these we strolled through crowds of gorillas, nor did I ever see another human being.

The citizens themselves tended to be shy and non-confrontational, with the exception of those who would make themselves at home with Dr. Chala, hoping to catch me for a few minutes' conversation. But even the scientists and politicians (who had not changed in a mere 900,000 years!) were easily dissuaded should I choose to excuse myself. The centuries of close living had given them a respect for privacy not unlike the Japanese, and I feel sure that many social gaffes on my part went unremarked.

I learned more about the apes by watching Timash than through conversation with him. He reminded me of my own friends of my adolescent days: everything interested him at once, and nothing for very long—unless it swayed and winked at him in the street, at which time he was wont to forget me completely in fascinated observation of what, in the apes, I found difficult to think of as "the gentler sex." (Although they likely could not have crushed my skull like an eggshell with a single blow of their massive fists, as could their forebears, I did not doubt that one could lift me over her head and dash me to the ground with little effort and much the same result.)

When it came to the world outside, Timash was much more

informative, for he had lived there. Not all of the Tehanans lived in the mountain; some preferred the outdoors even with its unpredictable weather, animals, and occasional human interlopers.

"Most of them still think we're savages," he muttered one day as we strolled along a quiet, park-like lane. He had recently spied a girl of his fancy, and her dismissal of his advances had pushed his mood distinctly toward the morose. Apparently my company suited him. "Except for the conservationists; they think we should simply move into abandoned villages instead of building them ourselves."

"The conservationists? Who are they?"

His head raised a bit and he almost smiled. "They're the ones fighting with the Nuum."

I waited until my patience was out, and then I prodded him. "And...?"

"Hey! That hurt."

"Tell me about the conservationists," I said quickly. I had seen Timash aroused to anger and was not keen to repeat the experience. "I was shanghaied by the Nuum to fight someone. In fact, I had to escape them through the middle of a battle. Were those the conservationists?"

Timash turned to stare at me, a new light sparkling in his close-set eyes. "Really? A battle?" Only when I pantomimed seizing him by the throat did he collect himself. "Well, the conservationists are humans who've lived here a long time. Maybe as long as we have. They respect the trees and the jungle, the way the Nuum don't know how to do. The Nuum have been trying to move into the jungle and harvest trees and animals, and the conservationists are trying to stop them."

"Really..." I said, half to myself. "How long has this been going on?"

"Not long." Timash made a face, something the apes seemed to enjoy just for the exercise. "Maybe a year or two. I used to go up to their camp and see them, but Mother won't let me anymore."

"I thought you were old enough that you didn't have to listen to your mother."

He only grunted.

"It seems the conservationists are giving the Nuum all they can handle down here. That's why they brought us from up north. They said the black Nuum could not take care of their responsibilities, so it was up to the red Nuum to do it for them."

This time his eyebrows shot up. "Really? But the blacks and the reds hate each other!"

"That's what they said…"

"Shene must be massacring them!"

"Who is Shene?"

"Shene's the leader of the conservationists. I knew she was going to resist, but this is great!"

It was my turn to put on a face. "I thought your mother didn't let you go to see them anymore." He averted his eyes. "That's where you were going when we met, wasn't it? And when you saw me, you were hoping to take me prisoner!"

"Yeah, but the tiger spiders got in the way, and then we had to run, and things got all fouled up. It would have been great, but I guess it worked out all right."

His friendly compliment flew past me without recognition. What a world of possibility this opened! Until now I had been wandering, tossed to and fro involuntarily and without purpose. This was the first moment that the resentment of the Nuum that had bubbled inside me since the deadly riots had found vent to the outer world. Here, a hemisphere removed from where I had first witnessed their ruthless carnage, I had discovered a way in which I might strike back!

But no sooner had my mind embraced this great purpose than the clouds began to rise around my brain. Though I seemed to act the same from my viewpoint, I saw the alarm spread on Timash's face as far away I heard a madman's rising babble, and I realized faintly that the madman was me…

Strong arms gathered me up like a babe. As my conscious mind began to succumb, I heard the sounds of a gathering crowd of apes. Suddenly the rumblings of concern grew into a mighty roar, and for an instant my vision cleared. As in a dream, I saw myself standing on a great hill, while all around me thousands—humans, apes, and others at which I could not guess—cheered and shouted my name over and over until the ground shook under my feet. I raised one arm in triumphant salute --

-- as the last of my awareness sank into the mire and I was carried off to what destination I knew not.

Chapter 19
I Meet a Visionary

If losing consciousness and being rescued by hairy anthropoids was becoming a habit, waking easily and without discomfort was not. At first I thought Timash had taken me back to his mother, or to the hospital, for I lay on one of the apes' hard beds, but where I was and how long I had been there were mere tangential details compared to the pulsing, aching mass that was my head. I didn't dare try to open my eyes, but a moan escaped my lips. Leathery fingers cradled my skull with utmost tenderness. A warm, sour smell wafted in under my nose and a cup was placed against my lips. Hoping against hope that it was a swift poison, I sipped.

The warmth slipped down my throat like fine brandy while the vapors rose through my sinuses in a rush, and where they touched, the aching eased away. I opened my eyes to a softly-lit room and Timash watching me over the shoulder of a stranger. As he saw me come around, my friend sighed heavily with relief.

"If you'd died, my mother would've killed me."

"Nonsense!" huffed the other gorilla in a gravelly voice. He slapped both hands on his knees and stood up. "I taught your mother more medicine than she can remember."

"More than she wants to remember, you mean," Timash

retorted.

"That's enough of that, son. I also taught her to respect her elders." He regarded me, still prostrate with the memory of pain. "You can lie there all day if you want, but the tea's in the other room." And with that he turned and left Timash and me to our own devices. I queried my friend with raised eyebrows.

"That's my Uncle Balu," Timash whispered. "Well, actually he's my mother's uncle—I think. Anyway, his house was the closest place of I knew to take you, so…"

"A good thing, it feels like to me," I said, rubbing my scalp. I swung my legs over the side of the bed.

"Oh, yeah, Uncle Balu knows a lot of stuff like that. He wasn't kidding when he said he taught my mother a lot about medicine. He's been *everywhere*."

I began to understand the origin of Timash's wandering ways. However, my manners, impressed upon me almost a million years ago by my own family, suddenly snapped me back to the present and commanded me to join my host in the other room, preventing me from interrogating his nephew any further.

Uncle Balu sat in a straight chair before a window overlooking the city. His apartment was on the third floor, judging from the building across the way, which surprised me, for in a city of very close horizons, lodgings with anything approximating a commanding view were highly prized and notoriously difficult to obtain. Although directly across the road was another apartment building, I was to find that from his chosen seat, Balu could see obliquely one of the small but beautiful parks of Tahana.

On a small table beside the chair sat what I least expected to see: a dainty flowered tea set, with three cups set out on saucers. Not until I was quite close could I see that the flowers were not the English roses with which I was familiar, but flowering plants whose genus had probably not existed when I was born. But they were lovely nonetheless, and I was almost overwhelmed with an attack of homesickness.

Balu gestured for us to sit down, and as he poured the tea (which I was delighted to find tasted equally as delicious as those I was accustomed to), I took in the wonderful tiny museum that he called home.

In only four rooms, he had stuffed the memorabilia of a lifetime. The walls were covered with paintings and carvings of all sorts, although placed with such a masterful appreciation of each piece's uniqueness that they complemented each other perfectly without blending into a homogenous blur. I was pleased to see that none resembled the abstract art with which Hana had decorated her room, and I began to feel an affinity for this creature so unlike me. Hana's face arose in my memory, chiding me for my inaction. I shook my head to clear her away along with my guilt.

Where there were no paintings there were curio cabinets and shelves lined with objects of glass, metal, wood, plastic, and shell. Not cheap souvenirs from some backwater midway, these virtually shouted out to be noticed, absorbed, and their stories told. On one shelf I saw a long, hollow metal tube, ringed about the middle with semiprecious stones. Both ends were blackened and pitted. I could guess that it was a weapon, and very old, but how it might work I could not fathom—nor was I sure I would want to. A small glass globe held a replica of the Earth so finely detailed I could almost see myself on its surface, but the continents were subtly changed, and an unknown archipelago stretched almost the width of the Atlantic.

"Your tea will be getting cold," a gentle voice chided me, and I turned to see Balu and Timash watching me from their chairs. So lost in fascination had I become that I had arisen to walk about the room without ever noticing my own movements.

To proffer my apologies would have been insulting. I groped for words as I retook my seat, but anything I could think to say seemed inadequate.

"Timash told me you'd been everywhere," I managed at last. "I'll never doubt him again."

To my great surprise, he laughed, a roaring jungle-cry of a laugh, until he could hardly put his teacup down, and then he slapped both knees with his hands and laughed some more. I looked at Timash, but he was nearly as mystified as I, communicating without words his feeling that: "He's an old man, you just have to take him as he comes."

When Balu finally calmed down he took a moment to wipe a tear from his eye.

"Oh, Clee, I haven't laughed like that in years. *I've* been everywhere? What about *you?*"

I smiled self-consciously. I have never been comfortable as the center of attention; until the War, books had formed my shelter from the scrutiny of my fellow man.

"Most of my travels have been through books—or because of them. Even in the War, I went only so far as France and England."

Balu stroked his chin in an attitude of wisdom, and then said: "I have no idea what you're talking about. How far is it from England to France?"

Again, I smiled, but this time in response to the unintentional irony of his question.

"That depends. In distance, only a few miles. In culture, philosophy, outlook…the Moon is closer."

Balu nodded. "Then you have traveled far indeed. Cultures can learn from each other, even in war. I myself have learned a great deal in my travels, but nobody wants to hear about it anymore." He glanced at his nephew. "Except Timash, of course, and even he doesn't believe me."

"Hey, hold on—!"

"Quiet, boy. If you'd rather listen to your mother, who's never been outside this mountain, than to me, well that's your business." He sipped his tea, giving me a wink over the lip of his cup. Timash missed the wink and sank into a staring contest with the bottom of his cup. The conversation lagged.

"I did make quite a trip getting here," I ventured, trying to relieve the silence. "But I spent most of it inside a Nuum airship, so there wasn't much to see."

At the mention of the extraterrestrials, both generations perked up. Balu was the first to speak.

"The Nuum... What an odd bunch. Did I ever tell you about the time I worked on one of their sky barges, Timash?"

Timash started to speak, then thought better of it. I was getting pretty good at reading the apes' faces: his took on an expression of concentration, then puzzlement, and finally dawning surprise. I knew his answer before he spoke, and it required no telepathy.

"No, actually...I don't think you ever did." He put his teacup down and assumed an expression of real interest for the first time since we had begun talking.

For his part, I believe Balu was no less surprised than Timash to find that he'd never told that particular tale, but he concealed it more artfully. He set aside his own cup and rubbed his hands in preparation; I could tell that when he let go, his entire body would leap headfirst into the telling, his arms and legs windmilling and gesticulating. I quietly backed my chair to a safer range.

"Years ago, when I was about your age, Clee, the Nuum hadn't gotten on this crusade about apes that they have now, and it was pretty safe to travel around the countryside. Well, it was safe from the Nuum anyway, the tiger spiders and the breen and maybe some of the humans were a different story. But hey, if there's nothing out there you can't see from your front window, why go out at all?

"So there I was, minding my own business, somewhere up by Cantrenes, which is maybe five hundred miles north of here, and a pretty lively town at the time. About thirty years ago it got wiped out by the red weed, but that's a different story and I wasn't there then anyway. So I wandered into town one night, keeping to the shadows, 'cause some of the Nuum even then were a little nervous about a gorilla walking around after dark." He winked again. "I guess they were even more nervous before I got through. I wasn't lookin' to start any trouble; fact is, I was really looking to find some work—I was hungry—but who should I run into—and I mean that—but a Nuum.

"I almost knocked the poor fellow right off his feet. He took one look at me, and his eyes got real wide, and I was sure for a second we were gonna get into it, and he says: 'Hey, what are you doing here?'

"Well, I thought maybe I could scare him off, so I said: 'Looking for a job. What's it to you?'

"Quick as a wink, he tells me to follow him, and turns around and goes the other way. So I followed him. Before you know it I'm standing guard at the local governor's house with a brand new uniform tunic and a full stomach to fill it out. He tells me: 'Stand right here. Don't move and don't let anybody in unless I tell you to.'

"Seemed simple enough to me, so I did it. I found out later that the only reason they hired me was because the governor and his daughter were passing through town and they wanted to scare off anybody with a gripe against Nuum. They would've fired me the next morning—if I'd lasted that long.

"A couple of hours of standing there and I was getting pretty bored. Then I heard some noises from around the corner. I wanted to go look, but the Nuum who hired me had told me to stay put. So I did. A few minutes later, this couple came around the corner, all covered up in capes and hats and things. As soon as they saw me, they stopped.

"Now I knew as sure as I was standing there that they were up to something. I just didn't know if it was any of my business. I figured if they tried to come in, it was, and if they didn't, it wasn't. They walked by me kind of fast, and as soon as they went around the corner I heard them start running. But hey, I was doing my job…

"About an hour later the whole place started jumping and the lights came on and there're people everywhere. Finally one of them runs up to me, asks me if I'd seen anybody, and I told him about the couple that ran around the corner.

"He started screaming at me. 'Why didn't you stop them?'

"'Because I was told not to move. I'm keeping people out.'

"'You idiot! That was the governor's daughter! She's run off with a Thoran!' And the next thing I know they've got those weird guns all over me and I'm shipped off to a sky barge for 'dereliction of duty.'

"You ever seen one of those things?" I had to admit that I had not. Vaguely I had a memory of one from my night in the Library, just enough to know that the ship on which I had flown did not meet the same description. "They're just big open boats in the sky. They've got photonic sails and negative gravity generators, but most of the time they run on photonic oars. They Nuum use them for pleasure ships, mostly—the nobles like to ride around in them because they're slow and you can actually look around. That, and it gives them a place to put prisoners. They use them as slaves. You sit there all day and row back and forth. It's not hard, but it sure is boring."

He stopped to pour us all a new cup of tea, sipping some of his own to soothe his dry throat. "Well, after a while the novelty of the whole thing started to wear off, so I started working a little harder at it. Pretty soon my bench mates couldn't keep up with me, and that threw off the whole side of the boat. Couldn't row in unison, you see, and we kept spinning off to one side. All the time I just kept smiling like an idiot, so they wouldn't see I was doing it on purpose. What they didn't know was that we'd sailed almost all the way back home, and I figured if I was getting off it was now or never. What I didn't know was whether they'd get rid of me at the next stop—or just dump me over the side and be done with it.

"I guess they must've figured that dumping me was more work than letting me go, so they dropped me off in the middle of nowhere. They must have thought it was quite a joke; they forced me off at gunpoint like I was being exiled to some foreign land." He pointed through the window. "It was about ten miles from here. I was home for breakfast the next day."

Home. Would the word ever again hold any meaning?

Chapter 20
I Have Hope

In the weeks subsequent to my first visit to Uncle Balu's home, I became a frequent guest, both with and without Timash. In truth, I believe he found his uncle less spellbinding than I when subjected to his familial duties on such a scale. Somehow, I found that Balu evinced an understanding of my circumstances; more than once in his long wanderings he, too, had known cause to wonder if he would ever see his home again.

On top of that, though, I had Hana to think about. Had Farren's intentions toward her changed after my abortive attempts at rescue? Was he now holding her hostage against my renewed appearance? Was she even alive? Every day I was forced to remain in seclusion held the potential to drown me in a nightmare of worry; every day I was reluctantly compelled to the conclusion that the only sanctuary for my sanity was to put her dear face from my mind until I could resume the hunt.

In this Balu was a godsend. Twice he prevailed upon me to become an overnight guest, and although there was no danger inherent in walking the streets of Tahana at night, unlike some of the larger cities I had known, I grasped his offer eagerly. His store of treasures was apparently far larger than those on display in his apartment; each time I went there I would find new and different objects in place of those I had seen before. After a while it became a game between us, to see how long it would take me to pick out the new wonders in the museum that was his home.

It occurred to me at last to inquire how he had conveyed all of these fantastic objects from the far corners of the earth here, particularly given the Nuum's strictures against many of them. For that matter, how had he obtained them in the first place?

"I never reveal my sources," he chuckled over a cup of tea. (He seemed to live on it.) "But there are a lot of places in the old cities where you can stash mountains of things if you know where to look. Warehouses, vaults, chemical storage tanks… No one uses any of them anymore. There are more abandoned cities between here and the Nuum in the north than you can count on your fingers and toes."

I picked up a cup of my own and sat down, recognizing his expansive mood. Such moods never failed to be informative, or at the very least fascinating. "But what happened to all the people? Did the Nuum destroy them in the invasion?"

"Oh, no," Balu shook his head. "These people were gone long before the Nuum. Maybe they died, maybe they left—maybe they *became* the Nuum. Who knows?"

"And the cities are just deserted? Nothing lives in them?"

"Oh, no," he repeated, with greater emphasis. "I never said that. There are still things living there—not people, of course, let alone apes, but plenty of Things."

I smiled, unable to miss the capitalization. "Well, of course something lives there," I said, backtracking to cover my apparent naiveté. "I don't doubt there are animals, and insects, and a lot of things I wouldn't care to meet—tiger spiders, for example."

"Son," he said with sudden seriousness, "even a tiger spider will back away from some of the things that live in those cities. Have you ever heard of the breen?"

To this day I vow that it could have been nothing less than

racial memory that caused the chill that ran down my spine when he said that word—racial memory of the horror of a creature that had not even come to the light of Creation until millennia after I was born. It could not have happened, but it did. In answer to his question I could only shake my head.

Before he spoke again, he rose from the chair he loved so much, moving about the room to touch an object here and there. My apprehension grew; I had never known him to be reticent before about any part of his wanderings or the things he had seen—precisely the opposite. I normally had to preface my departures by at least an hour to allow him time to wind down.

"Nobody knows where they came from. They've only been around for about a couple hundred years, so the most popular theory is that the Nuum brought them. From what I've seen and heard, that's probably the best idea we're going to get.

"Breen stand just a little bigger than a man—about your size, in fact. They're covered with silvery short fur, walk on two legs, and carry claws on their fingers and toes that will cut through metal. They're fast and they're strong. But the most scary thing about them is their tenacity. You know how you never go after a rat in a hole? Once it's trapped, it's ten times as dangerous because it's got nowhere to go and nothing to lose. Well, the breen are like that all the time. They never back down from a fight, never give up. They're like wolverines—except they're your size. If one ever sees you, you're a dead man. They'll eat anything that moves, and nothing that you can carry can stop them."

"Why would the Nuum bring such creatures to Earth? And why would they let them run free?"

Balu shrugged. "The Nuum aren't exactly talking. But the story goes, in the early days, they used them to flush out pockets of resistance. Sometimes rebels would take refuge in a building that the Nuum didn't just want to bomb out of existence. So they'd pull back, let a pack of breen in, and wait. Problem was getting the breen out again. Pretty soon they learned that they might as well have bombed the building in the first place, for all the good it was doing them. So eventually, they abandoned the project and worked around those areas."

"And there are still districts in these cities where no one lives because of the breen?"

Balu chuckled and poured more tea. "Oh, no. That's where the Nuum outsmarted themselves. Breen are nomadic; they run in packs from place to place, moving whenever they hunt up all the food in their area—which is often. Pretty soon they started coming out of the buildings on their own —hungry. But they were smart too; as soon as they'd fed, they'd run back home. Nuum started moving out real fast, and by the time they figured out what to do about it, they were afraid to bomb the buildings because they didn't have any way of knowing if they'd gotten all the breen. They ended up evacuating a bunch of cities and hoping the breen wouldn't migrate."

"And have they?"

"Apparently not. They were bred for climbing and killing things, not for long trips through empty land. The story goes that they still live there, in the cities, feeding off rats and birds and whatever idiots happen to walk through." He grinned and tapped himself on the chest. "Like me."

I made a properly impressed face. "Have you ever seen one?"

"Oh, yes," he nodded emphatically. "And smelled him. The only good thing about a breen is that you can smell him a mile away. Thank god, or I wouldn't be here."

As much as I wanted to hear more about his adventures, with a mind toward their impact on certain future plans of my own, I was doomed to eternal disappointment by the frantic knocking that suddenly rattled my host's front door!

As I was the nearer, Balu gestured to me to answer the frantic summons. "It's just Timash, anyway."

And so it was, with his chest heaving like a bellows from his exertions. As I have previously noted, the apes are not heralded for their endurance over distance, but even so I had not seen one so breathless since the day Timash and I met under decidedly extreme circumstances. So it was that I was quite curious to learn the origin of his excitement, an urge I had to quell while the poor boy got air back into his lungs.

"My mother—" was all he could get out. Balu was on his feet instantly.

"Has something happened to her?" I cried.

Timash shook his head, still gulping air. "No, she—thinks she's found something. She needs you home right away."

Behind me I could almost hear Balu relax. "If it's that important," he asked, "why didn't you just call?" All homes in Tahana City were equipped with extremely sophisticated telephone systems.

"I wanted to tell you in person," Timash said to me. "She thinks she's found a cure for your virus!"

My friend tried to explain to me what he knew on the way back to his house, but I rather rudely broke into a sprint that he could not hope to match and left him behind.

I found Dr. Chala in her laboratory, the Librarian at her side. The good doctor jumped when I dashed in, panting, my legs buckling from the unaccustomed exercise.

"What did that boy tell you? Where is he?" she demanded. "No, never mind. What did he tell you?"

Her cautious look calmed me faster than a bucket of water. The Librarian's ubiquitous expression of bemused observation imparted nothing.

"Timash almost broke down Balu's door to tell me that you had found a cure for the telepathic virus," I responded. "I'm afraid I left him behind."

"Oh," Dr. Chala moaned. She turned to the Librarian. "You were right," she said. "I never should have allowed him to be the one to carry the news. But he was so excited…"

"The Sixth Age philosopher Ochre said: 'Never is a deed badly done when its genesis is love,'" he replied.

"I'll bet Ochre never had any children."

"Oh, she did. Thirteen."

"Any boys?" Chala asked.

The Librarian frowned a moment. "No, all daughters."

"Figures."

I watched their by-play with bewilderment, and interrupted the Librarian before he could reply with his usual literality. "I thought you were programmed with geographical and cultural information I could use on my trip. Why are you suddenly spouting philosophy?"

"The main librarian noted that your natural education was heavily weighted toward literature. That includes studies in philosophy, religion, logic, and history. I was supplied with subprograms on all these subjects so that you would have someone to talk to."

I shook my head in awe. As much as I had been given to know about computers and artificial intelligences, the knowledge seemed still to be filtering into my awareness. It floated on the surface of my mind, attached to, and yet not part of, my consciousness.

Dr. Chala cleared her throat gently, followed by Timash's second breathless arrival in the space of half an hour. The twin events helped me to remember why I was here, and I gave the doctor all of my attention. Timash, after a single wordless glare from his mother, did the same.

"There is very little in my literature concerning telepathic viruses," she began, "since there are very few cases of them any more. In the very young and old, they kill quickly, and no one else has contracted a case—well, probably since before the Nuum came.

"What I discovered in talking to the Librarian, though, is that the Nuum themselves have had a little more reason to do research. Apparently one of the rare side effects of space travel is viral mutation, and every once in a while, what they call a 'telepathic carrier' is affected. When that happens, the virus can spread, with results that I wouldn't even wish on the Nuum."

"And they've discovered a cure?" I asked, trying to control my eagerness.

"No," she said flatly. "In fact, they haven't even stumbled upon the procedure we used on you, even though our Thoran doctors have known about using it for centuries. I guess it never occurred to them that our archives could be good for much?" She directed the last toward the Librarian.

"Not for medical matters, I'm afraid," he admitted. "A pity."

Dr. Chala allowed that to pass without comment. "In any event, by pooling our information—since the Librarian has learned a lot more from our governors than they have from us—I've come up with a theoretical vaccine. The problem has always been that the viruses are so small, they can't be invaded by most pathogenic agents. The agents are too big. We could slice off pieces with an electron scalpel, but the pieces wouldn't be sufficiently toxic to do the job. I asked the Librarian to scan my pharmaceutical database to see if there was anything on hand that could be combined with something Nuum to do the job, but he came up empty."

"Then Timash had an idea," the Librarian said. "He suggested we scan the biological databases to see if there was a naturally-occurring agent more virulent than what we could synthesize, and yet near enough to obtain a specimen."

"And we found something," Dr. Chala resumed. The shining pride in her eyes completely eclipsed any annoyance she had felt at Timash's earlier rash action. "It's natural, it's locally available, and there's little doubt that it is toxic enough to do the job, even in microscopic portions."

My excitement threatened to consume me, until it was abruptly overshadowed by a horrible fear that they were not telling me something—something that would negate all of their marvelous findings.

"So what is it? What did you find?"

Before she could answer, an entirely new voice said from the doorway:

"Tiger spider venom."

Chapter 21
The Revolution Begins

Balu walked into the room on the heels of his announcement confident that his niece would not contradict him, a faith in which he was rewarded. The astonishment in her eyes must have been ambrosia to the weary soul of a man so used to being shunted aside. Even the Librarian appeared impressed.

"I could have told you that without your computers." He waved his arm to indicate the world. "We've always known that there are things out there that have medicinal use. Even the Nuum have figured it out. Why do you think they built that base on the edge of the jungle in the first place? To keep an eye on us? No! I'll bet you my Picadorean compass they're doing biological research. That's why they don't just bomb the conservationists off the map. They want to study the plants down here."

Dr. Chala digested this news, turned to me. "You were with them. Did they say anything about why they were here?"

I shook my head. "No, we were brought in expressly to deal with the rebels—the conservationists. All they told us was that the 'blacks' couldn't handle the situation. I was a little confused—I didn't see any black men among the Nuum—but that would explain why we were given staffs and swords instead of guns. The ray weapons the Nuum use would burn up the entire jungle."

"When the Nuum talk about the 'blacks,' Keryl," Timash informed me, "they're talking about people with black hair. All the Nuum with you had red hair, right? The reds and the blacks don't get along."

"Black *hair?*" I repeated. "I thought they were talking about skin." My voice trailed off as I tried to re-order what I knew of this spacefaring people. In my own life I had had little to do with colored people, and never had any of them given me reason to dislike them, although I knew my opinion was in the minority. But to discriminate because of *hair color*—? Suddenly I felt the need to sit down somewhere and think for a very long time—a wish not to be granted for many days to come.

"Of course," Dr. Chala was saying, "this is all theoretical, and unless you know how to catch a tiger spider, Uncle, it will most likely remain so. There's no way to synthesize the venom here in the lab. We have to have a specimen."

"And the only time I've ever seen one," Timash chimed in, "we were too busy running to ask for a sample. 'Course, if Keryl hadn't smashed that first one, I wouldn't have been running anywhere."

The room seemed to move in slow motion, with Dr. Chala and the Librarian and Uncle Balu all swiveling to stare at Timash, then at me, doubt and hope and wonder dawning in their expressions. Timash must have caught their thoughts, because he too turned to look at me until I shrank away from their concentrated attention.

"Keryl," Balu said softly, "did you really smash a tiger spider?"

"Yes…"

"With what?" he asked with disarming gentleness, like a man removing the casing from an unexploded artillery shell.

"My staff. It's in my…uh, Timash's room."

Timash was the first to escape from ensuing scramble and disappeared into his room, emerging a moment later with my staff balanced gently in his big hands.

"Don't touch the part where he smashed the spider!" his

mother commanded, and he shook his head, scarcely breathing as he gently laid the staff on an examining bench. The doctor pulled on her gloves, approached the desk, then paused long enough to pull a second pair of gloves on over the first. Even at that, she used long tweezers to pick away bits of the vermin that still stuck there. The Librarian watched intently at her shoulder.

"Good lord," I whispered to Balu. "Is it still dangerous? That staff has been standing in the corner in Timash's room for weeks."

"Nobody knows," he whispered back. "She just doesn't want to take a chance."

"I kept meaning to clean it up, but I never thought to need it again," I said, meaning the staff. "Now I'm glad I didn't."

"You should be very glad, Keryl, and I'm glad Timash was taught better than to handle other people's possessions," Dr. Chala said tightly from where she bent over her task. She had added a surgical mask to her regimen, and as she spoke she carefully set down her tools and procured a pair of goggles. "These remains should have been contaminated with bacteria by now. They aren't. I've got a feeling they're still capable of killing anything that touches them." She set a control on a console on the examining desk and stepped back again. A faint glow surrounded the desk and the staff. "From now on, nobody touches this thing. And I'm going to need to decontaminate the whole house. I don't think any of us are in any danger, but I'll want to run some tests."

The tests came back favorably, a great relief to me and especially to Timash, who had spent some hours describing to me the thoroughness with which his mother was wont to conduct her examinations. To me, his horror stories held no fright, compared to twentieth-century medicine. I thought about regaling Timash with tales of battlefield first aid, but recanted the notion: Either he wouldn't believe me, or he wouldn't sleep for a week.

Despite my determination that nothing short of a Hun battalion could keep me from being the first to hear the results of

Dr. Chala's tests upon the venom residue itself, my illness, combined with the excitement, laid me low. I lay down on my bed in Timash's room, eyes shifting fearfully to the spot on the wall against which the tip of the staff had rested (now scrubbed so thoroughly the paint had all but disappeared) for a brief moment, and I knew nothing more for nearly eleven hours.

As always, sleep refreshed me greatly, clearing the grey, hanging cobwebs from my mind, and I was warm and comfortable under the blanket someone had thoughtfully lain across me. Most days I had been wont to lie there for some time sifting through my dreams, but on this occasion I was up almost before my eyes were open. As quickly as I could arrange myself, I was searching the house for someone with news.

Timash met me immediately, leaping out of his chair like a dog caught on his owner's bed. No need to ask him; through no choice of his own, he had stayed with me rather than accompany his mother to her laboratory. We ran out the door without a word.

We would as well have walked.

"It doesn't work." Dr. Chala's dismally bare pronouncement was given without artificial preamble or couched in false hopes. "The venom attacks the virus, but it only bruises the outer protein sheath. I thought it would be strong enough to break through, but I overestimated the size of the virus. To be passed along by mere *thought*—you cannot imagine how small it is. Lord only knows how the virus lives."

"What about radiation?" Balu hadn't left the hospital since the virus was transferred. "Couldn't you use a focused stream of charged particles to breach the protein sheath? We know that nuclear radiation will destroy them."

The doctor was tired, but not too weary to bite back her initial response. She simply shook her head.

"It won't work. The virus is dispersed throughout his brain. We could never find them all, and even if we could, his brain would look like a honeycomb. It's got to be done biochemically, or not at all."

As the education bestowed upon me by the Librarian was the first part of my mind to fade out when the virus wore me down, I had been following the technical implications of this discussion only vaguely. Even sleep was insufficient to bring my senses back to what they had been before I fell ill, and protein sheathes and nuclear radiation were fantasy in the world where I had grown up. But then, perhaps that is why Dr. Chala's words should trigger in my wandering thoughts an association that my more learned friends had overlooked.

"Biochemical?" I uttered vaguely. "Isn't that what you said the Nuum were here for, Balu?"

"Oh my god," Chala breathed. "Oh my god, he's right! The greatest biochemical library on the continent could be sitting not ten miles away…!" She swept me up in a hug that threatened to finish the job of killing me that the virus had begun. "Keryl, that's brilliant!"

Amid the renewed celebration, it fell to Timash, with the clarity of youth, to ask the obvious question.

"Um, Mother, how are you going to get in?"

The sultry air of the jungle night and the soft susurrations of its insects were in my mind merely gentle invitations to danger whose sinister agenda was only slightly diminished by Timash and Balu's repeated insistence that tiger spiders were solely diurnal. They need not add, and I did not seek to know, that other creatures roamed in their place, creatures far more adapted to nighttime hunting than we were to evading them.

I had never feared the dark more than any other adult; perhaps it was the telepathic virus's fogging of my mind that caused me to revert to childhood terrors. Whatever the reason, I credit my companions' unyielding vigilance, in bracing me between them as we threaded along barely-worn paths, with keeping me on track to our chosen goal. Without them, I would never have departed from

Tahana City, and the most fantastic sights of my long journey—far stranger than any I had yet experienced—would have gone forever unwitnessed.

The Library I carried in my pocket. We had found that the Librarian, when visually manifested, shone in the dark, and so he must await our destination before participating in our plan. I thought he had submitted to our arguments with a touch of pique.

Having begun our trek while it was still light, we were now skirting the area Timash recognized as being controlled by the Nuum. Our goal lay partway around the circle of their influence. Along with Timash's knowledge of the terrain I relied upon his assurances that we could pass undetected.

"You're sure they won't know we're there?" I had asked as he mapped out our route.

"Absolutely." He spoke with the confidence of one who had not lived long enough to see how life could go wrong. "They can't use infra-red detectors because the jungle's too thick and too crowded. Even if the sensors were on, they couldn't distinguish us from a hundred other animals on their screens at the same time. The only things they can pick out for sure are the thunder lizards— and you don't need a night scope to know *they're* coming."

"Thunder lizards?"

Balu had shaken his head gravely. "Don't ask."

Now, committed to sneaking through the monster-infested dark guarded by two jungle beasts, I thrust my nerves into a back cupboard of my mind and focused on what lay ahead, both literally and figuratively.

The moon was thankfully just over half-full; any less and we could not have picked our way safely. As it was, I was constantly tripped up by low branches and depressions in the damp ground. Before and behind me, my guides' bare feet made little sound. Again and again hands reached out of the night to catch me before I could trip and break my neck. At last I learned to raise my feet more than was my wont and place them straight down when I stepped. It was uncomfortable, but I fell less often and made less noise. No sooner had I begun to master this new gait than we arrived.

A nearby shadow detached itself from the bush and greeted us softly.

"Timash," the man said. "You're lucky you weren't caught. Your friend makes more noise than a three-legged sloth in the dry season."

Timash grasped the other's outstretched arm briefly. "You won't care when you hear what he's got to say." He turned to me. "In fact, I can't wait to hear it myself."

"You don't know what his plan is?" There was suddenly an unmistakable tone of suspicion.

"We thought it best he not know, in case something happened to him while he was setting up this meeting," I whispered. "We're just being careful, just as you were when you insisted we meet you out here in the middle of the jungle instead of at your headquarters."

The dim figure straightened in indignation. "We have a good reason. We have to be careful if we're going to keep the Nuum off our backs."

"Seems to me if you were a little less…careful," Balu interjected, "you wouldn't have to worry about the Nuum at all."

"Who're you?" The guard turned an anxious gaze on Timash. "Who's he?"

"This is Keryl Clee, and that's my Uncle Balu."

"Oh," the stranger said with a knowing nod. "So this is the famous Uncle Balu. Timash talks a lot about you." Suddenly he held out a long strip of cloth toward me. "He's got to be blindfolded before he goes any further."

"Oh for god's sake!" Balu exploded. "It's pitch dark!"

"I don't want him memorizing the trail."

"Memorizing—!" Balu sputtered. "He can hardly memorize his own name! He—oh, you tell him, Timash!"

Timash leaned forward and muttered a few words into the man's ear. Once the fellow's head jerked up and I saw his eyes glinting in the moonlight as he looked at me.

"Really?"

Timash said something else, which apparently ended the dispute, because the guide abruptly turned and disappeared again as silently as the moonlight. My friend followed and Balu ushered me along in their wake. Stumbling again, I had to grin. A blindfold!

I could have assured the conservationists, when we reached the low mass of darkness that revealed their headquarters, that a blindfold would not have contributed one iota to my inability to retrace my steps at some future date. I could have told them, but I did not. Not only did they not ask, but I felt secure in the supposition that their sense of humor was sadly underdeveloped.

I was gladdened to note that the members of their council, as they referred to it, were older by some years than the man who had lead us here with such poor grace. It gave me some hope that my plan, untested and largely dependent upon faith, might be approved. As I stood in the soft light surveying the four unsmiling faces that awaited my hastily-rehearsed speech, I lowered my estimate of the odds against us from astronomical to merely huge.

My initial introductions were met with polite nods and little else. Although Timash had been here on more than one occasion—to which was owed the genesis of my idea—any courtesies extended to him in the past plainly did not apply to me, or for that matter, to Balu. Even Timash seemed puzzled, so confused that he had apparently not yet realized that his own welcome had worn discernibly thin.

The council consisted of one black woman, and three men whose complexions were the reddish tan I had seen on Bantos Han and most people I had met recently. The woman's aristocratic features and short hair made her an arresting figure, almost Egyptian. Something about the intensity of her gaze caused me to direct the bulk of my remarks to her.

"Timash has already told you why we're here, and if you weren't interested, you would not have invited me to speak tonight. We want the same thing: To be rid of the Nuum. I can help you to do that."

"And how do we know you're not one of them?" one of the male councilors asked.

Balu retorted before I could. "Are we going to go through this all over again? Keryl's been a guest of ours for weeks. If he was going to turn anybody over to the Nuum, it would be us in Tahana City, not you living in the bushes!"

The councilors were on their feet before I could act. It took Timash to restrain first his uncle and then the council—but then, when a bull gorilla demands the floor, you give it to him.

"Look! Everybody shut up!" He pointed to Balu. "Uncle, control yourself! You taught me better manners. And you—" he fixed the council with a glare "—didn't need to drag us ten miles through the jungle just to pick a fight. You know I've been coming here a long time, and I would never betray you any more than you would me. We've pretty much left each other alone all this time, but now Keryl thinks it's time we changed—right, Keryl?"

I nodded numbly. That was exactly what I thought—but I hadn't told Timash. Balu knew what I was about, but he and his mother and Tahana City's own rulers had judged it too sensitive and dangerous to entrust the information to a lad of Timash's years. Perhaps we had misjudged him...

But now was the moment to speak. Timash had calmed the crowd, and bullied them into giving me at least a few seconds' grace, but that time was quickly draining away. Mentally I threw all of my logs onto the fire.

"I know some things about the Nuum that you don't. Never mind how I know them. But I can tell you that they are fractured and disarrayed, and they are vulnerable. The troops they have sent here cannot handle the job they've been given; they're barely holding their own. Properly supplied and organized, we can take them. We can take back what is ours."

The black woman leaned over the table. "Are you talking about actually driving them away? About taking over the research station for ourselves?"

"Oh, no, madam," I replied. "I'm talking about a revolution."

Chapter 22
I Go Behind the Lines

My bald statement seemed to stun them, set them back on their heels even more than Timash's bombast. In that moment of eerie silence, like the eye of a hurricane, I could feel with a rush along my skin the fate of our world teetering out over the edge of the abyss. I teetered with it, as a man who has stopped just short of the precipice does not know if the crumbling rocks will hold him for that timeless, priceless instant before he can regain his balance and save himself.

Then the moment was gone and the voices crashed over me once more.

Had I resisted, the power in that room would have swept me away. I only stood fast; before long they would see their words flooding over and past me without leaving a mark, and they would cease of their own accord. Then and only then would they be mine.

It came as no surprise that the black woman emerged first from the din. She stopped in mid-sentence, abandoning her argument with the man next to her, and simply looked at me. She looked at me as though she had not seen me before, as though I had appeared in a puff of smoke, like Merlin. When I would have grinned fatuously at her, I restrained myself: I held Merlin captive in my pocket. I was becoming drunk with unaccustomed authority, and had she not waved her fellows on the council into order, I might have laughed in sheer delight. All that they had put me through to come here, and I held secrets far greater than they could imagine. Power is a dangerous thing, and arrogance is far worse. A few more moments of chaos and I might have destroyed everything.

"You have our attention, that much is obvious," the councilwoman said dryly. She let her words hang on the air, an invitation.

"If I had your names, I might do more," I countered. To be truthful, I only wanted to know hers. Plainly the power behind the council's democratic facade, she fascinated me personally as well. As a colored woman, I could not bring myself to admit any attraction, but as a human being her force of personality was undeniable. In my own time, for a woman to exude such authority was unusual; in this downtrodden age of Man I thought it remarkable.

She acknowledged my riposte with a nod of her head. "I am Shene. My fellow council members are Trell, Ribaud, and Jonn." We briefly nodded to each other in turn. They had not spoken directly to me since I entered the chamber, and seemed content to allow Shene to continue. I was equally content to address myself almost solely to her.

I am unaccustomed to public speaking; my last experience was in giving orders, not in persuading unbelievers. I cast myself back in time (in my mind only, alas) to my university days and the unsmiling professors on whom I had bestowed my theses of Robin Hood and Arthur and the role of the women who loved them. I spread my hands in implied gratitude for my audience and assumed my most ingratiating smile.

"Thank you, members of the council. Before we go forward, you have expressed questions as to my reasons for coming here. You have lived a long time under the heel of an oppressor. You have the right to ask.

"Some of you know that I am ill. My doctor tells me I have contracted a virus, a virus that has no cure in Thoran medicine." It would be too time-consuming to explain how I contracted a telepathic virus, so I did not try. The crowd began to shrink away, but I stopped them with a wave of my hand. "It is not contagious. No one here is in the slightest danger. But my doctor believes the Nuum may have a cure. I need to get into their laboratories and find out."

"Then what do you need us for?" Councilman Trell snapped. "Why don't you just go back to them?" He fell to muttering to himself. There was little doubt how he felt about my story, or about me.

"Because despite my appearance, I am not one of them." I projected my words directly toward him now. I could afford no doubters. "I come from a land very, very far away. I was known by a different name there, but one thing was the same: They too suffered under an invading tyrant. When I first came here, I was glad for the peace and quiet afforded me. I did not know of the Nuum, but it was not long before I found out. My first experience with them showed me a cruel, selfish people who delighted in abusing their own power. I thought perhaps I was only seeing them at their worst, that with time I would come to understand their point of view. But I was mistaken—I had not seen them at anything approaching their worst.

"Because of circumstances beyond my control, they took me to be one of their own. Even then they were cold and aloof. But I was caught up in their war. I was one and they were many, so I did what they wanted until I could escape.

"Now I have friends, friends who stood by me when I needed them. Now we are many. I'm tired of running and hiding. And I'm not going to do it anymore."

Somewhere behind me a foot scraped the floor. Someone coughed. The council watched me intently. I hadn't said a damned thing, and they were still listening. The Lord had evidently not yet tired of protecting fools. I cast all my dice on my next throw.

"You can live the rest of your lives in these tunnels, or you can fight the Nuum and live as free men. I can show you how to make weapons that will kill at a hundred yards without a sound." Jonn, or perhaps it was Ribaud, stared down at his hands. The others simply shook their heads sadly. I challenged them to speak their minds.

Shene spoke for them all. "Do you think we haven't thought of this all before, Keryl Clee? We know these trees better than anyone. There hasn't been a Nuum who could walk safely alone outside in years. Even their tractor-probes fall into our traps. But it doesn't do any good. They just send more men, and more robots. We can keep them from doing what they came here for, but we can never stop them. We don't have the technology."

I fingered the Library and pulled it from my pocket.

"And if I could give you that technology?"

Her eyes narrowed. Even Jonn looked up.

"What do you mean?"

I activated the Librarian. Before I left that room, I had an army.

As with, I suspect, all medieval scholars, I had at one time carried on a romance with the bow and arrow. Unfortunately, I had abandoned it some time ago in the face of more pressing concerns, but I was delighted to find that while not so simple as riding a bicycle, it was yet a skill that had not utterly devolved over time. Nor was I forced to realize my other fear, that of not being able to reproduce my weapon of choice. I had never been a bowyer nor a fletcher, and had envisioned an extended period of trial and error in creating both a bow of sufficient power, and more importantly, an arrow that would fly in something approximating a straight line. I need not have worried, for the marvelous engineers in Tahana City quickly picked up on my crude design ideas and machined both bow and arrows in a single night.

I was so impressed I considered moving straight on to crossbows, as they require less effort and deliver more power. I left off the idea for a simple reason: A archer can string and loose much faster than a crossbowman. If my men couldn't hit their targets, they could at least shoot a lot of arrows.

This is not to say that none of them were proficient. Given enough hours of practice, anyone, man or ape, can learn to hit a target at twenty or thirty yards. I tutored the men while Balu, my best ape student, assisted his own kind. There was no derogation intended; the gorillas simply handled heavier bows. Safety demanded we practice in different areas.

I should have been far better than any of them; I was simply reviving an old skill while they were still learning it afresh, but the virus interfered with my concentration and aim. Perhaps it was not so bad, then, that my plan called for me not to take place in the attack.

Two weeks were allowed for training. It would have taken far longer for the men to become truly proficient, but we only needed to win one battle, wherein if I did my part we would hold the advantages of surprise, numbers, and terrain. If I didn't do my part, our plan failed no matter how well we imitated Robin and the Merry Men.

The sky was still grey and the ground wet when I stumbled into the clearing around the bio-research station. My clothes were realistically torn and muddy from having walked several miles through the jungle at night without my guides assisting me. I was thin from several days' near-fasting, and the hunted look in my eyes was no play-acting: I was jumping from the monster-infested trees to the monster-infested buildings. I was not terribly brave, only terribly desperate. I simply let my true feelings show through.

I ran to the nearest door, pounding hysterically. No one knew what security measures the Nuum followed, except that they could monitor their own clearing. We were fairly sure that their sensors failed within the first few yards past the tree line, but since none of the conservationists had tested the defenses in some time and the Nuum ventured out so seldom, we could not be sure of that any more than we had been sure that they would not shoot me the moment I came into view.

Barely had my fist hit the door than it flew open and I fell forward. Several hands grabbed me, unceremoniously pulling me through, and the door slammed shut again. It was so close I felt the rush of air.

My rescuers pulled me up with a jerk among a babble of voices. I was surrounded by strangers' faces, their eyes wide, their mouths gaping.

"It is him! It's Clee!"

"That's incredible!"

"How did he do it?"

A more controlled voice took command, from beyond the crowd that limited my vision. "Let's get him to the infirmary." That was a voice I was happy to listen to.

I was half-escorted, half-carried to the infirmary with a solicitude well outstripping anything I had been previously afforded. From the whispered exchanges of my handlers, I gathered that I was a brand of local celebrity: Apparently my disappearance had gained me a notoriety I could have done without. It also granted the Nuum a humanity I was loathe to recognize. With an effort I divorced that concept from my thinking.

The doctor was easier to deal with, even withal that I spent more time with him, for his manner was professionally distant. Comparing him in my mind with the equally competent but more accessible Dr. Chala, allowed him to remain a facade, a figure of authority and learning rather than a person.

Even in wartime, people are never as easy to kill as figures of authority.

Suddenly the doctor paused in his examination, straightened, and stared quizzically at his instruments. Then he bent over me, pulling up one eyelid, and frowned at his instruments again. I tensed.

He looked as though he were about to speak, thought better of it, and turned away. I half-rose from the hard pallet that served as examining table and diagnostic tool. Everything depended on my ability to pose again as a Nuum until I could reach my pre-arranged post. If the doctor had detected some anomaly that marked my true birth... I glanced around quickly; if I couldn't find a surgical tool, I would have to use my bare hands.

My breath came shallowly. If he moved toward the door, I would assume the worst. But he didn't; he turned again to me—a gas syringe in his hand.

"Take it easy," he said, gently pushing me back. "You'll not be sharing your adventures with the mess hall gangs just yet." The syringe was pressed gently against my neck and released its contents with a hiss I felt more than heard. "You're sicker than you think. I don't know how or why, but something you ran into out there caused serious cellular damage. You weren't living in an abandoned building, were you? Some of those old wrecks still have active power piles, and the radiation leakage is something you don't want to think about." He pulled back my lower lip, then the upper. "You don't appear to have been exposed, but something sure was playing havoc with your immune system."

"I have been having headaches," I ventured tentatively, thinking he might be referring to my virus.

He snorted. "And a lot of other things, I imagine. Maybe it was a poison. Were you bitten by anything?"

I thought wryly of the vaccinations and warnings we had received before I left the Nuum ship. Apparently this doctor thought no more of them than I did. I shook my head. Better, I thought, not to go into my close escape from the tiger spiders.

"Well, something got into you. I'll want to do a tox screen, but first I need to get some cellular rejuvenators into you. You seem to have stabilized, but whatever it was, it was causing your cells to age at an accelerated rate. I don't think you'd have lived to see 80."

I could not help staring.

"Oh, don't worry about it," he said, busying himself again with dials and lights. "Just stay out of the jungle and you'll be telling this story to your great-great-grandchildren."

Chapter 23
I Am Given New Life

My original plan had consisted solely of infiltrating the Nuum station, stealing the information I needed via the Library, and getting out again. It was to have been quick and relatively quiet, my reappearance and subsequent re-disappearance an object of curiosity to the aloof Nuum, but not, I believed, a long-term consideration. In that I had been mistaken. I had not counted on the excitement accompanying my return, or the notoriety it would afford me. My re-disappearance would have the station's entire complement out looking for me—in force.

That original idea, however, had already been abandoned before I met the conservationists, as I came to consider the difference between the Nuum and the German hordes of my own time—which is to say, almost none. Each occupied a land in defiance of the people who owned it. Each used his power to enslave, and to kill when it suited his purposes. The only true difference lay in the fact that the Nuum had already accomplished what the Germans still sought: domination. The Earth of this day and age was a conquered nation, and every free American fiber of my being rose up in indignation and outrage at the thought.

And so I had come to be here, lying on an examining table,

contemplating how best to kill the man who had just doubled my lifespan.

I thought of the hundreds of Bantos Han's neighbors turned to grey dust on the streets of Vardan. I thought of French and Belgian villagers crushed by the Hun. Were he to realize that I was not Nuum, this doctor would turn me over to my enemies. If this were still 1915 and I were dressed in a stolen German uniform, would I hesitate?

No, I would not. But neither could I kill him in cold blood. Regardless of his uniform, he was a man of medicine, and a non-combatant. Unless he took up arms against me, killing him would be murder, no less a crime than the Thorans or the Belgians had suffered.

"Excuse me while I fetch another analyzer," he muttered suddenly. I tensed once more, but this time he disappeared into a small supply closet. Without thinking, I slipped from the diagnostic bed, slammed the door on him, and blocked it with a chair. He began to pound his fists against the other side, shouting for me to let him out. I risked someone hearing him, but that was the price I paid for my humanity.

The treatments he had administered left me feeling unsteady, compounding my confusion at being faced with the host of blinking lights and gaping data sockets. I pulled out the Library and placed it in the nearest socket, as the Librarian had told me to do. "All of the systems are so interdependent it won't matter where you plug me in," he had said. "The kind of computing power I need to accomplish our goal isn't even supposed to exist on this continent, let alone in the hands of the Thorans, so the security interdicts will be elementary."

Nothing seemed to happen for several minutes: the lights blinked on and off as before and no smoke came pouring through the consoles, so I was forced to presume that the Librarian was right, and three centuries of peaceful tyranny had left the Nuum complacent. The doctor's pounding had calmed somewhat, as he realized that I was not going to let him out, nor was anyone apparently coming to rescue him. This left me profoundly relieved, as I had dreaded the necessity of asking him to prescribe a headache remedy if he didn't stop.

Where the doctor's shouting had left off, the sudden sirens more than made up for him.

The plan had called for the Library to tap the central computer system, bypass the security blockades, and simulate a fusion core-breach alarm. The Nuum, fearing a malfunction, would flee the station—only to find the conservationists and Timash's people waiting for them. It would only be payment-in-kind—but it would still be a massacre. Meanwhile, I huddled in the infirmary, wondering how to explain my decision to spare the doctor. Perhaps the Library had failed, I thought with gallows cheer, and the core breach was real. That would solve all of my problems in one quick flash of light.

My problems were only beginning. The infirmary door flew open and a Nuum dashed in.

"Quick! We're evacuating! Where's the doctor?"

That question was answered without any help from me—the doctor began shouting and pounding the door once again. The safety officer saw the chair propped up and leaped to the correct conclusion in an instant, his sidearm erupting from its place at his side and holding me fast in its sights. He waved it toward the closet.

"Let him out." I started to obey, but suddenly he seemed to realize that I was going to have to move the chair, placing a potential weapon in my hands.

"Hold on—"

There was a noise at the doorway, and a familiar voice said: "Keryl?"

We both turned to look, but since the guard was between me and the door, that meant he was looking away from me—a costlier error than giving me a flimsy piece of furniture. I was on him in an instant, and swiftly rendered him unconscious.

"Harros!"

My former bunkmate shook his head in concern. "I heard you were back. What's going on in here?" He cast a glance toward the noisy closet.

My mind was spinning. I had saved the doctor for my own reasons, but now: The doctor, the unconscious guard, Harros—how was I going to protect all these Nuum from my allies...or explain it to them when I was done? Could Harros be trusted? Not that it mattered, I reflected bitterly, since I could not send him to his death outside when I had another choice.

"Come on," he urged suddenly. "I'll tell you about it later. The core is going to breach any second!"

"Relax," I said, sitting on the examining table. "The alert is a fake." I had to tell him; he would find out soon enough, unless he went outside, which I could not now in all good conscience let him do. It was no accident, however, that I was sitting where my body blocked his view of the console into which I had plugged the Library.

He took it better than I had thought, a sly smile stretching his lips most unattractively.

"That explains the guns and the doctor locked in the closet. I always knew there was something odd about you. You don't agree with the occupation either, do you?"

It was my turn to control my surprise. "I beg your pardon?"

He looked up and down the corridor before he responded, then stepped inside and closed the door.

"We do have to get out of here, you know. They'll be back."

I shook my head slowly. "No, they won't." As a precaution, the Library had sealed all of the doors. Possibly some would escape into the jungle, but no one would be coming back.

"You're amazing." He seemed genuinely impressed. "How did you do it?"

"I have friends," I said curtly. Not only did I not want to disclose the existence of the Library, but I didn't want him to think that the gun gave him any advantage. "They'll be here soon. You didn't answer my question: Why did you help me?"

"They threw me into confinement after you disappeared. I was feeling out others to see how they felt about the occupation and what we were doing here, and I must have asked the wrong man."

I sat silently for a time, waiting for developments and cultivating an attitude that would dissuade questions. It appeared successful, as Harros looked several times on the verge of speaking, but then the urge subsided and the silence stretched on.

I stood. "You'd better get behind me. When my friends arrive, you don't want them to draw the wrong conclusions."

"What if it's not them? What if someone else shows up?" he asked, hesitating.

"Then you still don't want to be between me and the door." I gestured with the pistol to illustrate my point.

Moments later the door slid open again. Although they had professed to loathe them, the conservationists handled Nuum armaments with great confidence.

I had a much less difficult time explaining the doctor's survival to my allies than I had in convincing the doctor himself that my allies were not bent on curtailing his good fortune. I had expected, perhaps naively, that my having spared his life, and the explanation of why we were eager to enlist his cooperation, would pique his interest sufficiently to overcome his anxiety. Unfortunately, he denounced my story about a telepathic virus as outlandish, and insisted that it was simply a cover for our real goal, although he could not perceive what that might be.

This presented a serious problem; Dr. Chala had performed all of the preliminary work on my case, but we had agreed that the gorillas' involvement in this must remain privileged information. (Originally, of course, that would not have been a consideration. Dead men tell no tales.) In the end, however, two circumstances combined to satisfy all concerns: First, a simple examination confirmed my viral infection; and second, the Librarian recommended a forgotten interrogation technique which, while harmless, would have such a pronounced effect on his short-term memory that nothing he learned about us would survive. It was agreed that once my cure was effected, all the prisoners would be drugged and delivered safely to a town whence they could make their way homeward. In the meantime, Harros and the guard who had so fortuitously discovered me were interned in the brig.

Together with the Librarian, the two physicians buried themselves in the Nuum database. It was not long before they developed such an attitude of mutual respect that I suspect they both regretted that their collaboration was to be so short-lived, nor was it much later that they announced the results of their work.

"It's not finished, Keryl," Dr. Chala confided to me. "But we're being told that we have to evacuate. Even though we've cracked their communications codes, the Nuum will be sending in fresh personnel soon. I can finish the serum back in Tahana City."

"That's good. Timash told me this morning they've been ferrying computer equipment, supplies, weapons, and bio-sensors out of here for days. We've got to smash anything that can't be moved, then we'll leave the doors open and the jungle can take care of the rest."

She sighed. "I wish we could take Dr. Sinh back to the city with us. He's a zoological research scientist as well as a physician." She looked at me hopefully, even though she knew it wasn't my decision to make, and I told her so. But she had reminded me of an errand I needed to undertake, so I begged her pardon and sought out the doctor myself.

I found him in his quarters; since he was confined there when not working with Dr. Chala in the lab, not finding him would have been cause for great alarm. He looked up as though he had been expecting me, which I suppose he had.

He wore the face of a condemned man. "Is it time?"

I had to smile. "It's not that bad. Dr. Chala and the Librarian have assured me that you won't suffer any ill effects. And you'll hardly be conscious until you reach the village. Considering the roads around here, that's all to the good."

With a sigh he arose and extended a hand. "I guess I didn't believe it was really true until just now."

"I meant what I said. But I need to ask you a question," I confided as I accepted his grip. "Why was Harros in the brig?"

For a moment his eyes dropped away from mine, and he licked his lip as he formed his answer.

"I probably shouldn't say anything, but the truth is, I don't know. All I know is that you should watch him. We tend to give our soldiers a lot of rope. Whatever landed him in prison, it must have been serious."

"Thank you," I said, turning to leave.

"No," he replied. "Thank you. I owe you a debt. You saved my life."

"It's no more than you did for me."

"You're wrong. I did what I did because I'm a doctor. I had to do it. You didn't."

But he was in the wrong. War is about more than deciding who dies. It is also about deciding who lives.

Chapter 24
I Take Companions

Once the groundwork had been laid, the finishing of the serum to cure my telepathic illness was quickly accomplished. Dr. Chala administered it, sent me to bed, and watched me for twenty-four hours. Before the end of that time, the fuzziness that had filled my brain for so long it seemed natural began to ebb, and the whispers of other minds floated around the fringes of my consciousness. It was as though cotton had been removed from my ears.

"I guess you're just meant to make history, Keryl," she told me the next day. "Your screens are almost normal. Congratulations. You are the first person in recorded history to survive an attack of a telepathic virus."

"I can't believe it's gone. It was almost as though I were growing used to it."

"Best you not think that way. According to your scans, it isn't gone; there's still a residue, but it's so weak I don't think it will ever pose a threat. Your shields are strong enough to resist; it's almost as if you've built up an immunity."

It was the difference between a reprieve and a pardon. I would take it. I squeezed her as hard as I could, exchanging hearty grins with Timash and Balu, who stood nearby waiting for the results. I told Dr. Chala that she was to be congratulated as well.

"Hmm, well, me and the Librarian and Dr. Sinh. But since I'm the only one around, I guess I'll just take their bows too."

"So what are you going to do now, Keryl?" Balu asked. He said it quietly, as if reluctant to hear my answer.

"You've all been more than kind…" I began, but I needn't have tried to soften the blow. They knew my choice even as I did. "…but my heart is in Dure."

Timash began to shift his weight back and forth, eyes downcast. I smiled gently, thinking that he was trying to think of a way to say goodbye—which only showed that even after all this time, I knew next to nothing about him.

Balu cuffed his nephew gently. "You'd better get to it, boy. It's now or never."

"What?" Chala asked sharply—with a mother's instinct, I fear.

Timash stopped rocking and looked me straight in the eye. "Keryl," he said, not betraying his soul-shaking nervousness (as he confided later), "I'd like to go with you."

My first thought was that he would make quite a sight strolling through the West End. His mother was more to the point.

"It was bad enough that we had to put up with your uncle parading all over the world, son. I am not going to go through that again."

Naturally, those travels by his esteemed ancestor were exactly the spark that had lit Timash's fuse of adventure, so this argument fell short. But Dr. Chala experienced no shortage of impassioned arguments where her only offspring was concerned. She railed. She cried. She gave ultimatums. And she peeled Balu's skin off in strips, up one side and down the other, for giving her baby boy the idea that trekking across unexplored wastes chased by the Nuum and the breen and Lord-knows-what could take the place of a good education and a long life visiting his mother for supper every Sunday. Frankly, by the time she was finished cataloging the probable dangers found just between Tehana City and Dure, I was more than a bit willing to reconsider the entire venture myself.

"He's only known Keryl a few weeks, and they've already fought off the Nuum and almost been eaten by tiger spiders!" (She had a point.) "What's going to happen to them if they go off alone?"

In the end, though, she had no defense against the same age-old argument that Balu's father had probably used against his own mate, many years ago:

"Chala, he's grown. You can't stop him."

Which may have won the argument, but I doubt to this day that she has ever forgiven him for saying it. Unfortunately, Balu had not the answers to all of my problems.

The conservationists had accepted the two Nuum as their temporary responsibility with poor grace, but they were in my debt and I was forced to hold them to it. I could not and would not bring them to Tehana City; I myself had only been accepted there under extraordinary circumstances, and to attempt to secure similar courtesies for Harros would have been an abuse of hospitality.

But they had been no happier with the arrangement than they keepers; Harros, especially, as he had already been imprisoned once, albeit by the Nuum. He were cared for by the conservationists, and if the conservationists treated them with less than the greatest respect, they could ask for no more.

Days later, they were a little the worse for wear, but they did not seem to have suffered any permanent damage. I forbore to make an issue of it.

"Get up," I said. "We're going." Neither needed a second invitation.

The Nuum guard, whose name I had never inquired after nor cared to know, accepted our plan to return him to civilization with all the grace that was to be expected, once Dr. Sinh had assured him we were telling the truth about the drugs to be administered.

Harros did not.

"I need to speak to you privately," he said in an urgent undertone, and more out of curiosity than necessity I acquiesced.

"I don't want to go back with them."

Inwardly I groaned. Little enough of this episode had pleased me, albeit I had emerged much the richer for it, but now that it was almost over I had begun to breathe a sigh of relief. *Almost over*, I reminded myself now, *but not quite*.

"You have no choice. You can't stay here."

"Why can't I go with you?"

Were I a more nimble-witted man, I would simply have averred that I was going nowhere, that I was remaining with the conservationists, and thus put an immediate end to his request and this ridiculous conversation. But then, a thoughtful man would not have ended up in my place at all.

"Because I'm not going back to Vardan. I have other business."

Harros looked off into the distance for a moment. "All right," he said. "You should take me with you because we have something in common." I arched my eyebrows at him, expecting him to launch into a tirade against the Nuum and their oppression of the Thorans, but he surprised me. "I'm a ghost, too."

I blinked, but before I could deny knowledge of this topic, he went on. "You can ask the doctor to check the 'sphere. He'll tell you I'm not lying. But if I go back with the others, the first thing the authorities will do is check my records—and I don't have any."

I asked Harros why he was not present in the datasphere; he replied he had not asked me my business, and I was forced to let it lie. Nor would he divulge how he knew I was not listed there either.

He was not pleased to find that Timash was also included in our party, but to his credit, Harros kept his feelings to himself, nor did he query me as regarded my plans, despite the fact that they now perforce included him. I was not, under the present circumstances, planning to divulge to him my own destination or my origin: He was still a Nuum, and might buy his way back into their good graces with my scalp. On the other hand, we were bound together at least until we reached some spot of civilization where he might be released with some chance to remain anonymous. After that, his fugitive life was his own. I explained that to him the first night as we made camp, parking our stolen Nuum groundcar beneath a spreading forest giant.

He had gathered wood for a fire, almost apologetically eager to pull his weight.

"I wouldn't mind sticking with you for a while. The Nuum have a long reach and a longer memory."

We had passed out of the jungle an hour ago. I stared out at the endless grasses of the great plain for a long time, more to keep Harros off-guard than to formulate my answer, which I already knew. The sun-painted sky glowed a deep vermilion more intense than the sunsets I remembered. The Library had told me the atmosphere had changed in almost a million years; it scattered light in a different way. It was very beautiful.

"Timash and I have a lot to see. We'll make sure you're all right before we leave you anywhere."

That was the plan.

* * *

I am not by natural inclination a talkative man, which served me well on the long days that followed, one from another onto the horizon. Timash was not happy that I had allowed another to join us, and a Nuum at that. I could hardly blame him for his taciturnity under the circumstances. Harros tried to bridge the gap, but he was rebuffed with silence. To have taken sides would have been divisive, so I kept my counsel. Either they would learn to get along, or not, and in any event we were not planning to remain a trio for long.

At first we had hoped to appropriate a Nuum flyer that could have covered the distance to distant Dure in a day—even if we detoured long enough to drop Harros in another town. This idea was stillborn: The flyer was available, but none of us could pilot the thing. Such practical but exotic information was outside the Librarian's programming and unavailable from the research station's database.

Ground transportation was our other option, offering more choices and controls that any one of us could have mastered with ease. One of our first tasks was removing as many identifying marks as possible.

I call it a groundcar, because that was how Harros referred to it, but in fact it was a marvelous invention that traveled through the air—albeit only two feet off the ground. In the trees, we had actually used retractable treads, but in the open we glided along with no more noise than a strong breeze. The controls were in the front; behind was a space somewhat larger than a Conestoga wagon, in which the three of us could sleep, if somewhat uncomfortably.

Ironically, and yet fortunately, the low vibration of the groundcar had an unaccountable and almost irresistible somnolent effect upon Timash. Try as he might, and fascinated by each passing mile as he might be, within a couple of hours of setting forth for the day he was dozing in his chair. (And perhaps each passing mile became less fascinating when it resembled nothing so much as the hundred miles behind and all those visible ahead.) Throughout the day he would doze fitfully, waking at unpredictable intervals and falling asleep again. The poor youth was highly embarrassed, but nearly helpless to resist. As penance, he took the night watches, leaving Harros and me with the sleeping space. (We had decided it was too dangerous to move at night; the catalog of nocturnal beasts was too long and too hideous to be repeated here.) At the time I thought this quirk of lower primate biology convenient and not a little humorous; had I only known then how much depended upon it!

In all of my civilized life I had never traversed such wilderness.

Although the groundcar carried us several dozen miles each day (any faster and it blew up so much dust as to be undriveable), at dawn on the fourth day we still had seen no evidence of human habitation other than a few stray abandoned dwellings. Built around ancient watering places, these had all fallen victim to weather and wandering animals, crumbling until in truth I could not say for certain that the builders had been human after all. In this world of wonders, I was slowly learning to put my preconceptions behind me.

Thanks to the Nuums' unintentional generosity, we did not lack for supplies, although their rations looked and tasted as though they might have come straight from my own time. Again I was struck by how little the passage of nearly a million years had changed the basic materials and devices with which Man sought to better his place in the universe. Unconscious of the irony, my companions nonetheless swiftly grew as tired of our unvarying fare as I, and desired greatly to sample the wild game we passed on our way. These animals showed little fear of us, and supplementing our diet would have proven simple had not the conservationists forbidden our taking any of the ray weapons with us. Limited as we were to a couple of Nuum staffs, the beasts had little reason to run.

Little reason to run from us, at any rate.

Harros was poring over the computerized charts while I steered our course; Timash was enjoying one of his frequent naps.

"We should be coming up on an old river delta very soon. If we follow the river south, we may find a town."

I nodded. "The land seems to drop away just ahead." I snuck a peek at what Harros was viewing. "Looks like an old sea bottom gone dry."

We reached the lip of the basin a few minutes later, and I slowed to a crawl. As I inched out into thin air, the soft earth gave way and we tilted forward at a dangerous angle. Harros and I were thrown into the controls, and the sleeping Timash tipped out of his chair, crashing heavily into my own. We slid forward several yards onto level ground again before the car could brake itself. A muffled whine came from below us that had not been there before.

Throwing the gears into neutral, I turned to see if Timash was all right, but one look was enough to tell me it was best not to ask. He was levering himself off the floor using the back of my chair, which groaned alarmingly, his teeth bared in anger.

"If that was somebody's idea of a joke, it wasn't funny."

I exchanged glances with Harros and spoke very carefully.

"It wasn't on purpose; we were going down a hill and something gave way. And I think something may be wrong with the car."

Harros seized the opportunity to volunteer to go outside, inching his way past Timash. I followed his example, and Timash, once he had calmed down, followed me.

The car had settled down onto the ground—mud really, from the embankment all the way across to a line of trees some yards before us. A river or stream, then, and one that had recently flooded. Water seeped up between the car and the mud.

"It looks like mud has gotten caught up in the fans underneath the car," Harros said.

"What do we do?" Timash asked him. There were few motorized vehicles where he came from. I was in no better position. Harros sighed.

"I'm no mechanic, but it seems to me the best thing to do is float the car and let it dry out. But I don't think we want to try to drive over this mud until the fans are clear; we'll just muck everything up worse."

Unable to offer a more sensible suggestion, Timash and I agreed. Harros clambered back into the car to start the engines again, explaining that the process might take some little time, so perhaps we would be more comfortable outside. Given my gorilla friend's recent burst of temper, I made no argument. We stepped away from the car as it geared up.

Laboring with a noise I had not heard before, the car rose to half my height, spitting out such quantities of mud from its underside that we had to retreat hurriedly, lest we be covered with sludge. Harros experimented with moving forward, but quickly gave it up as a lost cause. Waving to us, he sat back to wait.

We headed for the distant line of trees, by virtue of there being nothing else of even remote interest upon the horizon. Looking back, boredom would have been a welcome alternative…

The trees were set in a line too straight to have been natural, almost as though they had been intended as a windbreak. They had been there a long time; they towered above us and their boles were crowded about with lesser shrubs and piled brush, but through it all I thought I saw a glint of faraway metal. I moved faster, urging Timash along. Breasting the bushes, I saw much more clearly.

Across a narrow river sat a settlement, grayish metal walls surrounding squat buildings, some surmounted with flat-topped towers. Sunlight glanced off odd points on the walls, as if they had once been bright and shining, but now only bits of the original coating remained. My heart sank with the fear that this was nothing more than one of the many ruined cities of the south, then rose again with apprehension at what such a city might hold. In this new world, flyers more hostile than bats inhabited the high towers, and crawlers more deadly than spiders wove their cobwebs in the cellars of the long-deserted.

Timash, naturally, was all for going exploring.

I vetoed the idea immediately, but he insisted. "We don't even know that there isn't anybody living there. Maybe we could drop Harros off and get on with why we're really out here."

I was loathe to let on how much that idea appealed to me. I did not dislike Harros—in truth I had not formed a definite opinion of him, save that he was less onerous a traveling companion than I had feared—but he was an impediment to my quest to find Hana Wen. Moreover, as long as he was with us, I hesitated to remove the Librarian from my pocket, and the old man's counsel I missed much.

As I thought of him I reached down to retrieve the small sphere, but an abrupt, ugly sound from across the water stopped me.

"What was that?" Timash had heard it, too. He would have to have been deaf not to. "It sounded like somebody dragging a big sack of rocks on the ground."

"A very big sack," I agreed uneasily. "Let's get back to Harros."

Our intentions were sound, but the best intentions do not guarantee the best results. Before we could move, something moved within the city opposite us, something large enough that we could see it over the wall. All at once the Thing lifted its slate-colored head and screamed at the sky with a hundred teeth half the height of a man. Its shoulders topped the wall. I needed no explanation from Timash to identify it.

"A thunder lizard," he breathed.

Had he been there, the Librarian could have told us that thunder lizards have extremely poor eyesight, but good hearing and a bloodhound's sense of smell. Its head swiveled in our direction, and before our horrified eyes it jumped over the city wall, raised its fearsome head to the skies and roared its triumph to its prey: us.

Chapter 25
We Are Pursued

A hot, wet blast of wind from the creature's mouth, redolent of mud, dead fish, and even more foul odors to which I still dare not attribute a name all but choked us, but the thunder lizard's own cries were so loud as to cover our frenzied coughing, else it would have been upon us in another instant and this memoir would not be in your hands.

In plain view at last, it stood upright on two massively-muscled legs ending in yard-long claws tearing ferociously at the mud. Its upper arms, puny in comparison, appeared nonetheless strong enough to rend a bear—and its teeth would make a Burmese tiger run and hide. Twice the size of an elephant on its hind legs, its scales rippling rainbows in the sun, it was a nightmare come to roaring life.

Recovering his voice, Timash leaned close to me.

"Uncle Balu says they have very good ears and noses but very bad eyesight. I don't think it can see us in these bushes. Thank God we're downwind from it."

Indeed, although it had leaped over the wall giving every intention that it was about to swoop down on us, it now simply stood swiveling its head back and forth, its chest rising and falling like a giant bellows.

"You're right," I whispered back carefully, watching the monster to see if it reacted to my voice. "I don't think it knows we're here. It must use that roar to panic its prey into making a run for it." And judging from what we had seen of its celerity on foot, that would doubtless be the last move any prey would ever make.

"Uncle Balu also says they are very stupid."

I had an absurd notion of three or four thunder lizards under a circus tent while a man with a whip tried to teach them to jump through hoops.

"I have an idea," my friend continued. I gestured for him to tell me his idea quickly, because I honestly had none. He outlined it in a few sentences: It was foolhardy, extremely dangerous, and all in all better than remaining where we were until the giant lizard decided to cross the river.

We parted, moving carefully in opposite directions under cover of the trees—this was the "safe" part of the plan. So intent was I upon not making a sudden noise that I was forced to devote my entire attention to the ground before me; I had none to spend on the lizard. If it made a move, I would only have my ears to warn me. Two creatures out of their times playing cat and mouse by hearing alone. While I suppose it leveled the playing field, I doubt seriously that the lizard was any more interested in the philosophical ramifications of our respective situations than was I.

A sudden shriek brought me out of my self-absorption. The plan was for Timash and me to separate by about two hundred yards, start screaming simultaneously, then run like the devil back toward Harros and the groundcar. Whichever one the lizard pursued, the other would shout louder to draw its attention. If it was as stupid as Balu had claimed, we might confuse it enough to allow both of us to escape—if Harros had the groundcar ready.

But Timash had screamed before we agreed—and the creature was moving in his direction—fast. I choked back a curse against romantic bandy-legged youth and churned my legs as fast as they would go.

I broke through the bushes and ran into the water, splashing and shouting and waving my arms. For a moment I feared the thing would not turn—then it did turn and I knew fear of an entirely different kind. It leaped into the river and charged me like an ocean liner overtaking a sailboat.

I clambered back onto the bank, panting hard, feeling its hot breath already at my back. As I broke through the brush, I heard another scream and a mighty splash: In trying to change its direction, the lizard had lost its footing on the slippery riverbed and fallen in. Its head went down and came up again, spewing water and mud. A stunned fish landed at my feet. I didn't wait to see how the monster fared; I put my head down and ran.

Timash not being built for sprinting, he was still in sight when I emerged on the other side of the trees. I could hear the beast behind me thrashing about in anger, and those sounds lent my feet all the swiftness I could use, heedless of the sudden ache in my side.

I ran for the car, but was still many yards short of my goal when it rose from the ground with a gurgling growl and proceeded upriver away from me! Stopping involuntarily, I watched aghast as my only hope of escape, escaped—but then there was the thunder lizard again, shedding water from its bath and loping after the car!

I felt a rush of shame for my less-than-charitable feelings for our comrade Harros: His sacrifice was saving our lives. The car was not only noisy, but slow, and the hell-spawned lizard was gaining literally in leaps and bounds. No doubt existed in my mind but that this prehistoric behemoth would tear the metal car apart like an origami sculpture, leaving its occupant only a red smear to be licked up at leisure. Yet through it all, chest heaving and ribs aching, I could do nothing. The two ends of history would soon meet before my helpless eyes.

The lizard pounced as the car sputtered and whined, Harros desperately jerking the controls about in an effort to veer away—

an effort only half-successful, yet fully enough. The car spun on its axis and the lizard missed, half-burying itself once more, but this time not in the river, but in an ocean of soft mud. As in the tar pits of my own home time and place, the more it struggled the more it became ensnared. Its cloud-searing roars masked the sounds of Timash's approach.

"There's not enough mud there to drown it," he said hopelessly.

"No, but it might be enough to allow Harros to get the car away."

Our hope was quickly dashed: The car had run its last race. With a loud bang that startled even the thunder lizard, it settled into the mud. Harros leaped out the opposite side before it hit the ground, running, managing somehow to stay afoot until he could get a safe distance away. He needn't have bothered; the dimwitted dinosaur was so busy tearing the earth to bits in its frenzy to reach the car it hadn't even noticed him.

Abruptly it found its footing, reared over our transport—and fell on it. Inside something sparked—and the ensuing explosion scattered thunder lizard steaks for a hundred yards. When the smoke cleared, the decapitated monster lay across the shattered remnants of its final prey.

Harros was stunned but unhurt, as the force had hurled him head over heels onto the marshy turf. His front was covered with black mud, his back with grass and water-stains. We reached him at a run as he rose up on his elbows and looked back the way he had come.

"Good god," he muttered, staring at the carnage. "Good god."

The only survivor of the explosion was my staff—the damned thing was apparently indestructible. It did, however, require a long rinse in the river before I felt comfortable touching it again (and Harros made sure he bathed *upriver* of my cleaning).

After our respective ablutions were accomplished, we three

stood across the river from the walled city, watching its silent ramparts as the sun marched inexorably toward the point where our decision must be made.

When no other thunder lizards had broken the day's peace for perhaps five minutes, I spoke up.

"If we're going to be spending the next few nights there, I'd rather get started now, while there's still light."

Timash stared at me. "Who says we're spending the night in there?"

"It's going to take time to build a raft, and there may be tools we can use."

"What raft?" Harros demanded.

"What's a raft?" Timash asked.

I started down the bank, scanning the water for any sign of a ford; they followed me perforce.

"A raft is a wooden platform that you can sail on a river. We've got more than enough wood to build one, if we can fell the trees. Somewhere downriver there must be another town, one with people in it."

"Beats walking," Harros said, but Timash was unconvinced.

"On water?"

I ignored him and concentrated on using my staff to sound the stream bottom. Finding a shallow spot that seemed to extend further than others, I stripped off my jumpsuit and boots, held them above my head, and waded in, motioning the others to follow and keeping the staff outstretched. In this way we found a path across whereon even Timash, the shortest of us, could keep his chin above water. We tried not to think of what might be swimming about our legs, but nothing bit us.

The city-side of the river proved much drier, and we set a good pace around the walls, looking for a gate, for the method of egress used by the thunder lizard was unattainable by us. Up close the metal walls were far less impressive even than I had imagined: Flakes of rust the size of my head spotted the surface like a loathsome disease. How many years had these walls stood unattended?

My companions' thoughts traveled along the same paths—but they reached the end before mine did.

"Keryl?" Timash asked with unaccustomed shyness. "What did that thunder lizard eat before we came along?"

Suddenly the idea of carving and building a raft with our bare hands took on a new appeal—but one that lasted only a moment.

Somewhere on the other side of the wall, a woman screamed.

Chapter 26
The Dead City

As deeply ingrained as is the instinct for one's own survival in the mind of Man, how much more deeply ingrained might it become after the passage of nearly another million years of evolution? And yet, as was now proven to my grateful eyes, the instinct of Man (or ape) to protect the weaker sex had kept pace with that most primal urge to live, so that even uncounted millennia in the future, the first thought of my companions was even as my own: to succor the helpless originator of that cry, regardless of the unknown dangers that might lie in wait for ourselves.

In short, almost at once I was sprinting along our projected path, frantically searching for a way past the wall, for it is in my nature, and my nurture, not to stand by while a woman wants for aid. And my friends, for whom I could not speak on such a matter, were right on my heels; although Harros and I quickly outdistanced Timash, it was only through lack of leg, and not of heart, that he was left behind.

The ground under my feet abruptly changed from hard mud to smooth stone, albeit so covered with dust that only the altered sounds of my boots on the ground alerted me. I stopped so suddenly that Harros almost knocked me down. Had not the wall curved so gradually that we were still in Timash's line of sight, he doubtless would have collided with the pair of us moments later, to the detriment of all concerned.

We stood on the flagstones of a partly-closed gateway, away from which at right angles to us ran an ancient road down to the river, a road now visible only in isolated chunks of masonry. The gate itself was a marvel of engineering, for while the city wall was fully three times our own height, the gate was equally that wide at its lowest point. And as it rose, the gate became wider; what mechanism could raise it we could not see, nor would we ever know, but that it was meant to be raised and lowered was obvious by the fact that it had stopped four feet off the ground. Deep grooves in the walls where the gate had once fit showed evidence of centuries of habitation by dust and wild creatures. It was not a place I was tempted to stick my fingers.

All this we assimilated in seconds, for this was the entrance we had sought, and pausing only long enough to catch our breath (and not nearly long enough to consider the probable consequences of our actions), we ducked through the gap and emerged on the other side, inside the city.

Instantly all sound ceased.

Rarely do we stop in our daily activities to take account of the myriad subtle noises of our lives; we have no time, and were we even to try, cataloging every day's surroundings would consume us. So we let most of the background slip by, concentrating on that which most concerns us, and the susurrations of life assume a position not unlike a sailor's unconscious appreciation of the rhythms of the sea. That is, until they disappear.

Ahead of us lay a continuation of the gateway plaza, opening onto a wide boulevard that disappeared in the hazy distance. Grass grew in clumps through the cracked stones of the pale red pavement. On either side of the avenue deserted buildings cast long, cool shadows; we stood in one such shadow, cocking our heads, but there was no sound, nothing; like the African veldt when the king of beasts prowls his kingdom and the other animals huddle, quaking, until he passes by. At that time the silence becomes a tangible thing, stretching out long past the point of breaking. This was the silence of the prey of the thunder lizard. Whatever lived here had fled the roar of the king of beasts—but what, then, had we heard?

I motioned ahead with my staff. I had no more idea than the others where the cry had originated, save that it was on this side of the wall, back in the direction whence we had come. It seemed now a ghostly illusion; there loomed the distinct possibility we were being lured to our deaths by a cunning predator. Still the urge that had stirred my breast would not leave me, nor could I depart this necropolis until I had tried, at least, to learn the truth.

We proceeded cautiously down a narrow street that paralleled the wall, curving inward as we entered the city proper. On either side of us balconies and catwalks crowded the upper stories; as in the olden Chester of my adopted England, the populace had once upon a time conducted their business on several levels, walking from building to building above the street along the connected second-story storefronts. I shuddered irrationally; their ghosts still strolled the elevated thoroughfares, but now their evil agenda involved stalking the living—in a word, us.

Strangely enough, I could not throw the odd feeling aside. I could almost hear their voices, sibilantly whispering in the shadows and the abandoned man-made caverns about us.

I stopped, secreting myself in a doorway and motioning my companions to follow suit. I could not shake that feeling! And soon I learned why.

Out of a doorway opposite us and a little further down the street trotted a squad of ragged men, variously equipped with blunt clubs and small bundles of rope that appeared to be netting. Without speaking and in almost perfect unison they crossed the road and filed into a doorway on our side of the street, without seeing us or even looking about. Their appearance caused me to stare: Pale-skinned and hairless, their limbs exhibited a leanness bordering on the emaciated. None seemed to lack for energy—yet withal there was a quality of lifelessness about them, as if the task before them absorbed their entire focus and no other consideration was worthy of notice. More than soldierly discipline, it was utterly sinister.

None of us questioned their connection to our goal; we were not such fools as to ascribe this apparition to coincidence. Allowing a few moments' time that we might not blunder into the patrol, I slipped out of my meager hideaway and down the road.

The trail was easy to follow; the dust inside this particular doorway was little disturbed but for the tracks of our quarry, and the shuffling of their many footsteps echoed in the high halls. I found to my surprise that light immigrated through many holes and windows, so that the pursuit was simple. Occasionally a gap would open in the flooring before us, but never without more than sufficient warning.

Then for the first time we heard voices ahead, their meaning twisted beyond recognition by the intervening corridors, but their tenor clear. A sudden slapping of feet on the floor, then a sharper noise followed by a short scream, cut off quickly—and an abrupt cry of defiance and victory: a woman's voice!

A wiser man would have reconnoitered, surveyed the numbers and arms of the enemy before engagement, planned and plotted and mapped his strategy instead of barging into an unknown battle in which he had no stake nor even knew whose side was right— but that wiser man would never have been me, and in this instance he might have delayed until his objective was lost. With Timash and Harros at my heels I burst through a set of broken double doors into the first room I had seen with working artificial light, and that was fortunate because otherwise I might have doubted my own eyes—and almost certainly I would have lost my life.

At a raised dais to our left stood a lone woman—a Nuum, by

her stained orange jumpsuit—armed with a thin sword. Before her and spread about were the men we had seen above—and their friends. Fully two dozen of the pale warriors filled the room, clubs and nets at the ready as if they were bearers on a safari of which the woman was the prey. Four or five bodies prone before the steps of the dais testified to her skill with the sword and explained her opponents' hesitation in charging her. I believe they were about to do so anyway, but our arrival changed all that.

She stepped back, dropping her sword for one exhausted moment upon seeing us, but her greeting smile fell when she saw that, whomever she had expected, we were not they. But it gave her a moment, for the pale men, as one, stopped what they were doing as well and turned to face us in eerie silence. Not one face showed surprise, anger, or fear. One of the men simply motioned and the bulk of them immediately fell upon us, clubs and nets at the ready. The balance rushed the dais. For all the ferocity of their attack, none spoke, shouted, or even scowled. They were the most serene antagonists I had ever faced.

But if our enemies were lacking in drive or passion, we ourselves were not. With a cry I charged them, and the same tactics that had scattered the conservationists at the research station worked to similar effect here—save that at the research station I was intent only on escape, and I did not have a bull gorilla at my back.

Our battlefield was too small to allow swinging my staff, so I shortened my grip and used it as a polearm. The novelty of this tactic against my foes proved itself again and again, as their clubs had a shorter range and many a man found himself knocked to the floor by a solid poke in the face or belly.

I felt a club graze my arm and I turned straight into one of their nets. Flinging up the staff in front of me, I managed to catch the edge of the net and bat it aside, but it left me open to attack. Off-balance I kicked one man and literally fell out of the path of another's club.

On the floor all legs looked alike, but since Timash's gaudy pants were not among them, I poked and tripped with abandon. Some fell on me and tried to pinion me—much to their own harm, as I was fully as much stronger than they as I was any other Thoran, and a better shield from the pummeling of their fellows I could not have asked.

I reared up, battled my way to the opposite wall and turned to fight again with my back secure. Timash was at the center of a rising pile of bodies, holding a man by the neck in each hand. He shook them around until they went limp, then dropped them and grabbed two more. The woman had leaped down from her perch and was slashing indiscriminately, blood flying, covering over older stains on her clothes and face. I could not see Harros.

It was over within moments, the last man falling to my and Timash's superior strength or the sword of their former prey. As it ended, Harros burst through the doorway.

"I was carried outside by their rush," he explained. "But I chased them off." He glanced past me, and I turned. The woman crouched behind me, her sword still ready.

"It's all right," I said slowly. "We came to help you." I lay the staff on the ground and backed up a step. She glanced at us, then at the staff, straightened, and made a motion with the grip of her sword. Instantly it contracted in on itself, forming an eight-inch rod which she placed against the leg of her jumpsuit. When she removed her hand, the rod remained in place. She bent to pick up my staff.

"That was nice work; thanks. But why didn't you just use the sword?"

I blinked. I had no idea to what she was referring, and I fear it showed in my expression. To be sure, my sudden idiocy was not entirely due to ignorance: As she pulled her fingers through her coppery hair, it became apparent even through the stains and the blood that this woman was extraordinarily beautiful.

Her features were bold without insolence, her skin a

translucent olive, and her figure, obvious enough even in utilitarian Nuum uniform clothes, was modeled more on the women of my own time than the thin, boyish females of this tragic earth. I felt a stab of guilt in knowing that even Hana Wen would take a back seat to this woman in any beauty contest I might judge.

Perhaps she was used to the male reaction, because she waited for my answer what seemed many moments.

"My name's Marella," she said at last. If there was any more to her, she was not prepared to say. "What's yours?"

I shook myself, hearing Timash smother a giggle behind me, and introduced us all.

A man at her feet stirred; she knelt down, unclipped her sword/club, and clipped him smartly on the side of the head.

"We'd better go. There'll be more of them."

At Timash's suggestion we took refuge in one of the upper floors of a building some distance away. As he pointed out, the unique architecture of this city (whose name, it came out, was as much a mystery to Marella as ourselves) gave avenues of escape in various directions even on the second and third stories, while giving us likewise a greater field of view. I think he also relished the possibility of climbing; ever since that day we escaped the tiger spiders, he had resurrected the arboreal habits of his ancestors at every opportunity. Even Balu had thought it odd.

Practical as only a woman could be, Marella had torn shreds of cloth from the clothing of some of our late opponents and was now busily scrubbing and scraping such stains as she could from her hands and face. She had offered us some, but as we had just bathed (twice) in the river, we declined. Nor were we as greatly in need; neither Timash nor I had spilled any blood to speak of, and Harros was almost fresh.

Keeping watch from inside the window, I inquired of Marella how she had found herself in this situation.

"I was on a sky barge crossing the plain on my way home. I'm from Dure." She paused, as if to await our reaction, but all she received was three blank stares. I understood why Timash and I failed to react, and apparently Harros was not much of a traveler himself, but Marella found us all incredible. "Hello? You know— Dure? The Island Continent—across the big water?" She shook her head. "Men…" After a moment she recollected my question and decided, whatever her personal opinion of us, civility did demand an answer.

"Anyway, I'm a force field tech on the barge. It's called the Dark Lady. We're ferrying some nobles home, and one of them sees this deserted city down here, so naturally, he has explore it." She shook her head again, her opinion no less obvious for being unspoken. "Well, no sooner do we set down the schooner than this big—" she looked around at us, set her lips, and changed what she was about to say— "*really* big thunder lizard comes crashing out of nowhere. Of course Lord Masinto is the first one back on the schooner, screaming at everybody to shoot the thing and take off at the same time, and meanwhile the officers are trying to get everybody on board but the thunder lizard's on their tail and so they take off and I'm still on the ground," she finished in a rush. "I got away from the lizard okay, 'cause he was watching the schooner (and probably laughing his ass off at Masinto), but I was looking for some water when those jokers you saw started chasing me and cornered me in that basement."

"We were outside the wall when we heard you scream," I explained.

Her brows knit. "Did I scream?" I nodded. "Huh. Must've startled me."

"I'm sure it was involuntary, and quite understandable under the circumstances," Harros assured her. I didn't like the tone of his voice —it struck me as rather more oily than our brief acquaintance with the lady warranted—but as she didn't seem to take offense I let it lie. If she were a lady sailor, as I gathered, she had probably heard worse.

She ignored him, in any event, and turned the tables on me.

"So what's your story? How come you're out here in the middle of nowhere?"

I explained that our vehicle had broken down and we had approached the city looking for shelter. I had thought to omit our own encounter with the thunder lizard lest Marella take it as the trumped-up tale of a braggart, but Timash was all for telling it, so I let him.

When he had finished, Marella turned again to me. "That's your idea of 'our groundcar broke down?' Flattened by a thunder lizard? What do you do for excitement, wrestle breen?"

"Don't say that word!" Timash scolded. "It makes my nose itch."

A moment later, as if on cue, Marella's eyes became very wide, and then I smelled it too, a wet-dog pungency that I had never smelled before but knew at once:

Breen.

Chapter 27
I Am Caged

Timash, near the window, lifted his nose to sniff the air once more.

"It's awfully faint," he reported hesitantly. "They may not be anywhere near here; maybe they just spent the night here or something."

Marella's mien was grim, her baton again extended into a sword.

"I don't care if they haven't been here since the King's last birthday. I don't want to be in the same city with them."

"You can stop worrying so much," Harros announced with unusual celerity. He stepped into the room holding a ragged bit of something that might once have been cloth—or then again, it might well have been fur, or something else better not dwelled upon. "This is where the smell is coming from."

Taking his orders from Marella's disgusted expression, Harros quickly exited the room, taking the offensive odor with him, nor did he return for some minutes. While he was gone, Marella retracted her blade, turning a puzzled eye upon me.

"You know, you did pretty well back there with that staff—but why didn't you just use the sword? I mean, the quarters were pretty tight—and they were using nets. I may not be much good with a staff, but even if I were I wouldn't have used it in that situation."

I had been watching her, and I knew now that she controlled her baton by use of differing hand grips: one made the sword blade extend, another made it retract. Except in these respects, her weapon looked just like my own, and that made me wonder. I held it out and gave her a sheepish grin.

"Actually, I don't know very much about this thing. I was a librarian before they shanghaied me onto a ship and brought me down here to fight Thorans."

"You were a librarian?" She cast a glance at Timash. "What was—never mind. You must not have had a whole lot of overdue reading crystals." Shaking her head, she turned her attention to the staff weapon. "It's really simple if you know the trick—and it was designed to keep energy weapons out of the hands of the Thorans. Twist like this, and you've got a sword; like this, and it's back to a baton for carrying; like this, and—you've got a staff. Here, you try."

As she had promised, once the basic holds were mastered, it was child's play to move from one to another configuration, as long as you remembered always to return to the basic "baton" position; you could not switch directly from sword to staff, but with that minor impediment, it was a marvelous close-in weapon— or rather, three weapons. Testing the balance of the two, I quickly learned to prefer the sword over the bulkier staff.

Stepping back, I assumed a fencer's stance. Although my spoken *"En garde,"* was incomprehensible to Marella, she immediately took my meaning, and just as quickly set out to take my measure.

There was no flash of blades, no singing on metal slicing off opposing metal: our foils (for such they appeared to me; I later found them to have the strength of sabers) whipped and whispered evilly through the air, sliding off each other with a liquid smoothness that so took me by surprise the first time that I almost impaled myself on Marella's point. She was on the verge of calling the match, but I waved her on again, concentrating on relinquishing conscious control of my muscles and allowing the Librarian's tutelage, as well as my own long-ago lessons, to press my suit.

Marella toyed with me at first, but as I gained confidence, I could see the light in her eyes darkening with her own increasing effort, until at length we broke off by mutual consent, sweat staining our clothes anew. I saluted her as no opponent had been saluted in almost a million years, but after a second's hesitation, she returned my gesture with a shy smile.

Then she laughed. "A librarian. Right."

I shrugged, embarrassed.

"Uh, Keryl," Timash interrupted. "Where's Harros?"

And as seemed to recur with horrific frequency in that city of the dead and dying, we heard a scream in the near distance.

We found Harros in a nearby courtyard, panting and down on one knee, surrounded by four men of the race of our recent adversaries, all dead. A bloody club belonging to one of his late antagonists lay at his side.

"I was looking for a place to bury the rag, and they came at me out of that doorway." He pointed weakly. "I managed to grab the first one's club and fight them off." He paused, catching his breath. "It looked like they were trying to take me alive."

"Was that one of them that screamed?" Marella asked, eyes darting to and fro. When Harros nodded, she said: "We'd better get moving. There could be more of them."

As I was to learn, Marella had an almost preternatural habit of being right. As if by magic, every doorway and every overhanging balcony was suddenly crawling with pale and emaciated men. We were trapped like rats.

Even after a relatively short time enjoying their forced

hospitality, I was compelled to admit that the Vulsteen were the oddest human beings I had met in two eras. And when you come to realize that I include in my definition of "human beings" an entire city of talking gorillas, that is quite a broad statement.

Notwithstanding that our capture meant the containment of those who had murdered (from their point of view) a number of their fellows, or that it capped a campaign which had commenced with a concerted effort to net Marella and ended with an additional three prisoners, it was with a distinct lack of enthusiasm for victory that they disarmed us and marched us through a maze of dusty tunnels to their home ground. I had been prepared at first to meet my Creator, and even when they made it plain that, as Harros had guessed, they meant to take us alive, I still apprehended the mistreatment to which we might be subject at their hands, most particularly Marella, the abuse of female prisoners being a constant throughout history that I had little hope of having been discontinued before now.

Yet nothing of the like occurred; we were herded in a single line by our unspeaking captors into the subterranean city of the Vulsteen, which to my knowledge has no name, or at least none was ever used in my hearing. Doubtless the inhabitants, a phlegmatic people to say the least, have never perceived the need, since they neither communicate with, nor seek, others outside their own community—except as prisoners, and those rarely.

At first the city itself was as uncommunicative of the life of its people as were they themselves. The Vulsteen were burrowers; generations long dead had been driven underground by their own fear of the thunder lizards and the breen, and by their own lax ambition, too lazy or unimaginative to mount an aggressive defense. This was my assessment of the winding, crudely-hewn halls, frequently broken by finer work where the tunnelers had incorporated existing basements and foundations into their own work.

Then imagine my surprise when, in one of these rocky

corridors, I came face-to-face with a mural of surpassing beauty! Red and orange predominated, blazing away from the other, duller hues as though the wall itself had caught fire! And then, as suddenly as it had begun, it stopped, half-way up a wall, a few lone streaks trailing away as though all at once the artist had lost interest in his project and simply walked away.

The Vulsteen marched impassively past this startling sight, but my companions, too, stumbled with shock, causing one of our captors to shove Harros in a mechanically nonvindictive fashion. At intervals we came upon more examples of such work, each as passionately emblazoned as the last, yet each abandoned in mid-stroke. And each lay upon the wall of a relatively flat portion of the unfinished tunnels, providing sure evidence that these, our inert guides, sprang from the same loins as the race that had authored those works.

The long march gave me ample time to puzzle over these questions, and at length an answer sprang forth in beautiful simplicity: The men and women who had painfully carved these tunnels many years gone had also been Vulsteen, but even in their decline one among many had retained a spark of mad artistry, one in a thousand who had attempted to arouse in his fellows some grand passion by the expression of what passed, under these distressed circumstances, as great art. The paintings' abrupt endings bespoke a sudden, grisly end to these brave souls; I could easily believe that the forefathers of the men who had captured us could kill in fear of such grand gestures.

Strange as it might appear, I found this explanation comforting, for it allowed me to categorize my enemies, assign to them a known quantity that might be used in our efforts to escape. Men who would burrow underground rather than fight, kill their own rather than think, these were animals with brains. Marella, Harros—and yes, Timash—and I were brains in the bodies of animals. Our inspiration, our courage, would see us quit of these lifeless barbarians—even if we could not count on the Librarian for help, and if the situation warranted, I would not hesitate to reveal even that secret to Harros and Marella.

Thus fortified, I walked with a lighter step, my eyes darting to and fro, taking the measure of the Vulsteen and finding them wanting. Their ingrained societal numbness would prove their Achilles heel. I almost smiled with the irony of it all as I passed yet another mural...

...until I reached the far end and saw the fiery red paint still dripping and wet.

I smelled our destination before I saw it. Here, in a world where the walls literally formed the edges of civilization, every foot of circumscribed space was precious. We did not warrant much. At one end of the "city," yawned an open pit, whose odor advertised what seemed a community dump and charnel pit.

"Oh my god," Harros yelped. "They're not going to throw us in there...?"

Much as we might have deplored the panic with which Harros offered his opinion, we were nonetheless unanimous in our agreement with it. I dug in my heels and the others did the same, but there were far too many Vulsteen pushing, and we tumbled, one by one, into the pit.

It was not the fall that filled me with sudden dread. The bottom of the pit was coated with muck and debris; disgusting as it was, it broke our fall so that none of us was hurt. Nor was it the specter of renewed capture; I had been a prisoner before, and I knew escape would present itself: We had not been herded down here simply to be discarded. When our captors wanted us, we must be ready; that was all.

No, the horror that rushed up to meet us all transcended the mud, and the loneliness, and the smell of the hundreds that had come and gone before us. In the pit it permeated and suffused and overcame all other smells, all other senses.

It was the overwhelming smell of breen. And even before I

hauled myself off the ground and looked about, I knew that we were completely surrounded.

Chapter 28
Living with the Man-eaters

We stood stock-still, fully aware of the slippery footing beneath us and the sheer, wet walls that towered twenty feet over our heads. I judged the far end of the pit to be about thirty yards distant, albeit the dim subterranean light made such measurements chancy. But it was no lack of light that made the counting of breen difficult; rather it was their numbers that confused the issue. Still, argued the remaining rational portion of my brain, barricading itself against the primitive caveman pleading to be let out so he could run, run from the sabretooth that had invaded his home—what difference did it make? My entire infantry division would have had little enough chance against these creatures. Ten or a thousand, my companions and I had been dumped into an underground abattoir. The Vulsteen's use for us had become horribly clear.

The breen stood silently in a loose curving line about ten yards away. Terror stretched out the final seconds of our lives. Would we feel it when those claws and teeth tore through our entrails, or did the breen kill quickly with a swipe across the throat? I wish I could say that I was more concerned for my friends than for myself, that I was tempted to throw my body between that horde and Marella in a doomed attempt at chivalry—but I was not. Even before I came to this world, I had been a soldier, and in the dark, bloody world of war the only way to keep your life was to keep your head down and, yes, sometimes you pray that the whistling sound you hear overhead will end in the body next to yours instead of your own. And to be truthful, the man next to you is hoping the same thing.

And still the breen did not charge us. Even in the adrenaline-flooded attenuation of time that comes with impending death, the seconds still pass. Slowly I came to realize that we had stood thus for a span of moments, unarmed and unprotected, surrounded on three sides by beasts that by all accounts would stand with the shark and the piranha as among the most vicious predators ever to stalk our world—yet still we lived.

I allowed myself to breathe.

A breen broke ranks with his fellows, carefully placing his feet as he walked slowly toward us, outstretched hands ending only in fingers, not claws. I mirrored his action, stepping away from my friends to meet the breen in the center of the cleared space between us. If this were the ceremonial beginning of the kill by a tribal animal, then I was walking to my death—at least then it would be swift—but I thought otherwise. Breen hunted among thunder lizards, but no breen would walk up to a thunder lizard open-handed and alone!

As we approached, it—he—put out his right hand, palm up. I could hear Timash's breathing behind me. With only a trace of a tremor in my fingers, I reached out and gingerly placed my hand atop the breen's.

Clasping my hand gently, he smiled—or at least so I took his baring of shark-like fangs to be, for I still lived. My heart was hammering and my face so numb that even an automatic answering smile was beyond my ken. And then he did the most unexpected thing of all.

"Peace," he said.

It had been surprising but certainly not unpleasant when they lead us from the muck of the pit onto dry ground, although the smell attached to our drying clothes (on top of everything else) would remain, our host explained apologetically. Even with the amenities the breen had earned or built for themselves over the generations, washing facilities were unknown. Unlike man, the breen had never incorporated original sin into their rise to intelligence: they wore no clothes. Not that they were dirty; like cats they groomed themselves, and like Timash's ancestors, they groomed each other as well, but trapped here there was only so much they could do for themselves.

Understandably skeptical at first, my companions had slowly come around to the notion that we were not about to be eaten. The breen were patient with us; they had gone through much the same process with every one of the previous humans who, wandering occasionally into the clutches of the Vulsteen through some great error or accident, had been as unceremoniously tossed in among the great beasts even as had we. When I asked what had befallen them—for there were none but breen here now—our guide explained they had all been done to death by the Vulsteen. Further he would not say.

We were conducted across the pit, quickly discovering that only one area was thick with muck and mire; the rest of the floor had been scraped clean and the debris piled up where the Vulsteen routinely dropped their victims. It seemed an entirely civilized practice for a mob of hairy, naked man-eaters, but there was much to these breen that I had yet to learn.

For example, they did not all live in the pit all the time; they had tunnels and chambers underground, just as their captors. The four of us were even given our own space, a three-walled open room with no furniture, admittedly, but still ours to use. Again, our guide apologized for the cramped quarters, but four prisoners at once was quite rare—most came in singly, survivors of some awful crash, who had fought their way past the thunder lizards and bloodbats of the upper world only to be dragged down here like lost souls into hell. The breen, of course, did not put it that way, but our continuing descent into the bowels of the earth was disquietingly similar to Dante's. However, since my fellow inmates would not have appreciated the comparison, I was forced to keep it to myself.

What the breen failed to give us was a name: They didn't have any, another sin that they had avoided, perhaps. Nevertheless, I felt its lack when referring to our guide, who appeared to be chief among them, and so after some thought I took to referring to him as Uncle Sam. Timash and Marella looked upon my announcement as evidence that I was losing my sanity, but Harros seemed to find it amusing, even if he could not have gotten the joke.

We spent our time sitting listlessly in our cell, having explored the limits of our confinement within the first hour. Simple creatures at heart and by necessity, the breens' rooms were not segregated for separate tasks, as they had few tasks to perform. They wandered freely about, but the only opening in the warren was the pit itself, and there was no escape through the walls. The irregular tunnels were defined by the foundations of the original buildings above us, and nothing we could bring to bear would even scratch their surface.

The lack of openings meant a lack of air circulation, and the breen-scent hung everywhere. Over the course of what appeared to be several days—we had no means for reliably measuring time save for eating and sleeping—our noses came to accept and ignore it, but even the breen could not stand it forever, any more than we would enjoy living in a locker room. Wandering about the open pit was a favorite pastime that we did well to emulate.

It was during one of these excursions that Harros sought me out. I tried to hide my annoyance, as solitude after a fashion had been my aim; as much as I liked Timash, even we had had too much of each other of late. Still, Harros' sudden sociability was so entirely unexpected that my irritation was equally balanced by curiosity. Living in that cage had started exceedingly dull, and gone downhill rapidly.

As it turned out, this was the crux of Harros' conversation.

"Are you bored yet?" he asked with false humor.

I raised my eyebrows. "In this five-star palace? No wants, no needs, room service—" we were fed twice daily a steady diet of mushrooms and tubers grown elsewhere underground— "plenty of exercise and no responsibilities. And I haven't had a vacation in years!"

He nodded sympathetically. "Yeah, me too." His eyes darted about, as if seeking someone, and when he didn't find him, they came back to me. "Uh, seeing as we're stuck here…"

"I'm sorry about that," I interrupted. "If it wasn't for me you wouldn't be here. I should never have brought you along."

"What, I'd've been better off with the conservationists? If they'd known any breen, they'd've fed me to them in bite-sized pieces." He shook his head emphatically. "Uh-uh. I asked to come along. I knew it wasn't gonna be a picnic. But listen, that's not what I wanted to talk to you about. I wanted to ask you about Marella."

"Marella?" I frowned. "What has she to do with me?"

"That's what I wanted to talk to you about. See, it's getting really dull down here, and if truth be told we might not be leaving on our own two feet, if you know what I mean. So I was wondering how you'd feel if I tried to…make a move. On Marella."

Truth to tell, I was not sure for a moment how I felt. Harros must have caught a flash of my thoughts, or perhaps they were reflected on my face, because he retreated half a step, but then I shook my head and caught his shoulder.

"No, it's all right. You're a gentleman for asking, but I already have someone else." *Yes,* my moral sense scolded me, *you do.* Marella was a beautiful woman under all the dirt and danger, but I had embarked on this journey to rescue Hana Wen, and to turn my heart away from her now would be unconscionable, notwithstanding whether or not I continued on to Dure. "For a minute there, I was jealous, but it wasn't because of you. We've been through a lot together, and if you want to try to find some comfort with Marella, then God speed you."

For perhaps the first time, I saw Harros' face broaden into a full, genuine grin, and clapping me on the shoulder, he was off, searching, I assumed, for Marella. I stood alone, as I had wanted to be, and hollow.

My solitude was soon ended for a second time. Feeling a presence at my elbow, I turned to find Uncle Sam standing there. I was hardly an expert on breen emotional states, even after studying them at close range for a few days, but even I could see that he was nervous, agitated more than I had seen before. Come to think of it, he and the others so far had resembled the Vulsteen in some respects, as if their masters' wooden equanimity had rubbed off upon them. Up until then I had never questioned exactly why these breen were the way they were: The sheer relief of finding our lives spared by some of the most feared carnivores on earth had chased away concern for the reasons. Now I sensed that my unasked questions were to be answered. I doubted I would like it.

"It's going to be soon," he began cryptically. "We can tell the signs. The Vulsteen are going to come for us soon. You need to gather your friends and stay out of the way. That's the only way to keep from being hurt."

"Hurt?" I seized his shoulder but immediately let go. The muscles under his fur were tight, rolling with nervous energy. "What's going on? What do the Vulsteen want?"

"Listen carefully. The Vulsteen have kept us here for generations. The only time they let us out is when they take us to the arena. They have some sort of object there. They point it at us, and we go wild. Something takes hold of us and it's just like we were outside again." He glanced up at the far ceiling, but he was seeing the sky. "There's fighting, and killing. Not all of us come back. That's what's going on; everyone's scared because they know the Vulsteen are coming to put us in the arena. If you don't stay out of the way, you could get hurt before they even pull you out."

"Pull us out? Why?"

He paused a breath before he told me. "So they can put you in the arena with us."

Uncle Sam looked up again, and stepped back quickly. An instant later a loop of tough cord yanked closed around my upper arms and I was hoisted into the air!

Chapter 29
In the Arena of the Mind-Mutants

The rope bit into my triceps; my heels kicked the side of the pit while they pulled me up, heedless of my pain or shock. It was all over in a few moments and the rope was removed, but I was surrounded by armed men. Angry as I was, that would not have stopped me, but the small remaining portion of my mind that could still claim rationality told me that I stood too close to the precipice and less than a shove would be more than enough to end any impromptu rebellion.

Thus restrained, but in no way calmed, I allowed them to bring up my companions, whom Uncle Sam had fetched. At least they were not taken by surprise, so their ascent was easier than mine. Even as Harros, the last man out, cleared the lip, I could see that Uncle Sam had done the right thing; the breen were milling about, growling and bumping each other. The smallest had already fled to the comparative safety of the rear chambers, and those who remained appeared, if anything, eager to work themselves into an ever greater frenzy. And Uncle Sam had told me they did not go truly wild until they entered the arena!

Our hosts, meantime, spared no time marching us away toward our fate. Through more halls we were lead, alternating between dust and rock, fine finished stone, and the occasional lunatic mural, but this tour was shorter than our first. We were herded into a small chamber through a heavily barred door, which was quickly shut behind us. Ahead another door, also barred, lead to a lighted area. I could feel a cold breeze through the bars. That door lead to the surface!

Closer inspection revealed that we were not in a chamber at all, but a cage, not unlike a large prison cell. Outside our jailors stood for a moment staring at us, then they all but one filed away. For the first time, we heard a Vulsteen speak.

"You are going to die," he said in a voice dry as a hacking cough. I could almost hear his leathery jaw muscles creaking in protest at the unwonted exercise. "We find it heightens the experience if you know why."

All reasons to the contrary aside, I was fascinated by his narration. To hear a Vulsteen speak of "heightened experience"— notwithstanding the novelty of hearing one speak at all—drew me like a moth to flame. Perhaps this would explain the psychotic art splashed across random walls! At the very least it would explain why we had been kidnapped, and why the Vulsteen had gone to such lengths not to kill us (although I admit it was a near brush with death by fright when we were thrown in with the breen). After all we had suffered, they owed us this much.

"Years ago," he continued in the same distracted tone, "we lived on the surface, as other men. But the land changed, and the thunder lizards and the breen and the bats came and we were chased beneath the earth, where they could not reach us. We were safe, but the confinement drove many mad. Our scientists perfected a method of draining out all volatile emotions. This allowed us to live underground without sun, without air, and without madness.

"But as time passed, violence began to break out. Men murdered without warning, without reason. We found that emotion could not be drained, only suppressed, and that when it built up, like fluid in the brain, it must be allowed to escape or it would explode in violence.

"It became a conundrum: that we must express emotion to survive, but quash it to live. We discovered, at last, that we could draw emotion from others and rebroadcast it toward ourselves. With this catalyst, we could experience our own emotions in a powerful but harmless burst of energy. For a few hours we are gripped by strong passions, but they can be channeled, and then we return to the serenity and calm order of our lives.

"For our emotional subjects, we chose the breen: bestial savages but with manlike emotions that could be drained and reused. They have served us for generations, even though left to their own devices they would do naught but kill each other, and soon we would have none left. But the breen prefer killing outsiders to fighting with their own kind. So when we find travelers, we bring them here, and we loose them in the arena, where they fight for their lives. It takes only exposure to the outer air to whip the beasts into a frenzy, and you Nuum, when you are threatened, are particularly vicious. We will absorb your energy and use it. If you live, you go free—but you will not."

Three us stood stunned at this matter-of-fact lecture on the rationale of our execution, but Timash was having none of it. Throwing himself against the bars, he reached one sinewy arm as far as it would go, clutching air inches from the Vulsteen who, I am certain, had chosen exactly that distance from the bars for precisely that reason.

"You see?" he rasped. "It works." He pointed to the far set of bars, which slid upward as at his signal. "Go." He pointed at Timash. "You are the largest. You go last."

Unwilling to march to our own horrible deaths, none of us moved. But the Vulsteen must have seen it all many times.

"That door will remain open whether you leave here or not. The breen will find you regardless."

There is not a man worth his mother's pain who would not

rather die in the open than in a cage. I lead Harros and Marella onto the sand of the arena, and whirled when we heard the bars crash down behind us, a second ahead of Timash's anguished roar. Again his arms plunged through the bars; his hands grasped them in a futile attempt to move the door, but it was adamant. I took his hairy paw in my own.

"Courage!" I hissed at him. "This is all planned. Find out why they left you there and use that knowledge to help you to escape!"

Several soft thumps sounded behind me and I turned to find that our weapons had been thrown into the arena with us. Even as I seized mine I had to admire the Vulsteen's ruthless consideration for the conservation of their resources. Armed, we would survive a few moments longer, providing a few more precious drops of passion for their dead husks of souls.

I twisted the handle of my staff until the sword leaped out, ready to do battle as was Marella's, while Harros stood bravely with a club and net. But even as I hefted it, I saw myself pushing the point between the ribs of the breen I knew as Uncle Sam, and my rage grew at these arrogant ghouls who threw friend against friend in a battle to the death only because they lacked the courage to make their own way in the world.

I raised my head to shout my defiance at the crowd—and stopped, speechless at the sight of hundreds of pale-skinned living skeletons perched on their stone benches, burning eyes pinned on me in rapt anticipation of their upcoming feast upon my soul.

Sucking in my breath, I resolutely turned my back, forcing my emotions deep down in my breast and taking the last calm moment that my life might ever know. Across the way, I saw a barred door lift away and the breen emerge into the light. Pushing and snarling, they broke onto the sand singly and in fractious pairs, raising a small hope that perhaps they would, after all, break into a riot before they even saw us.

These were not the same animals with whom we had lived the past several days. In the last moment before my hopes were dashed and terror descended upon us, I stole a look at the grandstand, and there I saw men clustered about a gray metal contraption of patchwork tubes and circuits. It could only be their emotion machine, not pointed at us, but at the breen, and I knew then that the Vulsteen had lied. It took more than a return to their wild environment to turn these creatures into killers—the Vulsteen left nothing to chance.

My newfound knowledge, however, gave no comfort when the first of the breen saw us, and giving a high-pitched cry, hurled himself across the arena!

Naturally, my first thought was to run headlong to meet him.

Chapter 30
I Conceive a Plan

For all that my rush implied a desire for swift suicide, the Bard himself would have approved the method to my madness. In the instant after the breen had charged and before I dashed ahead to meet him, I had caught Marella's eye, and an instant understanding passed between us. As I ran, so did she, flanking the breen. Separated from its pack, under assault from two directions at once, the poor beast's head whipped back and forth as it tried to decide how to deal with this unprecedented problem: other creatures ran away from breen, not *at* them.

By the time it faltered in its charge and turned on Marella, I was close behind. Clumsy in the sand, it swiped at her with its claws and missed; I did not. My sword entered its body below the shoulder and plunged straight into its heart.

I pulled the sword free even before my victim hit the sand, dead, and I backpedaled furiously. The wondrous material of which the Nuum made their weapons allowed for no sticking in the body; it slid in and out as if the target were water. Blood itself hardly clung.

The remaining breen stood bewildered in their tracks. As Marella and I retreated, Harros moved to join us. I could hear

Timash cheering us on in the background.

The breen suddenly surged forward—and halted again. Even the subsonic buzz of Vulsteen telepathic "shouting" stopped. Some subtle but palpable alteration tugged at the edge of my consciousness, like a background noise suddenly silenced. I whirled, turning my back on the most dangerous creatures in the world, and saw my thoughts confirmed: Where before the Vulsteen technicians had surrounded their device, now they swarmed over it like ants. The undercurrent that had signified the operating of their machinery was gone.

I fell to my knees as though exhausted, dropping my chin in an attitude of despair. Whatever the cause of the instrument's failure, its creators must not suspect that I had divined even a part of the truth. Let them think that I believed in heavenly deliverance, but if they were unable to remedy the problem, we would live to fight another day—unless they simply decided to execute us.

And then the hand of inspiration reached out and touched my pitiful brow. Throwing my arms out, I pitched full-length onto the sand. It was as dismally histrionic a performance as was ever hissed off the London stage, but I gambled that these passionless monsters would lack the experience to see through me. Against the sand, the whip-like sword was nearly invisible to me, let alone any watchers in the gallery. One-handed, I retracted the blade.

"Come help me," I muttered to my friends, and when they moved in close I threw a handful of sand in Harros' face. As he clawed at his eyes, I staggered to my feet, palming my club and sliding it down my sleeve.

Open-mouthed with shock, Marella nonetheless followed me back to the cage where Timash waited. My heart was thumping wildly; if the breen were to rouse themselves now, Harros would die blinded and alone. But (so my reasoning went) if the breen came alive again, we were all dead in any event.

"What did you do that for?" Marella demanded as we reached the wall. "What's going on?"

By this time Harros had cleared his vision and was stumbling in our direction. I needed no telepathy to see that if the Vulsteen had gotten their connivance operating at that moment, they could have picked up from him alone enough emotion to power their society for a year.

Harros came to a stop a few feet in front of me, blinking angrily, club hefted but held in abeyance out of respect for the sword I had carried. He had had no time to note its apparent disappearance.

"It was a trick," I hissed before he could speak. "I had to distract them." I dared say no more for fear of being overheard, and the many eyes still upon us prevented my showing my prize, but he must have read the truth on my face, because he dropped the club and net. Marella dropped her sword as well, and with their voluntary disarmament the bars rose behind us. It took a great deal of composure not to shout out loud. Safe!

For now.

A Vulsteen was awaiting us; whether it was the same as before or another I could not tell, since their gaunt features and monotone skin gave little individuality to any of them. Even the voice was the same.

"You." He meant me. "You did not leave your weapon outside?"

"I dropped it on the field. Didn't you see me?" Thousands of years of telepathic communication and generations of suppressed humanity had erased any facility the Vulsteen possessed for lying, or for perceiving it in others. He lowered the outside bars again and left us there.

"Boy," Timash marveled when we were alone. "I don't know what you guys did, but it sure made them crazy!"

"What do you mean?" Marella asked.

"Well, I was up against the bars, trying to bend one or something, and they must have been right above me because I could hear them talking the whole time." He snorted. "Not that they were whispering. They're a pretty rude bunch."

In telepathic communication, as I had learned early on, your "voice" can carry much further than in mere speech—and through walls, to boot. Evidently the Vulsteen had tossed the baby of manners out with the bathwater of emotion.

"All of a sudden," he went on, "they really started yelling and carrying on and like that! Something about how the meter was only showing a third as much input as they expected, and it wasn't balancing the output, and all kinds of other technical garbage that I couldn't make heads or tails of, and somebody said something about throwing the switch and the next thing you know the breen are all standing around like statues and the whole place got real quiet. For a minute I could hear them up above…it sounded like they were working on some kind of computer or controls for something…and they didn't sound happy. Then they stopped and you guys came back."

I nodded, comparing what Timash had told us with what I myself had seen. Something had gone wrong with the Vulsteen's plans; their infernal emotion-sapping machine had not functioned as planned, and I suspected I knew why. From what the first Vulsteen said, it had been calibrated for Nuum emotions, Nuum minds. My variant brain chemistry had proven resistant in the same way it proved resistant to certain forms of telepathy. I chuckled dryly to myself. Let them try to figure out what had gone wrong! They'd be at it for a million years…

Harros stared at me, eyes narrowed. "What's so funny?"

"Just wait," I assured my companions mysteriously. "It's all going according to plan."

For the subterranean dwellers of a dead city, there is no night or day, and for the emotionally parched Vulsteen there was no sense of increased tension or alarm following our visit to the arena, so awaiting a propitious moment at which to begin our escape would have been an exercise in procrastination. We were hustled back to the pit soon enough, when someone could be bothered to remember us. Once there I sought out Uncle Sam without delay. I found him at the funeral.

The breen were gathered at the spot where their dead friend had lived, crowding quietly into that little space while some spoke softly in turns. I came upon them suddenly, unaware of their intent. When I realized what was going on, I backed away and listened from a distance—I was, after all, the deceased's killer.

If I had foreseen ill will, I was correct, but it was not aimed toward me. Rather the Vulsteen took the blame for the death, and in the breens' words I heard an echo of my earlier sentiments: that these our slavers were cowards, living through the deaths of others the lives that they could no longer feel for themselves. I heard the words of these man-made predators, and looking at their claws and teeth I wondered if my plan was so very clever after all. My sympathies were hardly with the Vulsteen—I have always despised those who force their will upon others—but with Timash, and Marella and Harros: If I unleashed this force of nature and used it to topple our captors, would we be pulled down as well?

The ceremony was short, befitting a people who had never been meant to know humanity, let alone been allowed to experience it freely. When it was over, I went to Uncle Sam and told him what I had planned: Several breen would form a pyramid against the wall of the pit. The others could climb over them out of the pit. There were no guards; I was astonished that no one had thought of it before.

He turned me down.

"It will not work," he mumbled, turning away from me. I looked to the others around him for help, but none would meet my gaze.

"There's nothing above for us," one said morosely. "At least here we are alive."

"And as far as they were concerned, that was the end of it."

"They weren't even willing to try?" Timash's youthful world view could conceive of no more bewildering possibility.

"Maybe we could do it ourselves?" Harros suggested. "The walls are about twenty feet high; between the four of us we could get that high."

"I don't know." I hesitated. "None of us has ever done this before, and if we don't get it right the first time, somebody could get hurt."

"Hurt?" Harros echoed. "As opposed to what?"

His point was well taken. "All right. Timash, you're on the bottom, then Harros, then me. Marella, how are you at climbing?"

"Terrible." Marella had listened intently throughout, but now she slumped down and turned her face to the wall. "Uncle Sam's right. It'll never work." She picked at the dirt with her finger. "And even if we get to the top and get out of here, the bloodbats'll be on us before we get two blocks—if the thunder lizards don't eat us first."

A chill ran through me. In prison, despair passes from person to person like a disease: If it could infect Marella, how long did the rest of us have?

I took her face in my hands as I would a child. She did not resist my touch.

"Marella," I said. "Remember how we found you. You were alone, fighting for your life in a room full of Vulsteen. You weren't afraid, you were angry. What has changed? This is our chance! You aren't alone anymore."

There was no response, not even an angry shrug or a declaration of her right to be left alone. My words washed over her and fell away like waves from a rock.

"Let me try," Harros suggested. "We've been—spending a lot of time together." He hunched down next to the girl, speaking in whispers. After several moments he stood again with a deep sigh. "That's not the same woman we met a few days ago," he stated with certainty. "That's not even the same woman who went into the arena with us."

"What do you mean?" Timash demanded.

"He means the Vulsteen have been using their ray on us," I guessed.

Harros nodded. "That's why the breen have never tried to break out before. It's on all the time. It keeps them in line, except when they're in the arena. Then the effects are reversed for the show."

"So why aren't we affected?"

"Marella is a woman," I pointed out. "Their emotions are more easily manipulated than ours."

Harros stared at me. "What century are you from? But the question is, can we get out of here without her help? If we can find a rope, we could come back and rescue her whether she likes it or not."

"That's not good enough," I said. "We can't leave the breen here to be enslaved—and the next poor devil who wanders in here will be thrown to the same fate."

Harros stared at me in astonishment. "We're not even out of the pit and you want to overthrow the Vulsteen and free the slaves? Let's get ourselves free and get out of here."

My face was getting hot and I was on the verge of doing something which might have jeopardized all our chances for freedom when Timash placed a leathery hand on my shoulder.

"I've got a solution. It's going to take all of us to climb out of the pit. After that, each man is on his own. I'm sticking with Keryl. If you want to take Marella out and try to fight your way past the thunder lizards alone, be my guest. But if we can help the breen, then I'm willing to bet they'll help us. And if it doesn't work, we're no worse off than we are right now."

There is something about a reasonable compromise, which, when suggested by a full-grown gorilla, is well-nigh irresistible.

As our escape was problematical if we could not first leave the pit, we resolved to find out just how difficult that would prove. To this end, Timash stationed himself next to the wall. With our help, Harros hoisted himself onto Timash's broad shoulders. That part was easily enough accomplished, but the next was not.

We soon discovered that climbing a ladder composed entirely of other men is even less simple than anticipated. Merely gaining Timash's shoulders required a helping hand, and once there I had precious little to hold onto, never mind finding placement for my feet: Timash made no secret of his preference that I not use his head for a stepping stone. After I shed my boots and tried climbing in my bare feet (at his suggestion), I found purchase more readily, but had we not chosen a spot in the marshy, debris-cluttered end of the pit for our trials, they would have ended far sooner with much less happy results. Timash might have been the one holding up the weight, but it was I who took the tumbles.

Finally Harros suggested that Timash stand a bit away from the wall, allowing the two of them to lean in, partly resting their weight on the wall and giving me a more gradual climb. What we lost in height we gained in stability, and it was not long before I was relatively steady atop Harros' shoulders.

I was also a good three feet short of the top.

I reported my situation, and heard Timash groan.

"Come down then. You guys are gonna break me."

I started to obey, glancing down to check my landing, when something caught my eye. Just about waist level there was a crack in the wall. Crouching, I bade my companions hold on a bit longer.

"If I can get my baton in there, I can use it as a step. From there I should be able to reach the top." It was slow going, every moment stretched by the knowledge of what Harros and Timash were going through, holding me up. The blunt end of the rod made a poor pick, so I extended the sword. It was even more clumsy, but at least it boasted a point.

"Can we stop for a while?" Timash pleaded. "You guys are crushing me."

"Almost there," I hissed, and I was not lying. Digging

frantically I cleared a narrow space that I thought would serve. Retracting the sword I jabbed the baton home, holding on with both hands while I tested its hold.

That hold was all that saved me when my living ladder suddenly vanished and I found myself dangling fifteen feet above the floor!

Chapter 31
Battle in the Control Room

I sensed more than heard the Vulsteen stop short of the edge of the pit only inches above my head. The strain of sudden weight tore at my shoulders, but I bit back my hiss at the burning pain and concentrated on keeping my body pressed against the wall. If he saw me, there would be nothing I could do to prevent his summoning aid and confiscating my baton by force. His foot scraped the ground as he stepped closer.

Suddenly he cried out and backed away. I couldn't see what had startled him; I could only presume he had spied me hanging there and was calling for help—but after his initial outcry, nothing. After a few moments, I felt Harros rising up beneath me, his shoulders finding their way under my feet and relieving the awful strain.

"What happened?"

"He was about to see you. Timash threw a handful of garbage in his face."

"And it was sticky garbage, too," floated up a comment from far below. Timash sounded a bit put out by the sacrifices demanded by his own quick-thinking action. I had a feeling that I had not heard the last of this.

Taking the path of Isaac Newton, I was able to reach the lip of the pit by standing on the shoulders of giants (and my baton). I stretched out on the edge and reached down for it. Harros was trying to hoist himself up to use it as I had.

"It won't work," I warned him urgently. "There's nothing else for you to hang on to."

"I can do it," he panted. "I know I can."

"It won't work," I repeated. "Timash might do it, but you can't lift him. Give it to me—that Vulsteen might return at any moment!"

"Give him the baton!" Timash growled, and caught between a rock and a hard place, Harros pulled the baton out of the wall and stretched until it touched my outstretched fingers. I grasped it and climbed to my feet.

The corridor was deserted for the moment; as soon as I was far enough from the pit I reached into my pocket and withdrew the Library.

"It is good to see you again, sir," the Librarian said as he materialized beside me.

"You, too," I answered, and as I said it I realized it was more than simply an automatic response. The Librarian had been programmed to resemble men I had known, and I could not help but like him.

"You realize, of course, that if you deactivate the emotional sequencer, the breen may revert back to their natural state. In that case, Timash, Harros, and Marella will have no chance."

"I know. But if they were going to revert without help, the Vulsteen wouldn't have wasted the energy preparing them to fight in the arena."

The Librarian nodded. "Still, they are a fractious species, and the wrong word could set them off. Even if you are correct, it would be a mistake to leave the others in a confined space with them for long."

"Exactly. So—do you know where the control room is for the

machine in the slave pit?"

"No, I do not. But I noticed when they brought you back from the arena, they used a different route than when they took you there. And each time the path was unnecessarily torturous. I have extrapolated a more direct route that lies between the two you took. It may be that only one control room directs both the arena and the slave pit emotion projectors..."

"And if that's the case, it's probably smack between the two." The Librarian was a dear man, but sometimes he took the longer route himself. "Which tunnel?" He indicated his best guess, and I followed it. To avoid being seen, he vanished, leaving me alone once more. I drew my sword and hugged the wall.

The guard gave it away. I had covered more than half of the distance I estimated lay between the pit and the arena, seeing no one—I had fortuitously chosen a Vulsteen sleep period; most were in their chambers—when I chanced upon a man standing before a door some way ahead. Casual loiterers being rare in these tunnels, I marked him as a sentry.

The Vulsteen would have done better to leave well enough alone; had they never posted a guard, I would have tried the door, been stopped by the lock, and moved on. But his presence was a lighted signpost.

Men without emotions make very poor sentries: They lack fear, nervousness, caution...all emotions that would have caused a normal man, upon being confronted with an unknown person in a restricted area in a forbidden city, to call for assistance. Having none of those survival factors, this sentry did not, even when the Librarian suddenly appeared in the corridor, and refused to advance when so ordered. So the guard left his post to intercept the intruder.

Eventually he returned—at which point I left him lying senseless in the control room, after letting myself in with the key he so thoughtfully provided. The Vulsteens' lack of experience in security matters was about to cost them dearly.

The room was entirely filled with machinery vital to the Vulsteen—or so the Librarian told me as I was about to place the library sphere into one of the universal access indentations on the control panel for the air ducting system. He directed me to another panel, plain but for four blinking blue lights and an access indentation, across the room. I reached for it...

Concomitant with the disadvantages of totally emotionless guards is the advantage that when they awaken, they do not let loose with outraged screams that alert the intruder who previously rendered them unconscious that such a state of affairs no longer exists. In other words, when the guard I had knocked out woke up, he smartly slapped the Library from my hand before I could place it in the interface.

Perhaps he was still groggy, in that he did not simply club me over the head and take possession of both saboteur and sabotage equipment at the same time. But even so, I barely scrambled out of his way across the slick floor before he flung his net and nearly entangled my still-numbed hand.

I had been holding the Library with my right hand, the same with which I usually held my sword, but for that moment I had transferred the sword to my left hand, and now it was with that hand that I was forced to defend myself. I moved in close to seize his net with my aching right hand and use my sword as a long knife, but he flicked the net at my eyes and blinded me for a second. I thrust regardless, and he swept my blade out of the way with his club, but at least I delayed his charge until my vision returned.

The Library had rolled into a corner beyond anyone's reach. We circled the room in silence. I could not reach the control bank, and he could not summon help lest I carry out what I had come to do.

My breath was coming short and fast; time was on his side, and the moment one of his fellows happened upon us, I was finished. He knew it, but where a normal man might have smiled at my predicament, or given some sign of his nervousness, the Vulsteen's face was an expressionless mask. No excitement pulsed through his veins; no fear made his heart pump harder. I looked at his skeletal visage and wasted limbs and all I saw was a breathing mechanical man.

And then, with the seeming rashness that had more than once saved me, I jumped back, my fingers dancing on the invisible control buttons of my sword hilt. Had I consciously thought about it, I could not have effected my weapon's metamorphosis before my foe was upon me, but my hands had a life of their own and I was holding a stout staff in place of my sharp blade before he could close with me.

I charged into him, my staff pitched straight out like a lance. He tangled it in his net, drawing it to the side and rendering me helpless—until I let go the staff, its weight dragging his net aside. He tried to bring his club to bear and I seized it in one hand before he could summon up any momentum. In a mob against lone Thorans, the Vulsteen were dangerous predators; one on one against me, he had the strength of a palsy victim. I wrenched his club from his grip as I would from an unruly child. True to his nature, he showed no emotion whatsoever right up to the moment I slammed his face into the wall.

Moving quickly, I gathered up the Library from the corner where it lay.

"Are you all right?"

"You needn't worry about me," the little sphere whispered pedantically. "I am thoroughly laced with plastimetallic alloys and I have no moving parts. Place me in the access pit directly to your left."

I did so without any fear that my actions would be interrupted a second time. As far as I could tell, nothing happened. Then the Library spoke again.

"I have isolated the subprogram that controls the emotion sequencer. I can turn it off at any time, but I would advise you to remove your friends from the pit first."

"Can you change the settings? Perhaps we can use the Vulsteen's machine against them."

"I'm sorry, no. I am basically an advanced database. In light of your situation, the main Library programmed some—additional—capabilities, but that one is beyond me. I can turn the machine on and off, but I have not the analytical superroutines necessary to change its pre-set parameters."

I hesitated, calculating how long it might take to find a rope, return to the pit, and haul my friends out—assuming that I ran into no further Vulsteen on the way. I instructed the Library to give me ten minutes' grace, then deactivate the machine. I was well on my way back to Timash and the others when I realized that I might not have a chance to return to the control room.

Without the Library I was trapped in this century, but without my friends I would be unworthy of living in any event. I take pride in the knowledge that I hesitated hardly a moment before continuing on toward the pit—notwithstanding that my heart was racing back to the control room to retrieve my only guide to my slim chance of returning home.

Whither the Vulsteen might keep a rope or a ladder I knew not, but common sense dictated that they did not carry them around, and common sense, it seemed, had survived the past million years. Taking a stout cord from its hanger out of reach of the pit, I quickly lowered it.

Harros was the first to try and his weight nearly pulled me back in and dashed all our plans.

"There's nothing here to lash the rope to," I reported hastily. "Marella is the lightest; send her up and she can help me hold on while you climb up."

"She won't go," Timash hissed back. "She's still under their influence."

"Well, she won't be for long—and neither will the breen. I fixed the machine to turn itself off in a few minutes, and then it's going to get crowded down there."

Timash's eyes got very wide. "You turned off the machine?"

"In a few minutes. I—"

Timash waited to hear no more. Backing up, he took a running start, leaped straight into the wall, and started clambering up without my help. Within seconds his paws appeared at the edge and he scrambled upright next to me.

"Let's go!"

"How did you—?"

"I've been climbing trees since I was a baby. C'mon, Harros, let's move it!"

Marella was still dead weight, so he looped the rope around her uncooperative body and we hauled her up like a sack of rice. No sooner had we dropped the rope again than Harros seized it, practically running up the wall faster than he could have slid down it.

"They're starting to get restless down there," he imparted breathlessly. "I think the machine's turned off."

Indeed, Marella seemed to recover her spunk even as we stood there. Blinking her confusion away, when apprised of our situation she voted for an immediate departure; Harros seconded her.

"I have to go back," I said. "I—left something in the control room."

Marella stared at me. "What? Whatever it is, I'll buy you a new one! Let's get out of here!"

"You go on. I'll move faster alone."

"Oh, no," she said. "We stay together. You've got the only weapon." Although Harros seemed ready to protest, when Timash backed Marella he wisely kept his own counsel.

I tried to give her my baton, but she would not hear of it, nor would the others. We all realized that only in a group might we have the strength to fight off any Vulsteen we met between here and the surface. I was about to lead us back to the control room when I glanced at the pit, and watched in a mixture of awe and horror as the first breen, clawed hands and feet throwing gashes of mud in its wake, raced up the side of the pit and stood truly free for the first time in generations!

It turned, saw us, and bared its fangs...

Chapter 32
Fight for Freedom

In the moment between the time the breen beheld us and its predatory instincts took hold, another breen scrambled out of the pit. It put out one hand against the other's chest and growled a few words in their own language. The first breen's lips reluctantly slid back over his teeth, even though the fiery hunger in his eyes burned unabated.

"Stay there," the second breen advised us in its coarse voice. It crossed the floor and stood with us as others climbed out of captivity, demonstrating a facility for scaling the walls that made Timash seem clumsy by comparison. It was plain that the pit itself had played no part in the slavery of these beasts; only the emotion sequencer had held them in thrall all these years. The pit must have served the Vulsteen more as a psychological separation than it had served to keep the breen in their place. We were quickly surrounded by furry bodies, some antagonistic, needing a growl from our protector to ward them off, but most seeming to ignore us, wandering the small space as though they had never seen it before—as indeed they never had.

The very last breen to come forth was Uncle Sam, and all the others, save our guard, gathered about him. He lifted his arms to take them all in. They leaned forward as though to hear him better, and I could almost smell the bloodlust on their minds. But for all his people's ferocity and righteous vengeance, he had a different answer.

"It is over. Let us return to the surface and see the Vulsteen no more."

I feared a slaughter, that one of the young bucks would leap out of the crowd and strike him down, crying for vengeance and blood, but none did. Instead he walked through the crowd and they parted for him, obediently allowing him to lead them away from this place and back into the sunshine.

Caught up in the tide of retreating beasts, I could do no more than stay my place as they streamed by; try as I might I could make no headway against them, and as a result I found myself on the fringe of the crowd, watching them go. Uncle Sam, leading the pack, had not yet noticed that we were not among them, and I am not sure that he would have stopped for us had he known.

"Go ahead," I ordered my companions. "I know where I'm going, and I can catch up before you reach the surface."

Marella started to protest again, but this time Timash sided with me.

"He's right. You're better off with the breen. We'll catch up."

Thus it was that Timash and I, scurrying in the opposite direction from the straggling breen, were the first to come upon the Vulsteen army.

Contrary to our initial impression, we had not run headlong into the entire population of Vulsteen, but in that crowded corridor it seemed as though we had. We met at an intersection, neither party knowing the other was there until we had almost run each other over. They were not armed with the usual complement of clubs and nets, but wide, straight swords—they were not out to gather prisoners this time—but apparently the Nuum's strictures against machines had affected even these subterranean hermits.

How the Vulsteen knew that their slaves had escaped we did not know, nor did we ever find out. My best guess is that we set off an alarm when we turned off the emotion sequencer; it is inconceivable that no precautions would have been taken against its failure.

Their mass proved their undoing and our salvation. Flooding the confines of the small passage, they had little room to wield their own weapons, while we simply lashed out at whatever got in our way. Timash, especially, was good at this, bulking thrice as large as most of our opponents, who, unable to fly backward from his fists as would have befitted the force employed, crashed into their still-charging comrades, causing riotous confusion.

There was no science to what we did in that hallway, only a frenzy of swinging limbs and slashing swords. The Vulsteen fought and died without sound, without visible emotion. Perhaps that is why Timash and I lived and they did not.

As suddenly as it began, it was over, and a dozen of them lay about us, some still breathing, some not. Who killed them, I do not know—in those close quarters some of them may have stabbed each other.

We reached the control room without further incident. I grabbed the Library—which came loose at my touch, although no one else could have moved it—and returned to the room where we had left the breen. We moved much more carefully on the way back, but the Vulsteen patrols appeared to have already passed. Only the dead remained at the site of our skirmish in the hall.

There were sounds coming from the chamber ahead. Screams that came from no human throat, ripping noises whose origin I did not want to imagine.

Timash and I looked at each other, plainly and unashamedly afraid to rush into what could literally turn out to be a bloody hell, yet goaded on by our obligations to our companions. Had they made it to the surface, or were they trapped in the midst of the carnage?

And then it stopped.

Warily, we crept to the entrance to the larger chamber and peeked out. A very bloody hell, indeed. Even in my days and nights in the awful trenches of France, I had witnessed nothing to rival this. Bodies and pieces lay everywhere, blood coated the floor, dripping into the pit, smearing the fur of the victors. For those standing were breen, more than a match for men who despite their superior numbers had been limited by the edicts of Thora's alien conquerors to weapons that only approximated what the breen had been given by God. The smell overtaking us made me want to retch. I saw nothing standing that was not breen, neither Vulsteen nor human.

But even as I was casting about in my mind for a route that might bypass these bestial killing machines, a small knot of breen on the far side of the room opened and I saw Marella and Harros step out, unharmed but no less horrified than I by the abattoir that confronted them. We, at least, had been spared for the most part the awful sounds that accompanied so much death. Even as this thought crossed my mind I saw Marella throw her hands over her ears and bury her face in Harros' chest.

None of the breen had noticed us as yet. Thinking it unwise to appear suddenly in their midst, I called out to Uncle Sam, whom I recognized in the throng near my friends. Heads jerked around, teeth bared, but a shout from their leader brought them to heel, and we were allowed to cross the room unmolested, although I confess that my skin crawled icily along my shoulders the entire time. We walked through the breen as through a forest of lions, each gazing hungrily at our tender flesh but held in check by an invisible power. We were careful never to brush against even a single individual, for fear that the touch would drive him over the edge and the entire room would erupt in savagery once more. From the slight sigh that escaped when we reached him, I believe that Uncle Sam had dreaded that same possibility. Indeed, he lost no time guiding us to a passage to the outer world.

Our goodbyes were of necessity swift and informal, but Uncle Sam's thanks were no less genuine.

"Where will you go now?" I asked. "None of you has ever lived outside before."

His answer surprised me.

"Back to our people, of course. We have wandered these plains for thousands of years. Just because men fear us doesn't make us animals. We have many tribes, many nations." He nodded. "And we have long memories. Our people will be glad to welcome us home."

"But—but..." Harros sputtered. "I mean, will they accept you? I mean, won't you be *different?*"

Uncle Sam lifted one lip in his imitation of a smile. "Not so much as you think." He laid a clawed hand on my shoulder. "Remember, my friend, the breen have long memories."

And with that he was gone. Not far ahead we saw daylight. It was morning, and we sat in one of the long shadows while we waited to our eyes to become reacquainted with the sunshine.

"So, Keryl," Harros spoke up. "If the breen have such long memories, do you think one of them could tell us how to get home?"

Mentally I slapped myself for forgetting that our transportation had been smashed to pieces the day we arrived. How could I know that this would soon emerge as the very least of our problems?

Marella got to her feet and looked out into the morning sky, shielding her eyes from the glare. Apparently satisfied with what she saw—or what she did not see—she returned to sit with the rest of us in the shade.

"What's so interesting out there?" Timash asked querulously. "That's the third time you've been out there."

"Just looking for something to get us on our way. We're not doing any good sitting here."

In discussing our options, we had decided not to return underground to the breen for assistance. Not only did it feel wrong after our triumphant exit, but the breen had only one thing to offer that we lacked, and the idea of marching for several days—and nights—escorted by the most ferocious killing machines ever to walk dry land left us more comfortable relying upon our own resources, scant as they might be.

I was beginning to wonder about the steadiness of our own group: Marella was still a stranger, Harros had long overstayed his anticipated visit, and Timash had shown unwonted surliness ever since we emerged from underground. I had known him in the past to exhibit the moodiness of youth, but never such raw ill temper. Given his past animosity toward Harros and the latter's lack of diplomacy, I feared they might come to blows ere we camped for the night.

"Let's go for a walk." I stood up and cuffed his shoulder lightly. He looked up at me with angry red eyes, but I refused to back down. "Come on."

"Where are you going?" Marella asked as Timash got to his feet. "It's dangerous out there."

"We won't be long," I said, and walked into the sunshine without looking to see that Timash had followed.

He had to shield his eyes again. "It's hot out here."

"You might as well get used to it. We're going to have to move out sometime."

"Then we oughta travel at night."

I responded with an annoyed look. After several nights on the plains in the groundcar, he knew as well as anyone why we couldn't travel at night.

"What's wrong?" I asked bluntly.

He looked at me, lowering his arm as he put his back to the sun.

"What do you mean?"

"You're growling and complaining so much I had half a mind to leave you with the breen. You could bite *their* heads off instead of ours."

"It's nothing."

"I've seen it before, you know. Back where I come from. I told you I was taken from the middle of a war. I was an officer, and I used to see this reaction sometimes after men went through their first battle." When he failed to rise to the bait, I took the plunge. "It was you or them. It's no sin to kill in war. That's what happens in wars. If they don't die, you do."

"But I didn't have to like it!" Once the dam burst, there was no stopping the flood. "Back when we attacked the research station, they made me stay back. I watched everything, but I was more concerned with my friends than with the Nuum. I even pulled a couple of them out of the way when they were hurt, and I thought how great it all was, with the shouting and the fighting and here I was saving lives. But I didn't hurt anybody! It was just like Uncle Balu's stories, so when I got a chance to go with you, I saw myself charging around, having adventures—but I never thought about what it would be like to kill a man. Back there, in the city—I know, like you said, it was them or us...

"But Keryl—when you and I were down there, trapped in that hallway with the Vulsteen coming at us and we started swinging and slashing away and they—I liked it! It was my greatest adventure, fighting evil and helping people and—and there you were next to me—I felt so great! People were dying at my feet, I could feel their bones breaking, but I liked it! I liked the feeling of power. But then, when we got back to the pit, and I saw all those bodies and all that blood..."

Like a phonograph record, he ran down until his voice was inaudible.

I put a hand on his hairy shoulder. "Timash, let me tell you something. When I was a boy, I read the same kind of stories you did, all about heroes and knights in shining armor." From his expression, he had no idea to what I was referring. I let it go. "And I joined the army for the same reasons you wanted to come with me: Grand adventure, fighting evil. But I'd never killed a man, never even gotten in a real fight, until I went to France, and the first time I saw the enemy marching across no-man's-land... I will never forget the feel of my rifle against my shoulder, and the kick of the recoil, and the sight of a man falling backward, dead because I shot him." I had to stop while the damned moving picture played through my mind again. "Very soon afterward I learned there are two kinds of men in war: Those who kill because they have to, they're soldiers. Those who kill because they want to, they're murderers.

"How do you feel, right now, about what you did?"

"I feel like I'm gonna be sick."

"Congratulations. You're a soldier."

Whatever my speech meant to him, he had no time to tell me before a huge shadow swooped down and someone began shooting at us.

Chapter 33
I Am Shanghaied

The snap of the whip on flesh was short and ugly. Unlike the shells and the bullets, you never heard the whip coming, never knew when it was flying at you, or the man next to you, until it struck, the sound sharp when it split the air, wet and flat when it flayed your skin. It didn't hit me, but I flinched. We all did.

"Put your backs into it!" Garm shouted, as though he were the overseer on a slave galley and we were the human engines. And so he was, though we were not. This Nuum sky-barge depended no more on our muscles than Garm needed his ancient leather whip to keep order. But both had their uses.

I snapped my head, tossing my hair about to keep the sweat from my eyes. My hair was longer than it had ever grown, even as a child, certainly longer than my days in the British army. My hands, chained to the oars, were helpless to wipe my brow. My mind, numbed by the incessant push and pull of rowing through thin air, fought to rise above the fog of misery, but it failed, sinking once again into the comfort of the past...

Our shouts had been drowned out by the engines of the descending airship, and we could only scatter before it crushed us.

As it was, the hurricane winds from its hoverfans kicked up such dust that we had no breath for shouting in any event. I held one hand over my mouth and eyes as best I could and staggered in the direction I hoped was shelter. I could not see or hear Timash.

Those shots had been meant only to frighten, not kill; had it been otherwise, we would have died without ever knowing we were targeted. The second the craft touched down men boiled out of the hatch, some coming for me and others, I assumed, seeking Timash. With the wind dying away, I could see them approaching; I had run into the open, not toward cover, and one look at their firearms told me that a dash for freedom now would likely end quickly and painfully. I stood carefully still.

They were a motley pair that closed in on me, sporting garish baggy shirts and pants that complemented them only in a drunkard's nightmare. To a man the landing party wore beards, an affectation I had not seen in this era. They held their pistols loosely, but with an air of confidence and familiarity. Their ship was the size of a house, roughly triangular, but plainly a larger cousin of our own late groundcar.

"Look, boys, another one! And he's a big one, too!" A barrel-shaped man in green shirt and purple trousers, sporting a bright yellow waist-sash holding a wide sword, rounded the ship and put his hands on his hips while he looked me over. His dress, manner, and the careless way his own pistol was thrust in his sash, inevitably reminiscent of a Caribbean pirate, was more evidence of the cycles of history. Behind him several more men escorted Timash, their pistols held in a less cavalier manner than my own guards'.

"What's the meaning of this?" The meaning was quite clear, but having no wish to seem meek in front of these men, I followed convention. I probably should have kept my tongue but there was no sign of Harros or Marella—and not far away camped a small army of breen. If I could make enough fuss, rescue was not out of the question.

The big man thought my question humorous but undeserving

of an answer. Despite his red hair and beard, he did not fit my usual image of a Nuum, and some of his men were black-haired. A few of them, I was sure, were Thoran, but each one held guns supposedly forbidden to all but the overlords. There were six raiders altogether, bad odds even without the guns.

Their leader jabbed a thumb toward the front of their ship. "Porky, get us going. I don't want to have a lizard breathing down our necks while we on-load."

"Aye-aye, Durrn." One of the crew ducked back into their ship. Durrn followed, waving to his men to bring us aboard.

"Wait!" I said, startling my guards. "What about our friends?"

Durrn spun about, eyes narrowing.

"Keryl!" Timash shouted. "What are you doing?"

"Yes, what are you doing?" Durrn walked up to me, peering into my eyes.

"We left two friends in that building over there." I motioned with my head, feeling it unwise to use my hands around the nervous guards. Meantime I was trying to tell Timash telepathically, *Trust me!* with little success. Perhaps it was as well. "We can't leave them here."

"They might not agree with you."

"Whatever you've got in mind, it can't be any worse than what we've seen here."

Durrn chuckled. "You might be surprised."

I laughed right back at him. "So might you." That unnerved him, but when Marella appeared from the shadows and shouted "Stop!" at him, he completely went to pieces.

As I have stated before, in moments of crisis my body leaps ahead of my mind, taking the initiative when the more settled of spirit would have withheld action pending rational consideration of outcomes and consequences. Not so I. This time my body literally leaped without conscious impetus, and the consequences were severe.

As soon as I had seen we were outnumbered, I had slid my

baton up my sleeve and held it there. Our captors had not gotten around to searching us, and now they paid the price.

I spun, sliding the baton in my hand as I did so and resting it with some force against the side of a guard's head. When he staggered, I grabbed his sidearm.

My fingers wrapped themselves around the grip in a practiced habit a million years old—but when I reached for the trigger there was none. I pointed the gun at the remaining guard and wished I knew how to fire it.

The gun flashed and the guard went down. Deep in the back of my mind the words *telepathic trigger* echoed faintly, but I was too involved to appreciate the Library's far-ranging education right then. I whirled, searching for targets.

There were none, and too many.

Timash's guards had turned at the sound of Marella's shout. One lay on the ground, one writhed in the ape's grip, but the third had trained his weapon on the girl. Timash was between us. At the last second, Harros appeared, chasing Marella. The guard shifted aim, fired, and Harros went down.

"Nice shooting, lad." Durrn had appeared in the hatchway, his gun leveled at me. "But you won't have time for another."

And then he shot me.

In the hands of an experienced marksman, a Nuum phase-pistol can render a target unconscious for a number of hours without any appreciable after-effects. I survived Durrn's attack because he wanted me to; knowing how long I would need to recharge my pistol, he took the time to adjust his own, to my everlasting benefit.

A few moments' careful listening with my eyes closed lead me to believe that I was in no immediate danger, so I allowed myself to look about and examine my surroundings. That they were strange to me was no shock; prisons were becoming a familiar sight. The room was small, seemingly hewn out of thick logs. Light was provided by a heavily-barred electric lamp in one corner of the ceiling. That Timash was napping in a corner, wearing thick chains that matched my own, was likewise not unexpected, but the absence of Harros concerned me. Several empty sets of manacles lined our jail, but they bespoke nothing of any recent occupancy.

"Are you awake?"

"Unfortunately." My friend opened one eye. "I was hoping you wouldn't wake up. I was hoping maybe you were having a dream and I got caught in it." He touched one hand lightly to his closed eye and winced. "I didn't think it was true."

"Are you all right?"

He grunted. "I'll live." Then he winced again. "Oh. Bad choice of words."

I felt cold. "Harros?"

Timash and Harros had never gotten along; I knew that, but my friend's voice showed genuine concern.

"He was shot in the head. Maybe it was an accident; I don't think they meant to kill us. They brought him on board, but he wasn't moving—and if they know anything, they're sure not telling me."

"On board?" I repeated. There were no windows in our cell, and there was no sense of movement. I'd no idea we were inside a vehicle.

"We're on a sky barge." He couldn't keep his hand away from the area around his closed eye. It was as if the pain would eventually convince himself that his plight was real, and then he could do something about it. "They're a Nuum invention. They use them to ferry themselves around—the rich ones do, anyway."

"A sky barge? Are we airborne?" I tried to feel my surroundings, placing a hand to the deck, but there were no vibrations, no sounds of engines.

"Yeah. Don't ask me how they work. We've seen them on occasion flying over our mountain. They never make a sound, just sail over like a huge balloon. Uncle Balu says sometimes they fly so low you can see the rowers."

I recalled now that Balu had told me about sky barges once, but our conversation was interrupted by the arrival of four motley jailors, two of whom exchanged our fixed manacles for others, while the remaining pair guarded us from a distance—with *cutlasses*. At first I believed all an elaborate dream after all, that I was trapped in a Morphean landscape out of Robert Louis Stevenson, but I was to learn that the gaudy play into which I had been involuntarily cast was all too real. Everything in this surreal world had its place and its purpose: I was to be thrust into my own niche very soon.

We were forcibly marched up several flights of what appeared to be wooden ladders before being pushed into daylight. I stopped; I could not help it. The vision before me was so incongruent as to overwhelm me as I had not been since my first days in this looking-glass world.

I stood upon the deck on a Spanish galleon the size of the Titanic. Masts like redwoods towered above me, and sails of a shimmering silver stretched for what seemed miles in the bright sun. To my immediate left, seated below the level of the deck, I saw the rowers Timash had mentioned, swaying to and fro to a beat I could barely hear, though they were but scant yards away. And beyond the rowers, beyond the limits of the ship itself...

...were the clouds. We sailed, without a doubt. We sailed the sky itself.

I stumbled forward as a heavy hand shoved me in the back.

"Enough gawking! Move along! We got a place for yah!" And I was herded to an open spot among the rowers and chained again into place...

My memories exhausted, I did not return to any conscious appreciation of my state. I rowed. My body rowed. Whither my mind had gone, I had not the wit to say.

Chapter 34
I Am Robbed

When my shift was over, I was reunited with Timash and introduced to my crewmates. We were in no condition to exchange polite greetings; our labors had pushed us well past the edge of exhaustion. I had fancied myself well-conditioned, and Timash— Timash was a gorilla!—but we fell limply to the deck the moment our jailors pushed us through the door to the "crew quarters"—a euphemism at best. Technically it was not even correct, since the real crew, those skilled "air sailors" who truly operated the ship, had their own separate and far superior quarters above decks.

We were slaves. We lived communally, always chained, rotated on and off the rowing details as our masters wished. We lived to work, and we only stopped when we died. These things I was to learn over time, but the first thing I learned was the *raison d'être* for this flying circle of hell: It was a prison, and all of the men around us were convicted criminals. This I had discovered very quickly indeed.

I awoke with the exceedingly unpleasant sensation that I had tried to eat a woolen blanket in my sleep. I rolled over, spitting our bits of Timash's fur, and banged into a wall. I didn't have to roll far.

My first sensation had been a bad taste, and my second had been pain, but the third was the most disturbing, as it stole upon me gently but insistently. As Timash rolled away from me—thank god, or he might have crushed me—the last feeling became at once more pronounced: I was cold. All over.

My clothes had been stolen while I slept.

Levering myself painfully into a sitting position, I tried to clear the dreams from my head and ignore the eyes I could feel upon me. Behind closed lids the pressure of foreign minds beat against my shields. Those too feeble to take my physical possessions were attempting to make do with the crumbs and tidbits of my unconscious mind. But they were weak, and I had overcome the dreaded telepathic virus. I shook them off like fleas. Their panicked feet beat a tattoo on the deck. Someone laughed, but it was dry, like a splintered stick. Suddenly, opening my eyes felt like the last thing I wanted to do.

We sat in a cleared space, away from other sleepers and away from the door. Had we been dragged to an open space to sleep or simply pulled out of the doorway so others would be saved the trouble of stepping over us? It did not matter, since we had most likely been robbed by the same good Samaritans who gave us a place to rest. Timash had been stripped and left on the floor even as had I; I shuddered to think of strangers' hands all over my senseless body. They had left me my shorts, but filched my coveralls and boots.

A low growl from behind me said that Timash had awoken. He had exhibited a more aggressive side since leaving Tahana City than I had seen before; I did not know if it was a sign of his continuing maturity (sometimes I had to remind myself that he was still much younger than I), or the loss of the civilizing influences he had known all his life. In either event, this seemed both the most obvious, and the least desirable, time for him to test his newfound capacity for anger.

Next to opening my eyes, confronting a outraged, half-naked

bull gorilla ranked as one of the worst choices in a day that had already reached calamitous proportions—and I had only just awakened.

I rotated, crablike, without getting up, hoping to avoid any more notice than was inevitable. Timash was more jumpy, his shoulders twitching with the thought of what he would do to the unfortunate soul he found wearing his clothes. I swallowed hard; my weeks in the city of the apes had not inured me to their behavior as much as I had thought. Still in the back of my mind they were the savage beasts of my own time, beating their breasts only when safely contained within iron bars. This ape had yet to begin beating his breast, but he wasn't separated from me by thick iron bars, either.

Many of the men who were awake at this moment had congregated toward the far end of the compartment, talking and arguing amongst themselves as men will in close quarters with no diversions. In the trenches of France, even with the closeness of sudden death—or perhaps because of it—men weakened by months of freezing weather and scarce food had suddenly erupted into riots over inconsequential playing cards or another man's picture from home. Sometimes only the shrieking of the incoming shells had stopped the madness. And sometimes the only way was to substitute another form of madness: Not all suicide charges could be laid to blame at the door of an incompetent rear-line command.

So I knew the gunpowder that lurked in a mob chained into a small space, and I knew that the fastest way to ignite them, to unify them against the newcomers in their midst, was to charge in. However righteous our anger, however strong our arms, we would be torn limb from limb.

This news was not welcomed by Timash, but I made him listen. I used my experience leading men to ease his brow and calm the twitching of his shoulders, but deep down, his still eyes burned. I told him to keep that fire banked, because sooner rather than later, we would need it. He asked me why.

"Because whoever stole my clothes also has the Library."

Now indeed my plight had surpassed the merely calamitous and traversed the realm of the catastrophic. Possession of the Library was a capital crime; even if it remained hidden from the Nuum, its possessor held the key to both the secret of my origin and to my ever returning home. Its retrieval was not only imperative, but must be accomplished in such a way that its true nature—its very existence, if possible—remained undiscovered.

"We should find some clothes," Timash suggested gently. "All we're going to do is draw attention to ourselves otherwise."

Forcing my other problems into the back of my mind, I nodded. Naked, we were marked. Clothed, we could begin to fit in.

"The men who stole ours must have had some before," I said. "Let's find them."

Timash smiled, showing fence rows of teeth. "Yes, let's. We'll want to give them back when the time comes."

Although lying in an exhausted stupor we must have appeared helpless—as we had been, and I reminded myself that we had been lucky to awaken at all—once we had gained our feet our true sizes became apparent to all. Never a large man, I was nonetheless the tallest of the galley slaves by several inches, and Timash outweighed any three of them. Any thought of further hazing evaporated, and even the crowd at the end of the compartment shifted, however reluctantly, to let us by. We kept a close eye out, but no one was wearing familiar clothing. Either it had been stolen by the crew—which I doubted, as the Library would then have been found and I would not be here—or the thieves were taking their turn up on deck.

New clothes we found without undue trouble, so worn and torn that they actually fit me after a fashion. Timash was forced to tie together a sort of loincloth. We turned next to learning the lay of the land. Timash volunteered to find us a tutor, and I let him. His method was simple and effective. He picked one of the loners lying pathetically against a wall and dangled him from one hairy paw.

"How do we get fed around here?"

The poor devil's eyes rolled and his jaw clacked like he was afraid Timash was about to feed upon *him*, and for a moment I had doubts myself. I looked around to see how the others were reacting, holding their distance with carefully averted eyes. But they were watching all right, and Timash was giving them a show they wouldn't forget. On impulse, I turned my back on him and stared at the others. After a moment, they turned their attention elsewhere. I kept on staring.

Within a few minutes, my friend had all of the information he was going to get, and I had marked in my mind several of our fellows who had flinched under my gaze, as well as two or three who hadn't. Timash and I retired to our "spot" to compare findings.

"The crew pretty much doesn't care what goes on down here, as long as nobody gets killed too often—it's too much trouble finding replacements."

"That's probably what happened to us. What about the captain? Is he the type who might listen to reason? Can we explain we don't belong here?"

"My friend Wince over there didn't think so, but then he strikes me as the type who keeps his head down. It's a lot safer that way. All he knows is that the captain holds the crew in an iron hand, and the crew likes to take it out on the rowers. There's a gang of about a dozen that runs this whole Hold—that's what they call it, the Hold. Wince says they used to call it the Hole, but I guess the boss down here wanted to make it sound a little better."

"Does this boss have a name?" I asked. "And more to the point, does he have our clothes?"

"Yes to both. He calls himself Skull." I stared, frankly

incredulous. "No kidding. Nobody knows his real name; he's been here about a year, and he beat the old boss to death the first night. According to Wince, he's a brute—bigger than me, even." He stretched his massive chest self-consciously, as if I needed any reminder. "Anything that comes down here that Skull wants, he takes, and that's what happened to our clothes. If we hadn't been so wasted, he would've have beaten us up first, but we saved him the trouble."

I could have read the thoughts dancing across Timash's brain without any telepathic powers at all. I bit back a grin and focused on our problem, lest he mistake my amusement for enthusiasm for an immediate pitched battle.

"We'll have our chance, my friend. If Skull realizes what the Library is, he won't rest until he knows how to use it—and if he thinks *I'm* going to tell him, he's in for a sorry surprise." I stopped for a moment, staring at the opposite wall. Even when you haven't a clue what to do next, it's best not to let your subordinates know. Leadership demands an air of mystery. "But we have to choose our battlefield. Right now he holds all the cards: numbers, experience—and he may get privileges for keeping the rowers in line."

"But we don't have a lot of time. He's sure to have discovered the Library by now—and when he gets back down here, he's gonna come right to you to find out what it is."

Slowly, I shook my head. "No, he won't. He'll be tired, and we'll be rested. His kind never strikes unless they have the advantage. He'll want to rest a while, perhaps wait for us to turn a shift upstairs, then pounce on us while we're weak…" I thought about those who had turned away rather than meet my eyes, and those who had not, and suddenly I had an inspiration. "Go back to Wince," I suggested, "and ask him how many of Skull's men are here right now."

The door at the far end of the Hold opened precisely when

Wince had predicted it would, and, again exactly as foreseen, Skull was the first man through. He was easy to spot: He was wearing my clothes.

"Do they look as ugly on me as they do on him?" I whispered to Timash.

"Worse," he assured me. Oh, but he was in a rare mood.

We sat atop a pyramid of five of Skull's gang. Three had been among those I spotted earlier; the remaining pair, part of the short-lived mob that saw crushing our insurrection as a chance to enter Skull's good graces. "Short-lived," I call it, because when the majority saw how quickly we dispatched their brave fellows, they melted away like an August snow. Our attack had been sudden, brutal, and totally unprovoked. And it had worked. Timash with his temper up was…remarkable.

Skull stopped short as the conversations around us halted and the stragglers drifted to the sides of the room. His dark eyes darted all about, his brain whizzing furiously as he assessed us, his unconscious men, and the mood of the room. Facing them, I could see what he could not; that he still held the obedience, if not the loyalty, of the fifty men who had served on his shift and had not seen our earlier victory. If he called upon them to charge, our triumph was short-lived, as well.

In an all-or-nothing toss, I made the most unexpected move I could think of.

Chapter 35
I Fight

"Skull! So pleasant to make your acquaintance at last!" With my hand outstretched and an entirely lunatic grin on my face, there wasn't a warrior in recorded history with the wit to utter the words that would bring me down. By the time I stopped, hand almost in his face, he had recovered enough to scowl. "Sorry about your men," I babbled on, "but we had a little fracas and we didn't know there were yours until it was all over. Some of the other fellows told us. Bad manners, I admit, but how were we to know?"

Up close, Skull was not the overwhelming specimen I had feared—to me. To his contemporaries, at a scant two inches short of six feet he was a giant of a man. He looked up at me, and it was easy to see he didn't like it. He bore a shock of dark, wild hair; I had expected him to be shaven bald. But I had also expected an older man—he was barely out of his teens, his eyes glaring with the hate not only of me, but at the loss of an entire world to which he believed himself entitled. He shook himself out of his stupor, his labor-hardened muscles shining with sweat. Here was a young man who did not intend to die a slave.

In an instant my trepidation was replaced by sorrow. But if I were to live, Skull's dream must end.

He picked out one of the bystanders and snapped his fingers. "What happened?"

"I told you," I interrupted. My plan depended on keeping Skull off-balance. "We got into an argument with some of your lads, and one thing lead to another, and... You know how it goes. If they'd only said they were with you, we'd have backed off straight away."

He turned his attention back to me. "Why? What's so special about me? You've never seen me before."

I shrugged foolishly. "Of course not. But it didn't take long to find out who was boss around here: Skull. So the last thing we wanted to do was get on your bad side. We were kind of hoping to get in with you, if you know what I mean."

"Yeah, I think I do." He gestured contemptuously to Timash. "Is that monkey man with you?"

Perhaps Skull wasn't the thinking man I had given him credit for being.

"Shh!" I waved him to keep his voice down, even though Timash had certainly heard. "I'm trying to keep him under control. If he had his way, he'd take you all on."

This was a challenge Skull could relate to. His chest swelled just like the ape's whom he was insulting.

"No, no!" I said quickly. "I'll take care of him." I turned around halfway, as far as I dared. "Timash, apologize to Skull."

"Ha!" He stood up, flexing his shoulders. "He's not worth it." And he sat down again. *Thank you.* "He's so weak you could fight him yourself."

I glanced back at Skull, panic all over my face, to see how he was taking it, then at Timash.

"Will you be quiet?" I pleaded. "This guy could tear my head off!"

"Yeah! No problem!" Skull chimed in, right on cue. He had taken the bait.

"Prove it," Timash demanded. The trap snapped shut—with Skull and me inside.

Up until now, our strategy had unfolded flawlessly. By luring Skull into a one-on-one challenge, we had neutralized his entire following. Timash could easily have crushed him, but for that very reason, had Timash challenged Skull, he would have been within his bully's rights to call down his whole mob—and Skull would never have challenged Timash.

At the same time, we had kept his thoughts away from the Library. Now, if I could only defeat him in single combat, the others would be forced to accept me as their leader—particularly with Timash acting as my enforcer. The only unknown factor was whether I *could* defeat him, and both our lives hung on the question.

I had never been a wrestler, but I had boxed once. I bent my knees slightly, fists raised to protect my face. Given my lack of experience, I intended to stay outside Skull's reach as much as possible, away from those hawser-like arms.

Skull had no such intentions. He partly turned, speaking to one of his lieutenants, then spun on me with no warning, charging and taking me in the midsection. We went down hard on the floor, with me underneath. I barely kept my head from hitting the deck with enough force to end the fight at once.

Pinning me down with his legs astraddle my body, Skull tried to seize me by the neck while I clumsily fought him off with my hands. Time after time I knocked his grasp away from me; time and time again he thrust at my throat and face. He rose on one knee, attempting to drive the other into my body, but he couldn't find the leverage.

Half-pinned, I couldn't wriggle my way entirely out of his grip, but I could outlast him, and when he let up the pressure I twisted onto my stomach, gathered my legs underneath me and heaved upward just as he interlaced his fingers under my jaw and pulled— but instead of fighting against him I went along with it, using his own leverage against him. We crashed to the deck again, but this time I was on top. I heard his head smack against the deck.

I rolled over again and crawled away, feeling the strain on my neck, back, and knees.

Deep in my hindbrain, a thought was tugging at my mental sleeve, but I could not spare the time. Skull rose, bloodlust in his eyes, and charged into me, knocking me back, but this time I tumbled, keeping my legs in so he could find no purchase, then pushed him away hard. He backpedaled off-balance toward his own crowd, who split down the middle and made no effort to aid him.

His next approach was slow, wary. I had been fortunate thus far; he was a brawler and I was not, but he had underestimated me. All of his earlier opponents had been specimens of modern man; I doubt he had ever faced a foe with my "primitive" physique. Formerly bright and eager, now his eyes were hooded and flat. At the start, an easy victory would have served his purposes: humiliation would have sufficed to keep me subordinate. But this had taken too long; even if he won, there would be doubters as to Skull's supremacy, those who would eye him speculatively, wondering if it was time for new leadership. Skull had decided I was to die.

That same old thought was back, tugging like a child who's seen a balloon-vendor at the zoo. Awaiting Skull's next move, I retreated a step, breathing deeply, trying to control my racing heart and mind. Into that microscopic oasis of calm the little thought raced—and then vanished, winking out like a shooting star, nothing left but a streak of enlightenment.

Like a wind-up doll in reverse, I let my arms relax, holding them ready but flexible, as though they were hoses filled with water. Somewhere deep inside me a new facet of the Library's teachings was sinking into place: It was as if I had just read a book on self-defense. Suddenly I knew every move required to bring Skull to his knees—hell, I knew a dozen ways to *kill* him.

But I also knew that there was a vast difference between memorizing an art and mastering it. As the Librarian had warned me, "Muscle memory can only be learned over time." It could take years of practice for my body to catch up to my mind—if I survived the next five minutes.

And Skull was tired of waiting for me to make another move. There was no more time. I made my decision and met him head-on.

We grappled again, he going right for the throat—and I let him. Left hand on my neck, he fought to close in with the right, but I seized it in both of mine, twisting backward and counter-clockwise simultaneously.

Skull screamed and let go, rolling to his right. He couldn't help it, unless he wanted his wrist broken. I kept up the pressure, forcing him backward, then down, and all the time he was howling in agony that only became worse if he hindered me in the slightest. I could have lead him anywhere with that grip, and I made sure they all saw it.

Then I let him go. He had not surrendered; I had not demanded it. But the fight was over. Skull could not go on. His damaged wrist would throb for days, and ache for weeks. He could not even protest when I told him I wanted my clothes back.

I handed Skull my rags, making a point of looking him in the eye.

"You can wear these. And when your hand is healed, come talk to me."

He took them hesitantly. It wasn't the retribution he had expected, and, I don't doubt, better treatment than his predecessor had received. But it wasn't in me to kill the man in cold blood, aside from the fact that I wanted to keep as low a profile as possible. It occurred to me that if he did come to see me in a few days' time, I should have something to say. I put it aside. Our lives were not our own. It probably wouldn't matter.

Skull grasped my arm and muttered something puzzling under his breath. "It's all yours now. Hope you can live with it." Before I could seek clarification, he had retired to a far corner.

I slipped back into my familiar, if hated, Nuum garb, and casually slipped my hand into my deep pocket.

The Library wasn't there. It wasn't in any of my pockets. It was gone.

Chapter 36
The Dark Lady

Even before the cold, clammy hand of fatal dread had removed itself from my shoulder, I was examining the problem from all angles. Skull I suspected and quickly discarded; I had only moments before stripped him naked. Had the Library been in his pocket then, it would be in mine now. Nor could it have fallen out; it would have made a noise and I would have seen it.

Timash must have noticed my expression, because he came over and in a low voice asked me what was wrong. I told him.

"Skull?"

"No. If he had it he would have threatened me with exposure before he gave up his position. It must have been lost earlier. God," I said fervently, "I hope it's not on the deck somewhere."

"Unless Garm was to slip on it and break his neck."

This offhand remark might have proven sufficient to break the tension had not the door opened, revealing, with uncanny timing, the scarred visage of the hated Garm himself. I confess I jumped. What if that hideous soul harbored an exceptional telepath?

If it did, he hid it well. "Skull! The captain wants to see you!"

When no response followed, he took the time to look over the room. Skull huddled in a corner while I stood in center stage, my own clothes upon my back. "Oh," he said stupidly to me. "So that's how it is. Get your scrawny backside topside." He grinned at his own imagined witticism. "Move!"

I was escorted with no gentle grace up the ladders through the deck and into the aft housing where Garm and the real crewmen lived. Even here the motif of ancient times was continued, and the real machinery, as must exist somewhere for the comfort of these men, was so cunningly disguised that had these sailors been Thorans, the Nuum would have found nothing to alarm them. For my taste, the devotion to realism was taken to an extreme: I jammed a splinter into my hand on one of the ladders. Garm looked at me, but I merely pulled out the wood and kept climbing.

We walked and climbed for several minutes, the ship being, as I have said, of surprising size. My ears strained for sounds that were not there. Missing was the rolling of the ship at sea, but also the wind of the ship of the air. Had I not known by the evidence of my own eyes that we were some thousands of feet in the air, I would have sworn that we were entombed.

When we reached a level with no ladder leading further upward, I surmised we were nearing our destination, and so it was with little surprise that I was pulled to a halt at a wooden double door at the end of the short corridor. It was, in fact, the only door on this level. Garm rapped on it respectfully. At an unheard signal, he opened it.

"I brought the chief rower, Cap'n, like you asked." He must have received some further signal, for he turned to me. "Come on in. The cap'n wants to talk to you."

Given Timash's description of the "iron hand" and the coincidence of this summoning with the disappearance of the Library, for a brief instant I entertained the thought of jumping Garm for his weapon and taking my chances. I felt my legs tense to leap when the overseer, perhaps clairvoyant from his years as a jailor, dropped one hand on the handle of his whip. I relaxed. My window of insanity had closed.

Once more I had come upon a critical turning point in my life, and passed it by all unknowing, but still alive. Ignoring the crawling feeling in the flesh between my shoulder blades, I strode with a confidence I did not feel past Garm and into the captain's cabin.

The captain whistled. "You're right, Garm. He's a big one. And handsome, too."

Captain "Iron Hand" was Marella.

Garm wedged past me and muttered something in Marella's ear.

"Already?" she murmured, then held out a hand. "You owe me." Grumbling, he removed something from his sash and gave it to her. She placed it in a pocket of her own outfit and smiled.

Their by-play allowed me a few precious seconds in which to assimilate my surroundings, all of which passed in a dizzy blur — a spacious cabin, sparsely furnished with heavy chairs, a bed, and a desk Timash could sleep on; in place of art, tapestries and fabrics hung and thrown in an apparently random pattern—none of which remained upon my mind for more than an instant as my eyes were irresistibly drawn back to the most arresting object in the room: Marella.

The romantic interludes in my life have not been many; Casanova wooed more women in a week than I did in a year. But for all that, when I did fall my tastes and my affections were constant, and nothing in what my eyes beheld touched that place in my heart where only my lost Hana dwelled...but with God as my witness I had never imagined that the grease-streaked technician we rescued from an underground battlefield could metamorphose herself like this.

I stared, I admit it. In all likelihood I stared with my mouth open like a farm boy at a coronation. I could not help it.

Gone was the grease, the filth of the pit and the fatigue that had turned her skin papery and her eyes baggy. Now her black hair was washed through with strands of auburn that lit one by one as she swept her curls from her face. In dress, however, she had changed but little, favoring a deep red jumpsuit with a white stripe down the leg, rather than the fantastical motley that attired her crew. She tucked her suit legs inside of her thigh-high boots, rather than outside as was the style, a simple change which tightened and smoothed the fabric just enough to make her gender obvious to the most casual observer. Faint grease spots on her uniform marked long use, but I found them comforting, a reminder of the woman I had known and fought with days ago. Against her right hip lay the ever-present short staff, on her left perched a phase-pistol. I wondered—did that make her right- or left-handed?

"Garm," she said. "Wait outside."

While I stood, my mouth closed at last, she circled me like a shopper appraising a well-dressed model—or a shark her next meal. I felt a now-familiar tingle between my shoulder blades as she passed out of my sight. My questions scrambled all over each other trying to get out, but she had not yet given me a sign of her intentions.

When she strolled into my sight again, she sighed. "Sit down, Keryl. I know you're exhausted." I thanked her and did as she suggested. "I also know you've got a lot of questions," she blurted before I could ask, "but you have to wait. It'll be faster if I just tell you in my own way, and I don't want a lot of rumors starting. I have enough of that now."

My eye was caught by a pitcher on a side table, dewy with condensation. The mere sight made my mouth water. When Marella saw where I was looking, she flushed with embarrassment and poured me a glass of violet liquid without asking. I drained it. She smiled.

"That should take the edge off, in any case." Her hand began to make random circles on a tabouret next to her chair, and she watched in fascination.

"Perhaps you should try some, then."

She jerked her hand away. "I'm sorry. I'm just sitting here

wondering how much I can afford to tell you. I mean—well, after what we've been through, I shouldn't have to ask, but I need to know if I can trust you."

I rolled this over in my mind. True enough that we had been comrades-in-arms, and she owed me her life more than once, but all that seemed to me to have been tossed by the wayside since we came to this ship, and I said so.

Suddenly she stood and stretched, her arms straight out to her sides. I had to look away quickly; it had been a long time since I had seen Hana, and Marella's posture made the fabric of her jumpsuit stretch exceedingly tightly. If she had ever done that in front of the crew, I doubt she would still be captain.

"All right," she said abruptly, as though physical activity had released her worries. As she spoke she paced the cabin. "First of all, my name isn't Marella. It's Maire, Maire Por Foret." She pronounced it "Marie." Another of the Library's deep-seeded lessons floated unbidden to the surface of my brain: "Por" was high-ranking Nuum nobility, roughly equivalent to a baroness. I blinked. What other surprises was this woman about to unveil? "This sky-barge, the *Dark Lady*, is mine. I own it, as well as being its captain.

"I know what you're thinking: Sky-barge, female captain, pleasure ship. Crewed by convicts, but its only real purpose is so that I can fly around Thora doing whatever I damn well please because I can't find a husband. And you know something?" She stopped in front of me. "You'd be absolutely right."

She resumed her story along with her pacing. "Except that it's not that I *can't* find a husband, I just don't want to. Why should I? I've got my ship, my crew, and a whole world that doesn't have to conform to the Nuum way of doing things." I blinked. "Don't be shocked. You know as well as I do that our hold on this planet is tenuous, at best. Just look at the Vulsteen."

"I would rather not, actually, if I had a choice."

She sniffed. "You and me both. But I didn't have a choice.

That's what I'm getting to. I set down in that deserted city to do some hunting. We'd spotted the thunder lizards from the air, but I'm not into big game—I thought maybe I could bag a blood bat or a plains lion."

"Or a breen?"

Maire shot me a look of utter horror. "Are you crazy? Not if I was shooting from up *here*. Anyway, to get to the point, somebody stole my shuttle and left me there."

"Who?"

"I don't know. I was hunting alone—you know, big girl, big gun...big idiot—and somebody smacked me from behind. When I woke up my gun was gone. They left me my baton, for what it was worth. I was looking for shelter when the Vulsteen caught my trail, and that's when you found me."

"Someone was trying to kill you."

"Uh-huh. I've been questioning the crew. The word got around that I'd gone missing. They mounted search parties, but they couldn't look in the dark because of the animals. By the time they came back, the Vulsteen had caught up to us and we were underground. If they hadn't spotted you eventually, they probably would have given me up for dead and left."

"So that was why you kept looking at the sky."

"Uh-huh. Whoever dumped me had to make a really good-looking search before they gave me up—even then my father would have had heads flying—but I was hoping I could get some idea what was going on if I could see them before they saw me."

I reached for the pitcher again and poured another drink. "But we spoiled your plans. What was that all about, anyway? Do your men often swoop out of the sky and kidnap unsuspecting passersby?" She gave me a puzzled look, as if my question were entirely unexpected. I had blundered into some kind of faux pas, and I scrambled to change the subject. "That reminds me," I resumed quickly. "What happened to Harros? I know he was shot, but when I woke up in the dungeon I thought he'd be around."

The puzzlement on her face immediately gave way to grave concern. She walked over to one of the tapestries, and where I had thought would be only a wall I saw a room-sized alcove containing a large bed. On it lay Harros.

He was unconscious, his breathing regular but shallow. As I grew nearer I could see a clear gelatinous substance clumped around his right temple, a plasm bandage. Technically alive, it formed over a wound, feeding on bacteria and impurities so that it cleansed at the same time as it closed cuts and supplied nutrients by being absorbed slowly into the body. Once the injury was healed, if the plasm had not been completely absorbed, it simply dried into a powder and fell away. A faint scar showed through the gel.

"One of the men had his phase pistol set on high, unlike Durrn—the man who shot you. I don't know if he was aiming for me and hit Harros by mistake, or if he tried to pull his shot... It only grazed him, but he almost died before we could get him back on board. With all those witnesses the killer couldn't do anything but go along and follow my orders. So I know some of the crew is still loyal; I just don't know which ones."

"Is he going to be all right?"

"In a few days." She nodded sadly. "I felt responsible, so I had him brought here. Now you know what I meant about rumors."

I knew what she meant, all right, but I suspected also what she was not saying. Impertinent as it seemed to me, Maire had our lives in her hands, and I needed to know what she intended to do about us—her concern so far being subsumed to all appearances by her own self-interest. So I choked back my manners and prepared to be rude.

"It's going to be rough on him when he has to give up that bed for the rowers' quarters," I said with simulated pity.

"There's plenty of time for that," she replied brusquely. She took hold of the tapestry, giving me a meaningful look. We left Harros to sleep.

"There's something I have to know about you," she said. Standing directly in front of me, in height she came almost to my nose. Her eyes were dark and direct, challenging. "Why are two Nuum and an ape prowling around deserted cities alone with no guns and no transport other than a crushed groundcar? Come to think of it, where did that ape come from?"

Given the variety of humanoid mammals I had seen back in Vardan, I was surprised by the latter question, but as I could not answer it in any case, I ignored it and concentrated on the former. Harros and I had spent much time in the groundcar working on our story while the empty miles drifted by.

"We were part of an infantry unit detailed to fight the natives at a research station in the jungle," I said. "We came from Vardan on an airship. Most of the post was wiped out by the natives, but Harros and I escaped."

Her eyes widened, to my great appreciation. "You were at the research station? The entire Thoran newsnet talked about nothing else for a week!" I started to speak but she turned her back on me, pacing. Abruptly she turned again. "Escaped, huh? So where'd you pick up the ape?"

Damn. She was not going to let it go. "He helped us get away. The natives had him caged up. We freed him and brought him along. He's useful, times being what they are."

If she disbelieved a fraction of what I was telling her, she was a great actress, because she didn't show it. She began pacing again, and stopped.

"Garm tells me you've already taken over the Hold." She waited for my reply, but since the answer was self-evident, I said nothing. After a moment she went on, conceding a point to me. "You have any idea what that means?"

"As far as I can tell, it means that the next man you kidnap is probably going to try to pound my head in my sleep, so I should sleep with one eye open and the other half-closed."

"Well, yes...but more than that it means that it's your job to keep that bunch of killers, thieves, and cradle-robbers in line—and keep them from killing each other. That's your job as far as the rest of the crew is concerned, anyway—but I also need you. I need you to keep your eyes and ears open, to try to find out who's with me and who's against me." Her voice softened and her eyes would have melted a Prussian regiment. "Will you help me, Keryl? You've already saved my life twice; you're getting pretty good at it."

"And what about us? We weren't sentenced here; when do we get to leave?"

"You have a choice, my friend. You can either stay with me, or I can set you down at the next military outpost."

Chapter 37
Conspiracy

"I just can't figure her out." I had explained my conversation with Maire to Timash in low tones. I had to give him credit for keeping his surprise at her identity to himself.

My friend shook his head in sympathy. "Women. They never change."

I glanced at him to see if he realized just what he had said, and the blank look on his face was too comical to resist. I started laughing and I could not stop. It took only a moment for Timash to see why, and he laughed until he was bent over with tears running down his face. While it may have owed its origin more to hysterical fatigue than real humor, our emotional release was real.

Evidently laughter of any kind was not a common occurrence in the Hold. (I made a mental note to try to change the name of this place. It reminded me too much of the pit.) Those whose survival mechanism consisted of staying out of the way of their larger mates stole surreptitious looks of confusion our way, while their bolder comrades—in particular those who had formerly been allied with Skull—watched us with open disdain. One or two grinned wolfishly, perhaps believing that this existence had already worn away our sanity and openly awaiting their chance to regain the throne of the slaves.

Our mirth exhausted, we leaned against each other for a moment until we regained our breath. I took the opportunity to whisper into Timash's ear.

"I've got to get out of here and search the ship. You stay here and keep order. You think you can handle it?"

Very softly, he cracked his knuckles.

No one challenged me when I left, not that I had expected anyone to do so, but it still felt akin to sneaking into the dons' kitchen for a midnight snack. Trying to adopt a purposeful attitude, I straightened my aching back but avoided making eye contact with any crewmen. It seemed to work: perhaps they simply assumed I had been summoned to the captain again—or perhaps word of what had befallen Skull had traveled above-decks: Even among the Nuum, I was a formidable physical specimen.

I say this not in vanity, but simply as truth: As I had noticed soon after my arrival, the men of this age, whether through lack of physical labor, deliberate malnutrition, or simply evolution, were physically smaller than we of the 20th century. Even the Nuum, an alternate offshoot given generations of offworld development and access to better food and medicines, were smaller than I on the average. Harros was really the only Nuum I had known who rivaled my size, and I believe that I yet surpassed him in strength, although it had never come to a test.

All this time I had been wandering the corridors at random while attempting to look as though I had a definite goal. That could not last forever. For one thing, I had my work shift soon, and I doubted my status as the captain's pet rower would protect me from Garm if I missed my assignment. For another thing, someone was eventually going to ask me a question I could not answer, or find me in a restricted area, which would see me hauled back before Garm, if they didn't simply toss me over the side.

Garm had explained to us the first day, in his "orientation speech," that a force field rose up from the hull on either side of the ship to a point about ten feet above the gunwale. Its purpose was to keep anyone from falling out accidentally (he made it very clear that "anyone" was defined as the captain and crew), should the airship encounter unexpectedly rough weather. He had further intimated that it would not prevent the *purposeful* exit of a man from the ship, provided he were "assisted" by Garm. Then he snapped his whip and screamed "Row!"

Naturally I had carefully memorized each bend in every corridor and the placement of all the cross-passages I traversed, and so I set about to return to the Hold in complete confidence. Within five minutes I was totally lost; with the exception of the captain's quarters and where I really needed to be, I had no idea where I found myself. A vision of Garm treating me to a panoramic view of the earth from five thousand feet in the sky was beating down the doors of my mind.

Ahead of me stood one of the *Dark Lady's* few obvious modern features, a lift for transporting heavy cargo and machinery from the deck to the holds, and vice versa. If I could reach the deck, I could find my way back to my berth—or just stay there, as my shift would doubtless begin soon. As long as I stayed out of Garm's way he probably would not deign to notice me.

Once more my confidence soared. Every elevator I had ever seen on Thora operated the same way—I was as good as home. I stepped on, pressed the button to go up—and felt my stomach rise to my throat as I was dropped further into the bowels of the great airship.

There was no telling what was at the bottom of the shaft, but I needed no genius to know that rowers were not expected to be found there. My breath came shallowly as I waited for the car to halt; it was an express, and there were no controls for canceling its descent or stopping at another level. Finally it came to a gentle landing and the doors opened.

In fact, the doors both before and behind me opened: the cargo lift was designed to be entered from either side. My hand, hovering on the button, froze when I heard a voice outside:

"About time! Somebody should do something about the elevators on this tub."

"Leave it alone. The longer we take to get this regulator upstairs the longer till we get off."

I could not see either of the speakers; they were hidden behind a massive piece of machinery that was inching its way toward me. It would plainly fill the car. Quickly I tiptoed out and hid behind quietly humming heavy machinery until the doors closed once more.

Trapped in the nether reaches of the *Dark Lady*, late for my rowing shift, and trespassing in restricted departments, it was the furthest thought from even my impulsive mind to stir out of sight from the lift shaft until I saw those doors open again and an empty car awaiting me. Even then I ran the risk of being seen as I emerged, but there was no help for it. I must think on my feet.

It was, as I say, the furthest thought from my mind. Fate had other ideas: I was not alone.

I heard more voices in the distance, sensed other minds communicating, but they were on the far side of the lift shaft, and I relaxed. As I could barely hear them, I assumed they were working at the other end of the compartment; even if they heard the elevator return they would not see me get inside. I crept back to the lift button and had my finger over it when I heard one man's voice rise a bit above the others, and another quickly shushed him.

My "impulsive" mind took over. Whatever they were talking about, they wanted no one else to hear.

Drifting silently down neat rows of the identical humming machines, I satisfied in passing one curiosity: According to a warranty panel I saw in route, these huge devices were the anti-gravity motors that kept us all from making a big hole in the clouds. The Library had seen fit to give me only the loosest possible definition of their theory, so I had been inclined to dismiss them, much like the airplanes of my own age, as a convenient fantasy as long as they worked. If they ever stopped working, I would have wings to fly by myself ere very long.

The voices had resumed, and now that I had an idea of their location, I was able to hear their words with relative ease. The trouble was, their thoughts, forming the bulk of their conversation, were completely hidden.

I wondered if the anti-gravity motors' strong radio-fields interfered with thought transmission; the fact that the conspirators had chosen this spot to make their plans certainly lent credence to my theory. It was damnable luck, since my brain structure rendered my own thoughts practically invisible unless I wished otherwise, which meant under other circumstances I could have eavesdropped from scant yards away with little or no risk of discovery. But to lurk too closely courted disaster should they suddenly decide to break off their meeting and turn a corner right into me.

On the chance that the interference might be lessened if I could get alongside the radio-fields rather than amongst them, I sought out the bulkhead. I found some improvement, but not enough. I realized with disgust I would have to be *outside* the ship before I had any chance to "overhear" them.

Suddenly I squinted at a spot a few yards ahead of me on the bulkhead. I thought I saw door in the wall: it turned out to be a maintenance hatch. Attached to a cleat bolted to the bulkhead was a stout rope and harness. The door, designed to be used under emergency conditions, was manually operated. I donned the harness, slipped open the door and let myself out.

Bracing my feet against the ship, I slid the door closed as far as I could. As aircraft go, sky-barges are quite ponderous; the wind was no more than I could easily handle, nor did I think the breeze would alert the men inside, shielded from it as they were by the boxy generators. And even though my ears were now useless, I could understand almost every word they broadcast.

"—night," one of them was saying. I did not know the crew

well enough to distinguish their "voices," so their identities remained a mystery. But if I could just divine their plans...

"What about the rowers?"

"What about them?"

"I mean the ones that came on board with her. The Nuum's already sent Skull down to the mat, and what's goin' on with that ape-thing? I ain't never seen nothin' like him before."

Several others joined in agreeing with his last comment. Perhaps bringing Timash with me had been a mistake after all. I needed anonymity, and he prevented that on sight. No—without him I'd be dead already. For better or worse, he was along for the ride.

"Never mind them," the first man, apparently the ringleader, answered. "It's under control. If they get in the way..." I suddenly caught that over-the-side image once more. In my present position, it was quite uncomfortable. "That's it. Let's get topside before somebody gets suspicious."

"Say, wait a second," one of his henchmen objected. "How do we know Farren is going to pay us when the job is done?"

I almost lost my grip on the rope.

His boss chuckled. "You see this ship?"

"Yeah."

"That's how we're gettin' paid. When the job's done, we send Farren a note. We don't see him, he don't see us. He ain't even worried we're gonna finger him, 'cause who'd believe us? Instead we take this sweet little crate way up north somewhere, change a few registrations, and she's ours. To do with what we please."

"Like what?"

"You'd be surprised. You will be, if you don't get your backside moving and I toss you over the side!"

That broke up the meeting in a hurry. I hung there a long time waiting for them all to take the lift and disperse. Farren! What had he to do with Maire? Why did he want her dead? And who were the plotters scurrying about the ship awaiting the order to do his bidding? I was to discover the answer to this last question rather sooner than I expected and far sooner than I would have liked.

As I reached for the hatch to haul myself back inside, it suddenly swung open to reveal the toothy grin of Porky, the pilot who had flown Durrn's shuttle.

"Ah ha!" he laughed. "I thought I felt a breeze in there! And lookee here, they always said you couldn't do no fishing from a sky-barge! I guess they didn't have the right kind o' hook!"

His knife flashed in the sun, blinding me as it fell.

Chapter 38
Attacked by Night

At the very moment the door had slid open, I had gathered my legs underneath me in preparation for a leap—I knew that whoever was on the other side could not mean me well—so when Porky lunged at me, I pushed myself away from the side of the ship as hard as I could.

The rope on which I was suspended was not long, but I swung out far enough that he missed me on his first try. I quickly blinked away the spot in front of my eyes, and when he stabbed at me again I caught his arm at the wrist.

Porky leaned out of the hatch, straining to reach me with the knife in his right hand while he held on to the hatch with his left. I was stronger, but I was also hanging in a harness by no more than a stout rope, with no leverage. He could not press downward, and I could not climb up. Had he merely wanted to catch me, he could have left me hanging, called for aid, and seen me tossed overboard, but he was in this for the thrill. He would see me dead by his own hand.

But it was not to be. In a moment I saw the brutally simple—and brutally necessary—solution to my problem: I stopped pushing on his arm, and without letting loose my grip, I pushed myself once more into space. It was not far, but it was enough to unbalance Porky. He tumbled out of the hatch, and I let go.

I hear his scream to this day.

Fortunately, I was alone in this macabre honor; no one else marked Porky's death. Clambering back into the ship, I stowed the gear I had used and made all haste to return to decks I knew better. I decided to remain in the Hold through my rowing shift, using the time to fabricate a plausible story. My situation was uncertain. My duties here *might* outweigh my rowing responsibilities; at least, I could say that was how I understood them, and although it might earn me a lash or two, I doubted Maire would let it go any further. On the other hand, if I were to appear on deck now, any chance remark might bring my guilt to my face and that would be the end of me.

When at long last my shift-mates did come back, I found myself doubly fortunate: Not only did my status evidently grant me a certain grace in fulfilling more common duties—at least as far as Garm would admit in front of the others—but upon my failure to return at the proper time, Timash had concocted a story to cover my absence, a story which so closely resembled that which I had fabricated myself as to render any dissimilar details insignificant.

I filled him in on the conversation I had overheard as soon as I was confident we were safe. I omitted any mention of Porky. Best if Timash were as surprised as the rest when he came up missing.

"Do you think we'd better warn Marella—I mean, Maire?" Timash had not spoken to her since her transmogrification, and so found it harder to reconcile than I.

"No, it wouldn't do any good. She already knows that there is a plot against her—what she does not know is who, and I can't shed any light there. The only people she can trust are you, me, and Harros, and she doesn't know us very well, either."

Timash took on a guilty look. "Oh, I forgot! I saw Harros a while ago. He was walking around the afterdeck. He's got some plasm bandages on his head, but he looks all right."

I sighed. "Thank God. I was worried about him." I paused to consider. "We can presume that Maire will tell him about the plot, and that he'll help look after her. No one will suspect an invalid of being a bodyguard."

"How much of a bodyguard can he be? He's not armed. He looks like he can barely walk."

"You're right. But this battle won't be won through force of arms—at least not ours, since we don't have any. We have to think our way through. The assassins know that Maire knows about them, but they don't know that we do, too."

Our conference was abruptly cut short by a ruckus against the far wall. One of the rowers was attempting to bully another into giving up his rags. The victim huddled in a corner to shelter himself from the his tormentor's kicks while holding desperately onto what remained of his thin clothing. This was exactly why Maire allowed me to lord it over my fellows. I told Timash to stay put while I took care of the matter.

I had intended only to seize the bully by the scruff of his neck and push him on his way, but even as I reached him he hauled back and delivered his victim a vicious kick. The huddled wretch whimpered in pain but would not give up his tattered prize. His tormentor angrily grabbed for it again. I grabbed him first and spun him about.

He was a Thoran, as were all the rowers save Timash and me; I did not know him. I did not care to know him. At that moment, he represented to me all the strong—the Nuum, the Vulsteen, the *Dark Lady's* crew—who had wreaked their will upon the weak—Thorans, rowers, and me—since I arrived in this godforsaken century. When he saw me his eyes went wide and his wet lips began to blubber in fear. He wanted desperately to form the words that might save him from his just fate, but I never gave him the chance.

Slowly and methodically, I beat him. For Hana, I beat him. For Porky, I beat him. And for that nameless little mass of rags, I beat him even more. The rest of them watched, not the way they had watched me fight Skull, with bated anticipation, but with the horrified fascination of a man witnessing a landslide burying a distant village.

I was very careful not to kill him. That was outside the bounds. I backhanded him as often as I used my fists, so that the blows that did not land with brute force enough to fell him nonetheless blasted him with my contempt. In the end it was not nearly the beating I had intended to administer when first I clapped hands on him. It had been transformed from my own just vengeance into a horrific form of theater. When I was done, in what was probably only a few minutes, I let him lie in his own blood. No one approached him, either to help or to harm. The look in my eye assured that no one would.

"That," I said evenly, pointing to the corner where his former victim still cowered, "will never happen again."

The unfortunate I had rescued covered his eyes and cowered when I approached. It may have been an act—I had seen him watching me through his rags—but it suited me. If he was an actor, I was the director.

"Who are you, old man?" I asked.

He uncovered himself before he spoke, perhaps as a sign of rude respect.

"Wince, sir." Then he bowed his head again as though expecting new blows. I recognized him, now that I saw his face. Wince had been the man Timash had interrogated the other day when we awoke to find our clothes stolen. He was one of the periphery of men who, although sentenced as rowers, were completely unfit for the job. As far as I could tell, even Garm was content to leave them be, devolving their rowing duties onto someone else.

"Buck up, Wince," I said as I might have to a newly-arrived private a million years ago. "Nobody's going to bother you now. Neither you nor anyone else."

Wince muttered something that might have been thanks, or a

blessing, or just indigestion. I left it at that. Both he and his attacker had played their roles. I was finished with them, but later I noticed that Wince and several of the other "borderline" cases had moved their sleeping spots rather closer to my own.

As I walked back to where Timash waited—even he had not dared interfere with my lawgiving—I heard angry, low voices across the room where Skull and a few of his hangers-on still congregated. One of them was remonstrating with him, but I could not tell what they were saying. Skull put an end to the argument with a few violent words and an emphatic gesture. He looked at me, and I met his gaze, but he said nothing and turned back to his fellows.

Astonishingly, it was the next morning before anyone seemed to realize for sure that Porky was not on the *Dark Lady*. Even then it seemed not to create the storm I had feared, due evidently to Porky's lack of universal regard among the crew. Rumors of card games he had won too easily not only explained this feeling but also contributed heavily to the most popular theories as to why he was no longer with us. In any case, his disappearance had been noticed so far after the fact that no one would think to link to it any unexplained absence of mine.

I grew more bold in my explorations of the ship. As long as I stayed off the deck and out of the control areas, no one objected. I do not know if this was due to my slightly elevated status or just because none of the rowers had ever bothered to leave the Hold before, but I welcomed the opportunity to familiarize myself with my surroundings. If ever again arose the necessity to trespass on forbidden ground, I wanted to know my way about.

Nowhere, however, did I find a trace of the Library or a clue as to its whereabouts. I had to conclude that it was in someone's possession, probably the captain's. Why I had not been summarily seized I did not know, unless it were due to my rapidly-fading Nuum disguise. Time, immersion, dirt, and hazardous travel had all scourged my formerly red hair; it was quickly reverting to its natural yellow, and my beard was growing out as well. I was plainly not a redhead, as I had pretended, but since none marked upon it and there was nothing I could do to prevent it, I shrugged and let Nature take her course.

When I was not seeking the Library, rowing, or sleeping, Timash and I were concocting and discarding plans to aid the captain in the event of another attempt on her life—assuming that we were in any position to help her. Harros I had seen walking the deck with her on occasion. He waved, but we never spoke and if he was destined to take his place on the oar benches, it was not made known to me.

"I would've thought that if they were going to do something, they'd've done it by now," Timash whispered to me one night as the rest of the men were scattered about wrapped in their blankets. Some moaned in their sleep; it was a sound you either became used to or you persuaded the poor devil to be quiet. It reminded me of the trenches, but at least here I was dry. "The way you described that conversation you overheard—" he lowered his voice even further— "I thought they were getting ready to move."

"I think they were," I hissed. "Perhaps Porky's death put them off their plan."

"You think he was one of them?"

I could feel the heat of his gaze in the dark. I cursed myself for a fool, forgetting that I had not told him what I knew of Porky's last moments. Even now there might be some advantage to his ignorance.

"It makes sense," I said next to his ear. "It's too big a coincidence otherwise."

There was a silence, and then: "You know, if I was planning something, I'd be watching us—I mean you and me. We came on board with Maire. There's no telling what she might have told us. For all they know we could've smuggled guns on board."

I thought that unlikely, since Harros and I had been

unconscious, but he had a point. Could the plotters *afford* to ignore us? And if not, what would they be doing?

Nearby a man coughed in his sleep. Suddenly the dark was filled with menacing phantoms, assassins hunting our blood while their comrades played Macbeth on the night-cloaked upper decks. Placing a finger over Timash's lips, I quietly lead him outside to the corridor.

"The only way to watch us in the Hold would be to have one of the men spy on us," I explained. "Out here, since you and I talk mostly with spoken words instead of telepathy, they won't be able to eavesdrop."

"But who would they use? Skull?"

I shook my head impatiently. "No, not Skull. He wouldn't be malleable; he'd want something in return. Besides, Skull is never near me. They would need someone who could stay nearby but never be noticed. Someone inconspicuous, on the periphery."

The light dawned in my friend's eyes. "Someone on the periphery?"

As I ducked back inside the Hold, my quarry tried to hunker down and feign sleep, but his mental activity gave him away. It stood out among the real sleepers' like the beam from a lighthouse. I clamped one hand over his mouth and dragged him outside, pinning him against a bulkhead.

"Who are they?"

Wince's gaze jumped back and forth between Timash's face and my own. Neither seemed to offer the solace he sought. His thin tongue rubbed his papery lips.

"They'll kill me! They'll throw me over the side like they did Porky!"

"They killed Porky?" Timash demanded.

Wince nodded rapidly. "They musta! He was in it with 'em..."

Confusion to the enemy, I thought. "Listen to me, Wince. If they catch you, they'll toss you overboard. But what do you think the gang inside would do if I told them you were a spy?"

Even in the dim light I could see his face pale. We towered over him.

"You can't! That—that's your job...you gotta protect us! The captain said so!" He was trembling, almost crying.

I laughed softly. "The captain's the one they're planning to kill, Wince... Do you think she's going to care what happens to you?" I stole a meaningful glance toward the door to the Hold. "If I go back in there, the boys are going to throw you off the ship—one piece at a time."

Timash bared his teeth. That was enough.

"All right! They're gonna do it tonight! Midnight! Just don't tell 'em I told you!"

"*Who?*"

"Durrn! Durrn and Garm and some of the others! Maybe six, eight at most. Please don't tell 'em I told you."

I ignored the little traitor. Turning to Timash, I said:

"Stay here with him to make sure he doesn't leave. I've go to warn Maire and Harros. If they see she's on guard, they'll abort the plan and we can figure out what to do before they try again."

Knowing Timash, he would have argued if I gave him the time, so I did not. The fastest way reach Maire's cabin was not the way Garm had taken me, but across the deck. I climbed the nearest ladder so fast in the scant light of the ship's lamps it was a wonder I didn't dash my brains out on the ceiling.

Even that seemed bright in comparison to the deck, where the stars and moon were blanked out by a thick layer of upper-level clouds. The lamps here were few and far between, but since I had never walked the deck at night before I did not know if it was because they were designed that way, or if the assassins—mutineers, really—had turned them off. I made what haste I could in the dark, relying on my ears and my mind to detect any lookouts left to deal with unwitting witnesses.

I was at the foot of the stairs leading to the afterdeck when I heard a faint sound behind me. I froze, but it was not repeated. I put my foot on the step—and was suddenly struck from behind!

Some inner sense warned me at the last instant, and I ducked, taking an otherwise fatal blow on my shoulder. Blindly I rushed my opponent, but he sidestepped, tripping me up. Off-balance, I whirled and my spine slammed into the railing. My head snapped backward and encountered nothing—the force field had been turned off! Nothing but the railing kept me from following Porky those last five thousand feet to the ground.

Before I could clear my head, two hands grabbed me by the throat, cutting off my air and bending me back over the edge.

"I've been wanting to do this for a long time, but that damned ape of yours would never leave you alone! Farewell, Charles!"

The fingers tightened around my windpipe—the fingers of a man who knew my real name—*and who spoke English!*

Chapter 39
Mutiny

I knew that whispered voice—through the blood roaring in my ears, I *knew* it, but its low hiss disguised it and the onrushing darkness of death threatened to crash down on me in a wave so high that no other thought could be entertained but to focus on the glimmering, flickering candlelight that was my own mortality.

With desperate strength I struck back, but my foeman was no spindly Vulsteen or strength-deprived Nuum, but a creature with arms as powerful as those of any rower on this ship and fingers that choked away my air and my life. Low on my throat, they triggered my gag reflex over and over, what oxygen had been trapped inside me bursting against my blocked windpipe like an insane case of hiccups. I was convulsing with each aborted breath; the blackness of the night actually brightening as purple and blue inexorably filled my eyes with visions of asphyxiation. Still I beat fruitlessly against his body and arms, but with each passing second my blows were fading…

And then he was gone.

For long moments, retching and gasping, I could do nothing, and still the roaring in ears would not stop—but that was not what I heard. Gulping down the last remnants of my bile with all the precious air I could swallow, I looked up in time to see to see a snarling Timash charging—

—*Harros!*

His own lips drew back in feral anger as he climbed to his feet, braced against the wall of the aft compartments. His eyes glistened in the intermittent moonlight like a cat's. He sidestepped Timash's rush quicker than I had ever seen him move. Timash slammed into the wall and bounced back, stunned. Following up the advantage, Harros' hand flashed out in a chopping motion, and my anthropoid friend dropped to the deck.

My attacker stepped around the prone body at his feet almost with a dancer's delicacy. "That was easier than I thought. If I'd known he was that fragile, Charles, I would have killed you a long time ago."

Nothing about him reflected the man I remembered. Before he had loomed, almost too big a man for his own body, bulling his way along by sheer size. Now he radiated a cold confidence that made him appear more compact and sure. Every move was measured. I knew he had been sent to kill me before he said another word.

He wasn't a Nuum—and he wasn't Thoran. He was like me. He was from Earth.

Even with his face wreathed in shadow, I could see the curved white line of his teeth.

"Very good, Charles. How satisfying to know that all that time they put into making me up didn't go to waste." He would not let my questions reach my tongue. "Oh, yes, they made me up all right. After you sent the last of the time cops running back to the 23rd century with their tails between their legs, the department knew they had someone extraordinary on their hands. They spent fifty years getting me right—six generations of clones cultivated to create the best assassin who ever lived. Me."

"Someone will hear the noise and come to investigate," I blurted. It wasn't what I had intended to say. That seemed to confuse him.

"Well." He cocked his head to one side mockingly. "I don't hear anyone. Could it have something to do with the mutiny? I made a deal with them: I left the captain's cabin unlocked, and they left you to me. And before you ask—" he rushed on, "I *can* trust them. My fathers' pride and joy was my telepathic ability. I expect I'm the strongest telepath on the planet."

That explained my attack of telepathic virus: Harros had tried to kill me from a distance. He had nearly succeeded, if not for the reasons he expected.

"And since our brain structures are so similar," he continued, "I can read your mind even though these other simpletons can't." Suddenly he was right in front of me. "I also have faster reflexes, greater strength, and far better night vision than you."

"And a bigger mouth to go with it," Timash rumbled. Harros spun just in time to intercept a massive paw with his chin. He fell back against me, twisted, and seized my face in one hand.

The world exploded in smells of color and shapes of sound. Far away all the voices I had ever heard in my life twirled away down a drain. Scenes from my childhood burst like balloons before my eyes. My mother and my father towered far overhead, but when they looked down each wore Harros' face.

"I told you to play nice," Mother/Harros scolded. "You wouldn't stay in your own time, and now you must be punished."

"What's that you've been playing with?" Father/Harros asked sternly. "Good heavens, who ever gave a database like that to a moron like you? That's like giving a loaded gun to a five-year-old. I'll have to take it away from you. You can have it back when you're older. Oh, wait, you're not going to get any older!" I shrank back from their titanic laughter, retreated into the far back closet of my own mind.

"No, no, Charles," Mother/Harros tutted. She reached down with fingers the size of sofas. "Come along, it's—it's—"

And suddenly she was screaming and he was screaming and

Harros was screaming and a faint, cold, and familiar fuzziness was rising at the fringes of my mind. I threw all my energy into rebuilding my mental blocks so fast that my knees buckled, but the fuzziness melted away.

Timash helped me to my feet. Harros lay dead on the deck.

"He grabbed you, and then he just started screaming…"

"It was the virus," I choked out. "He activated it. It almost killed us both." I pointed to the stairs. "Maire's cabin—that's where they'll be. Once they kill her the rest of us are finished." Leaning heavily on my hairy friend, I directed him to the captain's cabin, where he had never been. I chafed at our progress, but I was still too unsteady to mount the stairs and my directions might not be good enough to send him ahead by himself.

Before climbing up to the last level, we peeked through the trapdoor. Another mutineer stood outside of Maire's cabin. Timash set me aside and finished climbing the ladder alone.

"Hey, buddy," I heard him greet the startled sailor. "Is this where I join up?" There was a sudden shuffling, abruptly ended, and then the luckless sentry slid head-first down the ladder. I stepped over him on my way up.

A small test proved Maire's cabin door was unlocked. We looked at each other, girding our courage. Barehanded, we were about to burst into a room whose layout only I knew, holding an unknown number of armed and hostile killers, to rescue a woman who in all probability had already had her throat slit. Timash grinned.

"Uncle Balu is gonna love this story."

And we went.

At the last instant, my normally phantasmal sense of survival erected a frantic barricade in my forebrain, and instead of crashing through, I inched the door open until I could peek inside. My eyes flew wide.

"My God," I whispered. "It's just like the Vulsteen."

Only in this case, it was but four against one: Maire had them outnumbered. Backed against the far wall, her sword waving tauntingly at the quartet of savages arrayed before her, her torn nightshirt told the story: She was a beautiful woman, and they had planned to take her by surprise in her sleep. They carried no sidearms—they had wanted her alive. The blood on her shirt and on one man's tunic revealed the outcome of that scheme.

I slammed the door open wide. All of them jumped, but Maire held the advantage of facing the sound; when the others instinctively glanced backward she reduced their numbers to three.

Rage darkened Durrn's normally ruddy face. "Take them!" he screamed at the others. "They're just rowers! They're unarmed!"

He was right, and his men knew they had us as they rushed the door and we fell back into the corridor, but in the moment that they came through the door and tried to change direction to follow us, they found we had not run far. In those close quarters we were on top of them before they could bring their swords to bear, and seconds later we were both armed and running to Maire's aid.

She needed none. Durrn's anger and strength availed him nothing in the use of the Nuum sword, at which she was clearly his master. But she could not press in close to finish him, and only belatedly I saw that some of the blood on her nightshirt was her own.

"Keryl," she panted. "Block that tapestry!" I looked, but I didn't know which one she meant, and Durrn took his opportunity to break free and run. Flinging aside one of the hangings, he banged the wall and it opened for him. He vanished through the hidden door and we heard him bolt it from the other side.

"That was supposed to be my escape route if I ever needed it," Maire explained wryly, dropping her sword. She put a hand to her side and hissed.

"Let me look at that," I ordered, but as I gently peeled the material away I realized that under her nightshirt she wore nothing. Embarrassed, I froze.

"Well, hurry up. We've got to get after him."

I could not move, but once again Timash came to my rescue.

"Let me do it, Keryl. My mother's a doctor, after all." I backed up and turned away as he lifted the nightshirt. I heard Maire whisper a question to him and he answered in the same tone.

"Great," she said aloud. "I've been stabbed, my crew's in mutiny, and he's shy."

"It doesn't look bad," Timash reported. "Just a scrape along the ribs. I'll slap some plasm on it and you'll be good as new."

"Thank God," Maire replied from behind my back. "If I had to depend on Dr. Do-nothing I could bleed to death."

"We're wasting time," I snapped, though I refused to turn about. "Where will Durrn go? Are there any weapons he can get to?"

She did not answer for a few moments—I almost turned to see what was the matter—and when she spoke, her voice was uncertain.

"No—they can't use energy weapons on a sky-barge. It could interfere with the anti-gravity fields. Uh—he may go down to the generator bay, try to hold the ship hostage until we agree to let him out somewhere. I don't know—ouch—it may depend on how many of the crew he has with him."

"Not as many as he had when he started," Timash muttered. "All done. You can get dressed now."

I was about to object—although I did not want Maire running about the ship in her present state of dishabille, we hardly had time to choose outfits—when she announced herself ready. She had tucked her nightshirt into a pair of trousers and grabbed her sword once more. Barefoot, she was ready to take back what was hers.

"Out the front way," she directed. "He could be waiting for us in the passage through the bulkheads. I could open it, but there's not much light in there."

I followed her down the ladder as swiftly as caution allowed.

"Where are we headed?"

"To the anti-gravity generator bay. It's the most likely place to run, and it's all the way on the other side of the ship. If he's hiding out anywhere else, we'll see him on the way." By unspoken agreement, we hurried our steps, sacrificing stealth for speed.

"What do we do if we find him?" Timash queried, rather unnecessarily, it seemed to me in light of the night's events.

"Then it's going to be him and me."

We opened the last hatchway and emerged into the night.

"Or...maybe not..."

Maire's words trailed away as we stood on the afterdeck bathed in the light of the ship's full complement of floodlights— floodlights glinting off the barrels of a dozen guns Durrn, Garm, and their followers were pointing unwaveringly in our direction.

The captain of the *Dark Lady* recovered quickly.

"You can't use those, Durrn. You know that as well as I do."

Durrn shrugged. "Way I see it, it really makes no difference. Die now, die later...dead's dead and that's an end to drinkin'." He assumed a mournful air. The penalty for mutiny was, naturally, death. The more things change, the more they stay the same. "Of course," Durrn resumed, "there might be a way out of this."

"I'm listening."

"Lay down your weapons and surrender, and we won't shoot you."

Maire, bless her, smiled as if she really were enjoying herself.

"And then what? We retire to my cabin so you can pick up where you left off? No, thanks."

"No, that wouldn't work," Durrn sighed. "We'd have to tie you up so tight it'd defeat the whole purpose. But look at it this way: If we start shooting, everybody on this boat dies. If you surrender, the rest of your crew and the rowers—don't."

From where I stood two paces behind her, I felt the tremor in Maire's thoughts. Gathered in a ragged bunch ten feet from the bottom of the steps, the mutineers were probably too far away to notice it, and even in the bright glare she did not evince the slightest outer twinge.

"Go to hell."

"Wait...!" Backing up, I held out a hand as if to ward off her words. All eyes turned to me. "You don't have the right!"

"Keryl—!"

"You don't have the right!" I screamed again, and rushed at her—then past her straight into the crowd of mutineers!

I should have died then, even with the grace of the single instant when the mob was caught off-guard—too astonished to use the guns they had never really wanted to fire—before I was among them. What I had hoped to accomplish heaven only knew, but at that moment the doors behind the mutineers burst open and Skull and the rowers flooded the deck!

Instantly guns and swords were reduced to nothing but clubs. Borne down to the deck, I flailed with fists and feet, kicking and punching at anything that moved. Friend and foe were indistinguishable from where I lay, only a morass of shadowy bodies kicking and punching and falling on me in return.

The ending was as inevitable as the sunrise. Outnumbering their former masters five-to-one, bodies hardened by months and years of labor and hardship and the whip, the rowers literally tore the mutineers to pieces. I learned later that, thinking quickly, Timash had seized Maire when she would have plunged into the fighting and both restrained and shielded her until the tumult was spent. Had he not, I am certain she would have suffered Durrn and Garm's fate.

When it was done, Skull himself helped me to my feet. "They locked the crew away, but they didn't bother with us." He shivered involuntarily in a sudden gust of wind. "With all the noise topside, I snuck up here to see what was going on. The idea of Durrn as captain... I grabbed as many of the boys as could help and waited for a chance."

I wrapped my arms around myself; it was getting cold. "I'm sure the captain will take this all into account. Something can be done."

He looked at me strangely, as if he were going to say something, then paused, looking into the sky.

"Storm coming."

I nodded. "It's getting cold."

"No, you don't understand. They've cut the force field! If that storm hits us without it, we could all go over the edge!" I turned to hail Maire, but Skull was ahead of me. "Brants! Go below and free the crew! Hanick! Check the field generators! Captain—" Maire had arrived, her face saying she didn't need to be told what he knew. "Who's your field tech?" He jabbed a thumb at the mess he and the others had left. "Tell me it wasn't one of them."

"It's not," she answered curtly. "It's me."

I blinked. She had not lied about that, in any case.

"They've cut the shields," Skull said. "I've got a man checking the generators. We need them up fast—there's a storm coming."

Maire vanished without another word. The boat pitched violently. I was thrown off my feet, but Skull took it in stride, knees bent, riding the deck like a barrel roller.

"Stay down," he advised me without taking his eyes off a hundred different tasks at once. "It's the safest place."

And then it was over, an abrupt calm descending like the eye of a hurricane, save that we were riding through an electrical storm high in the air on a ship that felt like it was anchored to a mountain. As I slowly stood again, untrusting of my footing, the storm blazed to life around us, jagged lighting pulsing across the clouds in mile-long tongues of fire, thunders passing over and around us like the bass of the largest drum ever devised by God. I jumped as lightning struck the outer shields, outshining the floodlights and casting fantastic shadows across the deck.

"Don't worry, it's fuel for the generators." Skull stood relaxed now, the crisis over. The men drifted back to him, drawn like iron filings to his leadership. It was natural, I thought. He had ruled them long before I arrived, and he had lead them tonight in their long-overdue vengeance. Perhaps I should have felt anxious, but I did not.

"It seems the captain owes you twice over, now."

He gave me that same strange look that he had before.

"Do you think she'd free me?"

I was wary of making promises for another, but in all honesty I saw little choice for her in the matter.

"I expect so. She certainly owes you that much."

"Hm," he said. "Well, since we've already saved her life twice tonight, I guess dumping her now would be pointless. Besides, she's a good force field tech."

"I'm sorry, I don't follow you."

"Take a look around, Keryl." The rowers were packed around us four deep. I saw Timash standing on the periphery, watching intently. "It's our ship now."

"And—what are you planning to do with it?"

"Well, that's up to you—captain."

Chapter 40
I Do Not Hesitate

"He who hesitates is lost." Nowhere is this more true than in the command of men in battle. Win or lose, right or wrong, a leader must *act*, or forego the confidence, the respect, and ultimately the acceptance of his men.

I was being offered this ship by those who had recently taken control of her, men who by the Nuum definition of things would be considered, I suppose, pirates. I had no doubt that piracy was a capital crime. For all its scientific advancement, this world in many ways reflected the barbarity of my own bygone era. Had I the luxury of reflection, I might debate within myself the efficacy of imposing a punishment which, even in my own time, had failed to make any appreciable dent in the capacity of men to wreak mortal harm upon their neighbors, but I had not the luxury, only an instant in which to weigh my decision: Should I assume a command for which I had no qualification, exercising dominion through discipline where previously the only supremacy had been attained through fear? Or should I decline this dangerous honor and lay the futures of my friends and myself bare to the tender mercies of the mob?

"See that the remainder of the crew is freed," I instructed. "But until we can determine their loyalties, they are to be watched closely. When Captain—when Maire returns, send her to—the captain's cabin."

Skull nodded and detailed a pair of men to liberate the *Dark Lady's* crew and acquaint them with the new order of things. His sure manner in relaying my orders and handling the men impressed me, and I said so.

"Thanks. I was mate on another barge, once. Even now, it just comes natural." As I turned away, he cleared his throat.

"Yes?"

"Captain, what about the bodies?"

Oh, yes. The mutineers—and a few of our own—lay where they had fallen. The deck should have been awash with their blood, but some agent was soaking it out, cleaning the "planks" as I watched. Still, the bodies remained, intermittently lit by the flashes of lightning.

"Make sure they're dead." Judging from their conditions, this was an unnecessary chore, but I would not have it on my conscience that I had failed to make the effort, not if I wanted to sleep at night. "Then dispose of them as you see fit." I turned again to go.

"We're over water," Skull said to one of his men. "Search the crew's bodies; we'll throw them overboard when the storm abates. Put our men into cold storage." I climbed the ladder to my new quarters. "And start with Durrn," he ordered.

"Wait!" I cried with such force that every man on deck stopped in his tracks. A wild surmise had entered my brain with the arresting power of a whisper in the dark, and I twisted in mid-air as I fairly leaped off the ladder. Striding quickly to where Durrn lay, I searched his clothes, and without a word I pocketed what I found there—but not until I was safely behind closed doors did I allow myself to examine my long-lost Library.

The Librarian himself materialized as I satisfied myself that the polished sphere was unmarked.

"As I believe I mentioned, I am more than capable of withstanding a significant amount of punishment."

I hugged myself with ferocious relief. "I've missed you."

"I do not find that surprising," he replied pedantically. "Although I was limited by my circumstances to extremely passive sensors, the passage of events was hardly difficult to follow. I will admit, however," he went on in a more relaxed tone, "that I was anxious about you, as well.

"And before you ask, both the mechanical and strategic elements of sky barge piloting were omitted from my program." He shook his immaterial head. "My, but you do often seem to exceed the parameters the main Librarian selected for you."

Before I could inquire as to whether this was a compliment or a jibe, someone tried to open the door, and only after finding it bolted did there come a knock.

"That must be Maire," I said. "She's not used to being locked out of her own cabin." The Librarian disappeared without having to be told so that I could unfasten the door.

Maire entered with unusual hesitancy, glancing about before she left the doorway. I stood aside in silent invitation. She was unarmed, and I credited Skull with initiative. Maire was unlikely to attempt to threaten me, given the odds and the debt she owed, but the psychological effects of allowing her to continue going armed would be bad both for the rowers and her own crewmen. I waved her to a seat.

"Harros is dead."

"I know." She nodded. There hardly seemed any way she could not have known, with his body sprawled in plain sight on the deck, but decency commanded me to show some concern. "Was he involved—in the mutiny?"

"It seems that way," I said economically.

"I thought so, when I woke up to find him gone and four men trying to crawl into bed with me." She glanced over at what had been, until an hour ago, her corner. "What are you going to do with my crew?"

As long as open warfare could be avoided, the rowers and the crew were better off divided for now. Tomorrow the integration could begin for those who wished to remain on board. I had not considered the question, but I saw no reason why any former crewman who wished to leave could not be set down by the ship's launch in an empty field near a town. I said as much to Maire.

"They're staying," she said flatly.

"Well, certainly, if that's what they want. But I want them to know they have a choice. Under the circumstances it is only fair."

"I appreciate your sense of fair play, but they'll stay with me. They're my personal retainers. They came with the ship."

I found myself rolling the Library between my hands to keep them occupied. Visualizing the Librarian rolling over and over inside made me smile despite the circumstances.

"Your personal retainers just tried to rape and murder you."

She misinterpreted my smile. "Those were sailors I picked up along the way," she snapped. "Half of my crew was drafted by another sky barge for military duty in the west. I didn't have any choice but to find new sailors." Changing the subject abruptly, she reached for the Library. "What is that thing you've got, anyway?"

I put the Library away before she could get a look at it, lest she recognize it.

"I'm going to need your help to pull all these men together. I have a mission for them and I'm going to need everyone to work together to get it done."

"What kind of mission?"

Following the ancient rule of command once again, I ignored her question. As a subordinate, she had no right to know my plans—not that I had any definite plans to know. But every commander knows: If you can't be wise, at least be decisive.

"I'll need to set up a new chain of command. Skull will be first mate; I'd choose Timash, but he has no experience. You'll be second officer. Your—retainers—will be your personal responsibility, at least for now. Keep them in line and Skull will keep them safe from others."

Maire was half out of her seat. "*Second* officer? To *Skull?* On my own ship?"

"Sit down, woman!" She fell back into her chair; she'd never heard my command voice before. "Skull has the respect of the men! He's done the job before. And if I put you in place as my second they'd all think it was because—"

"Because I'm sleeping with you?" Her eyebrows raised, Maire went on: "What do you think they think we're doing right now? 'Captain's privilege,' they call it."

I felt the warm blood rise in my face. "I'll put a stop to that." I sighed heavily. "By God, what do they think of you?"

"Oh, come on. They already know about Harros."

For a moment, I was nonplused, thinking of Harros, whose broken body waited with the others for the long fall to the sea. Then the light dawned...

"What do you mean, you and Harros? He was shot in the head!"

"Since when has a man ever let a little thing like that stop him?"

The blood rose in my face once again. "This is hardly a fit topic for discussion. I'll have Skull set the men straight."

"As long as you're setting things straight, there's something I've been wondering about, and as long as I'm going to be working under you for a while, I think I have a right to know." She leaned forward again, staring me straight in the eye.

"Who the hell are you, anyway?"

I found my reliance upon decisive action in place of hesitation to be wearing thin.

"What do you mean?" I thought it a reasonable question under the circumstances, and the best I could do. I was tired.

"You heard me. You're too big to be a Thoran, but you run around with a gorilla. You're a yellow, but you're dyed to be a red.

You're carrying a Library, but you don't know the first thing about not firing a weapon on a sky barge—and I can't find your address in the datasphere.

"At first I thought you were a spy," Maire continued. "Or else an assassin. But that didn't make any sense. If you were a spy you couldn't have found me in the Vulsteen city, and if you were an assassin you would have left me there. So who the hell are you, and how did you end up running my ship?"

"I won't be needing it long," I answered almost inaudibly.

"And then what?" she demanded, her maternal instincts aroused.

"And then you can have it back," I said harshly. "I won't need it after that."

"After what?"

"None of your business," I whispered.

"It damned well is my business!"

"You can have your pick of the cabins, after Skull," I told her. I knew it would infuriate her that I still ignored her questions, but I had more work to do and no time to indulge her. "Are we secure for the night?"

"Yes," she gritted.

"Good. Then please fetch Skull and Timash. We need to have a conference." When she hesitated, I added: "You will find that some of your questions may be answered."

She still did not move. "Not the one I want. There's something weird about you. You know the wrong people, you turn up in the wrong places, and most of all the 'sphere says you don't exist." She looked at me most queerly, as if seeing me through a microscope and discovering an unknown virus. "Are you from the homeworld?" she breathed.

"I was born right here on Thora."

Maire banged her fists on the table. "That's impossible! Then why aren't you in the 'sphere?"

I grabbed her wrists. "Stop pounding the furniture and do as you're told."

She did stop pounding the table; breaking free of my grasp, she wound up and swung at *me*, instead.

Again, I did not hesitate. I caught her hand, pulled her to me, and kissed her.

Chapter 41
I Betray Myself

When I finally dismissed my "senior staff" that night, I made sure to bolt the door to my new cabin, and still I slept neither in the bed that Maire had recently occupied, nor that used by Harros—though now it appeared that recently the two had been interchangeable. That was not, however, the reason behind my choice, nor was it squeamishness about sleeping where lovers had last lain before one of them died, even if that was more than sufficient in and of itself.

No. In the main, I apprehended assassination. Only hours ago an attempt had been made upon this room's tenant, and the change of landlords, to my mind, made a repeat of that scene more rather than less likely. Maire had calmed for the duration of the conference—amazingly, she had not only failed to attack me for the liberties I took with her while we were alone, she accepted them without comment and fetched Skull and Timash straightaway—but I, like most men, am only so far acquainted with the ways of the fairer sex that I admit the depths of my ignorance. Maire, while she had assured me that Durrn had revealed the only bolt-hole into or out of this cabin, might harbor darker motives than she would admit.

And even could I trust her not to attempt to take back her ship, her men might try something equally foolhardy. For tonight I had them under guard, but it was best to take no chances; without my command, the crew would surely dispose of them and sail away to their homes. I intended eventually that they would have that chance, but not at the expense of more lives lost.

Nor could I even rely upon my own men. I had taken Skull's pre-eminence by force; by force or stealth it could be taken from me.

I checked the locks again, and slept in a pile of tapestries in a dim corner. Despite all my precautions, had my killer sidled up to my side in the night, I would have died, for no sooner did I lie down than I was dead to the world until Timash rattled my door in the morning.

Groggily I staggered across the strange room, tripping on a worn piece of carpet. Timash was insufferably cheerful.

"You look like the wrong end of a rhinocehorse."

"Which side is that?" I asked, casting about for a sink in which to wash my face.

"Usually the bottom. Rhinocehorses trample their prey before eating it."

"Oh." I decided ignorance truly was bliss. "Where in heaven's name is the sink?" Now that I thought about it, there was much missing in the captain's quarters. Being the only woman on the ship, I doubted she had shared her sanitary facilities with her crew—especially as she was their captain, and a titled lady to boot.

Timash looked around. "You could ask the Library to ask the ship's databoard."

The thought of sharing my morning not only with Timash but with the supercilious image of a long-dead professor did not improve my mood. I said I didn't know where the dataport was.

"You could ask him that, too." Gorilla or not, if he offered any more help I was likely to throw him overboard if it meant cutting him up and shoving his body parts out through the porthole.

"I refuse to ask a computer every time I want to wash my face. Where I come from the washing bowl was always right next to your bed!" As if on cue a panel in the wall beside the bed slid soundlessly away, revealing the water closet. "See?" I demanded. "Some things never change." I disappeared inside to take care of my morning ablutions. As I said, some things did not change—thank Heaven.

I emerged with an entirely new outlook on life. It brightened even further when I saw how Timash had spent his time: breakfast was on the table. After all the time we had spent together in his mother's house, he even knew what I liked, odd as it seemed to him.

He watched me eat with a silence that conveyed much. Timash had never been disposed to pensivity. He had learned that I tended to eat, not talk, at meals, but he had never let that stop him before. I made an encouraging motion with my fork.

"Out with it."

"The men are wondering what you're planning to do—"

"And?"

"And so am I."

I wiped my lip to give myself time. I sighed and settled back in my chair to give myself some more. At length, however, I ran out of things to dawdle over and Timash was still awaiting my answer.

"I started out to find Hana Wen and bring her home. That hasn't changed."

"I'll give the pilot orders to make course for Dure," Timash acknowledged, but he did not rise from the table.

"Was there something else?" I asked coldly, for Timash's question had left my nerves on edge for reasons I could not pin down.

"What about after Dure? Are you still planning to try to find that time machine?"

My irritation made me answer his question with one of my own.

"Why? Did you have other plans?"

"Me?" He leaned back, hands wide. "No, I'm just along for the ride." We were both silent for a few moments, not knowing how to escape this swamp in which we had wandered. "I just thought maybe you wanted to do a little more with your life."

"And what the hell is that supposed to mean?" If I thought my attitude would cow him, I was surprised.

"It means that after the way you helped out the conservationists, I thought maybe you were onto something! I saw how they reacted to you, the same way I did. They wanted to follow you, and they didn't know you from a tiger spider! And Uncle Balu, he saw it, too! He was the one who said I should go with you in the first place. 'He's gonna go far, boy.' That's what he said. 'Follow him and the stars're the limit.'"

I shook my head. "I don't understand. What are you trying to say?"

He took a deep breath and plunged on. "Uncle Balu was right. Look what's happened since we met. You organized the conservationists and destroyed an entire Nuum research station. We got caught by the Vulsteen, and you made friends with the *breen*, for god's sake. Now we get kidnapped onto a sky barge, and a week later you've not only taken over the slave hold, you're captain of the whole damned ship!"

Put that way, it did seem rather extraordinary, but to my mind I had done nothing but that which was required to survive. And I pointed out that the captaincy of the *Dark Lady* was completely fortuitous.

"When we were starting out, you told me there was a saying in your time: 'Fortune favors the bold.' So be bold. I don't know about the rest of Tehana City, but I'm tired of living in a damn cave. Thora's tired of living in a cave. The Nuum have had us down so long they think we're a joke. The conservationists, my people, the breen, we're not laughing. We're mad. All we need is a leader."

"My god," I whispered, my eyes opening wide. "You're right! You are mad."

It was tragic to watch his untempered enthusiasm die its swift and undeserved death. He stood slowly.

"I'll take your orders to the pilot."

Maire had taken to heart my orders to bring her men into line with the more numerous rowers. Timash told me later that she and Skull had put their heads together earlier that morning, each coming away from the meeting with a grudging respect for the other's abilities. I don't know who impressed me more. The crews, however, were working together and that was what counted. Timash himself had taken on the cleaning up each former rower and outfitting him with a new outfit from the former crew's stores so that at first glance, it was difficult to tell who only yesterday had been the masters and who the slaves.

I don't doubt that there were problems. These men had much to work out, and even the combined personalities of my officers—which were formidable singularly, and positively overwhelming together—could never smooth over all the old animosities. But not a rumor of discord ever reached my ears, and if my eyes spied an occasional facial bruise and a corresponding bandaged knuckle, I could turn away and play ignorant so long as no one disappeared. In that requirement, life had not changed.

Maire consented to turn over to me all of the ship's records, save for her own personal logs, which she assured me had no bearing on my official duties, and I accepted her word with the air of a gentleman. She steadfastly refused to give me access to the Nuum datasphere. I turned instead to the Library without realizing how much my mere request had given away.

What I found in the ship's logs shocked me.

"These men aren't criminals, they're revolutionaries!"

The Librarian pretended to read over my shoulder. I suppose it was to make me more comfortable than knowing that he had scanned all the records beforehand.

"To the Nuum, they are one and the same."

"But these charges——!" I protested. "Their trials were kangaroo courts."

"Without recognizing your reference, I can presume your meaning from context. The Nuum are not interested in justice, but in preserving their way of life. These sky barges are designed specifically to destroy any cohesive spirit by denying the prisoners sufficient resources for all, thus pitting them against one another. It also disperses them across the empire."

I thought back to my own first days on board ship. "The system works."

"The Nuum thought it instructive that the populace understand the risks they took in revolt," the Librarian said. "My files include graphic representations of shipboard life. If they are accurate, Captain Por Foret was a very merciful jailor."

Timash's words haunted me like the ghost of Hamlet's father calling him to his task. I grinned self-consciously at the irony of drawing such a simile while sailing on a ship called the *Dark Lady*. When my professors had proclaimed the Bard immortal, they had had no idea…

"There is a great deal more to the captain than we thought," I mused.

"As she is beginning to realize about you, as well."

"What do you mean?"

"Come, come, sir," he said in his best imitation of an Oxford don. "You asked her how to access the datasphere."

"Yes?"

He sighed. "The *Nuum* datasphere." I looked blankly over my shoulder at him and he returned the favor until at last his eyes widened. "Sir, where you come from—they did not have a worldwide data system, did they?"

"Where I come from, they barely had airplanes. We had never heard of computers."

The Librarian walked around to the other side of the table so that I could untwist my neck.

"I begin to see. The Nuum datasphere is a universal system, open to everyone—everyone who is a Nuum, anyway. When you asked Lady Por Foret how to access it, she knew immediately that you were not a Nuum."

I closed my eyes and cursed softly. "Would you know if she had accessed the datasphere herself?"

"No, sir. I am not connected at all. If she carries an implanted datalink, she could download any information or contact any other person in the sphere without anyone else knowing."

"Which means she could call for help at any time."

There was an annunciator in the room; Maire had told me that much, and how to activate it without broadcasting every conversation the length of the ship. It came on now.

"Captain, this is Skull. Another ship has appeared on the northern horizon. It appears to be headed straight for us."

I now understood some of the vast potential of the datasphere. But I feared my comprehension came too late.

Chapter 42
Sky Raiders

"Is there any way to identify it?" I whispered. Next to me stood Maire, both of us gazing into the cubicle where pilot sat enveloped in a three-dimensional rendering of the sky and earth, down to the wispiest clouds and every migratory bird for leagues. No one but the pilot on duty was allowed in the cube; not even the captain. His view, I was told, must be unencumbered, for without sufficient warning, one of the larger Nuum airships like the one that had shanghaied me to the research station might blow by us and toss us in her wake like a leaf in a storm.

"And if that happened," Maire had assured me somberly, "our pitiful little force fields wouldn't keep half the crew from being thrown overboard—not to mention the disruption to the anti-grav generators, the photon sails, the oars..." Mercifully, she had stopped and let my imagination fill in the rest. Or was it mercy? Was she perhaps pointing out to me in her own needling way that I was the interloper on the ship she was literally born to command?

In answer to my question now, she pushed past me to a small console next to the door. A line of symbols and numbers ran across the scanner. I could read she was the *Eyrie*, out of Dure.

Maire stared at the screen and bit her lip. Even without reading her mind I could read her mood.

"What's wrong?" I asked with false lightness. "Not the rescue you were hoping for?"

"Hardly," she muttered, then my remark registered with her and she shot me a look of surprise and anger. "What's that—oh, never mind." Once again her attention was on the monitor. She sighed. "They shouldn't be here."

"Who are they?"

"The ship is from Farren House. It's the major house of Dure, the capital of Dure, where my family lives. But we're way out beyond any of the normal trade lanes for any of the southern families. That's why I came here, to get away. Farren House and my family have been friends for years, but there's no reason for them to be here."

"I can think of one," I said.

She turned on me, her brow furrowed with surprise. "What?"

I hesitated; there was more to my interest in Farren than what I was about to tell her, and I still couldn't trust my life and all my men to her uncertain loyalties. But the in viewscreen the other ship was looming larger and I had no time to debate the issue with myself.

Quickly I sketched in the conversation I had overheard in the gravity generator room. Maire stiffened when I told her that the mutineers had mentioned Farren's name. I said nothing of my own interest in the man; for all I knew, we could be talking about two distinct individuals—although I doubted it.

"How do I know you're telling the truth? How do I know this conversation ever happened?"

"Remember Porky—the crewman who disappeared?" She frowned, and nodded uncertainly. He was not the most likely member of the crew ever to have crossed her path. "After the others had left, he found me." With a little jerk of my head, I intimated the direction of Porky's last voyage.

Maire's gaze slipped back to the viewscreen. My thoughts were racing: Friend or foe? Was the *Eyrie* just stopping by for a visit with a friend serendipitously found along a remote pathway? Or had it been sent to make sure that Garm and Durrn had done their job? If the former, any face but Maire's could raise an alarm; if the latter, that same face would put the enemy on notice and leave us sitting ducks. How could we know?

Then I considered what I knew of Farren, and the men aboard his ship, and of my own Hana Wen, and I read therein the answers to all my questions.

Without a word to Maire, I whipped out of the pilot's cubicle, gained the deck, and collared Skull and Timash for swift orders.

"Timash, take Maire and her crew below decks. Lock them in a cabin. Then report back to me."

"Huh? But what if she won't go?"

I did not have time for this. "Do it! You're a gorilla…" To his credit he stopped arguing and started moving. "Skull—can they see what's going on on our deck?"

"Uh-uh. The force fields give us some privacy."

"Good. Arm the men and have them line the port side, but stay out of sight. And tell the pilot to bring us alongside." I paused long enough for him to send a man down with the orders. "Then have a force field tech standing by to bring down the fields on my order."

Skull stared in frank astonishment. "What are you going to do?"

I clapped him on the shoulder. "We're going to board her, Mister Skull! And we're going to set her rowers free." I left him standing flatfooted while I ran for my cabin.

"Ahoy there!" In all the millennia, my world's ancient sea greeting was sure to have changed, but in this era of telepathic communication, it was the meaning, and not the words, that carried weight. The crew of the *Eyrie* took my meaning well enough, if the manner of its delivery was unorthodox.

I stood in the *Dark Lady's* rigging, clinging to the mast with one hand while the other, hidden behind me, held not only Maire's pistol, but the rope I had hastily affixed to a cross-bar. I prayed my knot-tying abilities lived up to my expectations, for my entire plan (as well as my life) would soon hang by this thread. Across a few yards of empty air floated an air barge nearly the twin of our own, a product of the same nostalgia for this world's wild past that had inspired the lines of the *Dark Lady*. Their buccaneer days had featured flying boats, not floating, but nonetheless history had proven once more endlessly repetitive.

Twenty feet below me my crew crouched out of sight. The order to arm had been sudden and confusing, but welcome at the same time, and they had responded with more alacrity than I had hoped. I knew Timash's dark bulk would stand out among them, but I could not spare a look. Now that we were close enough for unaided eyes to see across the narrowing gulf of nothingness, I could not risk betraying everything with an unguarded glance.

And all eyes on the *Eyrie* were upon me. Its crew stood in curious clusters on the deck, staring upward. Both their mechanical and telepathic hails had gone unanswered by my order. Whether they expected a shipload of mutineers or a friendly face, they were not expecting a ghost ship, and this was what I was giving them. For now, the element of surprise favored the *Dark Lady*.

"We've had some trouble!" I called. It did not hurt that I was able to imbue my act with the unmistakable ring of truth. "Our communications are out. We have wounded who need a doctor!" I bit my lip. I had said "wounded" instead of "injured."

"I'm Captain Stoshi!" a man on the other ship's rear deck shouted. "Where is Lady Por Foret?"

"She's been hurt!" I called back, watching the gap between us. It was almost closed, but I needed more time. "Come alongside and lower your fields!" That was the telling point: With Maire's life reported to be in danger, no captain on a legitimate mission would hesitate for a moment to come to her aid.

Captain Stoshi did exactly what I thought he would do, and in all honesty, exactly what I had hoped he would.

"Stand by!" he called back, and headed for the stairs. That was a plain enough sign for me. I waited until he had turned his back.

"Now!" I shouted to Skull, and moments later the air shimmered as our force fields came down. I whipped out the pistol and fired.

The results justified every warning Maire had ever given about the danger of firearms on board ship. Violent red and blue lightnings danced around the periphery of the *Eyrie* almost too fast for the eye to follow, and more than one Nuum crew member who had been leaning against the shielding was blown back across the deck, blackened and twisted and dead. With a *crack!* the entire system shorted and the *Eyrie* stood naked to the elements.

I jumped.

There had been no time to measure the rope I used to swing across to the *Eyrie*, nor had I any way of knowing just how far I would have to swing. My arms threatened to explode out of their sockets as my full weight jerked the rope tight and I sailed with far more speed than I expected straight onto the deck on the other ship.

At the very last second I let go and slammed into a fortuitous knot of crewmen. All of us crashed to the deck, but at least I knew what was coming. I stumbled to my feet, shot a man, and got my back to a wall. If I could rouse the slaves, they could keep the crew busy at least long enough for my men to follow me.

"Rise, rowers! Fight!"

But they did not. They could not. The Librarian had not lied about their treatment. Filthy, emaciated husks barely looked up as the entire ship's complement charged me.

The pistol hardly gave them pause. I fired once more before it was wrested from me. The very suddenness of my assault had robbed them of the luxury of thinking of their own lives; they had become a mob, a mob intent on the blood of the man who had already tasted their own. I went down under their fists.

And then the *Dark Lady's* crew surged over the unprotected bulwarks and the battle was joined.

They took the Nuum from behind, and they were angry, but the Nuum were bigger and not sapped by months of deprivation. And they were all armed, where my men had taken what they could from the *Lady's* armory. Those with weapons lead the way, and those without massed behind. My pistol was gone. I used my sword to good effect, but not every foe had abandoned me and not all the blood that soon stained my costume was from another's wounds.

We'd had no time to plan our battle, and our only previous experience as a fighting unit had come by surprise, in the dark, against the outnumbered mutineers. Here again the Nuum were outmanned, but we could only bring against them as many men as could cross between the ships, and with the lack of any margin of error no man was eager to make that short journey if he could not be certain of his footing.

The ship was shifting underfoot as the pilot tried to break away from us. How our pilot was keeping close I had no idea, unless Skull had managed to rig boarding cables to tie us together. The absence of force shields added to the danger, but it was necessary if we wanted to board at all.

I was close-pressed by two of the *Eyrie's* crew. They were mean swordsmen, but not seasoned soldiers; had one dropped back while the other engaged me, he could have changed his sword to a staff and between them they would have had me dying on the deck or forced over the side in moments. Still, they had me trapped. Whether Skull or Timash had made the leap to this ship I did not know, but without one of us to lead it our attack would surely fail.

And then that which I most feared happened: With a flickering crackle and the scent of ozone, the *Eyrie's* force fields came back on.

A shout went up from the defenders. While our mates watched helplessly, the liberated *Eyrie* dropped like a rock, putting the *Lady's* own bulk between us and negating any attempt to repeat my short-circuiting of the shields. Its inertial controls kept us all on our feet, but the momentum shifted nonetheless.

With a sudden burst of energy I spitted one of my foes and kicked the other away at the cost of a sliced thigh. Scampering up a ladder at my back, I stood on the upper deck and shouted encouragement to my men.

It worked—so well that Captain Stoshi saw me and began shouting orders of his own. I couldn't hear them and I didn't need to. Half a dozen sailors broke from the combat below me and charged the ladder. I met them at the top.

Two of them went down before more reached me by climbing the ladder on the opposite side of the ship. So many men pressed me that they could not all reach in at the same time. Now the force field that had cut off all aid saved me, for it gave me a place to put my back, at the very aft point of the ship where two planes of force came together. One man fell on my sword; I pulled it out and used his body as a gruesome barricade. My world was a forest of thrusting points quickly turning my shield into a blood-soaked pincushion as none of the frenzied mob could find enough room to push his sword all the way through. My arm ached from my swing and the constant swordplay. The smell of the blood and the sweat in my eyes blinded my senses and I fought on solely because I had forgotten that anything else existed in the world.

I grunted in pain as one of my foes pushed past my guard and pinked my shoulder. My arm went numb and my point faltered. I was past conscious thought and my reflexes were too blunted to parry the next sword to seek my heart.

Chapter 43
I Renew a Friendship

A scream galvanized my last remaining spark of survival instinct to life. At first I thought the scream my own, that I had blacked out for an instant that would cost me everything, but when the foes about me suddenly scattered like tenpins from a whirling dervish, I realized it was the scream of a predatory bird unleashed on a flock of its prey.

Maire's staff flashed up and down, in and out with a speed and celerity that my weary muscles had lost. She capitalized on the element of surprise; all of her opponents were fighting with shorter weapons than she and none had seen her coming. Each seemingly slight blow flung a man aside or doubled him in pain. And then they were gone and we were for the moment alone.

"Where—?" I panted and gulped down air. "Where did you come from?"

"I flew," she grinned, and pointed upward. The *Dark Lady* floated almost directly above us. From her railing hung a rope which dangled a man-length above our heads.

"You dropped from the rope!" I accused her. "You could have been killed!"

"Hey, if you could swing, I can climb," she said impishly. "We just had to get the *Lady* directly overhead so I could get between the force fields. They don't cover the whole boat, you know."

"But how did you get out of that cabin? I had you locked in!"

"Oh, please… It's my ship."

Later I would have to ask her what she meant by that, but now my eyes went wide as a Nuum topped the stairs behind her. Without missing a beat Maire spun, caught him under the chin with her open hand, and pushed him head over heels back down the way he had come.

I had written off Maire's fight against the Vulsteen as a combination of desperation of their own reluctance to kill valuable hostages, but I could see now that I had done her a considerable wrong. By way of hiding my reaction, I said: "We should help."

"No need," she replied. She pointed out across the ship and upward. "Look."

I did. Fully a dozen lines now hung from the *Lady's* flanks, with Nuum crewmen and former rowers alike dropping to the decks like rain. The balance had shifted once more. The battle was over before I could decide where I might be needed.

Maire signaled the *Lady* to descend and come alongside us once again. As I painfully climbed down the ladder to the *Eyrie's* bloodstained deck, already cleaning itself, I racked my brains for the solution to a brand-new problem:

I now had two ships and crews. What in heaven's name was I going to do with them?

In the short term, this question presented less of a dilemma than I had feared, although its solution left me none the happier. Both ship's crews had taken losses. Obviously, the *Eyrie* had fared the worse; its crew had fought until almost the last man, and most of the survivors were among those Maire had herself batted away from me. Captain Stoshi was dead. Likely none of his officers had lived.

Among our men who remained had to be parceled the tasks of

securing the new boat, tending wounded, stacking the dead, rooting out any stragglers from the *Eyrie's* crew hiding below, and, not the least important, freeing the rowers. I tried to give the orders while Maire propped me up and urged me back to my cabin. Neither of us had much luck; I was near to fainting from blood loss and she was almost overwhelmed by my sudden and frequent tendency to become dead weight in her arms.

Relief came from a reliable source. Timash left off his own organizing to trade places with Maire. While she handled the clean-up crews, he bundled me back to the *Lady*.

"I didn't see you over there," I whispered half-jokingly, after we had made the crossing.

"I was up in the rigging most of the time." He stopped to tuck me over his shoulder while he mounted a ladder. Apparently Maire had never felt the need to connect a powered lift to her own quarters. Perhaps she thought the men would see it as effeminate. I wished she had thought again. Surely she had not dragged Harros up here like a sack of rice…! "I took a lesson from the tiger spiders."

He tried to lay me on the bunk as gently as possible, but it was a lost cause.

"You weren't the only one," I hissed, hoping to hide the pain. "Did you see how that crazy woman dropped from the sky?"

He chuckled. "I missed it. All of a sudden there were a lot more guys up in the lines with me, and I almost knocked a couple of them silly before I realized who they were." He left me for a few moments and returned with a box from which he removed a variety of tools, drugs, and plasm for bandages.

Dr. Chala's training and Nuum medicine worked so well together that even Timash was able quickly to staunch the bleeding and numb the pain. Wounds which would have lain me up for days back home would trouble me no more by tomorrow, and infection was not even a dot on the horizon. I was one of the lucky ones.

"I suppose I owe Maire my life."

Timash shrugged. "So now you're even. Or probably not. Who's counting?" He started to stand, but I put my hand on his arm.

"And I haven't thanked you yet, either. Every time I turn around you're playing nursemaid to me."

"Unless I'm rescuing you from psycho time-traveling killers… But like I said, who's counting? Without you I never would have done any of this."

"Without me you'd be home safe with your mother, sipping tea with Uncle Balu."

"Without you," he said, gently removing my hand from his arm, "that tiger spider would have killed me. Get some rest."

He sounded just like his mother.

I took an inordinate amount of pride in the fact that I was up and about before Maire came in to see me. Knowing she would come, the idea of greeting her as an invalid proved so abruptly and overpoweringly distressing that I nearly tripped over the furniture in an incipient panic that she would open the door to discover me not only dishabille, but disabled as well.

Pulling on my boots, I fell wildly sideways, windmilling in a vain attempt to preserve my balance and succeeding only barely in finding a chair with that part of my anatomy built for the purpose when the door opened. I smiled, the picture of careless ease.

"Didn't I lock that?"

She smiled lightly. "Even if you had, it wouldn't have made any difference. How do you feel?"

I waved off her question, intending to ask instead about the men, but the sight of her had temporarily numbed my tongue. Cleaned up, somewhere she had found another outfit, a deep red blouse tugged tightly into midnight black leggings. Where she kept her omnipresent baton was an enigma I hoped not to unravel. How she had waltzed through the men on deck without causing a riot was likewise a mystery I thought better left alone. *Why* she had done herself up like this was enough of a concern, although I thought I knew the reason.

She sat down across from me, rushing into the vacuum with her own report, taking my tongue-tied silence as an invitation—or perhaps simply as her due. Her recent adventures aside, she *was* a pampered princess from a master race.

"We lost a handful of men, not nearly as many as we should have, but we had the element of surprise—thanks to you. I've never even heard of a sky barge being hijacked before, let alone by someone swinging in over the force fields and climbing down the mast to deactivate them by hand while fighting off the ship's crew with a sword in one hand and pistol in the other." I started to protest but she waved me off. "Don't get mad at me. That's what they're saying…"

"That's ridiculous!" I burst out. "Where did they ever get an idea like that? They saw me, for heaven's sake!"

"Use it," Maire advised. "The more the men think you walk on air, the easier it is. Believe me, I know."

I shook my head. "What about the *Eyrie's* crew?"

"About eight of them are still alive. None of them are officers. We checked the crew manifest and accounted for all but one. We think he may have fallen overboard in the fighting, but we're checking belowdecks. The survivors're all locked up, but I don't know how long they're going to stay that way."

"What do you mean?"

Maire took a deep breath without seeming to notice its effect on me, and slumped in her seat.

"Remember how I told you conditions on other barges were worse than here?" I replied that I did and Maire continued grimly: "I wasn't kidding. The rowers on the *Eyrie* were half-starved, and beaten daily. They're weak now, and confused by what's happened, but they won't stay that way. When they're rested and fed, their minds will turn to revenge."

"Do you have a guard on the door?"

"Of course. But they won't let that stop them."

I turned her words over in my mind. I couldn't spare enough men to guard the prisoners effectively, even if I had that many. And I couldn't very well allow them to barricade themselves inside...

"Bring the prisoners over to the *Lady*. We can lock them up here. If we do it now, before the *Eyrie's* rowers feel up to anything, we should avoid trouble."

Maire's eyes widened in admiration. She saw me as a vagabond, a renegade wanderer smiled upon by Fortune and placed in a—temporary—position of authority. As Maire used the annunciator to relay my orders to Timash, I smiled back at her; I hid mysteries of my own that I had no intention of disclosing. She had no idea that I had commanded men in battle eons before her forebears' planet had even been discovered by Man.

I wonder, if in all those millennia over which I skipped, any bigger fool was ever born than I.

"Have you decided to tell me yet what your plans are?"

What I had decided was not to tell her what she really wanted to know.

"Right now my plan is to find someone who can take command of the *Eyrie*. We can't sit here like this forever. Somebody is going to notice that it's missing."

Maire sat up straight in her chair. "Why don't you take it? I'll take back the *Lady*, and you can go wherever you want. I won't say a word."

I had to laugh. "That's very generous, but I was thinking of Skull. He's the logical choice."

"For what?"

"For—"

"Captain!" the annunciator interrupted tersely. Upon my response, Timash said: "We're trying to transfer the prisoners off the *Eyrie*, but the rowers are putting some up trouble. I don't want to hurt them, but..."

"Understood. I'm on my way."

The other barge was deceptively calm when we came outside, floating a few feet away with its shields still down to accommodate the inter-ship traffic. Now that both were under common control, we had tied their computers together with the result that their relative positions were fixed and we had installed a short footbridge between them. The ingenious little device was completely collapsible right down to the handrails. Its magnetic attachments were incredibly strong, but if the ships were violently wrenched they would snap like sticks. We crossed quickly.

You could feel the tension aboard the *Eyrie* as soon as you stepped on deck. My men stood stiffly on guard, nervous and uncertain as to their loyalties if their fellow Thorans tried to rush the Nuum ostensibly under our protection. The rowers had been unchained; many were shedding their filthy rags and washing themselves where they stood. Instinctively I tried to shield Maire from the sight, but she seemed not to notice, and I realized belatedly that there were more urgent issues here than those of propriety.

I collared one of my own sailors. "Why aren't these men below? They shouldn't have to wash themselves here."

"Sorry, captain. Skull says there's no room below. He told us to give the rowers whatever they needed to keep them quiet."

"No room?" I turned to Maire. "What does he mean, no room? There's got to be room…!"

Maire took me firmly by the arm. "No, there doesn't. I keep trying to tell you that. Now let's get moving. I've been in two battles in two days and I'm not going for a record."

Any sensible man—nay, any *sane* man—would have let her lead him wherever she wanted to go. But I have always been cursed with a mulish stubbornness disguised as principle. The same condition which had lead me to France under a foreign flag now rooted my feet to the deck. It got me into several fights as a child, and probably will get me killed some day. It almost got me killed right then.

"I'm going down below. I want to see the rowers' quarters."

Maire's fingers dug into my skin, and the sailor cleared his throat.

"Uh, captain, I've been down there. Maybe you don't—"

I stopped him with a glance. Perhaps my emotions were beginning to boil over, because he just stood there with his mouth open. Even Maire's grip relaxed.

"Go see Timash," I ordered her. "See if you can make transfer. Heaven knows that outfit of yours should distract the rowers."

I left her gasp behind as I strode toward the double doors leading to the companionway. I must still have been radiating my feelings, because the rowers actually looked up as I passed. A slow buzz rose about me, traveling first behind, then with me, and finally preceding me down the rows.

"It's him! It's the Ghost!"

I halted in my tracks, half-turning to look at those dirty, smelly wretches who rose unsteadily to watch me with too-bright eyes in their smeared and tired faces. I turned about, and the other side of the ship showed the same rows of beaten and haggard men's eyes unblinking upon me. But it wasn't fear, nor hostility, nor anything that I should fear—it was worse. To a man, they were almost worshipful. I knew without reading their thoughts that every poor devil on that ship saw me not just as his rescuer, but as his savior— and I had not the slightest idea why. And then one called to me.

"Keryl! Keryl Clee!"

I was at his side in an instant. "Bantos Han!"

And that was when the man next to him tried to kill me.

Chapter 44
Return to the Dead

The attack was so clumsy and hurried I was in little real danger of being hurt. I saw the knife blade glint in the sun as the assassin drew it from his shirt; had he been clever enough to dull its shine with the same grease he used to disguise his own face he might have stood some small chance of success.

As it was, in immersing himself among the freed slaves he had taken a spot next to the rail, the better to conceal himself, but putting him in the position of having to strike at me over Bantos Han. I don't even know why he even tried, unless he believed that I possessed some superior telepathic ability that would eventually unmask him. His mistake cost him dearly.

I pulled back even as he lunged at me. He tripped over Bantos Han, who fell heavily to the deck with a painful noise, but something must have warned him about the man, for he twisted hard as he went down, arms flailing to spoil the attack. As they tumbled in a heap, he seized the assassin's arm, and before I could help, Bantos Han was forcing the knife into my attacker's side.

The entire incident lasted no longer than it takes to tell. I was already helping my old friend out from under his dead burden by the time Maire dashed up from one end of the boat and Skull appeared from nowhere.

"Are you all right?" both of them demanded.

"I think I found your missing sailor." I took in all the other rowers, frozen in place by the sudden violence. "You're sure there was only one?"

Skull glanced at Maire, started to say something, then thought it over and started again.

"Get the captain and the prisoners back to the *Lady* right now, before something else happens. I'll search the ship."

I was helping support Bantos Han, who was looking from one of us to another to the next, vainly struggling to follow the conversation.

"Bring this man with you," I said to Maire. "I still have to see below decks." Both of my officers instantly protested, and I as quickly silenced them. "I'm just going to take a look. I want to know what's so terrible that none of my crew thinks I should see it."

I was being stubborn again. I should have listened to them.

Less than a century before I was born, European "traders" had trafficked in African slaves kidnapped and dragged to the New World in the hot, stinking bellies of ships upon whose decks walked creatures whose own souls mirrored the hellish conditions below. Hundreds of men and women and children were shoveled into dark holds until there was barely room to stand, let alone sit or lie down on the weeks-long voyage.

Nearly a thousand millennia later, Man still had not learned. Accompanied by Skull and another sailor (who would not let me go on alone despite my direct orders), I climbed down a narrow ladder to a short, dim passageway ending in a tiny, square chamber whose walls were damp and stained. Before I could unravel this mystery—having seen first-hand the marvelous technology with which Nuum kept the decks of their sky barges dry—Skull pulled open the thick door on the opposite side of the chamber and I gazed into the seventh circle of Hell.

I literally staggered from the stench, so foul that for a moment I had to close my eyes. When I opened them again I saw why my men had not let me wander hither alone. The wretches stacked in that hold like so many cords of kindling surged weakly forward; it was more of an easing of pressure than a concerted effort, but in their glittering, feverish eyes I could see the animal hunger for freedom. They would have overwhelmed a man alone and run amok up above.

"We don't even know how many there are in there," Skull said from far away. "As soon as we can figure out how, we're going to start letting them out and clean them up, but I don't know where we're going to find the room." He began to push the door closed again, and a mad moaning issued from beyond.

"We'll have you out soon!" I called to them, but they surged forward again and the other man had to put his shoulder to the portal before they stormed the opening. I felt faint and had to lean against a wall for support, but I jerked away from its slimy feel.

"What *is* this room?"

"It's a shower," Skull answered. "They stink so bad they're lead through here before they go up to row. The water pressure hoses them off so their masters can stand the smell of them."

I waved the two of them back with me. It felt like hours since I had seen the sun and breathed fresh air.

"How do they live down there?"

Skull looked none too well himself. "They have food," he said at last. "That's what the rowers have told us. And somehow the Nuum removed the dead ones. Nobody knows how. But there's no rotation, no set shifts. If you're lucky enough or tough enough to fight your way to the door when it's time for new rowers, you get to go up. If not, you could stay down there forever."

I walked back toward the bridge through the rowers who had been either lucky or tough. They lined both sides of the ship. I could see now why Timash had called for help getting the *Eyrie's* crewmen back to the *Lady*; it was a wonder to me that he been able to do so, even with Maire's help. There were hundreds like them down below; how were we to get them free?

My first mate had only one answer, and it was unwelcome: "We have to land."

I shook my head. "We'd be sitting ducks. Any Nuum airship within miles would see us and come to investigate, and that would be the end of that."

"And we can't set down in a town for the same reason. But we can't let them all out while we're airborne. They'd overrun the ship. Half of them would probably fall overboard—or jump. Even if we got the force fields back up the deck would be jammed full before half of them made it up here."

"Wait a minute," I said suddenly. "What if we could find a city where the Nuum wouldn't bother us? We could set down without being seen—at least as long as no one flew right overhead..."

Skull gave me a disbelieving look. "And where would this mythical city, with no Nuum and people who would allow us to set this bunch down there?"

I told him; he said I was crazy.

Crazy or not, I was the captain. We set sail immediately.

The former city of the Vulsteen looked peaceful from the air. The avenues were remarkably free of debris; the buildings that had collapsed seemed to have fallen in on themselves in an admirably tidy fashion, and whatever means the original inhabitants had used to discourage weeds and plant pests had long outlived them. Or perhaps the Vulsteen themselves had appropriated all the loose building materials years ago, and some voracious herbivore kept the streets clean with its early morning feedings. Whatever the case, our two ships sailed loftily and majestically over a scene of such tranquility that even Skull, speaking to me from the control cabin of the Eyrie, allowed that I might have been right after all in choosing this refuge for the beaten and mistreated former rowers.

And then our shadow crossed the path of a napping thunder lizard and his roar awoke every creature within miles.

I fancied I could smell its breath from even this height. At my direction, the pilot zoomed in on the beast until we appeared to be but a hundred feet away—near enough for my taste, even in this indirect form.

"You have to admire it," Maire admitted. "For what it is, it's magnificent."

"Oh, it's beautiful, all right." The irony in Skull's voice was not lost in the inter-ship communication loop. "And I'm sure it'll return the compliment—right before it eats us."

"Relax." I had to laugh. We were already drifting out of its sight, and with a final ineffectual snarl it turned away from the two flying irritants in search of something it could catch. "We're going to set down on the other side of town—miles from here. We killed the one that lived there, and there can't be too many—they're too big. So relax."

"Relax, he says..." Skull's voice disappeared as I waved the connection closed. Maire had covered her mouth as she tried not to laugh out loud at Skull's irritation, but her giggles were getting the better of her. Evidently she found my leadership methods amusing.

Although our words were flippant, we spent the better part of a day and a night floating above our intended landing spot, monitoring for life. During the day the streets remained empty but for small, scurrying animals. Daytime had been the haunt of the thunder lizard, and though we saw none, old habits die hard. Beyond the wall and across the river I could see the carcass of the thunder lizard that had pursued us and smashed the groundcar. Its bones had been stripped clean, and broken for their marrow.

On a whim I borrowed the monitoring apparatus long enough for a close-up. The bones seemed to be flowing back and forth with a rhythmic, liquid motion. On closer inspection, they were covered with millions of tiny, white scavengers, methodically moving back and forth, scouring even the bones clean. Surreptitiously exposing the Library to the view, I asked what they were, but he didn't know. I was suddenly glad that my duties had kept me from making a personal inspection.

Nighttime was a different story. While we sat fascinated, the drama of life and death unfolded in the dim light of infra-red. Even with computer enhancement, the scenes retained a spooky dimness. Swarms of bats with three-foot wingspans soared gracefully from ancient towers, inverted V-shapes like hideous geese swooping over and around the lower buildings in perfect formation—until one flock blundered into the path of another. Instantly all was chaos, winged devils diving and pouncing on each other like rival packs of sharks. In less than a minute, one flock limped away. The other lay dead on the ground.

But they lay not peacefully. Smaller shapes were soon skittering among the fallen, feeding on the dead and near-dead. Even between the scavengers there was competition, and battle, and some of the scavengers quickly became the scavenged.

"I think we were wise to stay inside at night," I noted to Maire, but she wasn't paying attention.

"Look!" she pointed, her finger penetrating the holographic cube itself. The technician quickly hid his annoyed expression. But we both followed her lead.

Peeking out of a doorway was a humanoid head. Even in this light we could see its silvery fur glint. It scampered into the street and another followed.

"Breen," I agreed. I turned to the technician. "Mark that spot. That's where we want to go."

I stood before the entrance to what we had firmly established as a breen burrow, bolstered both by the word of Uncle Sam that: "The breen have long memories," and even more so, I admit, by the assurances Maire had given me that not only could the *Lady's* fire computers stop even a charging breen with one shot, they could also differentiate between hostile and merely cautious movements. I needed the breen not simply to refrain from attacking me, but also to trust me. The memory of the poor, emotionally-scourged soul I had been forced to kill on the arena stage still twinged painfully when I touched it.

No one accompanied me; I was on this fool's errand all by myself. I shouted a halloo toward the building, squat and dusty, its windows gone. It would be surprising if the breen did not already know I was there, but the trick was going to be letting them know *who* I was. Far above I could feel the eyes of my crew, and the rest of them, jostling for a look at the monitor cubes or craning as far out over the railings as the force fields would allow. Their breath would be fast and shallow, their hearts beating heavily against their chests...they might as well have been here with me.

But they were spared the breen-scent that clung to the walls and the bushes and the very ground all about me. I knew it would stick to my boots when I went back—and when its pungency rose suddenly like a musical crescendo, I knew they were here.

They stood back in the darkness, not from fear, but from having lived their lives underground. Normal breen were not nocturnal, so I was fairly certain I had met the right clan. If I had not, I would soon be meeting my Maker instead.

"Come in." Sweat trickled down my back. Mangled by bestial mouths, most breen speech was garbled at best, and telepathy among them appeared rudimentary. I strode forward and hoped I had not mistaken "Oh, look, breakfast," for an invitation.

I could almost hear the screech when Maire realized what I was doing.

My vision disappeared completely the moment I walked through the door. I could not see a thing. The scent remained the same, my nose having given it all the credence it was warranted. One clawed hand gently—so gently!—encircled my upper arm and I was lead away.

"All the same, I thought Maire was going to jump ship and go after you when you went inside."

"What was I supposed to do, Timash? I wanted them—I needed them to trust me, and I needed to know that the men would be safe with them. If they killed me, at least you'd have known not to bring down the rowers."

"If they had killed you, we would have turned around and left your bones rotting in the sun!" Maire slammed the cabin door behind her. One look at Timash and he beat a hasty retreat. I raised my eyebrows at her and took another sip of my beer with a sigh. Man had lived a million years, but he could never get tired of beer.

"And what's that to you? I thought you wanted your ship back."

Now it was her turn to raise eyebrows. "What? You think Skull would just hand it back to me? 'All's forgiven, dear. Forgotten all about that slave-rower nonsense. See you around?'"

I nodded in beery satisfaction. "So you need me. And judging from that reaction a minute ago, maybe you even like me a little?"

"Let's stick to 'need' for the moment." She stuck out a hand. "And speaking of needing…"

With no little surprise I passed over the mug. At least I did not have to worry about her taking too much; the mug simply made more, until I told it to stop. And it kept the beer cold. *Lord, I prayed, if you could just let me go back home with this one little thing, I could stop all wars forever. Amen.*

She gave it back, licking foam from her upper lip. "It tastes like you."

I stopped short of another sip; thank goodness she hadn't waited another second to say that, or I would have choked on it and made the whole argument moot.

I thought of the other day right there in that cabin, when I had kissed her.

I couldn't help myself. "You should know."

Maire leaned forward, a wicked smile playing at the corners of her mouth. Shadows gathered at the opening of her blouse.

"If you ever try something like that again, you'll wish the breen hadn't given you back."

With God as my witness, I could not help myself.

Chapter 45
I Become a Ghost

To my knowledge, it was the first and only time Maire ever lied to me: Kissing her did not make me wish the breen had filleted me for lunch. It was, in fact, an uncommonly good kiss, for all that my experience in such matters was limited. Still, it is a uniquely subjective judgment in any case.

Only afterward did I feel horrible.

"Great," Maire murmured. "Now I really am the captain's woman." She opened her eyes. "What's the matter?" We had just broken off our kiss—or rather, I had done so—and I inhaled her breath when I spoke.

"I can't do this—!" I pushed away from her as though to push away the past few moments with her.

But neither she nor the past would let me go. "What? What's the matter?"

I inhaled deeply, grabbing the arms of my chair and looking anywhere but at her.

"I can't do this. I'm in love with Hana Wen. She's the entire reason I've come out here; I can't just abandon her."

A mask fell over Maire's face, instantly erasing all traces of the concern and—lust? affection? love?—that had previously suffused her face, as only a woman can do. Now it was she who pushed away, and rising from her chair, made to leave. I thought I had mortally offended her—and with good reason!—but as usual I had misjudged the fairer sex.

"I'm sorry," she said to the wall. "I thought you just needed a little encouragement." Abruptly she faced me again, a brave smile playing her delicious lips. "If we could just forget all about this, I'd appreciate it."

I hesitated; I had never known a woman to apologize for being forward to a man. But she stood frozen in a stasis of embarrassment until I should release her, so I mumbled a few meaningless words of pardon and allowed her to retreat with what dignity she could muster.

At that moment, had another of Farren's ships suddenly appeared on the horizon, I would gladly have boarded her alone.

Perhaps it is just another evidence of the cruel and ironic humor of Fate that the first person I met upon making the deck was Bantos Han. That he was the man I was seeking made me feel no less a cad. It was his sister that I had traversed half the planet looking for, sweeping up innocent lives in my wake and ending more than my fair share of them. Yet not five minutes ago I had kissed another woman.

The greatest shame came from recalling how much I had enjoyed it.

He and I had not been given an opportunity ere now to greet each other properly, and I returned his warm bear hug with equal sincerity. I asked after Hori; he said she had been well the last time he saw her.

"After the riots, things were never the same. The people were restless. All at once all of the malcontents and troublemakers seemed to find each other. Before we'd been afraid, but once we saw what the Nuum could do—what they would do, given the chance—we knew they'd taken their best shot. Even the threat of violence is less frightening once you've seen it actually carried out. Suddenly we thought, 'Sure, they're tough on a common mob, but with a little planning…'"

"'We'?" I interrupted.

He grinned. "Uh-huh. I still had the gun you left. And we're not quite as cut off from machinery as the Nuum think we are."

"What do you mean?"

"We have access. The Nuum still need us to do their labor, like Hori works in the library. That means we use machines during the day. When you've had as long as we have to work it out, it's not hard to get around the alarms that guard them at night. We've been making copies of your gun for weeks, and hiding them around the city. When we have enough, the Nuum are going to be in for a surprise."

A sick fear roiled in my stomach, the fear of untutored men with unfamiliar and very real firearms. Bantos Han must have read my thoughts in my face because he moved quickly to reassure me.

"Don't worry! We made very sure we knew how your gun worked before we even started making copies. Nobody touches one without plenty of supervised practice."

"But where do you practice? Those guns make a lot of noise."

"Oh, computer simulations. And we've made some improvements: range, accuracy, noise." He winked. "They're really pretty crude, you know."

"But they make a hell of a mess, even so. I can guarantee that," I said. "But what happened to you? How did you end up on a sky barge?"

Bantos Han shook his head in disgust. "Bad luck. That's all there was to it. The Nuum have started running patrols around town, picking up anyone out after curfew—there's a curfew now— and they found me walking home after a meeting. They didn't even know who I was. They didn't even ask what I was doing. They just picked me up, dumped on a transport, and next thing I know I was on the *Eyrie*." He shuddered. "Keryl, you don't know how bad it was. I got lucky and managed to stay near the front because I was new and I still had some strength. I've only been on board about a month; if it had been much longer I could've been lost in the hold and never come out."

"I saw it," I said quietly. "But you're out of there now. You're part of my crew. The *Eyrie* is going to stay here with the rowers while they regain their strength before they go home—" I fixed him with my gaze—"and we're going to Dure to find Hana."

Joyful tears filled his unbelieving eyes and he pulled to him once more. Why didn't I feel the same?

Seeking to change the subject as much as anything, I lead Bantos Han to the railing where we could speak privately.

"What was all that excitement when I first boarded the *Eyrie*, right before I saw you? All of a sudden the rowers started acting very oddly, and some of them were yelling something...?"

Bantos Han stared at me quizzically. "You don't know? You haven't heard? I would have thought that with all this—" he indicated my boat— "you'd have access to the datasphere."

I snorted without much humor. "My access to the datasphere is a touchy subject. And I don't think," I added after a moment's reflection, "that it's going to become any less touchy any time soon."

"Oh..." Bantos Han was evidently taking more than a moment to assimilate this new information. For the life of me I could not understand why. At last he blurted out: "Then you don't know anything!"

I blinked. The last time I'd heard that was in one of my first-year seminars, uttered by the same don who, four years later, proudly hung upon me my scholarship medal. I wondered what had ever happened to it.

"Keryl," my friend prattled on excitedly, "you're a ghost!"

"I've come close more times than I care to think about," I agreed.

"No, no." His hands fluttered in frustration. "I mean, you're a ghost. A—a non-entity. Someone who doesn't show up in the datasphere!"

My blank look was all the response I could muster.

Bantos Han took a deep breath. "This isn't easy. The datasphere is like the sun—it's always been there. Nobody ever has to be told what it is."

"I know what it is," I said testily. "The Librarian told me; he just didn't think I was ever going to have a chance to use it."

"The Librarian? You mean Hori?"

"Never mind. What's a ghost in the datasphere, and why did it create such a sensation?"

"A ghost... Like I said, it's somebody who doesn't show up in the datasphere. It happens sometimes; everyone knows someone who knows someone who heard about somebody in town dropping out of sight—I've heard there are places in the East where whole cities have dropped datasphere connections, but I don't know if it's true or not. The point is, when the Coremaire research station was ransacked, you missed a camera. Apparently it was in the infirmary; I don't know why, maybe it was to record surgical procedures. After you left the Nuum found it, ran the disk, and saw you. So they ran the data through the 'sphere for ID, and you didn't register. You couldn't—because you aren't in the 'sphere in the first place."

"So now the Nuum know what I look like?"

"Well, yes...but they haven't got the faintest idea who you are. Some of our people managed to tap the 'sphere and picked up some of the messages about you—and boy, are they going crazy!"

The import of this information left me a bit less elated than it seemed to leave my companion. Heretofore I had considered myself a phantom member of society, unknown and unlooked-for. Now that I had been formally designated a "ghost," I found myself photographed, cataloged, and no doubt highly sought after. At least in evading the Silver Men we had both been playing on an equally strange field!

"Can anyone access this information?"

"Oh, no," Bantos Han assured me. I relaxed. "Only the Nuum."

This brought less than the full joy of total security and comfort.

"I meant, can any Nuum access this information?"

He bit his lip in concentration.

"We don't know. The Nuum have secure areas that not even their own people can peek into, but we don't know how badly they want to find you. Theoretically, by now they could have dumped your picture into the mailbox of every Nuum on Thora. On the other hand, if they haven't, only certain people would have access. The Nuum have been acting very strangely the last few years— even for them. And if they suspect we can tap into the 'sphere, they might not want this information getting around."

"Why not?"

"Because things back home are already in a mess. We've used the datasphere ourselves to get in contact with Thorans in other countries—even Dure, where this ship is from. The people are ready. If word got out that the man who destroyed a Nuum research station was also a *ghost*—the rumorcasters would go wild. This planet is seething with revolution..." His voice trailed off and his eyes took on a feverish shine I did not like. "You could do it. You could be the spark that sets the world on fire!" Suddenly our surroundings seemed to take on entirely new meaning in his brain. "All this... A few months ago you didn't even know how to communicate! Now you've destroyed a Nuum installation, stolen two of their sky barges... Keryl, do you realize what this news could do?"

"Yes," I said honestly. "It could get me killed." Bantos Han's news had shaken me, but regardless of the justification for my feelings I could almost feel the ghosts of ten thousand generations turn their backs in scorn and shame. I plead with them. "You have to understand, I have a war of my own to fight. I left men behind in my own time. If I can return to them, I can save them. The people of this time have to save themselves."

But to Bantos Han, the men I had left behind had never been real, only dust for a thousand thousand years.

"I see," he said quietly, and then he, too, turned his back upon me.

"I have an obligation to your sister!" I reminded his retreating form, but his reply, if any, was lost in the wind of our passage.

Chapter 46
We Enter Dure

The landscape passed below us with measured tread, strolling steadily northward as we passed south. At first I woke in the night, dreaming that we had been overtaken by another Nuum aircraft, a shining, swooping metal bird of prey with wings like the craft that had taken me out of Vardan. But in common with the mariners of times past, we saw no one else on this vast sea, and as we progressed toward our destination my rest became less troubled, even as our chances of discovery grew greater. What we would do if hailed depended on the caller: Maire still trusted her family's oldest allies, proof she was sure against any leverage Farren might apply, and those she would greet personally. But if we were contacted by strangers—or worse, Farren's own household retainers—our tactics must be determined by our situation. We could bluff, run, or fight—but we would not know which was best until the choice was put to us.

I spent much of the days in my cabin, leaving the ship's running to those more competent than I. Timash took to sailing with the curiosity and enthusiasm of youth, and Maire seemed glad to teach him if it meant she could spend less time with me. Bantos Han had taken it upon himself to help organize the rowers, mediating disputes (with Timash's backing) that once would have ended in fights. The rowers themselves still rowed, for they needed something to do, but their shifts were humanely limited, and their quarters had been improved as far as was in my power.

Nights found me often on deck. Modern technology had dispensed with running lights, and the dark suited my moods. There were no rowers and only a skeleton crew which was glad enough to leave the captain to his musings as long as he returned the compliment. So far I had contented myself with the cooling breeze on my face and trying to memorize the changed constellations, but at last I forced myself to face the truth: The warm winds were drying out my skin and I had never really been interested in astronomy.

There was no one for me to talk to about my feelings. Timash was asleep, and, I feared, too young to understand—notwithstanding that I was not much older. Bantos Han would probably not appreciate being disturbed. And Maire—my soul reeled at the thought.

In the end, old friends are the best. I pulled out the Library and held it in my cupped hand. Then I asked it an unfair question.

"What do you know about the human condition?"

The Librarian did not materialize, of course. He was a secret I still held close to my heart.

"I hold nearly 117,000 novels in my memory cache." He replied so softly that I could not quite be sure if the irony I heard was really there.

Though the little sphere had no face, I stared down at it anyway.

"I thought you were just a branch library. You told me you were only programmed with information I might need on the journey."

Had it shoulders, it would have shrugged. "Boredom is a danger on any journey. And you would be surprised how many novels can fit in one krypton molecule."

"Hm." Behind me I heard the scrape of a shoe, and I stopped talking long enough for one of the crew to slip by me on his way to the forward hatch. When he'd gone I asked: "No psychology books?"

"Certainly. But psychology concerns the mind. You asked about the human condition. For that you need to read novels."

"And have you?"

"Most of them."

"That's a lot of work."

"I read quickly."

"Hm." Come to think of it, how long could it take to read a molecule? "So what's wrong with me? Up until a few days ago, I wanted nothing more than to kick the Nuum off this planet. Now I just want to be left out of the whole mess."

Can a machine sigh? Evidently so. "Keryl, Keryl, Keryl..." It had to be something bad; he'd never called me by my first name before. "If I told you, you'd never believe me."

I hate it when people tell me that. I told him so.

"All right, then. Your problem is you're in love."

I squinted down at him. "I know that."

"Do you?" There was an almost imperceptible pause. "Yes, I suppose you do."

"What is that supposed to mean?"

"According to your body telemetry, you are telling the truth."

I stared in sudden anger. "Maybe you're right," I said, pocketing the Library. "I don't believe you."

The next morning we awoke to the sight of Dure, the Island Continent.

Maire was already in the piloting room when I got there. Timash moved out of the way to allow me room to see the holo-charts. They showed the island from our perspective, tiny flying dots whizzing about like manic fireflies. Even from here the buildings on the shore were enormous in comparison.

"Normally, we'd be in the grip of traffic control by now," Maire said without looking away from the plot. "But the computer still broadcasts my ship transponder, so TC doesn't bother us. One of the perks of power."

I scanned the view anxiously for signs that any of the dots were growing larger.

"Do they know we're here?"

"TC has to keep a lock on us so it can move everybody else around us, but my father stopped getting automatic reports on my whereabouts when I took my title." According to Nuum law, Maire had not inherited her own title until she reached the proper age, so this was the same as saying she had attained her majority.

"Farren must know by now that the Eyrie failed," I said. "He probably has someone watching for us."

Maire nodded grimly. "Probably through the datasphere. He'd have no trouble patching in."

"Could we turn off the transponder?" Timash ventured.

Maire grimaced. "Then we'd be subject to traffic control. We'd be like everybody else. We could end up berthed anywhere."

"Yeah. Exactly. We leave as the *Dark Lady*, we come back as…?"

I liked it. So did Maire.

"Do it," I ordered.

"TC," the pilot murmured. "We have lost transponder. Request repair depot berthing. Aye, TC. Thank you." He looked up at us. "It's done. They don't have a clue who we are." An instant later he frowned and his face again took on an attitude of listening. "Say again, TC." A few moments later he signed off. "Traffic control has taken over our approach," he said slowly. "Once we dock we are to stay on board until we receive further instructions."

"What?" Maire asked. "Why?"

"According to them, Dure is in a state of martial law."

I looked at my officers. "Conference in my cabin. Now."

Maire shook off the effects of lengthy immersion in the datasphere and gave us a worried look.

"I can't get through to my father at all. The news reports say he's been sick, and nobody's seen him for at least three weeks."

"What about the martial law?" I asked. "Who's running the country?"

Maire's voice was small and afraid. "Farren. He's stepped up in my father's absence, and the Council of Nobles has given him discretion because of some problems in the north. They think there may be a general uprising coming."

Given the substance of my talk with Bantos Han, Farren and the Council might be more on top of things than Maire had thought.

"Farren's probably holding my father hostage in case he needs him, but if he was willing to kill me, he might not think that way."

"Which means you're the best guarantee your father has to keep on living," Timash pointed out.

"He's right," I said. "Farren isn't the kind of man to leave loose ends—that's why he sent the *Eyrie* after us, to eliminate the men who were supposed to have killed you." I was just talking off the top of my head, but it did make sense. "But at the same time, Farren's a coward. I should know; he hit me from behind and ran." I rubbed my head at the memory. "He'd want an ace in the hole if anything went wrong—he may even have convinced your father that he is sick."

The fear began to recede from Maire's eyes as her natural inner strength reasserted itself. Slowly she took on the expression of the woman I had first glimpsed battling a horde of Vulsteen all by herself—and winning.

"You're right," she said slowly. "Both of you. I've known Farren a long time. He's been trying to convince my father to marry me to him for years—of course my father wouldn't agree. He's a cunning little brat, but his family is one of the most powerful on

Thora. Half the Council is a cousin either by blood or marriage."

Timash glanced from one of us to the other. "So what we do? We're going to dock pretty soon."

"Normally in situations like this, we'd be boarded and inspected." I ignored Maire's questioning look. Let her wonder at my familiarity with wartime protocols. "If that happens, we have to assume that either Maire or I—or both—would be recognized. We can't let that happen."

"Do you think they'll inspect the entire boat?" she asked. "Maybe we could hide. I know some places."

"Too risky," I said. "They might know the same places." I rubbed my chin. "We're just going to have to make sure we aren't on the boat when they board her."

"And how are we going to do that?" Maire demanded.

As I expected, she did not like my answer.

"You actually did this *in flight?*"

"Shh! They probably don't have surveillance cameras, but they still could hear you!"

Even if I were disposed toward giving Maire the gruesome details of the last time I sat precariously in a maintenance harness outside one of the *Lady's* access ports, this would not be the time nor place. We were shielded from casual detection by virtue of hanging on the side of the ship closest to the wall of our docking hangar, but there was nothing above us save the side of the ship itself. If one of the boarding party took it upon himself to look over the side, we were sitting ducks.

We had come to rest in one of the skyscraping docking towers that ringed Dure's capital city, aptly enough also named Dure. These mile-high structures were little more than immensely tall tubes, pockmarked with landing bays ranging from the private, barely large enough to hold a small manor house, to the public, gigantic maws which could swallow half of Trinity College, where stacked air barges and flying ships entered to be attacked by giant

Brian K. Lowe

tubular arms that locked on like eels. The arms retracted into the building until the ship was fastened to the side of the bay by gravitic magnets. I had counted on the magnets not covering the maintenance hatches.

Our particular home was an arena-sized repair bay, where we could stay, Maire assured me, "as long as the crew can come up with excuses—and my credit balance holds out." When I asked how she could access her credit when Farren had doubtless frozen her accounts, she had explained that the custom was billing on departure; with the ship itself as collateral; everyone paid one way or another.

"How long do you think they'll take?" she whispered. Her voice sounded strained; I didn't blame her.

"It depends on how seriously they take their duties," I replied. I was about to elaborate when we both felt a humming vibration through the soles of our feet, planted against the ship's hull. "What's that?"

"It's the ship's engines!" Maire hissed. "We're moving!"

All at once I saw the outermost docking magnet release the Lady and retract just enough to let her slip out of the bay. Enough to let the ship get by, but not us. In a few seconds we would be swept up against it—and we'd be crushed!

Chapter 47
The Invisible City

"Jump!" I cried. There was no time to see if she did so as I pushed off from the hull and launched myself into space, jettisoning my harness as I did so. At the far point of my swing I let go, and after a frighteningly long six-foot fall, I landed flat-footed on a narrow ledge I had noticed when first we climbed out of the maintenance hatch. At almost the same moment Maire landed next to me, each of us instinctively reaching out to keep the other balanced.

Quickly I glanced upward to make sure no one had noted our impromptu trapeze act, but no curious faces were bending over the side of the ship, so I supposed we had gone unnoticed. That was a relief, for I'd half a mind that the shifting had been deliberately designed to trap us.

"What happened?" This time the question was mine.

Maire shook her head. "I don't know—unless the docking authority wanted the ship moved forward so they could get to the transponder array."

"Well, they got more than they bargained for, then." I pointed to the maintenance hatch. It was now half obscured by one of the great magnets. Even if we could climb back up there somehow, our pathway home was blocked.

I looked at Maire. She looked at me.

"Not a problem," she assured me, and as I watched in complete bewilderment, she proceeded to roll up her sleeves, tie back her hair, daub on a few strategic bits of grease (of which there was no shortage), and become a different girl—and an old friend.

"Why, Marella, it's been a long time."

"Follow me," she ordered, and strode away along the ledge as though she owned the entire docking tower. A door slid back for us and we were inside.

Low-ceilinged and grey, they were designed for utility, with no thought for decoration. Ventilation was not a priority; the warm air was redolent with the smell of oil and ozone. Marella muttered something and a pulsing green stripe suddenly appeared on the wall, accompanying us, turning at various cross-corridors and leaping through space at others to await us further along.

"We probably don't need it," she said, motioning to the green light. "I've been walking these corridors for years. But they change sometimes, and if you get lost you could wander around for days."

We often walked by others on their own tasks, almost all following the lead of a pulsing light-guide. Some carried small square panels lit with colored lights or moving pictures. Once we had to flatten ourselves against the side of a hallway as two short, squat, hairy workers maneuvered a long piece of machinery past. Marella sighed when they had gone by. "They're supposed to use the cargo tunnels," she muttered to me. None of the passersby, Nuum, human, or otherwise, paid us more than the most cursory attention, although now and again one would nod toward Marella as in recognition. She would nod back, but we never stopped to talk.

"Marella?" A cheerful blond Thoran stopped in mid-stride, a welcoming smile lighting his handsome face. "I didn't know you were back!" I thought his interest more than passing. He spared a glance up at me. "Friend of yours?"

"Kenns. Good to see you. This is Keryl."

He offered me what passed for a handshake among his people. I squeezed hard on purpose. He gasped. Marella glared at me as I mumbled an insincere apology.

"Don't mind him," she assured Kenns. "He's just a barbarian. He doesn't know any better." She patted his injured hand and his pained expression fled. My mood grew worse. "So what's going on here?" she asked confidentially. "What's with all the security?"

Kenns shook his head in friendly disbelief. "How can you not check the 'sphere more often? Don't they give you breaks down in the grav pits?"

"Somebody's got to do the work. No, seriously, what's going on?"

"Who knows?" He shrugged. "All I heard is the Council's in town and they're all cooped up in Assembly Hall. Nobody's seen the duke in days, and Countess High-and-Mighty is off on her boat somewhere whipping the slaves."

I thought I was going to choke, but Marella only *tsked* in sympathy. Kenns made his excuses, gave me a plausible, "Nice to meet you," and went off on his own rounds.

"I thought you were going to smack him."

"Why?" she looked genuinely puzzled. "He was right about her."

"It's amazing these people have no idea who you are."

Marella shot quick looks up and down the hall before she backed me against the wall by poking me in the chest.

"No, and don't you blow it for me! I've been coming down here for a long time—how do you think I learned to be a grav tech? Bloody boring at the palace all day..." She looked down the hall again; someone was approaching. "Nobody" —poke— "knows about this." Hard poke. "*Nobody.* Now come on."

We soon reached a voice-activated elevator. She said "Marella Aujan," into the speaker, and the doors opened. We stepped on, and few moments later they opened again—on an empty countryside. Off to our left was a narrow beach and a sun-gilded ocean, but there was not a building in sight.

Maire took this astonishing development in stride—literally. Once we emerged from the docking tower—which a swift whirl assured me still stood where to all appearances it had bulked since the first Nuum set foot on this planet—she set off at a determined pace on a northward course, parallel to the water. Just as astounding, the foot traffic in this area, as motley and dense as that surrounding any metropolitan transit center in my own day, treated this abrupt phenomenon with equal equanimity!

"Are you coming?" Maire had stopped several yards ahead and awaited me with an expression mixed of equal parts impatience and puzzlement. As if there were an invisible tether stretched between us, none of the intervening pedestrians would cross our line of sight, leaving us to converse in an open tunnel of ostensible privacy. How different the customs of this world from the New York or London of my native epoch!

Either my mind was finally succumbing to the fantastic experiences through which it had been thrust, or this was simply yet another of the incredible scientific achievements undreamt of in my own time that the people of this age took completely for granted. And, as standing and gawking at the scenery would mark me as a stranger no matter what the culture, I hurried forward to join my companion.

"Sorry," I said as I reached her. "I was just…admiring the view." To be honest, this was a credible excuse. Without the intervening buildings, the lush hills around and inside the city could be clearly seen in innumerable shades of green, with large patches of gold, red, and even light blue interspersed. Not a single hill bore the scars of development; either the buildings thereon were completely blended into their surroundings, or they had been banned altogether. Unless they were simply invisible as well…?

She beamed with self-conscious pride. "It is beautiful, isn't it?

When the first pioneers arrived on Dure, they thought they must have traveled back through time." She seemed not to notice my sudden start. "That's why we paid so much for the camouflaging techniques. Even back then, the equipment and systems were hideously expensive, but everyone agreed it was the only way to preserve the landscape, so we went ahead and did it. It took seven generations to pay the bill." Abruptly she turned to me, her beautiful smile frozen on her face. "You don't have any idea what I'm talking about, do you?"

I was paralyzed with paranoia and indecision. For me to disclose the truth would subject me to her complete power; here in the heart of the city of my world's overlords, the merest whisper from its princess' mouth could rain down upon me an army—and I knew for a fact that the truth about my origins pertained directly to a subject the Nuum would pay dearly to explore. And yet Maire was my comrade-in-arms (and friend?). I had saved her life, and she had returned the favor. I had stolen her ship, but I had never made her a prisoner, and now I had delivered her to that place where she most wanted to go. People flowed around us in an unending river, their thoughts drifting against my mind. Each was like the passing seconds, piling up and up in silence. The growing impatience in Maire's eyes became ever more stony.

Abruptly she ended my torturous procrastination. Grasping my elbow with all apparent gentleness, she tugged me toward what, once my attention was upon it, materialized as a graceful glass tower.

"Come on," she said with false camaraderie. "We'll tap the 'sphere."

Inside Maire lead me to a spacious alcove off the lobby, which sealed itself behind us. A small table with four chairs formed the sole furnishings.

"All right," she announced briskly as soon as we were alone. "Nobody will bother us here. This is a public datasphere lounge— but then, you should know that, shouldn't you?" I was trapped, and we both knew it. Memories from the Library's early indoctrination now swam to the surface of my brain, but too late. Since I had no way of accessing the datasphere, my education in its niceties had been neglected. I couldn't blame the Librarian; I had strayed so far from our original, simple plan!

"You've been hiding something from me from the start," Maire continued, her voice rising as she went on. "Timash, the Library, just being out in the middle of nowhere when you found me—not to mention Harros' trying to kill you. And then at the same time you don't understand the simplest machines, like the annunciator on the *Lady*—let alone the datasphere. Just tell me one thing: Who the hell *are* you?"

My brain, which had for the past several minutes been entirely incapable of making any connection with my tongue, finally got a signal through.

"It's a long story," I warned her feebly.

"Tell me," she said flatly. Then she sat down at the table, crossed her arms, and waited.

I edited considerably, feeling that under the circumstances the details were unimportant—and some, such as the existence of Tehana City and Bantos Han's involvement with the Thoran underground, were not mine to disclose. Still, when my summation was done a few minutes later, it left me feeling as though a great weight had been lifted from my shoulders.

Maire/Marella was frankly incredulous.

"I don't know which is harder to believe: Time travel, telepathic viruses, tiger spiders, assassins... It's too much."

"You saw the assassin yourself. You—met him. And you can ask Timash about the virus and the spider attack. He was there."

She shook her head, speaking almost to herself. "But time travel...?"

I sat down opposite her. "Read my mind."

She made a face. "No! That's disgusting!"

"Try," I implored, reaching across the table. "Just try. I know it's not done in polite society, but…just try."

Mind reading, as opposed to mental communication, in a telepathic society is a gross violation of accepted ethical codes of conduct. Without the most stringent limitations, privacy would be impossible. Perhaps that explained the way pedestrians outside had avoided interrupting our line of sight; even the idea of an accidental intrusion was anathema to upright individuals. From Maire's reaction it was plain that in her circle, at least, the notion had expanded from merely illegal to distasteful as well. Still, at my insistence, she took a deep breath, averted her eyes, and attempted to comply with my request. I could feel her shy touch skimming the very outskirts of my mind. After a moment she frowned and turned toward me.

"There's nothing there," she said at last in a confused tone of voice. "It's like…not like you're blocking me, it's like you're invisible." She touched my hand as though to reassure herself that I was not, after all this, a hologram.

"Now do you believe me? According to the Library, the telepathic ability was only latent in my time. I learned to use it when that part of my brain was stimulated by being here amongst all of you, but my brain structure is so different from yours that you can't pick up anything I'm thinking unless I want you to."

"A time traveler with an invisible mind," she breathed. "I sure can pick 'em."

"I beg your pardon?"

"Oh!" She jumped. "Sorry, I was just thinking out loud. Hold on a second; I'm wondering if I want to risk a call to some friends of mine."

"It should be safe, shouldn't it? You said no one knew you by this name."

"Yeah. But by the same token, nobody's going to take my calls, either… Come on."

Once Marella explained to me the principle behind the neural camouflaging, I had no further difficulty seeing the city for the buildings. She also explained to me that the project had been simplified (and the cost minimized) by situating all commercial and municipal buildings either completely or substantially underground. Beneath our feet was a warren of subterranean avenues, plazas, and moving sidewalks "almost as beautiful in its own way as the surface," although since our travels did not take us down there, I had no way of determining the objective truth of her words.

The sidewalks themselves were visible, even above ground. This was fortunate, given their tendency to move you along at their pace, not yours. Had they been camouflaged, they would have presented a significant hazard. As it was, they offered an opportunity to enjoy the passing scenery at a brisk, but not breathtaking, rate.

The sensation of passing by buildings I could not see was odd. At times I heard sounds coming from an apparent void, and other times the wind would blow harder for no evident reason, the result of being forced between two adjacent structures. If I concentrated in the slightest, they shimmered before me like fairy towers. Even when I wanted to see them, they were insubstantial curvilinear edifices of glassy steel, the easier to adapt to the camouflage, yet so far as I could tell, privacy was never sacrificed. Mostly, I relaxed and let my mind wander over the scapes that Nature had built for herself.

Our journey ended far north of our starting place, before a low, walled manor on a bluff overlooking the sea. As soon as Marella named it as our destination, I could see it clearly. Unlike the skyscrapers of "downtown," this two-story structure reminded me of the ranch houses of my native California. All of the ocean-facing walls were clear, the afternoon sun glinting in a hundred facets. We crossed the wall through an open gateway, immediately veering past the formal gardens, to our left.

"Where are we going?" I asked. "The entrance is over there."

Marella kept walking around the side of the building. "We have to go around to the servant's entrance. It wouldn't do to have anyone see us march straight up to the front door. Lords and ladies don't have grav techs and—" she glanced at me— "whatever you are, coming to dinner."

There was no annunciator at the side entrance, but an actual pushbutton. I will call the man who answered the summons a footman, for lack of a better term. He was Thoran, as all the servants proved to be.

"Yes?"

Marella said nothing, but merely stared at him with uncommon concentration. Whatever telepathic communication passed between them was unintelligible to me, but within a few seconds the footman had stepped back to allow us entrance.

"Follow me, please. I will inform Mr. Beene."

Mr. Beene, obviously the senior houseman, collected us without a word or change to his aristocratically serene face. We were lead for a short while along airy halls, some interior, some exterior, the former decorated with the sort of dark, overly dramatic portraits that the rich had favored even in my own time. I was again impressed to see how little Man had changed. Eventually we were asked to wait in a comfortable sitting room while Mr. Beene summoned "his Lordship." For a moment as he left his composure slipped in the most minute degree and I caught the merest wisp of thought: He was hoping we wouldn't sit on any of the furniture.

Nor was that the extent of his distrust. Surrendering to my paranoid leanings, I tried the door. It was locked. We were trapped.

Chapter 48
In the House of a Friend

Marella was more sanguine than I concerning our plight, when I informed her of the locked door.

"Well, naturally he locked us in," she said, rolling her eyes as if suddenly realizing that I lacked the breeding to be admitted into the homes of quality. "My cousin would fire him in a minute. He has no idea who we are; he can't leave us to run around the house unsupervised."

I frowned. "Then why did he let us in?"

"I knew the password. But even that will only get you so far." She glanced around at the walls. "What do you think of his pictures? I think they're ghastly."

In subject they were not so different as those decorating the walls of the manor houses of England (or at least those few to which I had been granted entry), which I supposed not surprising given that the human (or Nuum) visage has not changed all that much, even in a million years. I stared particularly at a grand lady whose disapproving brows glowered over the hearth (another innovation that had come down from the caves). My eyes ran over the lines of the drawing and puzzled over the subtle wrongness of the piece. I stepped closer and realized that there were no brush strokes—but that wasn't it. Not until I was standing quite close did I see that the woman in the picture was breathing. I jumped back with a start.

"What's wrong with you?" Marella asked with more amusement than concern.

"She—she's alive!"

Marella tsked. "Hardly. She's been dead for over a hundred years. And good riddance, from the looks of her."

I slowed my breathing, eager to recover quickly in the face of my companion's disdain.

"She does appear to have been an old battleax, as we'd say back home. I wonder who she was."

"My great-aunt," Marella replied carelessly. I was saved from further embarrassment by the opening door.

The man who stepped into the room was tall and thin, with receding copper hair. His skin was an almost shocking shade of white, his nose so aquiline it could have been copied from a Roman coin. His green eyes flickered over both of us without recognition. Behind and to one side, Mr. Beene stood in a stance more bodyguard than servant, and thinking back on Marella's words, I had little doubt my impression was accurate. His lordship's eyes focused on Marella.

"You wished to see me?" His voice blended courtesy with command, neatly masking the impatience he could not resist radiating. "I have guests..."

Again, instead of answering directly, Marella simply stared deeply into his eyes. And again, although I could pick up nothing of the private communication, its import was immediately clear.

His eyes widening and his mouth open in a wordless cry of joy, his lordship swooped Marella up in his arms; she returned his embrace with a sob. Out of the corner of my eye I saw Mr. Beene retire from the room. The door silently slid closed behind him.

"Maire!" his lordship breathed when finally they released one another and he held her at arm's length. "Where have you been?

How did you get here?"

Maire, for that was who she apparently was once more, wiped a happy tear away, reached for me and pulled me forward.

"Allow me to introduce Keryl Clee. Keryl, this is my cousin Lottric Valeuse, Baron Altaiv." We exchanged greetings, and I saw the baron's face go slack for an instant in what was becoming a familiar expression: He was querying the datasphere about me.

Almost as familiar was loss of color he showed a moment later when he realized I wasn't *in* the datasphere.

"Maire, he's a ghost!"

"Farren sent one of his barges to kill me, Lottric. Keryl saved my life."

"He should be arrested!" But Lottric was relaxing even as he said it. "This does explain a great deal," he said more thoughtfully. "Do you have any proof?"

"No." Maire shook her head. "And I don't know if it would do any good if I did." She tugged at her cousin's tunic. "Lottric, what's happened to my father?"

Our host waved us into chairs, not without one last wary glance in my direction.

"I'm not sure. The official word from the palace is that he's been taken ill, but no one's allowed to see him—not even me. The Council of Nobles has been swarming into the city like ants, but I don't know if even they've been allowed to see him." Seeing the look on Maire's face, he rushed on. "I'm sure he's all right. Not everyone on the Council is a friend of Farren's—a lot of them have known your father for years. Farren wouldn't dare try anything unless he was sure of his position."

"Which explains why he wanted you out of the way, Maire," I contributed. "Until you're gone, Farren can't have himself appointed your father's heir."

Lottric shot me a look. "What are you talking about? Do you know something?"

Maire, knowing as she did that my understanding of her

country's political structure was negligible, was staring at me with even greater surprise.

"It only stands to reason," I said. "It's been done a hundred times before."

"Where you come from, perhaps," Lottric muttered darkly. "But not here."

"No," Maire said slowly. "He may have something. Farren's been trying to marry onto the throne for years. Maybe he just got tired of waiting."

"Or perhaps he's looking to turn the Thoran situation to his advantage. The Council may be willing to listen to a new voice," Lottric mused, "but that only helps Farren if he can get on the Council."

"Which he could do if he took the throne of Dure!" Maire finished.

Lottric nodded. "He might, I suppose, if we can't produce you soon. If the Council thinks your father is really ill, they'll want to appoint a regent, at least. And with Farren's connections, he'll be in."

"It should be you," Maire said.

Lottric nodded unhappily and sighed. "But it won't be. Which is why you have to get to the palace and present yourself to the Council. Farren won't have a chance if you're around."

"If she's alive, you mean," I cut in.

"Surely you don't think Farren would shoot her right in front of the Council of Nobles!"

"What if he did? Who'd stop him?"

Lottric drew a breath as if to protest my thought, but Maire spoke first.

"He's right, Lottric. You have no idea the lengths Farren went to, to try to assassinate me. He not only bribed my crew to mutiny, he sent one of his own to clean up after them and eliminate the witnesses. If Keryl hadn't stopped them, I, my crew, the rowers— we'd all be dead, and Farren would be on the throne already. I don't think he'd stop at anything."

"But I still think if you should present yourself to the Council…"

"Even if I could, I don't have any proof that Farren's done anything."

"But there has to be a way…"

"If you would allow me," interrupted a soft, pedantic voice that I had learned to love, "I may have a plan."

And the Librarian materialized in our midst, an impish smile playing around the wrinkled corners of his mouth.

Chapter 49
Before the Council of Nobles

I kept my eyes straight ahead, only their involuntary blinking betraying the difference between me and the android statuary that lined the sides of the immense plaza before the palace of the duke. The statues, legendary heroes and historic leaders of the Nuum, assumed the poses and repeated the speeches of their models to whomever strolled near, a fantastical tourist attraction that would have held me spellbound for hours in more normal times. But today my duty held me even more inanimate than they—with the demeanor befitting a member of the personal guard of Valeuse, Baron Altaiv.

Both the baron and Maire had initially voiced skepticism over following a plan conceived by a computer, and a mere branch library, at that. I, on the other hand, had spent a year huddled in the mud and snow following the plans of fellow human beings who had far less knowledge than the Librarian, and whom, I had often suspected, cared far less for my welfare. At least I knew the Librarian's plan was based on historical research—he made a point of annotating each and every one of his ideas until Maire surrendered and Lottric's objections collapsed under the sheer weight of history.

At last our turn came and Lottric was ushered inside, close-followed by his personal attendants and guards; only six of us, but all he was allowed. The entire Council of Nobles was meeting in emergency session, and we were, it was made clear, simply a symbolic gesture. Our weapons were limited to the Nuum sword-staffs, but to be fair, such was the fear of the nobles of assassination that energy or projectile weapons of every sort had been banned from the chambers despite the protective scanners. I made a mental note to congratulate Bantos Han, should we be fortunate enough to meet again this side of Paradise: His partisans and allies had certainly made their presence known! I struggled not to show my pride on the surface before we crossed the threshold and underwent the mental scans.

Lottric had adamantly refused to believe that the servers would not detect my thoughts, and without being able to take him completely into my confidence, I could hardly blame him. In the end, it was only Maire's personal plea that convinced the baron to allow the plan to proceed; she could not tell him how I was to escape the scans, only pledge her complete faith that I would. He was even less enamored with the second part of the Librarian's plan, which involved smuggling Maire herself inside the palace, but on that point she could add assurances of her own: "I *live* there, Lottric. You think I've never sneaked out without Security knowing it? And sneaking out's no good if you can't sneak back in again."

I crossed the threshold, the line of no return, with my fellows, and nothing happened. If I felt even a tingling, it was my own "anticipation:" it would not befit my station to admit to nervousness.

In the first several moments of my habitation of this legendary building, I was unaware of any special attributes, as our marching orders kept me staring straight ahead. This was not the time to gawk like a doughboy on his first trip to Paris. And the bulk of my vision was occupied by the head of the guard who preceded me.

But the human mind is not limited to the sense of sight (nor even to a tightly-controlled telepathic sense). The skin on my bare arms prickled at the small but steep temperature decline as we moved inside, and my ears seemed to strain for something that they could not detect and I could not consciously identify. It took me a few moments before I realized that the *echoes* were missing.

In every cavernous hall, one hears whispers of far-off conversations, the shuffling of feet on the floor, the occasional banging of a distant door. None of these—save our own footsteps—were present, and even our steps seemed to fade away without ever returning in echo. Breaking orders, I allowed my eyes to flicker right and left. Let someone notice—my break in decorum was nothing compared to what would soon commence.

The hall was filled with ghosts.

Everywhere about us stood knots of phantasmal men and women in close conversation of which we could hear nothing; not their words, certainly, but nothing of their movements, their breathing, their rustling robes. I could see the frescoed walls through their bodies, but fuzzily, as through a thin fog. In other parts of the hall, entire sections were more heavily veiled, as if the conversants required even more privacy.

I later learned this was exactly the case. The human-machine "servers" that ran this building were of such sophistication that they could isolate any area at the whim of its inhabitants, providing as much security from eavesdropping or even observation as desired. What a boon to a public building where sensitive topics were the order of the day! No need for private conference rooms; any bare patch of floor could be converted to an intimate meeting place at a moment's notice.

It was a relief when a majordomo quickly emerged from the field of "spirits" and took charge of our small delegation with surpassing courtesy. While the baron was not a member of the Council, here in his own home country he was an honored guest, immune to exclusion even when those in charge would gladly have accepted his absence.

Our guide ceremoniously lead us past the covertly jealous hangers-on and would-be personages toward a smaller, though no less grand, doorway into the hall that currently served as the council room itself. Maire had described with great pride the design of the chamber where her family had received their subjects for the past three centuries.

According to Maire, the carved "Servants have no secrets from the served," above the entrance to this room held many meanings for the nobility of Dure. Firstly, it served to remind them that they were, in a real sense, only *allowed* to rule, no matter their titles. At any time, should their subjects—Nuum subjects, of course—so please, they could bring down the hierarchy of power with ease. I reflected that it had been done before, more times than these people could imagine. That motto also pointed up an interesting fact: This was the only room in the palace where "screens," those fog-like areas of privacy, were forbidden. Here, in this room, all was open.

The architecture of the chamber itself reinforced this ideal. Instead of a petitioner standing before a large, imposing throne, surrounded by unsympathetically stern courtiers and advisors like the kings of old, here a man stood on a raised platform of his own, equal to the duke—and if he chose to stand, a bit above. Any audience, other than the duke's own personal retainers, stood below and behind the speaker, giving an illusion of almost a personal conversation between governor and governed. A small part of my mind looked forward to seeing this, in hopes that someday I might introduce a similar egalitarian ideal to my own people. But once again, my hopes were to be dashed.

The raised platform I had been lead to expect was gone. A small army of hastily-erected but imposing chairs crowded the dais as closely as they could to the vacant ducal throne without actually touching it, their occupants buzzing with conversation among themselves, their sycophants, and sometimes the seemingly empty air. But most surprising of all was the faintly-glimpsed *privacy screen* near the rearmost wall.

The baron hissed between clenched teeth as he saw it, and I saw the back of the neck of the man in front of me stiffen. My own heart sank; if this did not mean the old duke was dead, it surely meant that his days were numbered. I longed to divert my eyes to glance at the slight figure marching alongside me.

We were lead without words to a spot on the right side of the chamber, near the front but several yards from the outermost of the chairs on the dais. There we assumed the positions that had been drilled into us—in my case, in the last few days. They had been frustrating, agonizing days, but necessary. Our plan had needed time to mature, but fortunately, certain of Farren's closest allies had been temporarily detained in their homelands to combat a sharp spike in Thoran underground activity: Bantos Han's contacts had been as good as promised. Now they were all gathered at last, and their own excitement filled the hall with an almost audible tension. Suddenly, a flicker of motion in the rear of the chamber told me that the offending screen had been dropped.

"My lords, your attention if you please." The voice came from everywhere, giving it a phantasmal effect all its own. It did not apologize for its chauvinistic form of address: Everyone in its range was a lord, or nothing. Contrary to the proud tradition of this place, we did not count. I almost smiled at the thought. The days of their complacency were numbered.

The councilors headed for their seats before the voice had to take the embarrassing course of asking them to do so. What intricate etiquette dictated their seating pattern I know not, but it worked with a minimum of jostling or delay. Soon everyone was in his place. The ducal throne remained empty. My fist clenched when I spotted Farren with his own retainers opposite us and just a bit closer to the stage. I doubted not that this, too, had not escaped Baron Lottric's attention. If even I could read the signs, how many could there be in this chamber who did not know outcome Farren intended for this farce? And of those, how many would do the right thing when the time came?

From behind the ducal throne emerged another man, draped in red robes that looked almost too heavy for him to bear. Even from our distance I could see the circles under his wrinkled eyes. The baron once more sucked in an angry breath, and perhaps I picked up on the wave of recognition sweeping across the hall: there was no other way I could have known that this was Lord Denis Maccen, the duke's chancellor. Even though I had never laid eyes on him before, I knew that he was not a well man standing before us today. I refused to speculate on what his master's enemies had done to him to persuade him to appear.

"My lords," he said, giving lip service to the assembled councilors but including by silent appeal all of us standing silent before him, "as you have heard, the Duke Foret is gravely ill." Another mental buzz greeted this information all had surmised, but only now had confirmed. I wondered if Lord Denis comprehended that his were the first official tidings, and if it might have made a difference had he known. "He is so ill that I—have been instructed to convene this emergency meeting of the Council of Nobles to consider the question of his successor." Was his pause merely for breath, or for deliverance? "Lady por Foret, the Duke's daughter, is missing from the capital, and unable to attend us. It is the Duke's wish that you, lord councilors, undertake the business of succession in her absence, and with all the authority that His Grace would carry could he be here."

That was it, then: the formal transfer of authority over the lands and citizens of Dure to the Council of Nobles. Maire and Lottric had predicted it, failing only to foresee the mechanism by which it could be done, the Duke's chancellor himself. However it had been accomplished, it was a masterstroke; the datasphere would carry the old man's speech to every corner of the planet. Even if they wanted to believe it, the people of Dure could never be sure whether power had been legally transferred, or wrenched away.

I shifted my feet. The baron whispered a calming thought. It was not yet time, the final die had yet to be cast. Not until the Council had committed itself...

From his seat nearest the throne, a councilor arose to speak to his fellows. A large, red-faced, balding man in a golden tunic and autumn trousers, his words only incidentally spilled over onto all of us who were the most affected.

"My lords, grievous as this announcement is, we knew already that only the gravest situation could give rise to this emergency session, when in lesser circumstances we could meet through the medium of the datasphere and share interaction with all of our peoples. The seriousness of our deliberations and our respect and affection for our comrade demand that we be here. But we would be foolish—and blindly negligent as well—to ignore the reality of the past few weeks. Thoran resistance to our rule has grown intolerable. After three hundred years a handful of malcontents has determined that they know what is good for the majority of the population, and they seek to bend us all to their will. Thus, despite the gravity of Duke por Foret's illness, we cannot linger. We must act now to protect the security of Dure, then return at once to our own homes to protect the sanctity of those as well."

You had to admire the man; he was using the very upheaval we had created to aid our plan to propel his own agenda!

"I like to say that desperate times require desperate measures. Our times are not desperate, but the longer we fail to contain the senseless violence that threatens our peace the more drastic our eventual response must be. We all must return home as soon as our task here is done. In the absence of Lady por Foret, we must appoint a regent to act in the place of the duke her father. We are fortunate that a candidate exists who is both competent and willing to perform this duty.

"My lords of council, I call forward Lord Farren."

The man I had hated for so many weeks and so many

thousands of miles stepped up almost before his name was called. Right on cue, the council voiced its acclamation, those few who did not approve conspicuous by their abstention. With only one formal step to be covered before he was named regent of Dure, Farren allowed himself a tight little smile.

The chief councilor faced the nobles of Dure for the first time. "If any disputes the right of the council to so nominate," he announced formally, "let him speak his reasons before us all!"

And that's when I made my move.

Chapter 50
J'accuse

"I object!"

I shouldered my way past the baron and his guards, presenting myself to the hall. No one had expected anything of the sort; the chief councilor had already opened his mouth to finish his pronouncements. He stopped in mid-breath and stared at me in horrified bewilderment. Only slowly did Farren realize something was wrong, and turn to see what it was.

I was already in the center of the long empty aisle between the crowded nobles, my ceremonial retainer's robe thrown back over my shoulders as I spoke. Maire and Lottric had both coached me carefully on what to say and how to say it; we had only one opportunity to act, and the slightest mistake could give the Council the opening it needed to remove me from the floor. Should they succeed in doing so, all would be lost. My journey, Timash's hardships, all the lives lost and the blood spilled on my road to this moment would be for naught and the nation of Dure would be plunged either into merciless tyranny or savage civil war. Everything hung on this moment.

And I didn't give a damn.

I faced down the entire Council of Nobles of Thora, turned to the man who had kidnapped Hana Wen, and gave vent to the hatred that I had waited all these long months to declare.

"Farren, you are a murderer and a coward!"

Literally, there was not a coherent thought in the room. No one had expected this; no one had ever seen its like. An entire planet awaited my next words, but my only focus was on the man I intended this day to see lying dead at my feet.

To give him credit, he recovered more quickly than any of them.

"Who are you?" His voice was calm, but I knew he was a master at masking his true emotions, and his mental shields were far more sophisticated than my own.

Denying him the satisfaction of a straight answer, I turned again to the Council.

"I am Charles Clee, Lieutenant in the service of King George of England." None of this meant anything to them, of course, but I hoped that uncertainty would work to my advantage. If nothing else, it certainly confused them. I could see them exchanging worried glances. "I have come to call Lord Farren to account for the abduction of one Hana Wen of the city of Vardan."

Farren almost exploded in exasperation. "Please! This man has come here with a private grudge over a *Thoran* girl! Guards! Remove him."

"Wait!" echoed through the chamber in such commanding tones that Farren's retainers froze in automatic response. Lottric—no, Baron Altaiv—stepped forward. "I would hear this man."

Farren opened his mouth to protest, but closed it again at the look on Lottric's face. I realized then that they must go back many years together, and even Farren knew when he had reached a line he must not cross. Not yet, at least. But that did not mean he was finished.

"Then at least sever the datasphere link to these proceedings," he commanded. "I deserve not to have these slanders datacast for all to see." His order was quickly carried out. We were isolated.

"Whoever you are, Charles Clee, and whoever you claim to serve," admonished the chief councilor, "it is not a crime to take hold of a Thoran woman and do whatever one likes with her." He glared at me, and then at Lottric for bringing me hither.

I drew his attention back upon me. "Nor is it for that, that I charge Farren with the intent to murder and with cowardice. The cowardice he displayed toward me on the day he took Hana Wen from her family. When I attempted to stop him, he struck me from behind." That hit home; I saw Farren struggling to remember, then puzzlement when he did so.

"But that wasn't you—he was a Nuum..." Too late he stopped. Not even his most ardent supporters could deny his confession. I saw it on their faces, and on his. It might not be enough to derail his plans, but it was a bump in the road.

"How fortunate you had them sever the uplink," Lottric noted wryly. Farren blushed furiously, and I moved to take advantage. Time was running out...

"But the most serious charge of all, my lords," I said, giving them their due at last, for now I had their complete attention, "is that of attempted murder—not of a Thoran girl, nor even of me... My lords, I charge Farren with the attempted assassination of *Maire por Foret, Countess of Dure!*"

That brought the house down.

I am told that despite the superb insulation of the great hall, the physical and mental uproar that resulted from my speech was heard in the street outside. The council was shouting, the chief councilor was calling for order, the nobles were aghast and babbling, and Farren was watching me with eyes that oozed loathing. Had he Harros' power, I would have been struck dead on the instant. I returned his gaze with cold intensity, for now we both knew there was only one way for this day to end.

"My lords!" he cried when the tumult had died sufficiently. "You see now why I asked that the uplink be severed. Can you imagine, judging from the reaction of this honored body, how this news would have been received by the world? I demand that this Clee produce evidence of his claims, or by God I will strike him down myself!"

No better invitation had been handed down in the history of Man. I reached into my pocket and produced my evidence.

"My lords," and by this I included them all, "I hold in my hand a branch library. As you all know, it is incapable of being altered to deliver false information. It can record only what it senses or what is programmed by a Librarian." Again, Farren moved to speak, but his time it was the chief councilor himself who waved him to silence.

"Farren, you will have your turn." He nodded sternly to me.

"This branch library has been in my possession for some weeks. For a brief time, however, it was in the possession of a man named Durrn, first mate on Countess por Foret's sky barge, the *Dark Lady*. While in his possession, the library recorded the following conversation."

Without any cue from me, the library replayed with perfect fidelity the conversation of the mutineers I had overheard while hanging from a maintenance harness outside the boat. I hadn't even known the recording existed until the Librarian told us all in Lottric's study, since when it happened I didn't know it was Durrn who had stolen the Library. I watched Farren as everyone there heard the mutineers' plan and their reference to him, and the slow drain of color from his face brought me an unholy pleasure.

When the record was done, there was no need for anyone to prompt Farren for his reply. Swift and slick as the cobra he resembled, he was ready.

"My lords, this means nothing." He spread his hands innocently. "First of all, if this recording is true, it places this man on the countess' sky barge among the rowers. There are only two reasons why he might be there: Either he is a criminal, or he is not a Nuum. If he is a criminal, then he is not to be believed, and if he is not a Nuum, then he is in possession of a forbidden machine, which makes him still a criminal, and for which the penalty is death. In either event, we need look no further for the countess' murderer!"

"Who said the countess is dead?" I challenged.

"If she is not dead, let her appear and take her rightful place as her father's heir!" he flared, but even before the echoes of his voice had reached the walls he saw my wolfish grin and he knew he had made a ghastly mistake.

One of the baron's other retainers walked up to the dais before them all, turned, and threw back her hood. There for all eyes to see stood Maire por Foret.

"It's a trick of the rebels!" Farren shouted, and before anyone could move, he seized an illegal weapon from inside his own robe and shot the figure before him straight through the heart.

I leaped forward, slapping the gun from Farren's hand with a swipe of my baton. Obviously a cheap copy intended for concealment and emergency use, it shattered when it hit the floor. Farren did not, even though I hit him a lot harder.

I twisted about to see where his errant shot had gone, relieved to see only a smoking hole in the steps of the dais, two feet from the nearest chair, in which the stunned inhabitant still stared down at the spot marking his brush with death. Of the woman Farren had shot, there was no sign. Holographic images cannot be harmed by gunfire, but her usefulness had ended and the Librarian had terminated her program.

"There's no uplink!" Farren screamed from the floor. "You fools! *There's no uplink!*"

And the battle was joined. Without a live transmission of the events in the hall, the victors could write their own history. Farren's men surged forward, frustrated in their attempts to seize me only by the obstacle of his body still on the floor. While he scrambled up from the slick tiles, I turned to the Durean nobles, on whose loyalties our lives now rested, and raised my sword on high.

"The countess lives! Down with the usurper!" And I plunged into the fray without knowing if anyone was behind me.

Farren waved forward his retainers as nearly the entire half of the hall at my back had surged forward, hoarsely shouting for Farren's blood. The noise and commotion died away as he and I entered into our own world, so completely it was as if we had called up a screen for our own private war.

My opponent fenced conservatively, feeling me out, a pall of caution having at last fallen over his arrogant confidence. Despite the Librarian's tutelage and my own recent experience, I was at best a decent fencer, whereas Farren fought as if the sword were an extension of his own arm. Only my greater reach was holding him at bay.

Suddenly the crush of bodies enveloped us, and we found ourselves chest-to-chest. He tried to shove me back, but I laughed at his weak attempts. I brought up my other hand, grasping his arm and forcing it backward. I could smell the sweat on his body betraying his fear: I was easily the stronger, and without his blade, his life was measured in moments. He tried to bring his knee up between my legs, but I was too old a hand to be fooled—until he stomped hard on my instep.

I staggered back, off-balance; I couldn't help it, but instead of pursuing his advantage he stepped back to catch his breath. Even as I gathered my feet under me, I heard a sound from the dais. The Council, still undecided, had yet to enter the fray. They stared as one at Farren, as if astounded to find him still standing, and took that as their sign. An instant later their heavily-armed retainers were pouring in from both ends of the hall, outnumbering the Durean loyalists by far. We were surrounded in seconds.

Farren took his opportunity and ran to the protection of the dais as we were driven back against the wall. I found myself next to Lottric, who batted aside a blade meant for me. I thanked him as soon as my own sword took the man down.

"Look," I pointed, for the battle had shifted for that moment to the edges of the crowd away from us. "He's getting away!"

Sure enough, obviously intended to escape while appearing a hero and saving his peers, Farren was leading the Council along a rear wall toward a small nondescript door. I raged helplessly while he approached it—and cheered when the door flew open in his face and Timash and Maire rushed in at the head of the crew of the *Dark Lady!*

The crowd boiled where the incoming warriors collided with the escaping nobles, but Lottric and I began a chant of Maire's name, which my crew quickly picked up as they swept the others before them—even if Maire's name was liberally mixed with cries of "For Thora!" and even my own name. We were still outnumbered, but here and there amongst the pockets of warriors one and another—whether taken by a change of heart or a reassessment the odds—abruptly switched sides, loudly proclaiming the name of their new leader.

As the Council's guards at the front of the hall turned on the new threat, those at the rear redoubled their efforts and the tide of battle swept us up again. For all that he was Nuum, Lottric fought as valiantly as any man ever by my side, and so often did we save each other's lives that no calculation could possibly have been kept.

In the midst of it all we slowly became aware of a pounding at the doors. At first the Council guards had held them secure, but the tumult had so turned the crowd that now it was we who were backed against them. They began to splinter and give way. Something from the other side tickled the telepathic sense in my brain. I couldn't smell it through the doors, but whatever was outside was strongly stimulating my olfactory sense through sheer mental association.

"Tell the men to fall back away from the doors at my command," I ordered Lottric on my right, and he did so while I passed the word to the men on the left. A few moments later I gained a second's respite from the fighting and shouted, "Now!"

Without looking to see if our men had obeyed, I spun about and torn the fastenings half off the doors, flinging them open to reveal...

...Skull and the crew of the *Eyrie* shoulder-to-shoulder with a score of breen!

Their stench washed over the crowd in a wave and every soldier stopped dead in his tracks. With our men spread to the sides, there was no one between the Council forces and the nightmarish man-killers. Men on both sides licked their lips and tightened fists on sword hilts. No matter the odds, the outcome of this battle was now a foregone conclusion—but how many would live to see it?

There was an abrupt commotion at the far end of the hall near the Council dais. Maire strode purposely and without fear straight through the ranks of her enemies, and such was her bearing that not one lifted a hand to stay her, but parted before her like the sea for Moses.

When she reached us, she handed her sword to me, turned to the breen I called Uncle Sam, and embraced one of the fiercest killing machines ever to walk the earth as she would her own father.

At first there was no sound at all. Then a sword clattered to the floor, and the man who owned it, clad in Dure's own colors though he had fought for the usurper, knelt with his head bowed. Another followed, and another, and then a dozen more and at last the only men standing in the hall were Maire's own.

The battle was over. We had won.

Chapter 51
Triumph and Tragedy

The sun set over the water that evening no faster, nor slower, than it had always done. Even with the vast majority of the planet now aware of the momentous change engineered (or prevented, depending on your point of view) this morning, pedestrians still hurried along on those individual errands insignificant to the cosmos yet crucial to their own lives. A dynasty had been rescued, but that did not mean bread would walk up to your table.

For all that a woman had embraced a breen in full sight of God and everyone —and the breen had refrained from biting off her head and tearing her to tender pieces—still mothers would chide their children into bed with stories of nasty creatures that ate naughty youngsters.

Farren himself had engineered an escape, along with a handful of his closest allies; how he had done so remained a mystery, but in the excitement of the breens' arrival, any decent pickpocket could have scooped up half the purses in the hall without fear. Other than this, our victory appeared complete. Even Maire's father proved further from death's door than she had feared, once his loyal retainers burst into his quarters. The guards Farren had left with the duke had not heard the news of their master's defeat, nor were they given a chance to learn it.

A calm had descended over the capital, as follows a huge storm leaving both destruction and survivors in its wake. Most of the Councilors had already taken their leave, and Maire was glad to see the back of them. They had served Farren's ends, and more likely than not they knew it, but she had no proof, and no one to take it to if she had. In the sight of the world they had sworn her their friendship, and that must be enough.

"We've never had a war amongst ourselves," Maire sighed.

"Do you think he'll come back?"

She sighed again. I looked sideways at her, still watching the water.

"The world's changing, Keryl. We haven't seen a ship from home for almost a century. We don't know if we ever will. Maybe it's time we accepted that Thora is going to be our home for good."

"But you were born here, weren't you?"

"I just said we hadn't had a ship in a hundred years," she snapped in mock offense. "How old do you think I am?" In a more sensible voice she said: "Yes, I was born here. Of a Nuum father and a Thoran mother."

The idea of mating between the two races forced to the surface a concern I had been at pains to submerge in my mind: Hana Wen. With Farren still alive, there loomed large the possibility that he would wreak his revenge upon her. Maire had opined that he would not bother, that she was beneath his notice and far toward the bottom of the list of his concerns, but I could not help but fear for her, the more so since there was absolutely nothing I could do.

"I was born here, too," I said at length. "But on Earth, not Thora. There were no Nuum, only people. And they were free." Hardly, but Maire didn't know that. She jerked as if I had slapped her.

"We have the most equal society on Thora! No one is a slave here!"

"Unless they work for Farren!" I riposted. "Or some other

noble…" She hissed as the full meaning of my words hit home. "No one—not Nuum, Thoran, white, black, red, green, or spotted—has the right to keep other human beings under his thumb. Even the breen have rights!"

She advanced on me. "Is that what you're planning to do, then? Raise an army of breen and Thorans and steal our sky barges and kill us all in our sleep? I've learned some things from you, and I thought maybe you'd learned some things about us, too! I thought we—"

Once I had thought what she described was exactly what I planned to do. Now…now I was very confused.

"You thought we—what?" I prompted.

Maire turned her back, muffling her voice. "Never mind."

We were interrupted by a signal from the door. I ordered it to admit whoever waited outside, and Bantos Han entered—leading Hana Wen! Another man trailed after, but him I hardly noticed.

Hana hugged me with a glad cry, and I held her to me with no less relief. A leviathan weight arose from my shoulders. I held her face and I kissed her—

—and she pushed me backward! Not violently, yet peremptorily, and at the same moment the young man I had all but ignored advanced upon us with an unmistakable stride as old as the first cave-dweller.

"Please, Keryl," she said, flustered. "There's something I—"

"No," I interrupted gently. Bantos Han had laid a restraining hand on the other man's arm. "I can see for myself." And I released Hana Wen to the man who had won her.

"This is Conner," Hana said shyly. "He was one of Farren's retainers. Now he's sworn fealty to the duke. He's taken good care of me."

Conner was a tall lad, broadly built for a Nuum, and I wondered if he, too, shared a Thoran heritage. I thanked him for his chivalry, and he thanked me for all I had done, "not only for Hana but for all of us." She held on to him tightly.

I smiled at the girl I had once thought I loved. "It's all right," I told her, and it was the truth. "Now that I know you're going to be all right, I can go home with a clear conscience."

Her eyes widened. "Really, Keryl? You're going home?"

"I'm going to try."

I heard a soft cough behind me and Hana looked past my shoulder.

"Oh, I'm sorry," she said. "I didn't know you weren't alone." I kicked myself mentally for my lapse of manners—I'd left Maire standing there without even an introduction!—but before I could remedy my error Hana had walked over and performed that duty for herself. At Maire's reply I heard her gasp, then saw her bow hastily, but Maire put a quick end to that. They turned away, speaking quietly for a few moments, looking over their shoulders to give us men several suspicious glances which none of us could interpret, before Hana returned to me with a guarded look in her eyes.

"What have you been doing to her?" she demanded in a low voice. I had never heard such reproach in her voice.

My mouth dropped. My throat was constricted. "I—I— What?"

Hana looked deeply into my eyes. I could sense her brother-in-law and Conner shifting uneasily in the background.

"You don't know, do you? You stand there boasting about your plans to go home—and she knows exactly what you mean, doesn't she?" I nodded defensively. "In that case," Hana said bitingly, her voice rising, "she'll know exactly what I mean when I say: Keryl Clee, you are the most fat-headed man ever to walk this planet! And I mean *ever!*" I thought for a moment she would slap me, but she just spun around and flounced out. Bantos Han looked from her to me, shrugged, and followed with Conner.

"What was that all about?" I demanded. "What did you tell her?" When Maire did not answer, did not even deign to turn, I stalked around until I was facing her. She didn't have time to wipe away her tears.

In an instant my world was sundered, my heart sank, and the scales fell from my eyes. God in Heaven, what had I done! I put my arms around Maire and held her. After a few moments I kissed away her tears. I prayed that she could not feel mine.

"I'm sorry," I whispered. "I'm so sorry. I didn't know. But I have to go back."

"But you can't."

"I must," I insisted. "Or at least I have to try. When I stepped through the silver door, I left my men open to an ambush. I have to try to save them. I can't abandon them. Perhaps, then... I can find a way back here."

"Keryl, your men have been dead for almost a million years. There's nothing you can do."

"No! You don't understand! To you they've been dead a million years, but to me it's only been a few months! And if we can set the machine correctly, I can return to the same time I left! I can save them!"

"No, darling, you don't understand. Even if you can find a time machine, and even if you can make it work—what about the Council?"

"Time travel is number thirteen on the list of those subjects whose research I am instructed to report to the Nuum."

"Oh my god." Everything I knew suddenly collapsed about me as I realized the truth that I had refused to recognize for months, the truth that—along with Hana Wen's rescue by Conner—rendered everything I had done completely meaningless. If I could locate an operational time machine, the Nuum could find it, too, and with it they would conquer all of history.

Perhaps if Maire destroyed it after I went through? I was grasping at straws, and I dismissed the unworthy thought as soon as it appeared, but Maire caught it as it crossed my face.

She smiled through renewed tears. "If I thought it would work, I'd do it, but the man I love would never trust anyone else to do something that important."

I nodded unhappily. "Captain MacLean would have agreed with you."

"Who's Captain MacLean?"

"An old friend," I sighed. "A very old friend."

Maire reached up and pulled my head down. She kissed me until our tears melded together.

"Keryl, I'm sorry you can't go back."

"So am I."

"But I'm glad you're staying."

"So am I..." And I kissed again the woman I loved, for the last time. Abruptly she became limp in my arms and our lips parted through no wish of our own. "*Maire?*"

It was not until I had lowered her gently to the ground that I realized there was another person in the room. He was slightly built, with a high forehead, and brown hair which did not match well at all with his silvery-green tunic and pants. In his hand he held a small silver box.

"Oh, no..." I thought, but the words had no time to escape my lips.

"I'm sorry," he said. Then he aimed his weapon at me and I knew no more.

Epilogue

The Silver Man was sincere in his apology when I awoke—as were his superiors. Having not expected to wake up at all, I could hardly say that their pleas for understanding caused me further surprise. This is not to say, however, that I was not astonished—or that I accepted their protestations at face value. In truth, they were forced to restrain me for as long as it took to tell me what had happened.

As it developed, I had not been captured by the same men who had sought my extinction, but rather their descendants, living 130 years later. In the intervening span, they had developed methods other than execution of dealing with rogue time travelers. While glad of their conversion, I questioned (to put it mildly) why they had gone to all the trouble to retrieve me at all.

It was a small blow to my ego when they said that, under other circumstances, they would not have bothered; I was to them a footnote in history. And as no one had ever gone forward as far as I, they had had a devil of a time figuring out how to follow. But the battle from which I disappeared was a crucial point in the war. Unless I returned, my men would be wiped out—including a Very Important Person whom they were scrupulously careful not to name. To this day I don't know who it was.

I was kept in their compound/prison for ten days on bread and water, not through cruelty, but to thin me down. Despite my adventures, the food and care I received in the future had put several pounds on me, and given me a healthy glow no one living in freezing, muddy trenches should possess. They knew nothing of my longevity treatment, of course (and they were careful not to ask anything that might give a glimpse of the future that was forbidden even to them), so their regimen failed to have quite the desired effect, but something about "the timing of the reinsertion window" forced them to act.

Naturally, they did not discuss these matters with me, but I felt no compunction about raiding their minds for any bit of information I could rifle. Maire would have been appalled, but I didn't care. It was my misfortune that none of the men I came into contact with were sufficiently familiar with the operation of the time door for me to make any progress toward returning to her.

When the day came for the "reinsertion," they gave me a pre-stained copy of my original doughboy uniform to wear. I put it on, and followed them passively to the laboratory.

The door shimmered into existence, and just before they shoved me through, one of them leaned forward to inject me with a drug designed to make me forget all of my "out-of-time" experiences. How it would have worked I don't know, but it hardly mattered, since I knew what they were going to do before they did it. I jerked backward, taking the men holding my arms with me, kicked the hypo into the air, broke free, and dove through the door.

The air on the other side was cold and wet. Smoke bit at my nostrils and mud was already oozing down my cuffs. I had come back in the middle of no-man's-land—but when? Instinctively I kept my head down, awaiting shells screaming overhead.

"Lieutenant?" I jumped at the word, but it was in English and the speaker was the Canadian lad I had sent back to warn my men before I entered the cave. "Lieutenant?" he asked again. "How did you get here?"

I was outside the cave, next to the ladder leading back to our lines. I babbled something about another way out of the trench and chivvied him along without further delay. We reached our line without incident, and I sent the boy off post-haste to report to the captain.

When no one took the bait, the Germans finally decided that we had not only not fallen for their ruse, but had ourselves retreated. When they advanced to take over our supposedly abandoned position, we were waiting.

It was called "a glorious victory" by those who had not fought in it, and "a slaughter" by those who had. Captain MacLean dressed me down privately for my insubordination, but stood by as proudly as a father when the general pinned a medal on my chest. That was the end of my fighting days. Heroes are too important to be risked in battle; they are much more useful back home to recruit other poor innocents, and that was how I spent the remainder of the Great War.

In the twenty years since, my life has progressed from paranoia to depression to occasional fits of usefulness. My continued youth has proven both a blessing and a curse, for men are superstitious and afraid, and every few years it becomes easier simply to move on than to endure what begin as remarks and jokes and ultimately grow into stares and whispers. Even today, I have aged outwardly hardly a year since I last saw Maire.

At first I was afraid the Silver Men would come after me again, but eventually I realized that had they wanted to, they could have seized me the same moment I appeared here and simply put me through the same procedure again. Perhaps they were afraid of further complicating the timeline, or perhaps they themselves are unsure as to why or how my life will affect the future.

I have a good living. I wrote down the story of my adventures and sold it as a romantic fantasy to a publisher. It sold well enough that there was talk of motion picture rights, but that went nowhere, as I am given to understand is typically the case.

Mostly I keep to myself, although lately, with the advent of troubles in Europe, I have considered offering my services to the government. My telepathic powers are largely useless in this era, when no one has the same ability, but I do have what appears to others to be an uncanny knack for knowing when someone is hiding the truth. Sooner or later, America is going to be pulled back into Europe's troubles, and on that day our counterintelligence agencies are going to need all the help they can find.

I have never abandoned the hope that Maire or Timash or one of my friends might find a way some day to bring me back. In our long nightly discussions, the Librarian and I have formulated hundreds of reasons why they might not have been able to retrieve us before now. (Oh, yes, the Librarian came back with me. The Library was in my pocket when I was kidnapped, and sensing something had happened, placed itself in a mechanical suspended animation. When analyzed by the Silver Men, it appeared only a featureless solid metal ball bearing. Dismissing it as insignificant, they had left it in my possession.)

I have, of course, never married. My heart remains in the future, loving a woman who will not be born until civilizations undreamt of have been raised and passed to dust and raised again. They say that love never dies. I only know that nearly a million years from now, my love will live again.

Thank You!

Thank you for reading our book and for supporting stories of fiction in the written form. Please consider leaving a reader review on Amazon and Goodreads, so that others can make an informed reading decision.

Find more exceptional stories, novels, collections, and anthologies on our website at: digitalfictionpub.com

Join the **Digital Fiction Pub** newsletter for infrequent updates, new release discounts, and more. Subscribe at: digitalfictionpub.com/blog/newsletter/

See all our exciting fantasy, horror, crime, romance and science fiction books, short stories and anthologies on our **Amazon Author Page** at: amazon.com/author/digitalfiction

Also from Digital Fiction

STEPHEN L. ANTCZAK

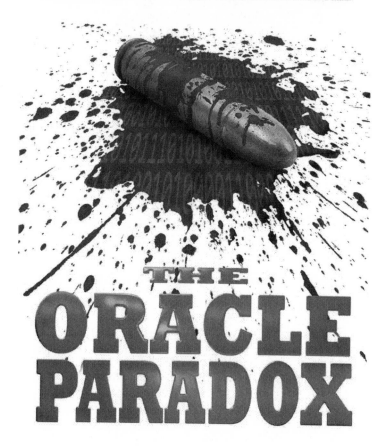

THE ORACLE PARADOX

About the Author

Brian K. Lowe has been writing since he was a child, the same time during which he was devouring the kinds of books that eventually he would write. A fan of comic books, pulp magazines, 1930s screwball comedies, and kaiju movies, he thinks he has a good grasp of what life must have been like in Depression-era America. He is almost certainly wrong.

Brian lives with his wife of 35 years in Southern California. He may be reached at brianklowewriter(at)aol.com.

Visit Brian's Amazon Author Page at:
https://www.amazon.com/Brian-K.-Lowe/e/B00D3V6FCU/

Check out his blog at:
http://brianklowe.wordpress.com/

Copyright

The Invisible City
Book 1 of The Stolen Future Trilogy
Written by Brian K. Lowe
Executive Editor: Michael A. Wills
Editorial Assistant: Ivy M. Wills

DIGITAL FICTION

PUBLISHING CORP